THE UNANSWERED QUESTIONS

The Unanswered Questions Series

The Unanswered Questions

THE UNANSWERED QUESTIONS

BOOK ONE

LAUREN D. FULTER

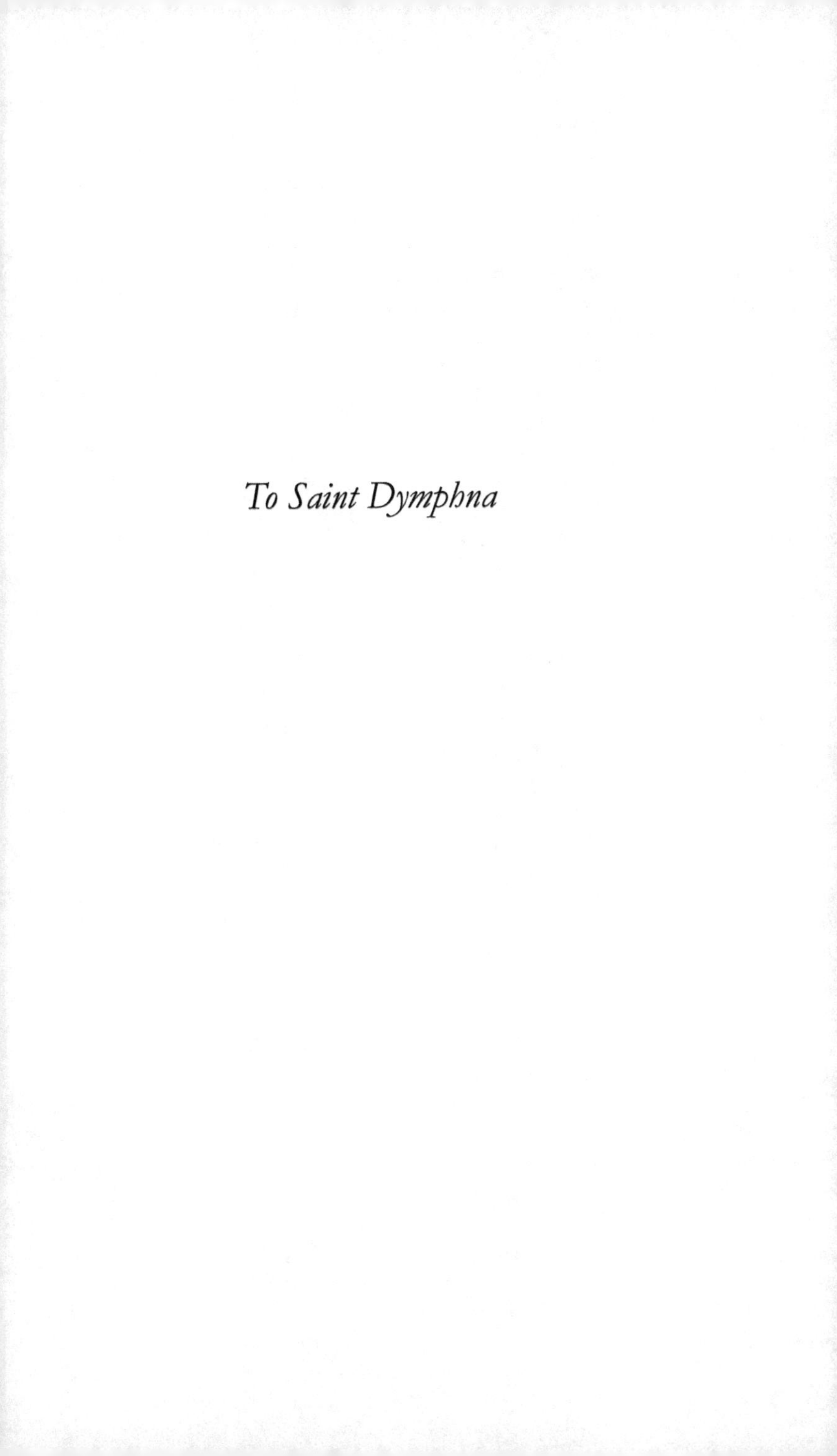

To Saint Dymphna

PROLOGUE

Once again, he was being sent to do the task practically everyone avoided.

Not because it was dangerous.

Quite the opposite.

The task was entirely trivial, and so far, unproductive.

A perfect match for his own performance score. He gave a loud, heavy sigh to the empty hallway, where nothing kept him company besides the cape fastened around his neck, flapping at his sides, and the quick, rhythmic pace of his footsteps.

He watched the numbered plaques along the wall, written in runes he'd known since he was a child, passing one by one. He stopped and turned on his heel, greeted with the appropriate plaque, labeled in basic Anglish as "4034, Cell".

Two months of that number, and it was ingrained into his mind.

He took a deep breath and pressed his hand against the wall.

The wall began to glow blue underneath his fingers, and flickered away to an open doorway, revealing a tiny room. The bright fluorescent lights burst on. The walls were painted a bland white. A small bed was pushed up against the far wall, the blankets still made and untouched. Beside it sat a small table, a few reading tablets stacked on top.

He stepped inside. The wall closed behind him. If he was lucky, he could say his lines twice as fast, and get out in approximately three minutes, and still call it an attempted briefing. A new personal record.

He turned his eyes to the corner, and as usual, the woman sat curled in a ball. He sat down on the bed and counted for thirty seconds, waiting for her to acknowledge him.

Her arms were firmly wrapped around her legs, her arms flexing a light muscled tone. Her hair was so light blonde, it appeared to be nearly white, and the ends were tinted grey. Her hair was also very long, hiding her face, scattered on the ground around her. Her entire face was hidden, only two peculiar, pointed ears could be seen poking out from her locks.

Thirty seconds of nothing.

He silently groaned. Just like the last sixty times he'd been forced to do this.

Now it was his turn to speak.

He cleared his throat, and adjusted his cape, checking the watch bound to his wrist.

"Hello," he said. She remained still. "Today would be a *lovely* day for you to say something. If you do, we can help you anyway in return."

Less than formal, but he barely cared. It wasn't like she even heard him anyway.

He began to count to thirty again for a response. "Fine," he sighed. "How about I simplify the request? Perhaps a name?"

The woman's head shot up.

He sprung back, hitting his head on the wall behind him. He lost count immediately, his heart ramming against his chest.

She stared straight at him, unblinking. Her eyes were startling. One a peculiar violet, and the other…a familiar grey.

He tried to speak, but he was suddenly out of breath. He straightened himself, swallowing hard. "A name?"

The woman's eyes narrowed.

He cursed himself. What had he said wrong?

What is your name? A voice thundered in his mind.

He looked around the room, bewildered. Her lips hadn't moved. Was he going mad?

"I-I asked you that--"

What is your name, little one?

His face flamed. "Did you just call me little?" He got to his feet. "I'm the dominant one in this conversation."

She continued to stare blankly at him. *Tell me your name.*

He started to open his mouth, but his mind willed the words back down his throat.

Tell me your name.

The order echoed in his skull. "S-Si…"

No! He was not a fool. What was he doing? He had to get out.

Tell me your name.

"Si-Si—" Hadn't he gotten into enough messes? He tried

to gasp for air, but it refused to come.

Tell me your name.

He couldn't give in. He had to leave. Get out. Never come back.

Tell me your name, or I will make sure you never see her again.

He froze, his sweat going cold, his heart ceasing in his chest. The threat was shallow. *He* was the one in power.

But his mind fought against his reason. His vision spotted, voices echoed, tearing at his mind. His eyes burned; his ears rang. Images flashed before him, screaming tore through, tearing them to shreds.

"Silas!" he cried, falling to his knees. "My name. My name is Silas."

PART ONE

THE LIGHT

1

If this has reached you, my mission is complete.

HER FOOT CAUGHT AGAINST SOMETHING IN THE DARKNESS, sending her slamming down against the wet earth. The flash in the sky, trickling down like a crack through the sky. She tripped, slamming onto the ground. Rain poured around her. Her heart beat against her chest. She shook her head, scrambling back to her feet, stumbling into a run.

The hands were coming for her.

She could hear them rustling through the trees. A rumbling sound crashed through the air above her. Her eyes darted here and there, trying to piece the darkness together. Tall thick… trees.

Her mind scrambled to understand it. Questions clouded

her senses.

She was jolted back, a cold hand around her wrist. She cried out, turning around to the empty darkness. She pulled free.

Keep running.

She tore her arm from the grip and ran.

The trees flew past her. Everything looked the same. The fingers scratched against her cheek.

Faster. Faster.

She ran up the rising slope. Her feet slipped in the mud and she began to fall, desperately scrambling for a hold.

Her hand slipped into a hole. It was a strange, cold, smooth surface. A word popped into her mind. *Metal.*

A hand wrapped around her ankle. With a cry, she pulled herself up, finding her grip on the earth. The hands tightened their grip. She kicked it away, crawling faster.

Her hand hit something hard.

She looked up. She had reached the top of the slope. A light suddenly burst on, and the girl turned her head toward it. The light moved slowly in her direction, revealing a slick black surface in front of her. A road. A path.

She pulled herself up onto it.

The light wasn't stopping. A low growl began to grow louder and louder.

Get out of the way!

She threw herself to the side, nearly falling backward down the slope. She grabbed hold of a metal bar, holding on for her life as the blur of light zoomed past. It vanished into the distance as fast as it had come, and she stared after it, stepping back into the road.

That had not been her light.

A flickering hologram caught her eye, and she turned to

look at the bar she'd grasped for support, and the words that hovered above it.

'*Entering North Cordell*'

Was this where she was?

The hologram flickered. Red.

'*High Alert. Bomb Warning.*'

Then the red flushed away, returning to its cold welcome. A bomb?

A hand slammed into her shoulder.

Run.

She tore away and ran after the light. Her feet slammed against the pavement. No mud clung to hold her back.

Faster. Faster. Run. Run and don't look back.

Another flash of light burst through the air. Her heart skipped a beat. The hands grabbed at her. She ran harder against their pull.

Don't let them touch you.

The light disappeared, and the girl clenched her jaw, not daring to slow her pace. She needed to reach the light.

The light was safe.

Faster.

The glow grew closer.

A building came into view, illuminated by the sign hanging from the porch over the step. It was a small building, a cabin, two stories high, creaking in the wind. The light seeping from the shuttered windows on the first-floor glowed red. The girl skidded into a harsh turn, running down the path. The hands clawed at her, desperately trying to keep her away. She fought them.

She ran for the door, then tripped, crumbling over onto the steps. Everything flew into focus.

The ringing in her ears. The damp warmth against her

cheek. Her desperate gasps for air and the pain searing through her chest as she breathed. Tears of pain burned her eyes. Her entire body shuddered.

Get up.

She pressed her palms against the step below her. It creaked as she pushed herself up and raised her head to see the flickering sign.

'North Inn'

The 'N' blinked in and out of sight, then steadied, and the rest of word took its turn to malfunction. A smaller phrase below it burst to life.

'Free Stay'

Then it all flashed away, replaced with, *High Alert. Bomb Warning.'*

The girl rose to her feet, tearing her eyes from the sign to the door and the red light that seeped from the cracks.

She glanced up toward the angry sky. She would be safe.

The sky growled again.

She bolted up onto the porch, grabbed the steel handle, and pulled the door open against the wind.

The door slammed her inside. Something crashed.

The girl froze, holding her breath.

Two pairs of eyes stared at her. A woman, with a bright blue pixie cut that framed her pale, delicate face, stood like stone, a metal bar at her feet. She wore a shirt with one longer sleeve and one shorter. The woman's lips parted, but it seemed not a breath escaped.

A man, his hair tucked away in the hood of the jacket and a shadow covering his eyes, stood perfectly still, staring at the girl with casually with his arms crossed.

An uneasy stillness rang through the room in the red glow of the hanging lights. A steel desk was set up in the center of the otherwise bare room, full of a neat stack of tablets. The place smelled of dust and wet wood. The girl scrunched her nose. A staircase ran along the wall, leading to the upper level, and a small hallway lay in the shadows beneath it.

The place was tiny.

The blue haired woman was the first to recover from the shock, scooping up her fallen device and taking a step forward.

The girl flinched.

The woman stopped mid-step. "Can I help you?"

The girl's eyes shifted to the male figure behind the woman. He tugged at his hood, shoving his hands into his pockets, a small smile crawling onto his lips as he slunk behind the desk.

"You look lost," the blue haired woman said with a sigh. "Third strangler we've had all night. Bomb warnings have everyone on edge."

"For a good reason," a crisp, deep voice muttered from under the hood.

The woman shot him a glare, then looked back to the girl. "I'm Sinni Hutson. Twenty-Eight. Court Illegia," she recited.

The girl blinked.

The woman, Sinni, gave a sigh. "Alright. Are you lost?"

Lost.

The girl tried to force her mouth open, but her body refused to listen. She gave a single, small nod.

"Where are you from, kid?" The man had adjusted himself to sit on the desk.

Where was she from? Even if she knew, she doubted she could make herself answer him.

His voice felt...off-putting. Everything about this place felt wrong. Her body told her to run. But she couldn't run anymore.

This place was safe. It had to be safe.

Sinni heaved another sigh, held out the metal cylinder, unraveling it to reveal a thin glass screen. It glowed red, like the lights. She tapped a few things here and there, looking up every so often to the girl, and then back to the screen.

Panic flooded through her. Was Sinni going to bring the hands back? Would she turn her away?

No. Not after she'd gotten this far.

The girl began to move for the door, but Sinni looked up. "We have a room on the first level. A bit broken. Heater's been malfunctioning all week since the funds have gone to all these bomb warnings." She frowned. "Do you want it?"

Leave now.

"Yes," her voice cracked.

Sinni nodded with a small smile. "Good. I'm guessing you're a Foundation Field kid. They barely offer any proper housing for the teenagers there."

The girl barely understood a word that left Sinni's mouth, but she kept quiet.

Sinni looked over her shoulder to the man, who was attempting to balance a stylus on the tip of his finger.

He looked up, the stylus falling off balance and clattering onto the desk. He scowled. "You messed me up."

Sinni continued to glare at him.

He shrugged. "Why are we staring at me like that? Is this about the Foundation Fields? 'Cause Sinni, I have nothing to do with the government's employment program. Far from it."

Government employment program. That's where they thought she came from?

Sinni growled, shaking her head. She turned back to the

girl. "I hope you will find this room a much more pleasant stay."

The girl gave another nod. Sinni gestured to a small hallway.

"To the left are the stairs to the upstairs rooms. It would be in your best interest to stay away, for the courtesy of those guests. The hallway straight ahead should lead you to room sixteen. The door might take a nudge."

"Or four," the man muttered.

Sinni shot him another glare. He shrugged.

She turned back to the girl, her screen retracting back into her metal cylinder.

There was another awkward moment of staring. The girl finally managed to pry herself from the door and shift toward the hallway.

"Hey kid."

The girl froze at the man's voice.

"What's your name?"

Her eyes widened. Her name? Her mind reeled. A name. A number tried to push its way to her lips, but she forced it away. She strode down the hall without giving a reply.

A name.

She looked down the hallway, at the doors rusted over, most strapped with tape. The numbers were out of order. 91. 62. 83.

A slow rhythmic beat loomed through the hall. A few doors had the red light escaping from underneath, and others were pitch black.

"What's your name?"

The floor creaked, drops of water falling from her and splashing to the floor. Each sound was a crashing echo against her skull.

Her name. *53*.

She stopped at the end of the hall at a door with a glass window. It was taped over, but she could still see between the strips to the four towering peaks, the clouds of rain swarming around them.

Another rumble. The inn shook.

Her name was short. Wasn't it?

53, her mind urged again. She pushed it away.

Her eyes narrowed, frowning. A small dot of light crawled up the mountain. It was running. She leaned closer.

Something clattered behind her. The girl spun around, and a door slammed shut somewhere along the hallway. She slowly turned to the side. There was the door, labeled 16.

Someone had been watching her. She barely breathed, grasping the doorknob, turning it with a quick jerk.

She pushed against it.

It barely budged.

She pushed again. The door burst open, and she stumbled inside. She caught herself, as the door slammed shut behind her.

She froze, remembering.

Her name was Nikki.

It crashed into her mind, a small gasp escaping her mouth, as she fell back against the door, sliding to the floor. She squeezed her eyes shut, her mind reeling, repeating the name over and over.

"Nikki," she said, opening her eyes.

That was her name.

She got up to her feet, feeling less sore and shaky than she had a few moments ago. The room was a tiny square. The walls looked like they had been painted at one point, but it had all been torn away. The window was boarded shut, leaving only a small gap.

She rushed to the window, grabbing a board and tearing it from the rusted nails. The room shuddered. She took in a deep breath, the cool air filling her lungs. She peered out into the stormy night. The landscape was shadowed in darkness, except for a small light. This light wasn't red.

Nikki blinked a few times, yet the light remained crawling up the mountain landscape. She leaned closer, pressing her face against the boards, peering out through the crack. The glow suddenly disappeared, and a roll of thunder crossed the sky.

Nikki backed away from the window. The room was as dark as outside, yet she could still see clearly. The tiny light intrigued her. Was it running too?

Did it need a place to be safe too?

She pitied the little light. A small part of her wanted it to come back. They were running, just like her. Did they know where it was safe? Or were they alone in the darkness, scared and alone?

The mountains remained dark.

She turned on the flickering bulb that hovered above the mirror, more of a jagged piece of glass, hanging on the wall's frame. Her reflection looked back at her, a frown creasing her brows. She touched her cheek, fingertips sticky with blood. She realized she was trembling, her body aching.

She quickly washed her wound in the sink that jutted out from the wall, then she sat on the bed, releasing a long, slow breath.

She shook the water from her hair and pushed her bangs from her face, running her fingers through the strands. Her hair seemed darker when it was wet. She hadn't noticed it before.

She flung the soaking boots off and crept back up on the bed. She wrapped the thin blanket around herself, forming a ball with her aching limbs, her back up against the wall, her eyes still shifting around at every movement and sound, letting the storm pass by.

Two days. That was how long she had been running. The memory of it came back to her like a sudden, vicious sensation of pain.

"You have one goal, child."

Nikki's eyes sprung open, her muscles tensing.

"Remember where you come from."

The voice again.

Her vision clouded, a cold, sharp, distant pain pierced her arm, her throat closing. The closeness of the Inn faded away for an instant, bright lights replacing them, a horrible cold overcoming her.

Then she stumbled back, gasping for air as she collided with the wall, her senses flooding back.

"Do not be frightened."

Something vibrated against her thigh. She slowly slipped her hand into her pocket, her fingers brushing against a cool, smooth surface. She pulled it out, cupped in her palm. It looked like a shard of crystal, its surface worn with time and scratched beyond repair, yet its striking beauty was undeniable. In the dim light, it seemed to radiate an eerie green light. Its familiar presence ran shivers through her body.

You have one goal, came the voice again.

This time it was unmistakably from the Stone, yet it only whispered in her mind. The voice was soothing, comforting almost, but it had a cold, sharp edge that sent a sudden shiver down her spine. She cupped her hands around it, holding it closer to her, the light glowing around her face.

"What do you want?" she whispered in a hoarse, raspy tone.

The Stone just shimmered.

A flash passed her window.

Nikki whirled around. The little light on the mountain had returned, but closer now than it had been before. She slid off the bed, her bare feet silently hitting the freezing floor.

"I can keep you safe."

The Stone began to move wildly in her hand, like a living, writhing creature. She turned and glanced out the window and watched the light disappear once more. When it had gone, the Stone seemed to calm in her hands.

Nikki looked back at the Stone.

"Safe?" she repeated, the word strange on her lips. The Stone dimmed, its presence growing cold. Nikki hurriedly pulled her boots back on.

"First," the voice breathed. *"You must give me what I want. You must listen to* me. *"*

She stared at the Stone. It was the only thing she understood in this new, strange world. Its voice soothing, its presence familiar…its offer tempting.

"If you want to be safe…you must listen to me."

Safe. She wanted to be safe. That's why she ran, didn't she? She cradled the Stone in her hands and watched it. "What are you looking for?" She asked.

"Something that belongs to me."

Nikki frowned. "What is it?"

"There is no need to talk so loud, child. Others can hear your voice."

"Voice," she repeated. Her hand slowly went to her throat.

The Stone sighed in her mind. *"You really haven't been out in the world long. Yes, the word is voice. You must have learned that at least."*

Nikki pressed her lips together and dropped her hand.

"I have freed you for a very specific mission. It is a shame the only one of you is merely an ignorant, innocent child, but all is well. Yes. I will get to it eventually. And yes, when our link is activated, I can read some of your direct thoughts".

Nikki gasped. *How?*

A groan. *"Far too complicated for you to understand now, though I feel as though it will be inevitable. I promise you your safety if you listen to my close directions to retrieve an item for me. Tomorrow morning you will need to travel to the small town nearby, and I will direct you from there."*

"What is this item?" she asked, making sure her voice was to a whisper, as to not annoy the talking stone again.

"Do you want protection from the ... hands as your mind calls them?"

Nikki nodded.

"Then you should know that information is mine and mine alone to reveal to you."

Felicity held the blanket tighter around herself as she hid underneath, not even daring to breathe. The slow blinking red light shone through the fabric. She couldn't bring herself to tear her eyes from it.

Something banged. She jumped, stifling her scream into the blanket.

She heard a sigh. "It's all clear, Liz. You can stop hiding now."

"Tell me your name."

"Real—"

"Now!"

"Tabitha Delorous."

"Finish the introduction."

Another sigh. "Sixteen. Liberty. Okay! Come on, Felicity,

it's me!"

Something slammed into Felicity's head. She tore the blanket away, turning her head to the other girl with her hands across her chest and a mischievous smile on her lips. She was of a short stature, with half of her golden-blonde hair dyed a bright purple. Her eyes were large and always staring, in a soft, brown color, though the girl was anything but gentle.

Felicity looked down to the pillow that had hit her, then back up to Tabitha. She couldn't help but smile and shake her head. "So, what happened?" she asked, slipping from the bed to the floor, sitting with her legs crossed, and the blanket draped around her shoulders.

Tabitha plopped down opposite Felicity. "Just a newcomer."

"That's the third tonight," Felicity noted.

"Because of the bomb warning," Tabitha said, shaking her head. "Not *everyone* is out to kill you, Liz."

Felicity looked away, taking a stray piece of her bright red hair between her fingers, brushing it up against her lip. "B-but the bombers—"

"I know, I know," Tabitha said, waving Felicity's words off. "But we're in North Cordell! Someone would have to be out of their mind to choose this place out of a whole other 95 regions. I'm sure they've already caught these 'terrorists' anyway. It's just a little squabble. Something to go down in textbooks and stuff."

Felicity's hand hardened into a fist. Tabitha raised an eyebrow.

"B-but they haven't," Felicity forced out.

"Stop being paranoid," Tabitha sighed, picking up a thin white binder from the floor and flipping it open.

"Don't be paranoid?" Felicity's voice cracked. Was her friend concerned about *anything*? "Tabitha!"

Tabitha looked up, looking bored. "Yeah?"

"There hasn't been an attack since the EarthShaker! Three hundred years."

Tabitha flipped a page in her binder, clicking her stylus—a curious contraption that had been adjusted to write on paper. "You know that's all propaganda and gibberish. There's always guys starting fights in Bōli and Glorgory."

"Tabs. Those are literally just little rebel groups who have great plans to take over the world and only last at most a week at a time before the local Defending Department put them out. They are nothing compared to what they've done in Imperial."

Tabitha began to scribble something down. "Yeah. Pretty smart of them. You know, to hit the Defending Department's base region."

"Tabitha!"

Tabitha looked up with a smirk. "Am I wrong?"

Felicity kicked her binder.

Tabitha snatched it, holding it close to her chest. "Hey. You know this paper is expensive. Hard to find."

"Use a Scroll like a normal person."

Tabitha rolled her eyes, a smile escaping on her lips. A scroll—an electronic device used for multiple purposes, of writing, researching, and practically every flat surface use—was not a particular device Tabitha had ever been fond of. She set her precious binder onto the ground in front of her, staring Felicity dead in the eyes. "Never."

Felicity couldn't keep herself from laughing.

"There!" Tabitha threw her hands in the air and applauded. "You smiled! Yay! You did something that wasn't being a depressed, dense potato."

Felicity shook her head disapprovingly, but her chest did feel somewhat lighter. Tabitha's mood often confused her. Her hardness often came out of nowhere, and her sudden bursts of sarcasm and amusement mixed in between them. Felicity wished she could read her friend's emotions as Tabitha seemed to read hers.

Thunder shook the walls again. She held the blanket tighter around her.

"What are you writing?"

Tabitha glanced up. "Stuff."

Felicity shifted under the blanket. "Sure," she said, looking over her shoulder to the tele on the bed, the red still slowly flushing throughout the glass. She didn't dare touch it. Just looking at the warning made her queasy.

Almost 48 hours of high alert now.

Two days of missed university classes. She'd tried to distract herself by studying on her tablet, but nothing worked. It only reminded her more of why she was trying to distract herself.

The whole room fell dark.

Felicity screamed.

Tabitha let out a groan. "So dramatic."

A light flashed on. Tabitha set her glowing tele on the ground between them. Felicity wrapped her arms around herself, digging her fingers into the fabric of the blanket, turning her eyes to the door.

Tabitha began to hum under her breath. Felicity could barely breathe. If her friend had resorted to her nervous hum, then something had to be off.

Tabitha began to rise, but Felicity jumped out, grabbing hold of her wrist. "Don't!" she said, her voice hushed.

"I'm just going to investigate," Tabitha said. "It's probably just—"

The lights burst back on.

"See?" Tabitha said, plopping back down. "An electrical problem."

Felicity looked back to the tele on her bed. Still red.

"News alert, Liz," Tabitha said.

Felicity whirled back to Tabitha, who was scrolling through her tele. Though the device was transparent, Felicity couldn't see through the back what was displayed on the screen.

"Bentsworth stuff," Tabitha said, with a raised eyebrow and a small smile.

"What?" Felicity squeaked out.

Tabitha cleared her throat, reading in a deep, obnoxious voice. "Gordon Bentsworth, addressing the recent attacks on Imperial, has announced at 23pm tonight, transports into the Imperial City will resume as regular after being on hiatus for the past two days."

Felicity raised her hand for Tabitha to stop.

"Alright. I got it. Good news," she said. "Liberty's not bombed."

Tabitha set her device down. "Sadly," she mumbled under her breath.

Felicity's eyes widened in horror.

"I mean…I…not for you… I was joking." Tabitha forced a laugh. "But see, your good old richest entrepreneur in the world is still well and thriving."

"Always a plus." Felicity shuddered. The room felt colder.

"Yep. Bentsworths," Tabitha sighed. Her voice seemed serious, but her face felt less than genuine.

Felicity instinctively shushed her.

"No one can hear me," Tabitha said, raising her voice. "Hey everyone! I'm here with a Ben—"

Felicity jumped on top of Tabitha, slamming her hand over her mouth, glaring hard at her. "Shut up," she said through gritted teeth.

Tabitha's face lit up with a smile, murmuring something against Felicity's hand.

"No," Felicity said, firmly.

Tabitha rolled her eyes and said something that sounded like "Fine." Felicity removed her hand and Tabitha sat back up, unable to wipe the smirk from her face.

"What do you want from me?" Felicity groaned.

"Let's go get food."

"Now?"

"A little rebellious activity?" Tabitha's smirk only grew.

"I wouldn't say I'm the slightest bit rebellious." Felicity shrank back under the protective cover of the blanket.

"But you're hungry," Tabitha said, leaning forward.

Tabitha wasn't wrong, but the idea of the cold, dark hallway and the empty openness around them as they'd move through the quiet didn't seem worth it. "You go."

"I went last time," Tabitha said, sitting back, crossing her arms. "Come on," she lowered her voice, "Bentsworth."

Felicity glared at her.

Tabitha held her hands up in defeat. "Okay fine. But now you owe me… caffeine."

Felicity frowned. "But remember the last—"

Tabitha's arms fell. "They got your order wrong. I know, Liz."

"And that—"

"They put meat in your sandwich. How were they supposed to know you were vegetarian?"

"I almost died!"

"You're not allergic."

Felicity thought on it for a moment.

Tabitha threw her head back and sighed. "Alright. I'll go by myself. But you'll be alone."

That idea didn't seem pleasant. Felicity would have been fine with it if she was in her normal upstairs room, but she'd moved downstairs yesterday to be closer to the ground. She straightened with a quick breath. She needed to prove herself. "I-I can handle it."

"Go screaming to Mathews if you see something in the closet," Tabitha said.

Felicity scrunched her nose. "I won't need to."

"Why? Cause you don't want help from the Foundation Fields kid?"

"Ray's more obnoxious than that."

"Truth," Tabitha said, nodding. "I'll be back. Don't die."

Felicity flinched but tried giving a confident smile.

Tabitha got to her feet, opened the door, looked to Felicity, then slipped out and closed the door behind her.

Felicity was alone again. She pulled the blanket over her head, held her legs to her chest, squeezing her eyes shut, and waited.

"They couldn't manage to give break one more day," Tabitha grumbled.

That morning had been a pleasant one, with the university announcing that classes would be resuming in mere hours, despite the high alerts from Imperial.

Felicity initially had been a mess, panicking, and pacing, trying to control her breathing. It took a constant reminder to herself that this meant things were going to be fine to push her feelings aside to control her trembling. It took small steps to overcome fears, she reminded herself.

She didn't believe the words.

Felicity stepped off the last step from the porch, quickening her pace down the path to the main road, cold immediately nipping at her face.

"It would be so much easier if we just took an auto," Tabitha grumbled, catching up easily after her. She slipped a bud into her ear as she walked.

Felicity shot her a glare.

Tabitha shrugged. "I was just saying." She sighed, combing her fingers through her uncared-for purple tips.

The road from the inn was more like a muddy river at the moment. She tried her best not to wet her shoes. Tabitha on the other hand, didn't have a care in the world, her bright red shoes soaked. They reached the main road without too much mud. She turned and looked toward the Inn. The four mountains reigned behind it, their peaks hidden by the clouds, and the dots of dark green trees splattered all among them. Uncared for fields of yellow grass swayed at the mountain's base.

She kept her thoughts on the mountains, keeping them from wandering on much else, thinking of the day she'd finally sit down and sketch them.

Felicity pulled her jacket up her nose. Tabitha moved quicker down the road, bursting into a small jog.

It was a fifteen-minute walk to the university building. That was if you were quick. It took a little longer to watch your every move, look both ways before crossing the streets, and check every street sign to make sure you're going to go the right way.

And now with the warnings going off, she'd make sure to

check twice.

Felicity took more like an hour.

Felicity usually fell behind Tabitha because of her extra caution, and because Tabitha couldn't stay still for more than ten minutes. Trailing behind her felt like a daily burden. Felicity pulled out her tele in a routine habit and checked the time. *5.56 (NC - GQ) IMPERIAL ONGOING—*

"Liz!"

Felicity jumped, her tele nearly slipping from her fingers. Someone laid a hand on her shoulder, and she spun around, her lungs freezing, a scream ready in her throat.

A tall young man looked down at her, maybe in his early twenties, with bleach white hair parted down the middle, his grey eyes piercing into hers.

She broke into a smile at the familiar face, all previous fury dissolving. "Silas!" she cried, throwing her arms around the man's neck.

Silas smiled and pulled her into a hug.

"Where have you been?" she asked when he let her go, tears burning at her eyes. "Have you heard the warnings?"

Silas's eyes softened. "It was just a work thing. I was nowhere *near* Imperial."

Felicity let out a sigh of relief, turning, and beginning to walk down the road, a little faster now.

Silas walked beside her, shoving his hands into his coat pockets and letting out a sigh.

Silas was the one of whispers of North Cordell, traveling all throughout the regions of the Joined World. He would always show up unexpectedly, stay a while, leave, and show up later for no apparent reason. He was interesting and reminded her of Liberty. A time before murky roads and creaky steps. He seemed wealthy, unlike many of the commoners who inhabited North Cordell, excluding the upper-class students like herself. He said he worked for his brother, his job sending him to extraordinary regions around the globe.

"That whole bomb warning thing has you pretty shaken up," Silas said.

Felicity tightened her fists. "This is the first time *anyone* has bombed in...what? Three hundred years? Since the EarthShaker?"

"That's what they're saying," Silas said, keeping his voice down, though his eyes fixed on her.

"The EarthShaker, Silas!" Felicity shouted. "When the world still had individual countries! We stopped that practice so we could avoid the aftereffects of *another* war."

"Someone pays attention in their courses," Silas smirked.

Felicity elbowed him, her face growing warm. "Someone has too! Someone has to understand our history. Silas, I don't know what's—"

Silas grabbed hold of her shoulders, stopping her. She nearly stumbled to the ground at the sudden touch. "Liz," Silas said, steadying her. "Calm down. We're *far* away from Imperial. And what do we even have here in North Cordell? They'll investigate and if it's over, then it's over. If it's not, then we'll learn to adapt."

Adapt.

She slumped forward into a hug, taking a deep breath and pushing the panic down. She would adapt.

"And besides, North Cordell's regional Defenders will protect you," he said with a shrug.

Felicity raised a skeptical brow. Was he serious? "You've heard the rumors."

"About what?"

She let out a breath. "The Sergeant. That they lost their mind a decade back, and that's why the North Cordell officers rarely show to emergencies."

"I heard she was friends with the Curatrix agents."

The Curatrix agents were practically legends among of the media. A team of five Defenders stopped some sort of uprising while just trainees. Felicity heard about them frequent enough to know practically every detail of their face, and public backstory. Two of the most favorite of the media to pick apart was Reyna Wents and Lyell Aguirre, the most famous of the five, and extremely controversial in some circles.

She didn't quite believe Silas's claims. If that was in fact true, they'd have to have featured the Sergeant in some interview or article. The North Cordell Sergeant was probably the least decorated, and probably worst in all of history.

At least, in Felicity's opinion.

"I didn't know you were into Defender drama," Felicity said, a smile quirking at her lips.

"It's hardly drama. A decade after their assassination it's apparently still relevant to the blabbering politicians," Silas sighed, his eyes looking off and down the road. "Perhaps that has to do with the Sergeant's rumored insanity?"

He offered his hand to her, and she took it. They began to make their way down the side of the road.

"Whatever it is, they are not doing their job," Felicity scoffed.

Silas squeezed her hand. "Everything will be fine, Liz. I promise."

His words mad the pit in her stomach lighter, and his smile made her worries only for a moment seem irrelevant.

He was back, and everything was fine.

She walked in happy silence beside him, taking in a deep breath of the air, tinged with the smell of rain from the night before.

"What are you doing back here?" she asked suddenly, looking back to him.

"I've just decided to come back for a visit," he said, his eyes turning to hers.

Felicity took it, his gloved fingers warm against her cold, bare hand.

"That's great news," she said, turning and continuing along the path. "I hope you can stay longer than your usual."

Silas nodded. "I think I'll be here for a while. I think I might check out that Inn of yours," he said.

Felicity burst out laughing. "You wouldn't want to stay there," she said. "Seriously. My door is already falling off."

Silas smiled. "I think I'd like it. I have crossed paths with its manager. Hutson."

Felicity nodded. "Well, I had no idea." She broke into a bigger grin. "Maybe she'll spare you from a rotting door and squeaky hinges."

Silas shrugged. "Let's hope," he said, his eyes seeming to sparkle as he stopped. "Looks like you're here."

Felicity frowned, then turned around, her eyes growing wide. They stood right in front of the huge university's golden, open gate.

"How?" She gaped.

Silas's eyes twinkled. "Time flies when you're having fun," he said, squeezing her hand. "See you later, Liz?"

"If you don't disappear." Her lip quirked to a smile.

Silas gave a groan. "Alright. Fine. I'll try not to disappear on you."

"Thank you," Felicity said.

Silas let go of her hand. He gave her a warm smile and a hug, before heading back down the street.

Somehow, she wasn't as cold as she had been. Today was going to be a good day. Silas was back. There was no need for panic.

She looked around. The campus seemed empty. She took out her tele.

6.03 (NC - GQ)

Six minutes.

But that wasn't the weirdest thing.

She'd gotten there before Tabitha.

Nikki felt replenished and energized, but her head still whirled, though she couldn't remember why. The Stone hadn't given further instruction, and deep down she was glad. She sat down on the floor, her back to the door and her fists clenched.

Her stomach growled. She jumped. Pain gnawed at her insides.

Eat.

Eat what? She couldn't dare go ask the woman, Sinni. What if she tried to attack her? Nikki realized she was awfully thinner than Sinni. She couldn't escape her easily.

She also wasn't sure why the bright light in the sky hurt her eyes. The feeling of it was just as warm as she'd imagined though.

She relaxed a little, taking a small breath.

"Hurry. Keep your head down and tell no one your name." The muttering thoughts of the Stone burst in her mind.

Her chest tightened. *What?*

"All will be clear in time."

Time. How much time? They would be coming for her. What she saw in the woods would be back, and the ones she ran from would find her. The clouded memories tore at her mind.

"Settle yourself. Get up and go down the road to the small town."

She obeyed.

Settle yourself, she thought as she left the Inn and strode down the steps.

Then she stopped in her tracks.

The Stone hissed in disapproval.

Nikki's face flushed and she burst into a steady run.

When she entered the small town, she slowed.

The town started abruptly. There was a road and a clearing, a few trees here and there, then the road turned to asphalt. The sidewalks were wide, with a few stands set up produce overflowing the tables. The sophs were nearly identical. All made of steel and glass, worn and weathered like everything in the town.

A shopkeeper, attending to a bot, looked up as she passed, his eyes meeting hers.

She turned her face away, her face growing warm. She kept her eyes down.

Most of the residents wore rugged and weathered clothing, except a few well-dressed misfits, many of whom seemed to be walking to a large, white building in the center of town. It had towering pillars around it, giant glass windows, and a door tall enough for four people. She watched the young people enter through the gates, and cross the small lawn, many in a hurry.

A shiver went down her spine. She looked away from the building clenching her jaw.

The feeling.

"Right this way!"

Nikki froze.

A small group of people followed a young man in a bright blue vest, all of them with their eyes glued to the devices—teles—in their hands. Nikki eased herself from the shadows, slipping into the crowd.

"North Cordell, a region known for its farming industry and our award-winning Education University. We're a Preservation Region, which means we keep forests. There are only thirty Preservation regions out of the 95 Regions in our world."

The group didn't seem to care much about the man's monotone speech, but Nikki couldn't help but be intrigued. Everything was bursting to life around her.

Her first observation was how she compared to the others around with her plain white, dirt-streaked shirt, and jeans. Her skin was a shade darker than the pale tourists, and hair a natural light brown shade unlike the many pastel heads.

"But the mountains," the man said, holding his hands out to the four towering mountains. The group perked up at those words, and Nikki followed his gesture to the landscape above. "Despite its gorgeous scenery and tense woods, no one goes into the mountains. Far too dangerous. Rumors have spread in folklore with the locals."

She frowned. She'd seen the little light in the mountains. Hadn't she?

The words "Foundation Fields" tore her from her

thoughts.

"Open for the working youth. They come from everywhere to help build up and restore the region. They can be of any age and . . ."

Someone rammed into her side, nearly throwing her off balance.

Another foreigner had stepped into the crowd, though she could barely see their face, with the hood of their jacket pulled down.

Leave, the Stone's voice thundered through her mind. *Get out.*

The stranger's head turned to her, brows furrowing.

Nikki looked away, her heart beating against her chest. She shifted through the people, pushing from the crowd. She looked over her shoulder, but the wash of relief sucked away almost instantly as a hooded figure also stepped from the crowd.

Her eyes grew wide. She turned away, trying to keep her head low, walking quicker. They couldn't be following her. She made it down three streets undisturbed, not daring to look back. They had to have been gone.

A hand slammed on her shoulder. She whirled around, coming face to face with the hooded figure, his lip curling to a small smile.

"Get out!" the stone screamed, the words echoing off her skull.

Nikki tore away, bursting into a run.

She tore down the sidewalk, people stepping out of the way. She skidded around the corner on her heels.

"Down there."

Nikki looked around. *Where?*

She glanced over her shoulder. The man was nowhere to

be seen, but she could feel him, just like the hands. He was close.

"There!"

She turned forward. To the side of the alleyway, she spotted a strange concrete incline, a few steps leading to a large metal door. She bolted toward it and scrambled down the steps, heaving the door up. She jumped inside; the door slamming shut behind her.

It was dark.

The place smelled wet, and the air felt moist. The hair on the back of her neck rose. She slipped her hand into her pocket, grasping the Stone. She pulled it out, the Stone glowing bright between her fingers.

The walls looked to be made of stone, painted years ago, though now it was mostly chipped away. A few wooden crates lay here and there, most of them broken in some shape or form. Other crates were full of empty metal cans and broken glass.

There wasn't much else.

The Stone gave a sigh. Nikki couldn't tell if it was from relief or annoyance.

What was that? Nikki asked.

The Stone didn't respond for a moment. *"Phase Two has begun."*

Nikki's ears perked up. Though she'd never heard those words before, her mind knew exactly what they meant, everything went blank. The Stone glowed its green light, every moment growing brighter. Then brighter. It felt like a substance was oozing from the Stone and into her skin, then throughout her. Nikki's mind began to panic. Run. She had to run.

"You will obey me. Stay still."

Nikki made herself obey. This was for the better. The cold, tingling feeling crept across her neck, and she suddenly couldn't breathe. The Stone hissed at her as she tried to inhale. Nikki held her breath and closed her eyes. She was drowning in something deep and thick and black. For a moment, everything was still, then her mind ripped with voices, screams, thoughts, and memories that she barely knew existed.

Flashes of a tiny room. A burning house. A strong, confident warm voice suddenly torn away by a shout and a number repeated over and over in her head.

53. 53. 53.

Pain pierced her arm, and her blood ran cold.

Everything was a blur.

Her mind was rushing back, pounding painfully at the sides of her head.

All at once, she could breathe again.

Nikki dropped the Stone, jumping back.

"You will not be rid of me that soon. I have healed your mind. You should be thankful."

Everything felt like it was spinning into place, becoming clearer than Nikki realized it could have been. The world was sharp and alive. She could barely blink, so mesmerized by every new sight and sound as she picked up the Stone and put it safely into her pocket. A draft blew through the room, sending a small shiver down her spine. The smell of rain was strong.

She heard a faint sound. A rhythmic high-pitched wail. She'd heard them the night she'd arrived.

Then a thud.

Another.

The Stone dimmed. Nikki held her breath.

Someone was coming.

Tabitha was on the verge of falling asleep.

More than three hours of sleep last night might have helped. Felicity and her bomb paranoia. She leaned back in her seat, stretching her arms out under the table.

It was her job wasn't it? To tend Felicity?

Her chair fell back into place. She clicked her stylus. It was cruel to think of it like that. But hadn't they told her to do just that?

So far, no one had missed Tabitha leaving Liberty. She didn't expect them to change that anytime soon.

She tried to focus on the professor in his striped suit to distract herself from her thoughts, but she couldn't make her mind keep up.

Something hit her in the back of her head, and she whirled around in her seat.

She shouldn't have been surprised. A boy in the desk behind her had one foot propped up against his desk. He looked too busy studying his tablet, but Tabitha wasn't convinced. She glared.

He glanced up, his stunningly bright green eyes meeting hers for only an instant before he quickly looked away.

Cole Johnson was seventeen, usually a level ahead of her, except for the one required course of history. He had broad shoulders, now hunched in an attempt to look small, and sharp defined features, his blond hair swept up from his face. He had looks in his favor.

Yes, he *acted* shy, but Tabitha was sure that was only a cover. The much more likely antagonist was the girl on seat two seats to the left whose tablet Tabitha had accidently stepped on that morning.

But she still glared at Cole.

"I'm watching you, Johnson," she mouthed.

He began to say something back, when a siren cut him off.

"EVACUATE THE BUILDING. EVACUTE..."

The lights dropped red, and everyone jumped from their seats, turning frantic, tearing for the door. Tabitha tried to gather her things, but was knocked from her feet, falling to the ground. People yelled and ran over her. She curled up, holding her hands over her head, squeezing her eyes shut. Someone stepped on her hair, another body nearly tripping over her, sending a blow to her side. She gritted her teeth her tears burning, as she held back a cry growing in her throat.

Someone grabbed her arm and jerked her to her feet, but her savior was swept away into the crowd before she could see who it was. She was pushed along with the students toward the exit.

Panic seared through her.

The binder.

She turned and tried to shove against the crowd. "Move! Let me through! Excuse me!"

She managed to squeeze past a few students before falling again. She scrambled, trying to get to her feet. Her hand grabbed hold of a handle.

The closet.

Without another thought, she tore it open, squeezing herself down on the bottom shelf. The door slammed shut. She was crammed alone in the darkness, but safe from the crowds.

Had Felicity been right? Were they really going to get bombed?

He tore her tele from her pocket. The screen burst to life.

NORTH CORDELL MONITOR ASSASINATED.

She let out a sigh of relief. No bomb. A Monitor assassination couldn't be linked. Monitors were literally only elected to represent regions and read off region reports to higher officials.

But it didn't mean the news didn't make her shudder. Tabitha accepted the pop up for more information.

North Cordellian Monitor, Lennon Cutler, was assassinated three days following the attack of Imperial at 13.00. The assassinator made it clear their actions were intentional. Officials suspect correlation to the Imperial bombings.

It is suspected the attackers themselves they alerted the authorities. The Defending Officers have not yet arrived at the scene.

A photo was shown, but Tabitha shut the tele off quickly, not daring to tempt nightmares with a horrific photo of a dead man.

She calmed herself with deep breaths, trying to keep herself from humming.

The Defending Officers have not yet arrived at the scene. Her stomach suddenly felt empty. Of course, they hadn't. She shook her head. No. She didn't have time for panicking. That was Felicity's thing.

She held her breath, listening to the world outside. It had gone quiet. It was safe now.

She wriggled herself from the shelf, reaching her arm out for the interior handle, cursing her stubby arms. She pushed herself out further, sucking her stomach in, grabbing hold of the door handle.

The door swung open, and Tabitha crawled out. The lecture room was empty. Tables were overturned, tablets and styluses scattered about. A lost handbag. A crushed scroll. It looked like a battlefield. She got to her feet, brushing herself off.

She scanned the room, finding her table. To her horror, it was one of the overturned. *How dare they.*

She made her way through the mess, careful not to step on any of the fallen belongings. She caught sight of her white binder crushed between the table and the ground.

She was just about to run for it when a hand clamped down on her shoulder.

"What do you think you are doing here, Miss Delorous?"

The crackling voice of the older woman sent a shiver down Tabitha's spine. She tore away, stumbling back against the fallen desk.

The professor's skin was stretched tight against the structure of her face, her attempt of a smile, pulling at her cheeks as her eyes widened to a horrifying grin. "What do you think you're doing?" she said through gritted teeth, leaning forward.

Tabitha could see the yellow around her eyes. She shifted back further. "Just grabbing—"

"This is a zero-tolerance time, Miss Delorous. I have to assume you in fault against direction orders of the region."

Tabitha tuned her out, turning to retrieve her binder. The professor was being dramatic. She didn't really have that authority. It had only been fifteen minutes.

The professor grabbed her arm, jerking her back. Tabitha tried to tear away, but the woman's grip was too strong. "Hey! Let go! What are you doing?"

The professor pulled her toward the door. Tabitha flung herself on the ground, shouting and kicking, but the iron-gripped professor just scowled, dragging her across the ground. Tabitha did her best to stumble back to her feet, and with a cry of desperation, threw herself toward the binder one last time, tearing from the grip. She slammed against the ground, her vision blurring, but she was up again in a moment. She scrambled to the desk, tearing her binder free.

The professor snatched her arm again, yanking her upward. "No tolerance time, Delorous."

"Prof—what are you doing?"

The professor froze.

Cole stood in the doorway, a frown deepening between his brows. "What are you doing?" he repeated, taking a step forward.

"Coleson Johnson," the professor said, with a smack of her lips. "You should be outside."

"What are you doing to her?"

"Safety precautions," the professor said simply.

Tabitha tried to take the opportunity to yank away, but the professor only tightened her grip.

"The alarm went off only fifteen minutes ago. Her activity should barely be suspicious. Why on *earth* are you handling as such?"

Tabitha had never heard the quiet boy say so many words. Tabitha was suddenly shoved to the ground at Cole's feet. The binder slipped from the ground, hitting the floor.

Cole knelt, reaching for her binder. She snatched it away, holding it to her chest.

"Don't touch that," she snapped.

They both got to their feet, turning to the professor. She stood watching them silently, not a single word escaping her thin, pale lips.

Tabitha glanced at Cole, biting her lip. She knew she needed to thank him, but she only managed a nod.

"Johnson!"

Tabitha and Cole swiveled slowly.

The professor advanced from the doorway and grabbed Cole's arm. "You're coming with me."

"But he didn't do anything!" Tabitha shouted.

Cole didn't move. He was a foot taller than the Professor and could have smashed her like a grape. But he didn't.

Of course, he didn't.

He gave a two-fingers salute of submission and the woman smiled wickedly. She let go of his arm and glared at Tabitha. "Get out, Delorous," the professor snapped at her.

Tabitha began to back away, too stunned to speak.

The professor led Cole the opposite way down the glowing red hall. Cole looked over his shoulder at her.

Maybe it was just the light, or her frantic imagination. But he looked furious.

And it terrified her.

4

HE TORE THROUGH THE DOORS OF THE SHOP, SLAMMING them shut behind him. The sirens were going off again. They had been perfect timing. He looked out the glass door, people rushing to get for cover. No familiar faces yet.

He smirked to himself at his victory. He locked the door, then looked around the shop. The owner was out for the week, due to that chaos in Imperial. Luckily for the boy, his part-time handyman position had earned him a key.

He stopped, stared at it, then pushed a produce stand over the door.

He wiped the sweat from his palms onto his pants.

Perfect.

He found a lantern among the crowded shelves and ran. The sensor on the lantern picked him up, the light bursting on. He tore through the door to the back room, locking it behind him.

He took a deep breath. A sigh of relief, and a laugh escaping under his breath. He rolled his shoulders and held the lantern up.

Crates of newly shipped produce stacked up in the corner. An empty bench up against the wall, bare hooks on the wall above. He turned his attention to the small door in the ground. He set the lantern down, kneeling beside it. Slipping his gloved fingers into the handles, he heaved the door up. Concrete steps led down into darkness.

So that's what was back here.

He stepped down on the first step, and hesitated.

The worst it could be was an old EarthShaker bunker.

But even that would be cool.

A bit of bragging rights.

He adjusted the bag over his shoulder. The door crashed open. He flinched.

"Mathews? Mathews! Where are you, cheater?"

They'd gotten through the lock.

He cursed under his breath. No turning back now. He grabbed the door, holding the weight up with his arm, lowering it every step he took down, till it gently slid back in place, and he was enclosed underground. He gripped the lantern. All there was another small door.

He grasped the handle, rust flaking off beneath his fingers. He pushed.

And to his surprise, it budged. He took a step back, then slammed himself into the door. It swung open, and he stumbled inside, his lantern slipping from his hand, crashing into the ground. He scrambled to his feet, turning around toward the door, but something caught the back of his foot, and he crashed down again.

Pain seared through his head. "Are you kidding me?" he groaned. His vision blurred. A dark figure seemed to be in the doorway. They were here for him. How had they gotten to him so fast?

He squeezed his eyes shut, pushing himself up to a sitting position. "Look guys. You see I got my fair share and you got yours and—"

He opened his eyes.

And it definitely wasn't a group of angry Foundation Field boys. Only a single, thin girl, her eyes wide and her fists clenched, braced in the doorway.

He blinked. "Well…um. You are *not* who I was expecting." He cleared his throat, getting to his feet. "The weather down here. Not great, is it?"

The girl's lip twitched, but she didn't shift from her position, her eyes locked on him like she'd never seen another human being in her life. Not a crack of a smile.

"Well then, mysterious...lady." He scooped the lantern from the ground and squinted at it. He scowled.

A crack in the bulb. And he'd just gotten his pay.

He held it up, the light shining over the girl. She cringed.

Her face was thin, but somewhat rounded. Her skin was a light shade of brown, her hair an oddly similar color. Her hair was frizzy, and fallen about her face, reaching to her shoulders.

He frowned, stepping closer.

Her eyes were…blue?

Blue? Now that threw him off. Her eyes didn't go with the rest of her.

And then he realized he was staring. He cleared his throat.

She jumped.

"Well, sheesh," he muttered, releasing a laugh that held more nervousness than he'd like to admit. "Tense much? How about proper introductions? I can't just keep calling you 'mysterious lady'. Really, that's a weird name."

The girl's shoulders seemed to lose a bit of their tension, but she kept her mouth shut.

"Well then. Hey. I'm Rapheal Mathews." He gave an exaggerated wave and a flip of his hair. "But call me Ray. Cause you know. That's what people call me. Not Rapheal. Raphie. None of that. Just Ray."

She frowned, her muscles relaxing.

"Well, mysterious lady…how about you?" Ray said, tapping away. "Are you some darkness warrior or something? Oh! Or maybe you're an Agent. Explains your attack on me. Wanna teach me that? Eh? Could really come in handy."

The girl raised an eyebrow, shaking her head.

"Well then, where *do* you come from?" he asked.

The girl still looked firmly confused.

No nod. No shake. Just *stare*. Was she even *breathing?*

Ray snapped his fingers in an attempt to take her from her trance, which just caused her to frown. Ray sighed but refused to give up yet. "So where are you heading?"

The girl hesitated for a moment. Would she speak finally? But silently, her eyes shifted south, then quickly away.

South?

"Ooh, you're going up the mountains?" he guessed.

The girl frowned again.

Ray groaned. "The mountains. Big lumps of dirt and rock, with trees on them. Moun-tains".

The girl's face softened.

He must have been right. He congratulated himself. "I

wouldn't go up there if I were you."

She frowned, tilting her head. "But you're not me."

So, she could speak! Ray shrugged. "It's kinda just an expression," he explained.

"Your face didn't change."

"An expression people say, like 'if I were you, I wouldn't go up the mountain.'"

"But you're not me."

Ray wasn't sure whether to laugh or just stare in at the girl. So, he ended up doing a combination of both. "Still, going up the mountain is dangerous. And people say" —he lowered his voice— "there's a curse."

The girl frowned. "What's a curse?"

"It's a thing," Ray said, quickly pushing past an explanation. "Purizies are rumored to still live up there."

The girl's frown deepened.

Ray groaned again. "You don't know what a Purizie is?"

The girl shrugged, turning back to the south, as if she could see right through the walls to the mountains...

Ray ran after her, throwing himself in front of her. "They're from the EarthShaker!"

She seemed unphased and turned to move past him, but he stepped in front of her.

He raised an eyebrow at her. "You know they fought in the big war, four hundred years ago?" he said, his small smirk growing wider. "Legend says they're still alive."

She didn't even look confused, like she hadn't even heard him, again trying to pass him.

Ray gave a dramatic groan. "No, but seriously. If I were you—I know. I know. You're not me yeah—but going up there is bad news. These people are crazy about it. The locals think the terrorists from Imperial came from *here*."

The girl didn't respond.

Ray sighed. "You're no fun, you know that?" He crossed his arms over his chest, gripping the handle of the lantern. "But you should take what I say to heart—"

The girl frowned again.

"Take it seriously," he rephrased. "You wouldn't want people suspecting you to be one of the Purizies, would you?"

The girl looked at him like he might as well have been a mad man speaking gibberish. Ray rolled his eyes, reaching into his bag and finding his comm, a thin, black device with a small glass screen, issued by the region to each citizen. A step below a tele being cheap to make and easy to replace. The screen burst to life, overflowed with threats and curses. He quickly deleted the messages. The warning underneath remained, though slightly adjusted.

"*NO IMMEDIATE THREAT DETECTED. KEEP CLOSE TO LIVING QUARTERS.*"

He put the Communicator into his back pocket. "Alright, girly. I'm going to head back to where I stay, cause those bozos who had the audacity to try to chase me down would never follow me to the inn. Too close to the spooky woods for them."

Her eyes lit up, and Ray guessed why.

"You're there too? Aren't you?"

She parted her lips, then closed them again in defeat.

Ray gave a grin, holding out his hand. "Coming?"

It was a solid minute before the girl moved again, though she didn't take his hand. She stepped past, heading for the door.

Ray dropped his hand to his side and had to run to catch up to her again. "You have a name?"

The girl flinched, glancing down at her clenched fist. She

turned and studied him, then she looked away and made her way quickly up the steps and heaved the door open.

Ray only managed to catch her when they finally reached the empty yard of mud behind the inn. He was out of breath, wiping the sweat from his forehead. "Just give me a moment," he said, sitting down on the back step.

The girl didn't even acknowledge him, beginning to walk away, when she suddenly came to a stop, her body going stiff.

Ray frowned. "You good?"

Voices.

The girl took a step back. Ray jumped to his feet, rushing to her side. He braced himself as footsteps approached and someone appeared around the corner.

Tabitha Delorous.

Ray sighed. "She's harmless."

Tabitha's jaw dropped, and she planted her fists on her hips. "Excuse me?"

Ray crossed his arms with a smirk. "Sorry, Delorous."

"Better be, Mathews." Tabitha's eyes moved from Ray to the girl beside him.

"Who's this?" The voice didn't belong to Tabitha.

A tall, young, white haired man stepped into view, the red-haired girl, Felicity, close to his side.

The girl slunk behind Ray, and he bristled, scowling at the newcomers. "So ... Silas Ridiculous is back?"

Silas ignored him, as usual.

"What are your royal highnesses doing back here anyway? You know you can go in through the front."

"What's the fun in that?" Tabitha shrugged.

"Sinni's out," Felicity explained, her voice soft and fragile. "The front door is locked."

Ray couldn't come up with something snarky to snap back, so he glared hard at Silas, whose eyes were concentrated on the girl.

Silas looked her with his gaze. "I haven't seen you around before, have I?"

The girl just clenched her hands.

"Does she go by a name?" Silas asked. "I'm Silas." He gave a polite nod.

The girl pressed her lips together firmly, then she tore away from the group.

Ray whirled around. "Wait!" he called out.

It was too late. She had already disappeared around the corner.

He growled, turning back to the others. "Great. You scared her off. Seriously. Very, very hard to even get her to *look* at me. Can you believe it? Who doesn't like looking at me?"

Silas groaned. Felicity cringed.

"That wasn't suspicious," Tabitha said, frowning.

Ray shrugged. "Eh. She's definitely not from around here."

Tabitha's face was pinched in thought and she shook her head.

"We'd better head inside," Felicity said, clearing her throat.

Tabitha's head bobbed up and she nodded at Ray. "Thanks," she said with a smile, turning for the door, following Silas and Felicity.

Ray frowned. "For what?"

She didn't answer him.

Ray scoffed. Of course, she didn't.

5

"YOU DID *WHAT*?" FELICITY STARED WIDE-EYED IN disbelief, leaning against the doorway as support.

Tabitha kept her eyes trained away from her furious, red headed friend, clutching her binder to her chest. "Look. I had every right. Her actions came out of nowhere. I barely did *anything* besides be a little late to leave."

"Sounds pretty bad," Silas said, standing beside Felicity, one eyebrow raised.

"You could have been expelled! What if they called Defenders? Or may—" Felicity stopped, pressing her fingers against her temples and taking in a deep breath.

"Look, I'm sorry," Tabitha said, her eyes shifting back and forth from Felicity to Silas. It felt she was being lectured by a second pair of parents. She would have been fine if Silas wasn't there, he made the shaming worse.

"You better be!" Felicity let her hands fall away from her face. "What about that other kid?"

Tabitha bit her lip. "Cole Johnson," she muttered.

Felicity raised an eyebrow. "That name sounds familiar."

"It should. He's in the far room of the Inn."

"The one with the keyboard?" Felicity frowned.

"I am studying music, Liz. Don't be too surprised some of my classmates are too," Tabitha said. "But yeah. That obnoxious thing. It's terrible."

"I think he's fine with it."

Tabitha snorted. "Sure. I'm surprised he stepped in. He usually…keeps to himself. And when I have heard him talk it's usually some stupid thing about the Purizies in the mountains or other weird stories."

"So, conspiracy theories?" Felicity said.

Tabitha shrugged. "Pretty much."

"And you didn't say thank you?" Felicity shouted, throwing her hands up. "He most likely saved you from being expelled, and you didn't so much thank him?"

"Mother. I would have," Tabitha mumbled.

A small smile crept on Felicity's lips. "Don't sass me, child."

A wave of relief released the hold of anxiety on Tabitha's chest, and she smirked back. "Sorry, mum," she said. "You saw the girl outside, right?"

Felicity glanced at Silas, who simply shrugged. Felicity looked back to Tabitha. "I guess I did."

"And did she seem…" Tabitha paused. "Suspicious to you?"

Felicity shrugged. "Maybe a little odd. Why?"

"She was the one in the hall. In the middle of the night

last night. She looked like she came from the *woods*, Liz."

Felicity flinched, but she settled her shoulders and shook her head. "What are you thinking, Tabitha?"

Tabitha shook her head. She turned down the hall, not waiting for Felicity to follow. Silas was there with Felicity. She'd be fine.

They didn't believe her.

That was fine.

She would prove she was right.

Tabitha froze outside the door, humming nervously under her breath. She'd been planning for twenty-four hours, replaying this moment over and over in her head.

Her first instinct had been to investigate the girl on her own. It sounded simple enough, but Tabitha soon realized she knew absolutely nothing about the woods. She barely trusted Ray's crazy stories, and the web was hardly helpful in providing her with anything other than random facts about the tiny town in a region no one hardly visited.

Her final resolution was one she despised. Cole Johnson.

She's thought about it all night.

From the little people talked of him, it was a widely accepted fact Cole liked conspiracies. Why else would he behind tablets all the time? He was quiet and cautious, and always observing. If anyone knew anything factual about the wood, it would be her bothersome, quiet classmate, who had just saved her from whatever the crazed professor had in store.

Tabitha took a deep breath.

Her fist was raised to knock, but she couldn't move it forward and actually *knock*. She pulled her hand away, shoving it into her pocket and shaking her head, turning on her heel. But then she whirled back around again. She took a deep breath and raised her fist.

And the door swung open.

Tabitha stumbled back.

"Hello—" Coleson stopped mid-sentence, frowning hard at her.

She straightened , though it barely made a difference as he still towered over her.

He sighed, turning away. "It's you."

Tabitha crossed her arms and cleared her throat. "Yes. Yes, it is."

He didn't seem to care in the slightest, reaching for the doorknob.

Tabitha jumped forward, pushing his hand away. "Hey! Wait! Cole!"

Cole stopped, raising an eyebrow, his light green eyes staring hard into hers, seeming bored with the conversation already. "What do you need, Delorous?" he asked, tensing as he spoke.

"I need your help…again."

Cole's brows furrowed. "What?"

"You saved me," Tabitha mumbled. "The professor."

"Yes, and she was crazy," Cole pushed the door open further. "Out of her wits. I don't know what her motivations were but something you did made her angry."

"I didn't do anything, Johnson," Tabitha scowled. "She's crazy like you said. Can we just make up? Look I wouldn't talk to your…nice face if it wasn't something important, right?"

She tried to keep herself from humming in the awkward silence.

Cole stopped for a moment, his eyes drifting off to his room. Then he turned to her. "No."

"No?" Tabitha said, frowning. "Woah, woah. Johnson, this is huge! There's a new person here and—"

"Delorous," Cole said. He didn't yell, but his firm, deep voice still echoed through her mind. "The answer is no."

Tabitha gave a frustrated sigh, clenching her fists. She'd forgotten for a split second why she hated everything about him, but now it all came back. She stepped in front of him, blocking his way. "Why?"

"Because I know your motivation."

Tabitha froze, seeing a fragile anger flash across his face, a small, defined line form between his brows.

"You're not the humble type, Tabitha," he said. He gently pushed her to the side. "Look. I helped you, and I hope it was worth it."

Tabitha gave no resistance, and he stepped behind her and into his room. She looked over her shoulder.

Cole began to shut the door, but he stopped for a moment and looked to her. "Was it worth it?"

Tabitha burned to snap something back, but her mind was cluttered and distraught. She could barely part her lips. She just gave him a glare as a response.

And with that, Cole shut the door, locking it with a *click*.

Tabitha gave a frustrated sigh, resisting the urge to whirl around and kick his door as hard as she could. "Fine! I can go to the woods perfectly fine without you!"

She dropped her clenched fists to her side, storming away.

She didn't need his help anyhow. He didn't know her. She could do it all on her own.

6

THE ENTIRE GROUND SHOOK, A SCREECHING BOOM splintering the air.

Felicity crumpled to the bedroom. Glass shattered, the remains of the windows showering over her as she scrunched up into a ball, her head in between her legs. She lay there for a solid ten minutes, trying to control her gasping breaths as the roaring settled into a stunned silence.

Bombs. It must have been the bombs.

She looked up, her body shaking. Glass was scattered all around her, and the windows were nothing but jagged shards in the frames. She swallowed down her panic and raced for the door, though her arms and legs were shaking as she tore down the porch.

Her jaw dropped. The road was cracked down the middle,

pieces seeming to have shifted out of place, or smashed to bits. Her vision spun, and she groped for something to steady herself on. This was the only main road leading in and out of small North Cordell town, now near impossible to use for as far as she could see. Who would do something like this in such a small, peaceful region?

"What happened?"

"We were attacked!"

"An earthquake?"

"Liz!"

Felicity turned her head in the direction of the voices. A pale-faced crowd stumbled from the door onto the porch, staring out at the destruction.

A white-haired boy ran through the crowd to the steps, his face drained and tired, his hair a choppy mess. He obviously had been woken by the quake.

She couldn't even form the right words. Her stomach flipped and she reached for him. One knee crumpled and she grabbed the railing to stop herself from falling.

Silas dropped beside her. His face softened; brows raised with a curious concern. He helped her sit down on the stairs, not saying a word.

She hugged herself, muttering "Thank you" softly under her breath.

Silas nodded; his eyes glued on the road.

They weren't the only ones who had rushed out. Almost everyone in the surrounding area was flooded to the scene. There were people shouting and screaming. The road to North Cordell was completely blown.

The authorities blocked the area, ordering the area to be cleared. People uneasily began to disperse.

The little child inside of Felicity wanted to curl up in a ball and cry. There was nowhere else she could go. She couldn't go home now.

It couldn't have been a bomb. Could it?

Silas's arm found its way around her shoulders.

She blinked the burning tears back, hiding her face between her knees and clasping her hands over her ears. Silas squeezed her. The affection only made her chest feel heavier.

She felt his hand slip into hers, gently pulling it away from her ear. "Come on, Liz," he whispered. "We're going inside."

She grasped his hand, keeping her eyes shut. He helped her to her feet, her legs wobbling as she took shaky steps forward. The walk felt like an eternity, the echoing of sirens running through her mind. Sirens. These ones weren't warnings.

Silas sat her down. She gripped the worn material of the old sofa with her hands, digging her fingernails into it. Her lungs screamed for air, but she couldn't get a breath in between the crushing panic.

"Liz," Silas whispered. "It's okay."

She pried her eyes open. The familiar view of the Inn's front room was flashing red, the lights going crazy. Her head grew light again, as she gasped for air. "Silas," she choked. "We're going to die."

Her vision blurred again. She leaned against the back of the couch, staring at the ceiling and counting her shaky breaths. "We're next."

"Felicity," Silas said, slow, but stern. "Calm yourself. It's going to be okay. We weren't bombed."

"Then what do you call that?" Felicity said, turning toward him, anger burning in her chest. "An accident?"

Silas's eyes shifted away. "An attack."

Hearing the words out loud made it worse. Felicity

shuddered, her breath hitching again. Counting breaths. She could do that. Just focus on counting breaths.

"They're going to handle it, Liz," Silas said, his hand brushing against her shoulder. "They're going to protect you."

"And if they can't?" Felicity said, looking up at him, strands of hair sticking to her wet cheeks. "We don't even have Defending Officers in North Cordell, Silas. Just some…untrained volunteers."

"Then I'll protect you," Silas said.

Felicity searched his sincere face. He was actually serious?

He met her gaze steadily, his brows straight and stern, his forehead creased with worry. "I'll protect you better than those officers ever could."

Felicity choked out a laugh, wiping her face, pulling her legs tighter to her chest. "T-thank you, Silas," she said. "F-for helping—"

Silas shushed her. She closed her mouth, and he gave a small, soft smile.

They sat alone in the room, watching the flashing red lighting, listening to sirens, watching people rush past them. Everything became a blur to Felicity.

A red blur.

Eventually, the siren shut off, leaving the red light as the sole beacon of the destruction.

Felicity blinked, her vision clearing, and she glanced sideways at Silas.

His hand rested on her knee, fingertips tapping a slow, repetitive beat against her skin. He looked up as the silence settled and turned to Felicity. "Feelin' any better, Liz?"

"I'll be better when all of this is over," she said, taking a deep breath and forcing out a small smile.

"One day, it will be better, Liz," he said. "Hopefully, very soon."

She placed her hand on top of his. "One day," she smiled.

He gave her a sad smile in return. "One day, Liz."

Felicity's heartbeat slowed. She tightened her grip on his hand, before letting her fingers fall away onto her lap. He finally let out a sigh. "I have to go, Liz."

Her heart lurched. She wished she could stay beside Silas forever, hiding her face away from the flashing lights.

They both stood. He hugged her quickly. "If you need help call me," he said. "Don't get too worked up and anxious, Liz. It's going to be okay."

"I will. I promise," she choked out.

She turned away from him and took to the stairs, her eyes glued on the floor. It was a mistake leaving his side. Now she was alone again. Fear began to creep up her throat no matter how hard she tried to swallow it down. And then—*bam!*

Tabitha slammed right into her.

Felicity staggered back, a cry tearing from her lips, but her friend grabbed her shoulders, steadying her before she could fall.

"Felicity!" Tabitha cried, throwing her arms around her and squeezing her till Felicity gasped for air and pulled at Tabitha's arms to let her go.

Tabitha stepped back. "We have to go, Liz."

"Home?" Felicity's eyes widened.

Tabitha smiled wide and shook her head. "To the mountains."

Felicity froze, arms hugged close to her chest, her lips quivering. "Are you crazy?" Her words only came out as a gasp, not the scream she'd intended. She needed Silas—

needed *someone* who wasn't insane—but he wouldn't have heard that pitiful cry. No footsteps came to her rescue.

"Felicity." Tabitha crossed her short arms over her chest. "I promise I know what I'm doing."

"It's about that girl, isn't it?" Felicity groaned. "Forget it, Tabitha!"

"I haven't seen the likes of her in. . . in well, ever! And she'd ran into the woods! Please, Liz! This *girl* could give us answers about what happening!"

"So now you want to follow some random girl who showed up at our creepy little Inn, in the middle of nowhere?" Felicity's hands began to shake. She clenched them shut.

"Exactly. And if there's nothing out there, and it turns out I was wrong and the girl's just a psycho, we'll come back and forget this whole thing ever happened. And I'll pay for all your hot leaf water for the rest of your life," Tabitha said, keeping her lips firmly pressed together, though her lips quivered with laughter.

Felicity sighed. "Fine. Ten minutes."

"Ten minutes?" Tabitha gasped, throwing her arms up. "No! An hour."

"Fifteen."

"Fifty-nine."

"Thirty and that's final." Felicity crossed her arms, the eroded step below her squeaking, the sound echoing through the hall.

Tabitha huffed. "Fine, thirty will do."

Tabitha wasted no time. The girl couldn't have gotten far, right? No one dared venture too deep into woods.

And was she crazy to bring Felicity *Bentsworth*, the girl scared of everything on the planet, with her?

Yes. Yes, she was. But it wasn't like she had a choice. She was in North Cordell for Felicity's sake, and there was no way she could justify going into the woods alone without her.

Felicity followed her down the back steps, timidly, her steps careful and slow.

"Come one, Liz," Tabitha said. "Thirty minutes, remember?"

Felicity opened her mouth in rebuttal, but shut in, with a forced frown.

Tabitha cracked a smile. She turned on her heal and headed into the feild of long, swaying overgrown grass, and broke out into a run. She heard Felicity cry out for her slow down, but Tabitha pushed it to the back of her mind. She could slow down later. Right now, she just needed her thirty minutes.

The sky thundered.

Tabitha barely wasted a glance upward to the grey stormy sky. Another storm. It wasn't anything uncommon, but it was strange timing.

She burst from the grasses, landing on the damp bank of the weak river. She spotted the small bridge, moss growing across the rotten wood, looking like it was as old as Earthshaker itself, with its missing planks, and rusted screws.

Felicity was still jogging her way carefully toward her.

Tabitha laughed. "Come on! Twenty-five minutes!"

Felicity shot her a quick glare.

Tabitha walked to the bridge, at a slow pace, giving Felicity her time. Her first step, the entire structure creaked under her weight. She cringed.

Another moment.

It held up.

She stomped her foot. A small shudder from the bridge, but nothing else. It was well built. She turned to the mountains. All air escaped her. She'd never been this close before.

They soured above her; the iconic four peaks hidden in the storm clouds. Fog trickled through the rows and rows of green ascending the massive earth structure. A gust of wind brought her back to her senses.

A shiver ran down her spine.

There's nothing to be afraid of. It's just some mountains. The townsfolk just say things to scare upper region visitors, She thought.

"They're beautiful, aren't they?"

Tabitha jumped at Felicity's voice. Felicity's face was relaxed, her head titled upward, her yellow-green eyes wide in astonishment at the sight, a small smile tugging at her lip. Of all people to not be afraid of the mountains, Tabitha would never have suspected Felicity.

Tabitha cleared her throat. "Let's go."

Felicity stepped onto the bridge. It swayed with her weight, causing her to scream. It stopped, but Felicity still stood frozen, her hands clamped to the rail.

Tabitha sighed, with a smile. At least now, she could be the brave one again.

She led Felicity across the bridge and to the other side.

"What's your plan?" Felicity gulped as they approached the trees.

"Twenty minutes to see if we can find a sign of the girl," Tabitha said.

"And after that?"

"Haven't thought much past that part," Tabitha admitted.

"But if I see her, I will have proof she's in the woods. Only lunatics come in the woods voluntarily."

"So, you're calling yourself a lunatic?" Felicity's face did not brighten with the joke, only becoming paler as the shadows thickened.

"No! I-I'm helping." Tabitha trudged forward; her head held high. A wet droplet hit her right in between her eyes. She reeled back, her heart racing. Another followed. Then another.

It was raining.

Lovely.

Something snapped.

"Did you hear that?" Felicity said, looking over her shoulder.

"Probably just a rabbit," Tabitha said.

"A rabbit? Have you ever seen one?" Felicity raised a skeptical brow.

"No. But they live in woods, so I can't be too far off." Tabitha turned on her heel and continued to march through the woods. The rain came down harder. *Fifteen minutes.*

Still no sign of the girl.

Probably because they sounded like elephants. Tabitha blamed Felicity. The girl would be scared off in a second, and from a mile away.

The wind began to whistle through the branches. A sickly feeling crept into Tabitha's gut. She gritted her teeth. She slowed her pace. *Breathe.*

"Tabitha Delorous, come to me."

What was happening?

"Tabitha?" Felicity ran to her. A boy jumped from the brush and grabbed Felicity back. Felicity shouted. Cole shot Tabitha a look, words forming on his lips.

Something dropped, the back of her head spiking with pain. Her vision blurred.

The world swayed.

And Felicity screamed.

7

THE LIGHT HAD BEEN THERE. SHE HAD SEEN IT. IT WAS AT the Inn, right before the ground shook and the red lights came back to illuminate the town. She'd watched the mountains all night, waiting for the little light to reappear. And it had.

And, at an all too convenient time, it fled.

"Are you trying to leave without me?"

Nikki nearly tripped and fell face first into the rushing river below. She caught herself against the support of the eroding bridge as it creaked under her weight and she whirled to the boy, who stood with his arms crossed and a dark brow raised at the end of the bridge. "Remember me?" he said, his lips curling into a smile.

Nikki's fist clenched. It was the boy, Ray, from the day before. He looked a bit more put together than the day before, his black hair smoothed back, his eyes bright and alive. He was dressed in three different shades of grey and black, and looked quite proud to have snuck up on her.

She turned away again, leaving the bridge for the soft earth on the other side. She looked up to the four peaks towering high into the dark, rolling storm clouds. They seemed to go on forever.

"Looks like a storm. You know what a storm is, right? Rain and stuff." Ray stood right next to her, looking up to the sky.

A growl rumbled through the sky. It sent a shiver down Nikki's spine, freezing in her place.

"And thunder!" the boy called after her. "Storms have thunder!"

"A storm?" she muttered.

Ray ran to her side, teeth flashing in a grin. "Yeah, a storm."

"Did a storm cause the broken road?"

Ray frowned. "A storm?" He burst out laughing, and she took another deep breath and marched onward.

The sky flashed, another 'thunder' following. The sky was a strange place. Little lights, gloomy clouds, strange sounds.

She broke into a run. Ray called out for her to slow down, but she had no such intentions. Something wet hit her face, then another. And then it was pouring down all around her. Rain.

The girl slowed, looking over her shoulder.

Ray slipped, falling over into the mud. He picked himself up, leaning against a tree and catching his breath, not bothering to scrape away the wet dirt that clung to his face. He waved to her, panting. "Hey. Please…no more running."

She turned away from him, looking up through the trees

and the wild brush, through the darkness that began to fall over them. A shiver traced her spine again. What were the 'Purizies' Ray had warned her about yesterday? She clenched her fists. He couldn't have been telling the truth.

She looked back to him as he was hopping around on one foot, his other shoe suctioned into the mud. He caught her eye and winked.

Something splashed.

Her body tensed, and Ray froze. Nikki whirled around; her fists clenched.

There was only rain.

"Who are you? You shouldn't be here!" The voice boomed from behind her.

She turned her head slowly to look over her shoulder.

A boy, about her height, pointed what seemed to be a bow and arrow like contraption right at her and stood only a few feet away from her, right behind Ray.

Ray's golden eyes shifted all around, and he half turned his head, but stopped himself almost instantly.

All three of them stayed still, waiting for someone else to move first.

The stranger's gaze darted between the two of them. Nikki watched him curiously. He was tall and had a wet mop of brown hair and the darkest eyes she'd ever seen. She couldn't tell his pupil from the color in the dim light of the brewing storm.

"What are you doing here?" he said, circling slowly toward her.

Nikki didn't respond, eyeing his weapon.

He lowered his bow contraption, pointing it at the ground and frowned at her. "Who are you?" he repeated.

Again, she silently refused. Despite his bow, he didn't

look much of a threat.

"Are you mute?" he said, walking closer. Now she could see his eyes were black.

"Her speech is limited to fluent confusion or weak threats," Ray called out. He managed to grab his shoe and pull it back over his foot, then he gripped his bag and strode over to them. Ray saluted, his smile as easy and casual as ever.

The boy flinched.

A sudden flash shot down and thunder rumbled. A distant scream rang through the air. Nikki's senses perked up.

"Felicity?" Ray called out, his eyes widening.

Nikki took off in the direction of the scream.

"Hey! Where do you think you are going?" the strange boy yelled after her. "We aren't done!"

Nikki didn't look back. Her senses overtook her mind.

"Wait up! You're still not out of this!" the boy shouted, sprinting after her, tossing the bow over his shoulder.

Nikki stopped at the top of a steep descent, staring down the steep slope.

The boy caught up behind her. "You think the scream came from down there?" he said, panting.

Her features twisted into a frown.

"How do you plan on getting down there?" he asked, a line of confusion deepening between his brows.

Nikki carefully slipped over the edge until she was almost lying on her side in the mud, supporting herself with the protruding root of a tree. She fumbled for another handhold, let go of the root, and maneuvered her way down slowly.

The boy followed, slow and hesitant, as he traced his way down in the slippery mud.

Another flashed bolted from the sky.

The boy's voice tore through the thunder. "Watch out!"

Nikki barely ducked out of the way of a falling branch.

So, the flash in the sky could hit things.

The boy lost his grip in the wake of the flash, and he slid downward, crashing into her.

Nikki tumbled down the hill until she caught a hold of a slim tree. She tried to breathe, the horrible gritty earth coating her tongue, she coughed, shaking her muddy hair from her face, coated in the filth, digging her fingers into the wet earth. She shot a glare at the sky. The flash -lightning as Ray called it- she decided, was not good.

The boy seemed to have had no better luck than she had. His entire body was coated in mud. Ray came tumbling down only a moment later, his body caked in the dark, wet earth.

The strange, dark-eyed boy stood up, shaking off what he could.

Nikki shot him a look.

He shrugged. "Hey, I most likely saved your life, alright?" he said, adjusting his bow contraption. "You could've been hit by the lightning next. So, don't be going around with that face."

Ray scrambled to his feet, shaking himself off, though it barely did him any good. "I could have managed it myself. Didn't need some little stick figure warrior boy to swing in and help. Right, girl?" He turned to Nikki with his brows raised.

Another scream brought her back to reality.

"Hello? Anyone?" The redheaded girl's voice came muffled in the darkness.

The farther they ran, the more fog began to build around them. The smell was awful now, stinging at her throat. She coughed, taking in another mouthful of the air. She nearly choked, covering her mouth.

Ray gave in to a coughing fit as they ran deeper into the smog. "What is this stuff?" he coughed out.

Nikki looked sideways to the outline of one of the boys beside her. The smoke was thick, and a silent, eerie chill ran through it. It twisted and flowed around her as she slowed her run. The boy stopped.

"Hello?" came another cry. This time it was a deeper, masculine voice.

"Two?" the dark eyed boy said.

Ray tore past them both. "We're coming!"

Nikki and the dark eyed boy broke back into a run.

Ray came to a stop as the fog cleared around another figure. Nikki frowned through the smog at the second figure crouched on the ground, and her chest seized.

She forced herself to run closer, then slowed again at Ray's side.

The red-headed girl, Felicity, stood with hands clasped over her mouth, her freckled face stained with tears, and her eyes strained in horror as they settled on Nikki. She looked like she was about to scream as she clasped her hands over her mouth, but no sounds would come out.

Then all the sudden, her voice broke out in a choked cry. "It's her! She's the one who bombed Imperial. She attacked the road. It's her! It's her fault!"

"Woah, Felicity! Chill!" Ray stepped forward and grabbed Felicity's shaking shoulders.

"W-what's—" a dreary voice came from the ground. The crouched figure made a *shushing* sound.

Ray's face paled, and Nikki followed his gaze to the ground. The shorter girl, Tabitha, lay limp in the lap of a young man Nikki hadn't seen before. His hair was blonde, rain sticking it to his forehead, his face stiff and concentrated, a gold medallion hung loose from his jacket. Tabitha was hurt. And the Felicity girl thought this was all *her* fault.

"She's hurt," the dark-eyed boy's voice came from behind her.

Nikki started to sink into a crouch, reaching toward the girl, but Felicity's shriek stopped her.

"Don't let that girl touch her!" Felicity screamed. "She'll kill her!"

"She's already dying," Ray said, pulling off his muddy glove and pressing two fingers against the girl's neck.

Felicity tensed at his words, her eyes wide but glowering at Nikki, like she would pounce at any moment.

"What happened?" the dark-eyed boy asked.

The boy holding Tabitha lifted his eyes to Felicity. The trembling girl's eyes were glued on Nikki and she didn't move to respond, so the fair-haired boy glanced at the stranger.

"I think they were attacked," he said, his voice strained. "They came out of nowhere. All I saw were dark flashes descending. I grabbed her, but--"

"It was her!" Felicity cried, pointing at Nikki.

"We don't have time for this!" Ray shouted.

They all dropped silent, holding their breaths. Tabitha groaned softly, before even she dropped silent.

Ray scanned the faces of the others. "We need to get her help, now!"

A violent wind burst through the air, the smoke swirling. The tendrils hissed like a thousand snakes, curling around the group as they stood frozen. The wind died down for a moment, enough to let them breathe, but then picked back up. Thunder greeted them with a roar from above.

"We need to get back to the Inn!" the fair-haired boy

holding Tabitha yelled.

"We don't have time! Even if we could see where we're going," Ray shouted over the wind.

"We have to do something!"

"We're all going to die!" Felicity cried.

"Calm down!" Ray yelled.

No one calmed down.

Nikki was frozen in place, her mind reeling. Her thoughts were sharp and clear but confused at the same time. She could feel it. A strange energy. The same energy the strange hands radiated. It was coming closer.

"We have to go!" she shouted.

Everyone dropped silent. Even she was surprised that she'd raised her voice.

The dark-eyed boy's eyes growing wild, muttering something beneath his breath. He must have felt it too. He unhooked a small lamp from his belt, shaking off the dirt. The light burst on.

The ground shook.

Nikki was tripped, slamming hard into the ground. The earth continued to shudder beneath her. Felicity screamed from somewhere overhead, and the wind whipped against them even harder.

Then the ground stilled.

Nikki stumbled to her feet.

The boy rushed up to her, holding up the light. It reflected little dots of white in his dark eyes. "I know a place where we can go."

"How far?" Ray asked, his eyes wide with desperation.

The wind whipped harder, and the fair-haired boy held Tabitha closer to his chest. In the light, Nikki could see the grey tone of the girl's skin.

"It should only take a few minutes," the dark-eyed boy shouted over the wind, his eyes shifting to her almost as if for some sort of approval.

She nodded.

They didn't have any other choice.

The young man staggered up; Tabitha cradled in his arms. She didn't even stir as he rose.

The dark-eyed boy hesitated, staring at her. "Did you get a clear look at them?" he asked. "The people who attacked her?"

"They were *flashes*, shadows," the fair-haired boy said, his voice growling through clenched teeth. "I don't even know if they were human."

"Purizies?" Ray suggested, brows furrowed.

"That's an old folk's tale!" the other snapped. "This—this is *real*. I got to them in time to see the shadows run into Tabitha. She disappeared from sight for a moment, then out of nowhere she just fell. She's been pasty and feverish ever since. And this fog…it's getting worse."

"It was her!" Felicity cried again.

"Come on!" Ray interrupted, cutting off any further hysterics. "We need to get out of here."

"We're here!" the boy said, leading them into a small cave.

Actually, 'cave' was a real understatement.

The place was more like a little cottage. Little shelves had been carved out of the sides, holding little tools, small gadgets made of stone, and spare parts. In the center, a fire pit had been dug out.

The dark-eyed boy stirred up the fire with an extra pile of logs, then grabbed a metal box from the shelf and hurried back to Tabitha.

Cole laid Tabitha on a tarp.

She was inhumanely pale, her veins a dark purple, and a tiny cut lined the side of her neck. Tears burned at Felicity's eyes. How had she let this happen?

Ray snatched the box from the dark-eyed boy, rummaging through.

"Are you a medic?" the boy asked.

Ray froze, then began pulling out little pouches of herbs. "Not officially."

"Whatever medicine you've not been officially trained to do won't save her."

"Isn't there anything we can do?" Cole looked up from Tabitha's pale face, his brows creased in helpless lines.

"Do you have any Pheomena Fleux?" Ray said, turning to dark-eyed boy, glaring hard into his eyes.

The dark-eyed boy frowned. "I don't think that's going to help—"

"Just tell me!"

"I think I saw a bush of it on the way here."

Ray turned back to Tabitha. "Someone needs to get it."

"A weed?"

"We don't have time for this! She can't breathe!"

Terror shot through Felicity, a gasp escaping her lungs. All three of the boys looked up like they'd just noticed she was there.

"Positivity," the older boy, Cole, muttered to the others.

"I'm going to search." The small voice came from the cave entrance.

Felicity turned her eyes to the soft-spoken girl in the mouth of the cave. The winds whipped the girl's hair all over her face and there was so much concern etched into her large eyes, that the hatred that burned in Felicity's chest wavered for a moment.

But she reminded herself that this girl was evil, and it burned brighter again.

The ground shook again, cutting off any response. Felicity stumbled into the wall, catching herself, dropping to the floor. She hugged herself in terror. The panic was creeping up on her again, her throat closing.

Breathe.

As soon as the earth steadied, Felicity pushed herself up. The quiet girl scrambled to her feet at the same moment and ducked from the cave. Felicity's heart skipped a beat. There was no way she was going to let that girl go alone.

Her legs were uneasy below her and her head throbbed, but she ignored it, grabbing the lantern and stumbling through the mouth of the cave. She tripped over her heel, nearly falling on her face, but someone caught her arm, pulling her up to her feet.

Felicity took a moment to catch her breath. Lightning flashed. Felicity jumped, looking up to the sky, raindrops pelting at her face. She whirled around to see the girl standing beside her. Felicity took a quick step back.

The girl had caught her.

Felicity had *let* her.

"I-I'm…making sure…you—you're helping,' Felicity stuttered.

The girl remained unphased.

Felicity realized she probably wasn't the most threatening person, even at the best of times. "I-I know what you did. I'm watching you."

The girl was still for a moment, then gave a single nod of her head, turned, and ran.

Felicity chased after her, slipping a few times, soaked and

caked in mud. Eventually, the girl jolted to a stop. Felicity pulled up beside her, chest heaving for breath. Her hands were shaking like crazy. She flexed her fingers, trying to force feeling back into them.

The girl started sorting through the shrubbery that crawled along a large boulder. Felicity narrowed her eyes.

The girl flinched and pulled her hand back.

Felicity's eyes widened. "You-you cut yourself," she said, unable to tear her eyes from the cut on the girl's hand as it lined with blood.

The girl ignored, tearing a fistful of the shrubbery and holding it close to her chest. She looked to Felicity as if for confirmation.

Felicity glanced back, then back at the girl. "L-let's go."

They both stood there. Felicity waited for the girl to start running back to the cave, but the girl just stood there, watching her. Was she waiting for *her* to go first? Her heart skipped a beat.

"Come on," she said, a little more urgently. "Let's go back."

The girl hesitated a moment, then burst into a run. Felicity's heart settled. They weren't lost. She ran after the girl.

The ground rocked.

Felicity shouted; her legs caught from under her. She slammed into a tree, pain bursting through her side. She tensed, clutching the lamp against her chest and squeezing her eyes shut, tears burning under her eyelids.

The shaking lessened, and a hand grasped her shoulder.

She didn't open her eyes.

Felicity slowly turned her head upward, forcing her eyes open to slits. The blurry figure of the girl hovered above her. The ground still trembled below them, and the thought of standing up was terrifying.

But Tabitha was waiting for them.

Felicity sat up, shaking. She leaned against the tree for support as she climbed to her feet. The ground trembled, like it would erupt at any moment. She looked up to see the girl, who turned her head to the soft light in the distance.

They were close.

She pushed away from the tree, steadying herself on her feet. The girl turned and ran, Felicity stumbling after her. Thunder echoed through the air, but Felicity kept her eyes steady on the glow.

They burst into the cave, Felicity crumpling to her knees again.

She looked to Tabitha, who lay on the floor of the cave, unmoving. There were no gasps for air, or meaningless muttering. She was still. Was she alive?

The girl pushed past the boys, dropping to her knees. Ray spotted the shrub held tightly in her fist and he held his hand out for it. The girl looked up to him with her wide, trembling eyes.

Ray took the weed from her hands, beginning to shred it, and rub it between his hands. The girl backed away from them, holding her cut hand close to her. Felicity's eyes shifted from her, to Tabitha, and back again.

Ray pushed the other two boys away, mashing the shrub in his other hand, and pressed the green mess against Tabitha's neck. A blast of cold air rushed through the cave. Felicity crawled back on her hands until she bumped against the back wall of the cave.

Tabitha wasn't moving.

Felicity's hand clenched to fist against the cold, hard ground. The flames flickered. Then the pebbles scattered over the ground began to tremble.

Not now. Mortals, please not now.

The earth rattled again, and Felicity curled in a ball, trying to control herself as her breath caught against the tightening pressure in her chest. She squeezed her eyes shut.

Something crashed. A shout. Thunder.

Then there was a gasp for air.

8

The girl was alive.

Even when the shaking stopped, Nikki's head couldn't seem to stop rocking with the thought.

Tabitha coughed up a storm, waking up in a drowsy panic. Felicity scrambled to her, and it seemed to take Tabitha a moment to recognize Felicity's face. She froze for a moment, then collapsed back.

Felicity fell to her knees, but the girl waved her hand drowsily. "N-no, it's fine," Tabitha mumbled.

The dark-eyed boy rushed over with his arms full of blankets.

Tabitha was too weak to resist being swaddled and set by the fire. Her eyelids drooped, snapped open, then drooped again and it was only a few minutes before she was settled against Felicity's lap.

Felicity sat tense beneath her, her long red hair soaked to a dark auburn, sticking to her face, and spattered with mud.

Ray tried to check the cut on Tabitha's neck, but she pulled away in her sleep, and Ray gave up, slumping onto the ground. There was an awkward distance between the six of them.

"How about introductions?" All eyes turned to the dark-eyed boy as he spoke.

This was the first time Nikki had seen him in the light that wasn't a waving lantern. He'd set his bow-like contraption on a hook in the wall, though he still had a metal arrow shaft in his belt. He wore a dark hooded jacket, faded and well-worn, the muddied sleeves pushed to his elbows. His roughly cut hair stuck up in a wet tangle of sandy brown strands.

"Now that we're all stuck in a cave, I think it might be nice to know how to address each other." He shrugged.

"You go first. You're the mysterious hunter boy, with death threats and all," Ray said, peeling off his soaked jacket and tossing it to the floor.

The dark-eyed boy raised an eyebrow and let out a breath. "Lincoln. Fifteen."

"That's it?" Ray frowned.

"What else is there?"

Ray cleared his throat. "Raphael Mathews. Fifteen. Glorgory."

The boy, Lincoln, seemed unphased, and Ray scowled, clarifying, "Name. Age. Home region?"

"I'd answer you if I knew." Lincoln crossed his arms.

Ray sighed, plopping down to the ground. "You can call me Ray."

Felicity looked up her eyes still wild. "F-Fel—"

"Her name's Felicity," Tabitha grumbled, pulling the blanket tighter.

Felicity nodded, closing her eyes, taking in a deep breath. "Eighteen," she stammered. "A-and this…this is—"

"Tabitha Delorous," the blond boy finished for her. "Sixteen. Both from Liberty."

Felicity's face melted to a frown, looking over her shoulder at him with a snort. The blond boy fiddled with a golden metal circle dangling from his neck. He was the least mud-caked out of all of them. His blond hair swooped up from his face, and his eyes were a bright green. So bright they almost glowed, shouting for attention.

"Liberty?" Lincoln frowned, glancing at Felicity. "Like one of the Capital regions?"

The girl froze, her arm tensing around her friend. She managed a shaky nod.

"Cole Johnson. Seventeen," the blond boy said, nodding to Lincoln.

"Part time errand boy too," Ray scoffed.

Cole rolled his eyes, tucking his medallion away under his shirt.

"You work at the Foundation Fields?" Lincoln asked, with a small frown.

"No," Cole said, glancing to Ray. "Raphael does. I just…work an extra job for the department stores."

Ray seemed to squirm at the mention of his job, clearing his throat, and turned his head to Nikki. "And you?"

Everyone turned to Nikki. It sent a terrifying chill up her spine. She felt the Stone flicker in her pocket, and the swarm of discontent swirled in her mind, clawing at her like a question she should know the answer to but didn't yet.

"N-nu—" she began, before shaking her head and

restarting, "N-Nikki."

There was silence, even the sound of the whipping rain and thunder seemed to dull into the distance for a moment.

"Nik," Lincoln said, suddenly. The word sent a strange shiver down her spine. "I'm going to call you Nik."

She didn't object.

"How did you know Phenomena Fleux would work?" Lincoln asked, turning attention to Ray.

Ray flicked a patch of dry mud from his arm. "I didn't."

Lincoln frowned. "What?"

His eyes moved to Nikki.

She froze.

Then he looked away and back to Ray.

"Back in the EarthShaker, they attempted to create genetically modified plants, that gave specific abilities. You learn this in base education," Ray said.

"Never went."

Ray paused. "Oh. Well, that explains it. The plants were just an experiment, the originally made a File to go directly to humans. It failed though, and the plants spread like weeds. My mom...she's a doctor." Ray began to tap his foot. "She had some of the pure P9F file. It's a powerful healing mechanism. The weed usually doesn't work that well."

Silence fell over them. It seemed to drag on forever.

Cole rose, stepping toward the mouth of the cave. "I'll keep watch," he muttered.

Ray whistled under his breath, sorting through Lincoln's box of medical supplies. Tabitha fell asleep again, and they laid her down by the fire. Felicity sat beside her friend, legs crossed, and her eyes stuck on Nikki with a glare.

Nikki sat with her back against the wall, her chin resting on her fists. The small cut had stopped bleeding, but still stung dully.

Lincoln came over to Ray, pointing to a spool of leather in Ray's hands. He mumbled something Nikki couldn't make out. Ray scowled, muttering something back, but Lincoln sank down to the ground beside him anyway, taking the spool of the leather. He whispered something again, and Ray shoved him.

"They're here!" Tabitha shot up, her eyes wide and her face coated with sweat. She was on her feet for a moment, then stumbled back to her knees, gasping for air and clawing at her hair.

Cole rushed over, catching her before she could fall on her face. He lowered her gently to the ground, his eyes wide and worried.

She stared into an invisible abyss, her lips quivering. She fought weakly against his steadying grasp, trying to push him away. "No," she cried, her voice cracking. "They're coming."

"Who?" Lincoln was frozen, crouched by the fire.

No one answered.

He stood and repeated his question, "Who?"

Felicity reached for her friend, but Tabitha pushed her away. Hurt flickered across Felicity's face and she pulled back.

"Dark," Tabitha muttered, staring up at the ceiling.

Silence.

Tabitha's eyes rolled back, and she slumped back.

Cole caught her head before it could crack against the stone ground, his breath shuddering in his chest as he stared down at her.

"She's dying," Felicity shouted, tears welling in her eyes. She twisted to Nikki. "She's dying! And it's your fault!"

"For the last time, it's not her fault!" Ray scowled, brushing Tabitha's hair from her face. He placed one hand against her face, and his other fingers pressed to her neck.

They all watched him in silence. Felicity brushed a tear away, glaring hard at Nikki.

Ray let out a sigh. "Her pulse is normal. She's okay."

Cole's tense shoulders relaxed, and Felicity fell back, scrubbing away tears.

But Lincoln still looked horrified, watching Tabitha. He blinked, shook his head, and moved to stir the fire.

"What did she see out there?" Ray asked, turning to Felicity.

Felicity shook her head. "I don't know," she choked the words out. "I don't know what happened…" She curled into a ball and hid her face, sobs shaking her shoulders.

Nikki felt wrong watching her, like her body was telling her to leave the girl alone, but she couldn't tear her gaze from the hysteric girl.

Lincoln silently stationed himself on the other side of the cave as Ray applied the herb to Tabitha's neck again, then draped the blanket over her, settling himself back into a corner.

Felicity caught her breath for a moment, glancing up, her eyes cold and hard on Nikki. Then she hid her face again.

The familiar shiver returned, trickling down Nikki's spine.

Felicity made it very clear that she held Nikki responsible, and she wasn't backing down.

The rain poured down and thunder continued to rumble for the rest of the night. The coals of the fire glowed dimly, still giving a gentle warmth to the whole cave. Nikki stared at the glowing remains and wrapping her arms around her knees.

Felicity had fallen asleep eventually, hidden away in the

folds of a blanket beside Tabitha. Ray was dozing in his little corner in the shadows, and Cole had finally stopped pacing in the mouth of the cave. Lincoln had offered to keep watch to let him rest.

"You're still awake?"

Nikki snapped out her daze, looking up at Lincoln who stood over the dying light.

His face was surprisingly soft, his eyes gentle as they met hers. "This must be unusual for you. I mean…getting lost and all," he said, a bit of sympathy in his voice.

She silently shook her head. She let her hair fall over her dirt-streaked face, peering up at Lincoln through the wet strands. His eyes really *were* black.

She had no idea why the idea was so fascinating.

Seeing them gave her that unsettling, anxious feeling inside again, but it was hard not to wonder. This was the first time she'd really gotten a good look at him since reaching the cave. His hair had dried, and his face was smeared with dried mud that he'd obviously—and unsuccessfully—attempted to scrape off. The hood of his jacket covered most of his face, though the loose waves of his sand-brown hair peeked through, his dark eyes shifting between the dying fire and Nikki.

She opened her mouth, but words failed her, and she shut it again.

His intent gaze slowly molded into a frown, a crease forming between his brows. Then he shook his head, his hood falling back and the dim light spreading across his revealed face. "Sorry," he muttered.

There was that word again. "What does that word mean?" she asked quietly.

Lincoln jumped at her voice. "Sorry?"

She nodded.

"It means I pity you. I feel bad for you," he explained simply, not questioning her ignorance. "It could also mean you regret something you've done to someone."

"What are you sorry for?" she asked, pulling her knees closer to her chest.

"It's just…" he hesitated, looking over his shoulder at the sleeping forms of the others before continuing, "No one comes out here. Ever. For a good reason."

He pulled his hood back up, looking away from her.

"You shouldn't have come." He squeezed his eyes shut. "You'll be dead by noon."

9

Felicity woke with a jolt.

The cold stone floor of the cave drew her back to reality, reminding her that she was not safe in her bed back at the Inn, but out in the middle of the forest. The fire had gone out, the last of the coals glowing red. The heat was barely enough to warm her fingers.

She looked to Tabitha, lying nearly beside her. The other girl was asleep, deathly still. The only proof she was still alive was the slow rise and fall of her chest.

"Liz!"

Felicity tensed, whipping her head around to the mouth of the cave. The wind had stilled the trees only swayed slowly against their grey night sky, the aroma of the light rain filling her senses. She slowly rose, hugging herself. She glanced from Tabitha, to the other sleeping figures around the cave, then finally to the outside.

"Liz!" the voice called again.

She knew that voice. Felicity stepped over Tabitha. Her name rang out again and she hesitated one last time, then took a deep breath, and slowly picked her way out of the cave.

The cold beyond the fire pricked at her face, almost painfully. It had stopped raining, but the earth was still wet below her. She hugged herself, trying to retain some kind of warmth.

"Felicity!"

Felicity whirled around and saw the source of the cry.

Silas stepped out from the shadows.

Her heart lurched and a muffled sob caught in her throat as she flung herself at him.

He dropped his lantern and hugged her, lifting her from the ground. Felicity pressed her face against his shoulder, trying to hold back the tears burning at her eyes. She took in a deep breath, then coughed as the smell of smoke stung her throat.

She pulled away from Silas. He looked more shaken up than she'd ever seen him, his usually neatly parted hair a mess, dark lines under his tired eyes. She'd only seen him hours ago, though it felt like it had been years.

Then all the questions flooded. "W-was there a fire? What are you doing here? How did you find me? Why didn't come sooner? Silas, Tabitha was hurt! How — *how* did you find me?"

Silas didn't answer her, picking his light back up and holding his hand out to her.

Felicity stared at it, then looked up to him. "Silas…"

"We can't talk here, Liz," he said, in a hushed voice, his eyes darting to the cave. "People are watching."

Felicity's heart skipped a beat, reaching her shaking hand out for his.

He grasped it, entwining his warm fingers with hers and squeezing gently. He gave her a tired smile, pulling her farther from the cave and through the cold, dark woods.

Felicity kept her eyes on the ground and her thoughts on the warmth of his hand. Why was Silas in the woods? Had something happened to North Cordell? She kept her eyes trained on the ground, refusing the panic that fought up her throat.

Silas came to a stop. "It's okay, Liz," he whispered. His voice was calm and soothing, calling her to lift her face to meet his eyes. They were wide and unblinking, his face drawn in pained lines.

He suddenly cleared his throat, pulling his hand from hers. "It's freezing," he said, slipping the dark coat from his shoulders.

Felicity began to protest, but she was almost glad that Silas insisted and slipped the coat over her shoulders. Warmth flooded over her and she pulled the coat close.

Silas' face softened.

"What happened?" Felicity said, shifting closer to him, frowning.

"Everything's fine. I promise." The shaking in his voice only worried Felicity more.

"Seriously, what's the matter?"

"Well, it doesn't really matter does it? Felicity. I've been meaning to ask you something." Silas's hands fidgeted like he wanted to reach out to her, but he held himself back.

Felicity's eyes grew wide. "And what would that be?" she

whispered, studying his face.

His expression unreadable, he reached out and gently touched her cheek, fingers brushing her skin so softly. She clutched his hand. She didn't want him to leave. "Silas?"

Again, Silas seemed to fight against his own throat to force his words out. "Do you trust me?"

Felicity stood, speechless. *Do you trust me?* Of course she did. There was no one she trusted more.

His eyes were wide, desperately searching hers. He pulled her closer and repeated his question, his voice breaking with desperation. "Do you trust me?"

Felicity squeezed his hand, with the slightest smile. "I trust you. I always will."

Silas nodded. His expression didn't soften. In fact, his face grew harder. He looked older. His lips curled into a small smile, though his eyes glinted with a half-veiled pain. He leaned forward, pressing his lips against her forehead. "Thank you," he whispered.

Everything went black.

A blindfold was pulled tightly over her eyes, as someone yanked her backward, wrists clamped in a strong, impossible grip.

Felicity screamed, trying to kick whatever was attacking her, but no sound escaped her mouth. Her heart pounded in her ears as she tried to scream over and over.

Not a sound.

Something frightfully cold slipped over her wrist. The bonds clinked together, slowly growing smaller to fit her wrists, though they dug deep enough to make her feel the burning cold. Someone pinched her shoulder, leaning close enough to her face that she could feel the skin of their cheek brush up against her own.

"Stop struggling," the voice hissed.

Her body obeyed his order. *Silas!* Where was he? Fear crawled up her skin, forcing its way into her mind. She couldn't fight it. *Silas, where are you?*

"Are you sure this is the Ewyon?" the same voice repeated, pulling her up off her feet harshly by the shoulders.

"Positive," another voice said. It was deep...and soothing. And strange.

Far too strange for her frightened mind to process it.

Her captor pulled her close until she could barely breathe. Everything began to whirl around her. The hairs on her arms prickled on end as the world spun faster, and faster. Her entire body was going to be ripped apart.

And then she was gone.

"SHE DIDN'T COME BACK?" RAY GROANED, BANGING HIS head against the wall. He stumbled back, shaking his head, wincing. "And you didn't do *anything* about it?"

The force and volume in Ray's voice brought a frown to Nikki's brows. Of course, she hadn't stopped Felicity. The girl wanted to leave, so why should anyone have stopped her?

"Someone…called for her," Nikki said, her voice falling to a whisper.

That sent everyone into a panic.

Except for Tabitha, who was still pale and shaken. She'd awoken earlier and proved quite loudly she could speak.

Tabitha pulled her legs to her chest, her face pinching with thought.

"We have to go after her," Ray said firmly.

"No!" Lincoln snapped, stepping in from the mouth of the cave.

Cole frowned, his hands curling to fists. "Why not?"

Lincoln looked around desperately, then whirled to face Cole again. "The storm," he said, glancing back over his shoulder. "The terrain will be too dangerous."

"Weak excuse," Ray scoffed. "Really. You could've come up with something more threatening. Like Purizies are coming for us or something."

Lincoln's eyes narrowed, glaring at Ray. "And what the heck are Peer…bizies?"

"Common tall tale. People think they fled and hid in the Preservations," Cole said, with a sigh. "They are commonly thought to be the opposing side in the EarthShaker."

Lincoln shook his head, laughing under his breath. "And you believe that?"

Something thumped above them.

Nikki flinched.

Another thump. Then another.

She looked around to see if anyone else heard, but they were all focused on their argument. "Hey, everyone…?" She tried to catch the boy's attention, but her trembling words failed to overrule their quarrelling.

"And you expect me to believe *your* silly excuse?"

Lincoln's face hardened, taking a step forward. "You have to listen to me."

"Shut up!" Tabitha shouted, meeting Nikki's eyes. "Nikki's trying to speak, you idiots."

They all fell silent.

Nikki blinked in surprise, then pointed upward. "Listen," she said, looking to the ceiling.

Thump.

Voices.

Someone was above the cave.

Everyone froze in place. The sound of footsteps grew, followed by more muffled voices. Lincoln's eyes grew wide with fear, his gaze darting around the cave, landing on his bow contraption that lay at Nikki's feet. His hand went for the lantern.

"They were chasing you," Nikki whispered to Lincoln. "You were the light."

Lincoln frowned for a moment, then nodded slowly.

The stomp of feet hitting the ground greeted them. The movements shifted around the mouth of the cave, though there was still no one in sight.

Nikki clenched her fists, her body tensing.

"Walk out now or we'll come in ourselves, Aviduous."

Lincoln's eyes began to frantically for an escape, but the enemy guarded the only exit.

Nikki slowly crouched and grabbed his bow from the ground. She examined it quickly before gripping it in her left hand.

Lincoln shook his head, frowned, then shrugged.

She didn't make a sound as she moved toward the mouth. She motioned with her head and movement flickered in the corner of her eye as Lincoln and Ray followed without a single hesitation. Tabitha tried to roll over and get to feet, and Cole dropped to his knees, helping her slowly to her wobbling knees.

Nikki nodded to Lincoln, who took a deep breath and stepped out of the cave.

"Hello again. So, do you think we can, you know, maybe talk about this?" Lincoln said, looking up to whoever was on the roof.

Nikki looked down to the contraption in her hand. Ray ran up to her, studying the bow with a deep frown creasing his forehead. She held the metal bend of bow and thin wire in separate hands, turning the metal part toward her. Ray frowned.

"Don't take us for fools, child." The person jumped down from the roof, landing flawlessly on his feet. His back was to the cave, his long black cape moving against the wind with a personality of its own, and two sheathed swords crossed along his back.

A tiny gasp escaped Tabitha before Cole clamped his hand over her mouth.

Lincoln crossed his arms and began to speak. "What do you need me for? Just a helpless teenaged kid, remember?"

Some of the others chuckled at his comment from above.

"Enough!" the leader shouted. "We are here to simply get the Aviduous and leave!"

Aviduous. What did that mean?

Half a dozen other men dropped from above the cave, landing neatly on their feet and advancing on Lincoln.

The boy stepped back, a smile flashing across his face as his eyes met with Nikki's.

Nikki forced herself to swallow. What was she doing? Come on! Shoot. She pulled back the cord. The tip of the arrow suddenly glowed red. That was strange.

The arrow flew from her fingers.

Her arrow shot right past the leader's head, catching the fabric of his hood and blowing it off. It sunk into the mud. Nikki's heart beat into her ears. She'd missed. She messed up Lincoln's plan.

The arrow exploded, sending chunks of clay flying.

Lincoln threw himself on the ground, tripping the caped

intruder in front as they dived for him.

The leader and several of the others whirled around, and Nikki's heart skipped a beat. They couldn't let them get to Tabitha. She still wasn't fully healed. Nikki looked to Ray. He smiled, nodded once, and they booked it out of the cave.

Nikki skidded into the open, aiming the bow at the leader once more.

"Hate to break it to you, but you're holding it wrong," Lincoln called out from the side as a few of the attackers stepped back.

The leader snarled. Wisps of his black hair flickered like flames across his face as his steel eyes bore into Nikki. "How convenient," he said, his disgust twisting slowly into a sly smile. "No need for violence." He seemed unthreatened by the bow aimed for his head.

Nikki didn't move muscle, her breathing rushed and rapid.

The leader lifted an eyebrow, muttering something in a language she'd never heard before. "Put down the weapon," he repeated, his eyes darting toward Lincoln.

The dark-eyed boy stood beside her now, staring down the leader with his eyebrows furrowed and his breathing rapid.

"But down the weapon, or the Aviduous comes with us," the leader said.

Ray scoffed.

"Don't believe them! They were going to do that anyway," Lincoln said.

Nikki didn't move, bow still leveled at the man. She'd already made up her mind.

Lincoln suddenly crumpled to the ground. Not like he fell, but like he was *pulled* to the ground. He let out a cry and fought against some invisible force pinning him down. His eyes darted to Nikki resisting the force that was trying to keep his head on the ground.

"G-go!" he shouted. "G-get out of here!"

Nikki's eyes shifted to him, and fear clenched her chest, but it was quickly replaced with a burning heat. She gritted her teeth. She maneuvered the bow into an awkward position and released.

It had to have been a coincidence. The mechanical arrow seemed to find its target all on its own. Incredible.

The arrow whizzed right by the leader's head, nicking the side of his ear.

He didn't flinch. A small smile flickered across his face as he brushed his hair back, revealing the wound. But it wasn't a wound anymore. The trickle of blood seeped right back into the cut, and the skin closed without even a scar. "You play my game quite well."

Nikki dropped the bow, staring.

The leader stepped toward her.

Nikki tensed, bracing herself for whatever the sly smile would bring.

Ray jumped forward, but with a quick flick of the man's wrist, Ray was slammed to the ground by another unforeseeable force.

The leader turned back to Nikki and waved the air between them, wafting the air toward him. An eyebrow lifted. "Strange," he muttered under his breath. His fingers traced over a silver pendant that hung around his neck.

Nikki's eyes darted from his pendant to his face.

The leader jumped toward her, a black energy shooting from the palms of his hands, his eyes growing wild. Her mind screamed for her to move, but her body wasn't fast enough to react.

Lincoln was.

Somehow, he managed to break free from the invisible bonds, and tackled her to the ground. She locked with his large, terrified black eyes. He'd saved her.

He pressed something into her hand, then he was jerked to his feet.

One of the strangers grabbed Lincoln's arm, pulling it harshly behind his back and slamming him against the ground.

Nikki scrambled up to her feet, breathless. To one side, Ray screamed for her to follow him. She ran. The last thing she saw was the leader raising the shining pendant, then the entire forest went wild, the wind howling, the thunder rumbling.

And the sky going black.

11

Tabitha felt horrible.

Not because her head throbbed and everything was shaky, but because she was stuck in a small corner of a cave while some kids got to fight people in capes. Capes!

Cole sat close to her, keeping a small gap between them and refusing to look at her.

It had to have been an hour since the noise, and the light, disappeared from the outside. The inside of the cave was pitch black everywhere Tabitha looked. It was like they'd gone blind, but Cole brushed it off every time she suggested it.

Tabitha took a deep breath, tapping her foot against the stone. Her body ached from sitting against the hard wall. Her eyes ached too, straining to adjust in the dimness. She could make out the vague shadows of the walls, and the blotch of black that made the exit. She hummed under her breath, trying to keep her mind off her situation. And the fact it was totally and completely her fault.

Felicity was lost, probably taken, because of *her*.

She should have known not to bring Felicity. She should have known she would break down and panic. That's probably why she left. But Nikki had said someone had been calling her. Who?

Cole's foot pressed down on hers. "Don't tap," he whispered.

Tabitha scoffed. "Why not?" she said.

"Can you just listen?" Cole hissed. "We can't run. You'd be too slow. If those..."

"Terrorists," Tabitha said, crossing her arms.

Silence.

"What?" Cole finally asked.

"Terrorists," Tabitha repeated, pulling her foot free from his. "Like the people who bombed Imperial."

"You think those...people are the same ones from Imperial?"

"They probably have a big crime organization."

"You've thought about this."

Tabitha scoffed. "Like you haven't."

"I have."

"Theories?"

"None I'm willing to share."

"Why? Because they're insane? Like Purizies living. Or mutated birds with claws to hold grenades." Tabitha smirked to herself.

Cole's sigh was agitated. "Just keep your mouth shut so your 'terrorists' don't come and slit your throat."

"They already tried. Remember?"

Cole didn't respond. Tabitha was sent back into the quiet darkness.

"What time is it?"

"15.32."

"Ten hours of waiting?" she groaned.

It echoed.

"Tabitha Delorous, please be quiet for your own sake, if nothing else," Cole said, with a deep, harsh breath.

She huffed, crossing her arms. She needed to stand up and do something.

Something dripped every so often, sending an echo through the cave. The wind whistled outside, the trees swaying. It was going to drive her insane.

The caped people who attacked them *had* to be the same ones who'd attacked her earlier. If only she could remember it clearly.

Bang!

An echo rang through the cave. Tabitha's heart stopped, and she felt Cole jump to his feet beside her.

"Hello?" a familiar voice called out.

Tabitha let out a sigh of relief. "We're here!"

Two sets of footsteps ran closer, then there was another thud, followed by a groan. "Anyone have a light?" Ray grunted. "Walls are out to get me."

"Felicity took the lantern," came Nikki's soft voice.

"Great."

"There has to be a fire starter somewhere around here," Cole said.

More footsteps, then something crashed. "Sorry!" Ray called out. "Just knocked something—"

The darkness lit up in a faint glow. Nikki held the lighter, like a thin metal match, her eyes wide in surprise.

Cole gathered some of the wood and kindling stacked in the corner of the cave and lit them to a small fire.

"So, you know how to make fires too?" Tabitha said, frowning. "Some university boy."

Cole rolled his eyes, pressing his lips hard together and keeping his eyes trained on the flames. "What happened?" he asked. "The sky…it just…"

"Went out," Ray said, snapping his fingers.

Nikki sat on her heels, keeping herself at a distance, her gaze on the floor. "He saved us," she whispered.

Ray groaned, throwing his head back. "I guess he did have a valid reason for not wanting us to leave."

"He tried to help us," Tabitha said, scooting herself closer.

"He didn't want us to go after Felicity!" Ray shouted, his voice echoing off the walls of the cave. "And those…things obviously knew him. They were searching for him, and he didn't want us to get caught up in it."

"And then he got himself captured," Cole said, looking up.

Ray scowled.

"A-aviduous."

They all turned to Nikki, who grew red under the attention. "They called him an Aviduous," she said, her voice growing small.

Ray went still. Cole knotted his brow, leaning back. "That can't be anything Anglish."

"So, they're not from around here, got it," Tabitha said. Then she stopped, her muscles growing tense. "D-do you think they took Felicity?"

Everyone was silent.

Tabitha looked to each of their faces, trying to pry an answer from them, but no one would meet her gaze. "We have to go after them!" she cried, trying to push herself to her feet, but her legs gave out and she plopped down. Tears burned at her eyes and she clenched her jaw. "We have to figure out who these people are."

"Tabitha, we can't just—" Cole stopped, his face twisting, seeming unsure what to say.

Nikki reached in her pocket, pulling something out and letting it clatter to the ground. A chain and pendant lay on the stone, illuminated by the flickering flames. The silver shimmered, the fire purple in its refection, in a diamond shape, three lines engraved into the surface.

Ray's eyes grew wide. "You…"

Nikki nodded. "Lincoln gave it," she said in a small voice. "Maybe we can use it's…abilities. Then we can fight them to get the others back."

"This is crazy," Cole muttered under his breath. "You're not actually thinking about going after them."

Nikki grabbed the chain and rose to her feet.

Cole sighed. "Alright, then. Here we go again."

Ray stood up and snatched the pendant from Nikki. "We'll both go. We do what we saw the leader do and see if it does anything. And then when we do, we get Black Eyes and Felicity back and get out of here."

"Where are you planning to execute your *brilliant* plan?" Tabitha asked. The entire plan seemed wildly far-fetched. There was no way it could work.

"Outside," Ray said. "You don't think this'll work in here, do you?"

"I'm going with you."

"No," Cole snapped. "You're not."

"So, you're just going to leave me alone?" Tabitha said, trying to use the wall behind her to push herself up.

"Of course not," Ray scoffed. "You have this Cole guy."

Though Cole wasn't looking at her, Tabitha shot him a glare. She looked back up to Ray, then to Nikki. "You can't possibly think this is fair."

"You are hurt," Nikki said, with a small shrug.

Tabitha sighed, leaning back and crossing her arms over her chest with a *humph*. "Alright then," she said, waving her hand. "Go do your thing."

Ray gave a small bow. "We intend to."

12

Felicity stumbled along in the cold, still darkness.

It was hard to keep her balance with her bound hands being pulled in front of her. The cuffs on her ankles made each step short and jolted, and on top of that, the blindfold was still tied painfully over her eyes. After running into quite a few walls, Felicity guessed the hall must have been quite narrow.

Her captor took a sharp turn, running her into another wall, then they stopped.

Felicity nearly fell over, but another pair of hands pulled her up by her shoulders. The hands were icy, and cold seeped through her coat. Something shifted in front of her, and warmth beat upon her.

She was roughly pushed through, then the blindfolded

ripped off her face. Felicity swayed and stared around the room.

A flame burst on a wick of a candle on the table in the middle of the dark room. Felicity jumped. Another candle on a tall golden stand burst to life on the right and then one on the left. The small flames lit the room quite well. The room had an earthy smell, and the walls were glassy, reflecting the flames and her own lonely figure.

She wrinkled her nose at her reflection. What had they done to her hair? It was tangled, and muddy, falling across her shoulders in a frizzy mess.

A figure appeared at the desk, simply materializing out of nowhere.

Felicity bit her lip, her heartbeat pounding in her ears as she scanned the rest of the room. These people could turn invisible? How many were hidden right in front of her eyes but out of sight?

He pushed back his hood, revealing his face. He was only a young man, maybe in his early thirties, with dark black hair and grey eyes, that bored into her. His very presence sending shivers down her spine. He was powerful, even if he didn't look anything out of the ordinary. She could *feel* it.

He pulled down the mask that covered the lower half of his face, and his lips pursed as if in distaste.

Felicity trembled, silently cursing herself for being such a coward.

The man frowned and turned to an empty corner with a scowl. "You reported she has none of the signs?"

Another hooded figure appeared in the corner, his head lowered in respect or perhaps shame. "Sometimes age can wear the signs," he said gruffly, his hooded face turning in her direction. "Her essence was hard to ignore."

"Who are you?" Felicity rasped, her voice shaking and worn. At least she could speak again now, not the impossible silence like before.

"She's weak," the second man added, ignoring her question. "But no doubt about it, she's stronger than most. Ewyon's are masters of deception."

"Why am I here?" Felicity asked, trying to sound more demanding this time, though her voice still cracked, turning to the newcomer.

"He doesn't have to answer to a child," the one at the desk snapped, his frown deepening with rage. "This child is nothing, but—"

"Lord Matthias Idicous!" Another hooded man stepped out of the emptiness, whipping off his hood. "If you are going to blame me for this mishap, take into consideration we may have a *Council Member* on our hands."

The lord snarled. "That Aviduous did have the wit to lie."

Felicity couldn't breathe, her chest seizing. Aviduous? Who were they? What was going on?

The newcomer turned to face her, a small, warm smile on his lips, but this time it was more terrifying than friendly.

No. This wasn't possible. Relief, then writhing, hot anger twisted in her chest as she stared into the dark grey eyes of Silas.

"Silas!" she gasped.

His skin was paler, his features sharper, and his eyes…his eyes looked almost ancient. His gaze shifted away, almost in shame, his shoulders tensing.

He wasn't here to save her.

He'd tricked her.

Anger overtook her fear. "You lied to me!" she shouted.

"You never asked," Silas responded simply. "So

technically I never lied."

Heat flushed to Felicity's cheeks as she pulled against her bonds though she knew they wouldn't move. The pain fueled her anger, pushing the fear back down to where it belonged.

Had he ever been her friend? What *was* he then? Why did his voice sound like that? Her head began to rock.

"What are you doing here? What is this place?" she demanded. "How—how could you not mention you were part of a-a cult! Magic! You—you were the one who attacked. And you had the *audacity* to comfort me." Her cheeks flamed.

"Prince Silas Idicous, actually," Lord Matthias corrected from the desk, and Silas's lips flickered to a sly smile.

He acted calm, but Felicity could see his clenched jaw and his tensed arms. So, *this* was the older brother he worked for. What *was* the 'family business'?

Tears swelled in her eyes, but she blinked them back. She wasn't afraid anymore. She was furious. "You *lied!* You're a coward! A terrorist—" Her words cut off like someone had flipped the switch and turned her voice off.

A sympathetic look flashed across Silas's face.

She wanted to scream, but any moment the tears would fall, and she refused to be weak. She wanted to hit that pretty face.

"Take this Unidentified to a catacomb," Lord Matthias said, standing up. The candle flames froze at his movement.

He shifted his attention to his brother, who was staring at the floor at his own reflection. "That Aviduous will pay dearly for his offenses, little brother."

"Did he have any magic words?" Ray said, waving the pendent around. "Anything?"

Nikki shook her head, trying to think back. She looked at the lighter they'd wedged into the ground. They're small source of light barely provided them with a few feet to see. Everything had happened so quickly. There had to have been something.

Or maybe it wasn't the man's pendant after all.

The Stone vibrated in her pocket. Her heart skipped a beat. Now? Of all the terrible things to happen in the past twenty-four hours, the Stone chose now to remind her of its presence.

You have no idea what you're doing.

It was a true statement, but Nikki ignored it.

Ray squeezed his eyes closed and jumped. He waited a moment, opened his eyes, and groaned.

The Stone sighed, sending an echo through her mind. *Pathetic. Leave now. You want to be safe.*

He kept me safe, she returned silently, trembling at speaking back. *I must repay him.*

The Stone made a low growl of disapproval but fell silent.

He thrust the pendant out to her. "This thing's freaking annoying," he said. "Have any brilliant ideas? Seriously, you have to be doing something in your silent shadow over there."

Her hand itched to grab the Stone, but instinct told her that she couldn't let Ray see it. She shrugged, taking a step forward.

Ray handed her the pendant, and she took it in one hand, chewing her bottom lip. What had the man done just before using the magic? She clenched her fist, then eased her hand, flicked her wrist, and jumped.

Nothing.

"Very cute," Ray said with a smirk. "But I already tried

that."

He took the pendant back to demonstrate. "Like so." He took a deep breath, flicked his wrist, and jumped.

And the world fell from under their feet, seeping through the earth into the darkness.

The sensation of falling was utterly terrifying.

Where was she falling to? Was Ray there too? What had he done differently with the pendant this time? Nikki hit a solid surface, flat on her back. Somehow the impact didn't crush the air from her lungs and her eyes burst open, jumping to her feet.

Ray stood beside her, his eyes wide in terror and his hands over his mouth. He turned his head slowly to her. "Th-that worked," he forced out.

They were standing in the middle of a dark hallway, the faint smell of earth lingering in the air. There were no lights, but Nikki's eyes adjusted enough to make out the winding hallways ahead and behind. It seemed as if all the walls were sealed with stone and glass.

They slowly made their way down the dark corridors.

She tried to map the maze-like hallways as they went. The walls seemed to stretch out forever, leaving her unable to piece any of it together.

No door.

No guards.

No light.

No sounds.

Just an endless maze of twists and turns.

She looked over to Ray and he gave her a toothy smirk and saluted. "Hey, let's split up to cover more ground. Find me when you're done, and we'll get out of here," he whispered.

He didn't clarify *how* she was supposed to find him, but he took off in the opposite direction before she could ask. Their plan was already unravelling at the seams. No, they didn't have a plan at all.

She ran her fingers across the walls, frost and dust collecting on her fingertips. How could it possibly be so cold? The walls felt hollow in some places and solid in others, but those were the only changes in the scenery.

Approaching footsteps finally broke the silence. A small glow of a torchlight made its way down the hallway.

Nikki froze in the shadows, too dark for the caped, masked men to see her as they marched around the corner.

Each carried a small flame, flickering in their palms as they passed., only illuminating their hooded faces and the path in front of them.

Nikki took a tense, shaky breath before silently following them, hidden in the darkness of the shadows behind the flickering flames.

Then, a way down the hall, they stopped. She pulled back further as they turned to a wall and slammed their burning palms into the wall. Veins of glowing blue crawled up the stone. A part of the wall vanished, and a glow of light flickered in to fill the gap. The men walked through the doorway quickly and professionally, silencing their hushed conversation.

Nikki hesitated.

There could be people waiting right outside the entrance. They would see her in only moments. She shook off her doubts. She had to risk it. The wall began to slowly reappear in the gap. Nikki darted for the door, slipping through the crack and dashing behind the first shelter in the room beyond, which happened to be a giant crate.

The room was huge, lit with giant flaming torches. In the center was a long table full of weapons, strange spare parts, packages, a few plates of food, maps with markings and furious scribbles, and long scrolls beside text tablets. Hundreds of projections were displayed on the walls, all displaying one room with hundreds of metal doors. The doors had no handles and were a small square shape. A projection focused on each door, and all seemed to be engraved with numbers and strange words Nikki had never seen or heard of before.

She recognized one word.

Aviduous.

The more she looked for it, the more she saw. There had to have been thousands of doors labeled with the word '*Aviduous*'. That's what they had called Lincoln. An Aviduous. Was it a person? A creature? She tried to force out the questions to focus on the room she crouched in.

The room was scattered with large dust-coated crates, sheets, and papers thrown about to the side. The wall opened again, and Nikki darted into the towers of metal boxes. She managed to position herself in between two with a dusty tarp draped over the top that left a small gap for her to see from. She lay on her side, peeking out into the room from her hiding place.

The two men she had followed had removed their masks and hoods. One had a crooked jaw, making his speech awful, though his piercing eyes made up for it. They were large, bright, and crimson red.

The other man's oiled, black hair had been put up into a ponytail, and the ends trailed over his shoulder as he examined the map that had been laid out on the table.

The new addition to the group ripped her hood off in a fury. Her hair was a striking green, and her lips matched the tone almost perfectly.

"Another Unidentified!" the green haired woman snapped, her accent sort of wispy and snake-like.

"'Em Defenders keeping 'emselves quite hidden these days," the red eyes commented.

"They're afraid, that's what!" the ponytail said, holding up the map. "Once we track down their base, we'll have all we need to meet the Lord."

"The little Aviduous brat hasn't been much of a help." Green Hair crossed her arms. "It's not every day we get a full-blood. Or a Member at that rate."

"The pure in the woods was full-blooded," Ponytail said. "I don't think we can give up on her usefulness anytime soon. Though I'm not sure she has Member material."

Nikki frowned. *Member*

"Pure full-bloods are a pain. Their essence is useless." Green Hair scowled, pulling a dagger from her belt. She slammed the knife into the table, a bolt of static running up the hilt.

"Am I interrupting something?"

It was the voice from the woods. The one who'd called for Felicity. He was here? Nikki's eyes grew wide, her heart skipped a beat.

He strode into the room, and all three dropped to their knees, bowing their heads until they nearly touched the ground, then jumped up just as fast.

"No, Prince Silas Idicous, sir," Green Hair said.

Silas scanned over the map that Ponytail had just placed back on the table, then looked back to the projections. "Locating the Defending Sergeant and the Officers, I see," he said, picking up the map and giving an approving nod to the ponytail.

Ponytail's stiff shoulders seemed to relax at the compliment.

Silas placed the map down, a pen literally appearing in his hand. He crossed out a section in the mountains and circled something else Nikki couldn't see. The three others crowded around it, blocking her view completely.

"Prying them out of their little hole is the best possible answer," Silas said, placing the pen down. "I have already spoken to the former Officer."

Green Hair scoffed. "Hutson? Didn't know the Departments gave her a piece of day."

Nikki held her breath. Sinni Hutson was in on this too? And Defending Department. The words felt strangely familiar.

Silas shifted. "She's tough to convince, but we have our…strategies. She's felt the consequences before. Locating the Defending Officers will be a top priority. I have already suggested some ideas to my brother. The force we need to awake is fast approaching."

"Then why hasn't Lord Matthias advanced?" Red Eyes asked.

Silas heaved a sigh. "He thought of it as more of a priority to catch the little Aviduous and set up his experiment to try to lure in the equipment we need," he explained. "I say we're wasting time. The faster we move, the larger the impact of the force's awakening will be."

Nikki wished he'd quit being so vague. What equipment? To wake what? So much information but no base to place them upon. Her hands tightened into fists, her fingernails digging into her skin.

The small group had fallen strangely silent. She held her breath as a cold chill prickled down her neck.

Silas frowned, looking up for a moment, his grey eyes growing darker with his expression. He turned his head to the towers of crates, then for a moment he froze on her.

He couldn't see her under the tarp's shadows. He couldn't see her. She repeated the words in her mind even as her thoughts screamed for her to fight and attack him now.

Finally, his eyes drifted away from the crates and to the projections. "Speaking of the Aviduous, he is the reason I am here," Silas said.

Green Hair gave a frown.

Silas looked at her with a small nod to confirm whatever she was thinking. "He is being brought to the Excenctial now," Silas said. "They have given you orders." He pulled a sheathed knife from the satchel that was buckled to the belt of his uniform.

Green Hair drew the wickedly long knife, a satisfied grin showing her teeth. The blade seemed to glint red in the flickering light.

"Kill him," Silas said simply.

Green Hair nodded, sheathing the knife, and bowed again. "I will make sure the blood is in your honor, my prince."

She was cramped in a small, dark space. Darkness pressed in around her so thickly she couldn't see a thing. She tried to call out, but her throat burned, her head rocking at even that slight effort. It was all too confusing. She wanted to move, but there was barely enough room to sit up in. She had to get out, but how? Her gut squeezed into a tight lump.

She screamed, kicking against the walls. Her throat seared with pain. "Help!" she yelled; her voice raspy. "S-someone help!"

Sickening fear began to crawl up her spine. She banged harder against the crowding walls. Tears began to slip down her cheeks. "Help! Please help me!"

Her arms fell. Exhaustion dragged at her breath, her

bones sore and her body heavy.

Felicity sunk her head between her knees, too weak to stop the tears. It was that *girl's* fault. Somehow it all had to be Nikki's fault. Then again, how could she have started all this? Felicity had been the one who'd trusted Silas.

The monster of fear howled in her mind, fighting its way back again.

That was the hard part. The part she hated to admit.

She felt so…scared.

She was always so afraid and alone. She couldn't fight it anymore.

He'd told her to trust him.

If she couldn't trust Silas, who *could* she trust? Felicity searched her mind for someone or something to blame for her problems. Her father, possibly. But even going back to Liberty seemed better than this. It scared her to think about it sometimes. She kept herself from there as much as possible to spare herself the anxiety attacks, but her heart longed for someone to trust again.

She probably wouldn't ever see a ray of sunlight again. She tried to brush away another tear and gritted her teeth. This wasn't the end. It couldn't be. She wouldn't let it be. She'd fight the monster. She'd fight Silas and every one of the creeps he worked with. There was no point in hoping, but the angry hope inside her was the only thing keeping her from completely losing it, so she clung to it with the strength she had left.

She had no control over these people. There was no way even her wealthy father could stop someone who could appear out of thin air and conjure fire with the snap of their fingers.

Felicity tried to solve the confusing puzzles of her strange captors, but nothing made sense. She touched the sides of her cell. Were there even other people here?

Something banged against the door.

She screamed and clasped her hands over her mouth.

Don't show fear. Don't show fear. They were back. The scraping continued as she tried to pace her breathing.

"Just leave me to die," she muttered under her breath. She couldn't face Silas again. She wasn't strong enough.

The thick titanium door fell to the ground and Nikki stood framed in the opening, staring at Felicity with wide astonished eyes.

Felicity's jaw dropped. How in the world had the other girl even gotten here?

Nikki motioned for her to get out, looking around for guards.

Felicity slipped out of the small cell. Her entire body ached from being cramped in such a small place for who knew how long. The cell door lay on the floor to the side, and the rest of the room was lined with equally tiny cells, all closed and silent.

"How in the world did you get here?" Felicity began.

"No time," Nikki interrupted, keeping her voice at a whisper. She set a crowbar on the floor. She heaved the door, rusted, bent up, fitting it back to the cell. She slammed herself into it to keep in place and Felicity cringed at the sound.

"That won't stay very long," Felicity said nervously, looking at the door. If they were caught, she'd be sent right back to the cell. The thought sent another chill down her whole body.

The cells were obviously made to never be opened. The cabinet-sized cells were like little labeled boxes of death.

They didn't even have handles. Felicity shuddered, wondering what lay behind those closed doors. What did the names mean? The numbers? She didn't want to stay and be the one to find out.

Felicity ran behind Nikki down the rows of cells. Did the other girl even know which way to go? Finally, a glass wall came into sight.

They'd almost reached the wall, when it began to pixelate and slowly fade. Panic lurched through Felicity. Someone was coming through. They were going to be caught.

A guard stepped through the invisible wall, then froze, his eyes widening as they found Felicity and Nikki. His hand flew to the weapon at his side that looked too like a pistol for Felicity's comfort, but Nikki didn't stop. The wall was materializing again more and more every second. Felicity ran blindly after her.

She heard something shatter.

Nikki shoved her past the guard, and pushed Felicity to the vanishing doorway. Another shot rang out and Felicity hid her face, trying to breathe.

"Run!" Nikki skidded out of the wall a few steps behind, just before it sealed shut fully. The girl fell onto her knees, catching her breath in shuddering gasps. Felicity didn't dare ask about the guard. Was Nikki alright?

The girl scrambled to her feet again and set off down the next corridor.

The hall was too dark for Felicity to see if she was hurt, but surely Nikki couldn't run that fast if she'd been shot. Pain throbbed in Felicity's ankle, stabbing up her leg each time her foot hit the floor. Her lungs screamed for her to stop. She couldn't do this. When was the last time she even ran like this?

It didn't help that Nikki seemed to be much faster than her.

Felicity never thought she'd envy someone because they could run faster than her and react wickedly fast to their surroundings. Left, right, right, left, right. Felicity had lost track a long time ago. She was just trying to not to trip and fall flat on her face.

Another right.

Nikki thrust herself to a stop, Felicity behind her. Her eyes widened, relief flooding through her.

Ray stood uncertainly in the middle of the corridor, but his face lit up as he turned to Nikki. "I knew you'd find me," he whispered harshly, then his gaze shifted past her to Felicity. "Felicity?"

Felicity shushed him, heart pounding.

Nikki's eyes were glued to a giant, arched entrance. A strange blueish-green glow flowed from the opening, carried on a cool breeze that sent goosebumps up her arm.

Nikki looked sideways at her.

Felicity knew what she was thinking. She was going to go through the doorway. She opened her mouth to protest, then shut it again. It was better than getting them both caught for being loud. Nikki couldn't be doing anything too reckless…unless she worked with Silas too.

Ray looked at Nikki. "It might be best, you know if I hang with her," he said, gesturing to Felicity.

Felicity could see right through his lies. He was terrified.

Nikki frowned and looked to Felicity, as if checking for her approval.

Felicity nodded, though she couldn't bear to watch Nikki's silhouette vanish into the glow leaking from the room.

Nikki stepped into the dimly lit room. Along the walls, black marble pillars towered above, and the floor was a clear white, with thick black veins crawling along in stark contrast. The veins met in the center, vanishing beneath an eerie fog that lingered over the room.

A steady murmur of voices flew around her head, but in such faint whispers she couldn't make out the words. The Stone hummed in an excited tone as she neared the darkest center, taking each step slowly.

"Don't step there!"

Nikki froze, her head jerking in the direction of the hoarse, raspy call. It had come from behind the pillars. She knew the voice. This had to be the place. She twisted from the center of the room and crept toward the pillars.

In the shadows beneath them, there were rows and rows of chained cuffs on the walls. The walls were streaked with red, and scratches across the floor made the hair on the back of her neck stand up. Two prisoners were half-masked in the shadows. One lay unconscious, their slim, ghostly body pressed against the wall. The other prisoner was very much awake, and very much alive. But it took her a moment to realize who it was.

Lincoln was hardly recognizable. His hair had fallen about his face, dirty and jagged. His face was streaked with blood, which must have come from his wrists as the cuffs had dug deep into them, soaking the ends of his jacket. He was awfully pale. She might as well have not seen him for years, not just yesterday.

"Didn't think I'd ever see you here," Lincoln said, his voice low.

Nikki looked behind her for any guards, then back at him.

The green-haired woman would be here soon to kill him. Did Lincoln know?

"I'm here to get you out," she whispered, stepping closer.

Lincoln's smile faded. "You'd have to be crazy. There is no exit or entrance for this place. Were you taken?" He leaned toward her as far as the chains permitted.

Nikki shook her head, kneeling next to him. She ran her hands over one cuff and Lincoln winced. "Key?" she whispered, the word suddenly taking shape in her mind. A key opened a lock..

Lincoln sighed. "It's DNA. There's no point. Even if I could somehow make an override, I don't have any materials. Not to mention the time."

He could make an override? She shook the questions off. Maybe they didn't need to remove the cuffs. Just the chains. She scanned the room again, and her gaze fell on an ancient display on the wall above them. A sword. She jumped up and tore it from the bracket. She wasn't sure how a sword worked, but the rusty piece of metal would to its job.

"What are you doing?" Lincoln hissed.

Nikki ignored him and without warning, sent the sword crashing down upon the first chain.

The bolt between the chain and cuff broke clean off under the blow.

Lincoln bit his lip back, half muffling a cry of shock and pain. He held up his newly free arm, the cuff still clamped around it, then glanced to the exit. "Hurry," he whispered.

The second swing snapped the old sword into shards, but not before it broke the second chain. As soon as Lincoln was free, he scrambled to his feet and ran. Nikki looked at the remaining prisoner, her stomach churning sickeningly, but there was no time. She turned and ran after Lincoln, trying to push down the nausea.

Nikki overtook Lincoln in a moment and burst back into the hallway.

Felicity heaved a sigh, but it turned into a squeal as Lincoln ran out behind Nikki, and she clasped her hands over her mouth in shock. Ray only smirked, like didn't expect any less. Lincoln looked equally surprised to see her.

"Halt! There they are!"

All four of them froze. The green-haired woman stalked toward them, her hood down, followed by a patrol of warriors. Felicity didn't move, her eyes stuck on them.

Nikki had no such delay. She grabbed Felicity's arm and ran.

"I guess this kinda ruins the secrecy and stealth method, doesn't it?" Ray shouted.

Nikki scowled. She calculated possible escapes, but each had a major flaw. They couldn't have been more than a few turns away from where they'd first appeared…

The hands.

The hands slithered over her skin, pulling her back. Panic rushed through her as she fought against the ghostly grip. Fight. *FIGHT.* She'd outrun them before. She had to resist. She couldn't give into them now.

Lincoln caught up to her pace, shouting, "Do you have a plan? Right now, would be a great time!"

"Raise the walls! Do it now!" The green-haired woman's voice thundered down the hall.

In front of them, a wall faded into view. Nikki glanced over her shoulder to see another wall closing behind them. The hands wrapped themselves tighter around her.

"We're going to be trapped!" Felicity yelled, panting, a verbal strain on her voice.

The dim light of the hall began to fade as the walls sealed them into a tight space. The hands slithered up to her neck. Nikki searched the darkness, biting her lip. *Focus on the pain.* If she could feel where the hands were coming from, she could fight them. She shut her eyes and stomped her foot on the ground.

The hands shattered and an inhumane roar filled the air as the world tumbled and tossed around them. Felicity's mouth opened in a scream, but Nikki couldn't hear it. She couldn't hear anything.

There were too many questions.

And too little answers.

PART TWO

THE SERGEANT

14

"THAT WAS STUPID!" LINCOLN GASPED AS WARM SUNLIGHT hit his skin. Pain rocked through his skull in time with his racing pulse, but the fresh air soothed some of the tension.

"The light's back," Ray said, shading his eyes to look at the bright sky.

It was much later in the afternoon than when they'd left the forest. Lincoln clenched his fists, his raw wrists stinging as the breeze brushed past. He took a small breath and urged himself to look down and examine the damage. His wrists were bloody, the skin worn away and the cuffs hanging clinging to his flesh, stained a dark crimson.

Ray sucked in his breath. "You're going to need those checked out."

"It's fine," Lincoln said, resisting the urge to flinch as he moved his arms firmly to his sides.

The older girl, Felicity, had crumpled to the ground on her knees, and Nikki had dropped to her side. Felicity stared out into an abyss, her eyes wide and lost, her hair frazzled. She was deathly pale.

Nikki touched the other girl's shoulder gently, and touch seemed to draw Felicity back to the present. She blinked out of her shock, gasping for air. Nearly toppling backward, she grasped at the earth with her fingers to steady herself, her eyes glassy as they began to take in the view around her.

"She'll be fine," Ray said.

"Y-your hands…" Felicity stammered, looking at Lincoln's wrists.

Lincoln nodded.

"Your face…mortals, you look awful." Felicity wrinkled her nose.

"Good to know," Lincoln said, taking in a painful breath.

"Wait!" Ray dropped to the ground, tearing a weed from the ground, with familiar forked leaves. "It worked wonders with Tabitha. It probably will help your wrist too!"

He ground the Phenomena Fleux between his fingers, and without asking, grabbed Lincoln's hand and drew his arm out in front of his him. He smeared the paste on the wound.

Lincoln flinched, his wrist stinging.

Ray waited a moment. "Huh. It did nothing? Not even relieve some pain?"

Lincoln shook his head.

Ray let go and stepped back, sinking into thought, his dark brows knitted together in confusion.

He finally noticed the smaller girl's eyes watching him. Nikki quickly turned back to Felicity, though Felicity just pushed her away and struggled to her uneasy feet, using a nearby boulder for support. She almost stood, but she lost her grip at the last moment and slipped back down.

Nikki watched her with curious eyes, her hand twitching as if she wanted to reach out and help but held back to keep what dignity she had left.

Felicity finally got to her feet and tried to dust herself off, though it didn't do much. "We need to get back to the Inn," Felicity said, catching her breath.

"You do need to leave. Now that they know that you know they exist, they'll be coming for your heads," Lincoln said, his eyes turning up to the clouded peaks and his mind scrambling. He hadn't been to the town in a while. With luck, his hunters wouldn't bother to look there for a few weeks. "They could already be on their way."

"Who are they?" Ray snapped.

Haunting danger loomed in Lincoln's mind, memories and fears that had almost come true. This wasn't good. Not at all what he'd meant to happen. He should have let it alone. He pressed his lips together and shook his head. "The more you know, the quicker you'll be dead." Lincoln began to turn away, but Ray jerked him back by his shoulder.

"Hey! And you'd just rather leave us to die slower? Maybe we know more than you think," Ray said, his voice shaking a little. "No one wants to die! Look they took Felicity! Why would they take her? We need to know."

"Actually— " Felicity stopped, looking on the verge of tears, her fingers digging into her arm in fury.

"Silas," Nikki muttered.

Felicity's eyes fell, tugging at a strand of hair, her face flushing red. Ray gaped, his eyes unblinking for a solid moment.

Lincoln looked between the two girls, his gut clenching. "Who?"

"Felicity's court mate," Ray put in.

Felicity shot Ray a glare, her hand raised like she might slap him at any given moment. "No. He was *not*."

"A friend. Fine. White hair. Mysterious, angst vibe sort of guy," Ray sighed, pushing her hand away.

"One of 'them'," Nikki said.

Angry tears began to fall from Felicity's eyes, but she tensed her features. "He took me. He is one of those... things."

Blood drained from Lincoln's face. This was not good. Not good at all. "Does this 'Silas' friend know any of your names?"

Ray frowned. "Why does that—"

"Yes," Felicity stammered, cutting him off. "Mine. And Tabitha's. Ray too. I'm not sure about Cole...I-I don't know."

This just got a whole lot more complicated. Lincoln cursed under his breath, squeezing his eyes shut as bile rose in his throat. "Gosh, you're as good as dead."

"Where are the other two?" Lincoln said, turning on his heel and starting in the direction of the cave.

Ray's eyes shifted nervously. "I told them to go back to the Inn if we got the pendant thing to work."

Lincoln's heart lurched. If they tried to go anywhere, they'd be caught. The cave was the safest bet, but how long would they have waited before leaving? They could have already been caught. How could they have been so ignorant? "We have to stop them!" He broke into a run, forcing himself to ignore the pain that darted through his body with each pounding step.

The others ran after him, but he didn't slow down for them to catch up.

"Why?" Ray shouted after him.

"They'll be after them!" The vague words came out wild and confusing, he knew, but there was no time to explain anything. Tabitha and Cole were in more danger each second he counted down.

"Dude, you do realize you're making *no* sense, right?" Ray yelled.

Lincoln didn't care. He tore past trees, his senses sharpening as he dodged a fallen branch from the storm the night before. The wet earth clung to his feet. He had to run faster.

There! The cave came into view. He scrambled up the slope and onto the stone ledge, careful not to fall as he made his way to mouth and burst inside.

Empty.

"They're gone!" His words echoed back, driving his point in the ghostly repetition.

He whirled around as the others finally burst in.

Felicity stopped dead in her tracks, her face losing all color. She looked on the verge of passing out.

"This is not good," Lincoln muttered, rushing to the shelves. How could they have been stupid? And where in the *world* were his boots?

Ray frowned, pushing Lincoln from the shelves. "But why? What do names have to do with anything?"

Lincoln glared at him, pushing past him.

Nikki suddenly gasped. "Tabitha and Felicity. He knew their names," she whispered. "They were attacked."

"Yeah. Freak chance!" Ray said. "Silas knows my name. I haven't been attacked."

"Not yet maybe," Lincoln said, shoving a few arrows into his bag and swinging it over his shoulder. He pushed past them and back out into the open. The fact Ray hadn't been pursued yet was curious, but there wasn't time to ponder it. They couldn't stay here; it was too dangerous. "Once they know your name, they can sense you."

"What are they?" Felicity called out, rushing after him.

"Oquelite." He clipped the word short, the taste sour on his tongue.

"That doesn't explain anything," Felicity said. "Slow down!"

Surprisingly, Ray had gone thoughtfully silent instead of demanding answers.

"It doesn't explain why they have magic powers." Felicity let out a *humph*.

"They're not magic." Lincoln quickened his pace as a shiver ran down his spine.

They were closing in.

"Seems pretty magical to me," Ray snapped, coming back to reality and quickening his pace to match Lincoln's. "If they aren't, what are they?"

"Oquelite."

Ray threw his hands up and groaned. Someone shushed him.

Lincoln looked over his shoulder.

Nikki had stopped. Felicity paused too, watching her.

Lincoln pulled to a halt; his chest tight at the delay. "What's wrong?

The girl didn't answer, looking around with wide eyes. It was like she could feel them coming too. Had she'd felt them before?

"They're coming," she said, her eyes turning to Lincoln.

He looked away, not meeting her gaze.

"I guess we'll just call them 'they' now," Ray grumbled.

Felicity's mouth gaped and she looked back and forth between Lincoln and Nikki. "I-I…how-how do you—?"

"She can feel it," Lincoln explained, the soft trembling at his fingertips warning they were growing closer.

"How?" Felicity's eyes were wide.

"They emit energy."

"Good to know," Ray sighed.

Lincoln tested the air again, the tingle running up his arms. "They're miles off," he decided.

Nikki frowned, obviously disagreeing, but she didn't protest.

Felicity's shoulders seemed to loosen a bit. "That's…good."

"We still need to keep moving." Lincoln turned again, setting a marching pace away from the cave.

"What do you mean by energy?" Ray said, falling into step. "At least explain *something*."

"It's known as essence. It's what allows them to have—"

"Magic powers?" Ray guessed.

Lincoln sighed. "Yeah." He decided not to run down the steeper terrain by the stream, not willing to risk falling, especially with an audience. He slowed just enough to take the precarious path safely down.

"Oh, and that's just a commonly known fact?"

"Actually, yes," Felicity said, her shoulders tensing as she eased herself down, her foot finding a secure place against a stone. "Although, I've never heard the word 'essence' used to describe it."

"Describe what?" Ray said, obviously tired being ignorant.

"The philosophical 'second bloodstream.'" Felicity pressed her lips together, her eyes drifting off to the stream as they came closer.

Lincoln was impressed. The girl was far smarter than she let on.

"That's gibberish. And physically impossible," Ray said.

"It's an idea," Felicity sighed. Color seemed to be returning to her face as she made her way down and onto the flat, stable ground. "That maybe the metaphysical aspects of humanity have physical forms we can't see. It's the topic of a lot of philosophy tablets."

"You listen to some boring tablets," Ray said, jumping down after her.

"Basically," Lincoln said, glancing past Ray to check Nikki made it safely down. He wiped bloody hands against his pants, hurrying for the bridge.

"Okay, but that doesn't explain why they're here," Ray countered.

Lincoln's chest tightened, a thrill of fear curling up his spine. "For the others."

"There are more?"

Lincoln sighed, crossing the bridge. "Later!" he called over his shoulder. He couldn't explain everything now. He wasn't ready to think it, let alone speak it aloud.

"Are you serious?" Ray stopped in the middle of the bridge, stubbornly crossing his arms and leaning against the post of the bridge.

Lincoln stopped, turned, and looked Ray straight in the eye, anger boiling as he clenched her jaw.

Felicity stopped beside Ray, and behind them both, Nikki looked from Lincoln to Ray, bewilderment dancing in her eyes.

"Very," Lincoln said, fighting to keep his tone controlled. "Your two friends are in *mortal* danger."

Ray gave a deep scowl, looking to Nikki like she would back him up, but she just moved past him. Felicity followed her. Lincoln broke out into a run again.

Ray's defeated groan followed him, but he quickly picked up his pace, his harsh footsteps following behind.

Beyond the steady pound of their feet, the only sound was the swift wind pushing against him, and the swaying of the long grasses. Silent relief from the barrage of questions, but it wasn't a good thing. It gave his mind too much freedom to wander to other things.

His pain decided it was a great time to make a reappearance.

He could barely resist the urge to flinch. He could feel new blood from the wounds wetting his palms and the cuffs scraping against his wrist as he ran. He gritted his teeth, shoving down the pain.

He'd have to bandage it…later.

Felicity's coughing fit brought him back to reality. He pulled himself to a harsh stop, taking in a deep breath. The air scratched at his throat, gritty and grey. He frowned.

"Fire!"

Lincoln didn't even have time to register who shouted it, but he jerked his head up, his eyes widening.

A building.

The Inn.

"Fire" was an overstatement.

There was nothing left of it but a few scattered, smoldering flames in the ruins of the first floor.

Felicity and Ray tore past him, not even stopping to take it in.

Lincoln couldn't believe it. They were too late.

Nikki stopped beside him.

"You aren't going to run to that place? No personal connections?" he asked, turning his head to her.

She turned her eyes to him, before shifting her gaze away and shaking her head.

"Together then?" he sighed.

Nikki studied him for a moment, like it took her a moment to understand him, then nodded.

They both headed for the burning building.

The fire was nearly out. One of the few standing walls was scorched black, the inside ghostly and bare.

It was gone. Stripped of all life.

Felicity crumpled to her knees, breaking into a coughing fit. "He did this," she muttered, clawing her fingers into the ashes as the coughs shook her delicate frame. "He smelled like smoke. They did this!"

Lincoln searched the area with his gaze, his heart beating faster. No one was around. But no one would just leave a burning building alone. Someone obviously had put out the free.

"We need to leave," he said quietly.

"No!" Felicity shouted, whipping her face toward him. "We can't leave!"

A light burst on. "Stay right where you are!"

Ray cursed under his breath.

"Turn around and put your arms out!"

They turned around slowly. Lincoln held out his bloody hands in front of him. What he saw was far worse than any Oquelite trying to kill him.

A woman, dressed in all black, the material tight and metallic. Her dark brown hair was cropped to mid-neck, framing her pale face, her dark eyes glaring hard at each of them. She held a gun steady in one hand, a light in the other.

A man, dressed in a similar black uniform, ran to join the woman. He stopped, examined them, then sighed. "Outown. They're just teenagers. Probably from the Fields, by the looks of it."

Ray snorted.

The woman, Outown, shot him a look, and Lincoln resisted doing the same. Ray wasn't exactly doing them any favors.

"Exactly my thoughts," Outown snapped.

"We didn't do it!" Felicity squeaked. "But you have to catch the ones who did! They're dangerous and they're after my friends. You need to stop them! You're Defending Officers—that's your job!"

"Right," Outown said, eyes narrow. She looked over to Nikki. "Hey. You! Hands out."

Nikki's brow lowered to a small frown, holding out her clenched fists.

"Out. Open your hands."

Nikki did so, slowly.

The woman gave an agitated sigh and turned to the man beside her. "Where the heck is Conrad?"

This was a waste of time. And a dangerous one. Lincoln cleared his throat. "Uh, Officer—"

"Quiet!"

Lincoln clamped his mouth shut.

The woman's companion muttered something under his breath as he turned on his heel, hurrying away.

"So, you're Out-a-town?" Ray said, a small smile forming.

Lincoln elbowed him. Hard.

Outown shifted her weapon toward Ray. "Oh. You're *so* original, kid. Don't make me shoot you out-a-this life."

"Let's see what we ha—" The man stopped in his tracks, his bloodshot eyes widening as he narrowed in on Lincoln.

Lincoln's heart stopped.

He didn't recognize the man, but something about the man's unshaved face, his greasy hair that fell over his worn, red eyes made his throat close. Something about that flicker that passed his gaze as their eyes locked.

"Disarm him," the man snapped, tearing the gun from Outown's hand and putting it into his own belt. "Bind them all!"

"What?" Felicity shrieked, her eyes wide. Then her face hardened into determined, angry lines, like she might actually get brave and attack someone.

Outown pulled out two magnetic cuffs. "I only have the two, Conrad," she said, grimacing. "I'll cuff the boys."

"No. Bind that girl and the dumb looking one together." The man, Conrad, gestured to Felicity.

Ray snickered, looking at Lincoln.

Until *his* wrist was clamped with Felicity's.

"Don't either of you think about running either." Outown shot dark looks at Lincoln and Nikki.

"We didn't do anything!" Felicity said, trying to jerk away, but almost resulted in having Ray crash face first into her. "You don't have any evidence against us. We're not even dangerous!"

Conrad ignored her. "Load them and take them to the Sergeant. I will deal with the Aviduous personally."

15

Nikki's breathing quickened, her eyes wide as Outown grasped her shoulders. She kicked at the woman's legs, twisting and writhing to pull away.

Conrad's hand reached for his weapon in his holster and Lincoln stiffened. He whirled around to Nikki. "Hey, it's okay," he said, mind scrambling. Would Conrad shoot her if she didn't calm down? They couldn't afford that. She would mess it up.

She froze, and her eyes darted to his, though they quickly fell.

"It's okay," he repeated. "No one will hurt you."

"Unless you act out," Conrad grumbled.

Lincoln ignored him, giving Nikki a small nod. It seemed to work. She let Outown clamp one cuff over her wrist.

Turning to Lincoln, Outown frowned at the cuffs already around his bloody wrists, but she didn't comment, swiftly clasping on the last manacle.

Lincoln flinched.

Nikki was jolted toward him, her bonds connected to his, by a magnetic force. She seemed to be holding her breath. Her hand twitched against his. She was resisting the urge to fight, but it looked like she was barely restraining a pounce.

But she kept calm, just as he had told her.

Conrad glared at them, with a disapproving sneer, muttering something about "Aviduous."

Lincoln tensed his fists. The pain was the only thing that could distract him. How many times could he be locked up in two days?

Outown grabbed his free arm harshly and dragged him toward a jet-black auto, Nikki being pulled along behind them. The vehicle wasn't as impressive as Lincoln would have thought the region's security force would have. It was a well-known fact that the North Cordell Defending Officers, or Defenders as they were so commonly referred to, were funded by the top officials and citizens, but the van looked like it was models old.

But it didn't explain the beat up auto, smeared with dried mud, the pain chipping, and the back door scraped. Outown flung the back two doors open, pushing Lincoln forward.

He froze, his confidence faltering. He would be trapped. Imprisoned. Again.

"Come on kid. We don't have all night." Outown sighed.

Lincoln resisted the urge to shoot the Defender a glare and clambered in. He and Nikki sat opposite Outown on a creaking metal bench, the bolts loose from the floor. The auto started with a jolt, and Lincoln and Nikki lurched sideways, slamming against the doors. Lincoln scrambled up, trying to move away from Nikki, who he'd practically crushed. She did the same, their panting breaths loud over the sound of the engine.

Outown seemed to have anticipated the lurch, fingers curled at the edge of her seat.

Lincoln found his seat again, watching Outown steadily.

She stared back, her foot anxiously tapping away. She finally leaned back, muttering, "Teenagers. Ridiculous," under her breath. She pulled out her Comm, glanced up to Lincoln, then shifted her eyes back.

He had a spare moment.

He looked down to his boot. His hand was bound, but he could reach it somehow.

Nikki's gaze prickled his skin and he winked at her and casually cocked his foot up onto his other thigh.

Outown glanced up.

Lincoln and Nikki immediately flattened themselves against the wall, looking away.

"Whatever you're trying to do—"

"What? It's just…uncomfortable." Lincoln shrugged.

Outown raised an eyebrow. "You're a terrible liar."

Lincoln held his breath, waiting for her to come and inspect him, but she just leaned back, looking at her comm again. Was that the tiniest smile curl on her lips?

He shook his boot ever so slightly. Nothing.

Nikki probably thought he was crazy. He shook it again. This time a small, sheathed blade slipped out, clattering onto the floor.

Outown didn't bother to look up.

He shook his foot again. A bobby pin came next. Then a tiny extra arrow that would explode when fired. Blowing up

Nikki and his arms wasn't exactly the best option. He shook again. The small vial finally peeked from his hidden pouch beside his ankle.

He looked to Nikki, who was staring curiously. He lifted his hand, moving hers with it, and raised his eyebrow to ask for permission to use her hand.

She nodded hesitantly.

He grabbed the vial, careful not to pull Nikki too far. He popped the lid of the vial off, but the cap slipped through his fingers and clinked to the floor. He cringed but fixed his gaze on the far wall of the auto.

Outown glanced up, only for a moment, before casting her attention back to the device in her hand.

He held the vial to his wrist, looking up to Nikki, whose eyes were glued on it. He turned the vial, the metallic dust spilling out over the chain that linked them together.

Nikki frowned, then her eyes widened as the cuffs began to glow and flicker.

Lincoln braced himself, watching the powder slip through the crack between the cuffs. Finally, they disconnected from each other. It worked! He didn't have a single moment to celebrate. He kept the cuff close to Nikki's.

She seemed to understand what he was doing, keeping her wrist still beside his.

The auto came to a jolting stop, and Lincoln braced himself again so he wouldn't pull away from Nikki too soon.

Outown stood, her eyes shifting to their bonds with a raised eyebrow, then turned and picked up Lincoln's bag. "Come on muskrats," Outown said, signaling them to follow, and she swung the doors open.

Nikki and Lincoln stood up, careful to keep the cuffs pressed together.

"On my signal," Lincoln mouthed.

She gave him no reply. Hopefully she understood.

Conrad leaped from the driver's seat, the entire auto creaking. He tapped his wrist band, a light bursting on it. It flickered. He shot them a glare, then scanned the blank wasteland before them. A few scrawny trees grew here and there, and tall weeds swayed in the dead, dry soil.

Nikki glanced sideways at Lincoln, her face stern and confident.

He nodded.

They pulled away and ran.

"Wing it! Outown, *wing it!*" Lincoln heard Conrad begin to shout. Lincoln didn't dare look back or try to figure out what "wing it" meant. A sharp whistle tore through the air. Lincoln tripped and slammed onto the ground, but he scrambled to his feet in an instant.

A lanky, shadowed figure reached for him, but he ducked out of the way, grabbing the tiny knife from his opposite boot.

The attacker blocked his first slash, grabbing Lincoln's wrist.

Pain seared up his arm and he wrenched away, ramming into someone behind him. He cursed and swung hand around, his blade scraping against something.

A beam of light flashed in their direction. Another Defender.

The first attacker grabbed for him. Lincoln slid to the ground, kicking the Defender's ankle and sending them crashing to the ground. Lincoln rolled to his feet.

"Don't kill him. Keep the Aviduous alive! Hey—" Conrad's voice broke off.

Lincoln whirled around to see the man catch himself on

his hands and knees.

Nikki had managed to trip him somehow.

Lincoln cracked a smile.

Another Defender lunged at him, gun in his hand.

Lincoln clashed his knife against the thick material around the Defender's wrist. The attacker pulled away, the gun slipping from their hand. Lincoln dived for the weapon, his finger finding the trigger.

He shoved to his feet again, pointing the gun at the Defender. His breath heaved in his chest.

"I wouldn't shoot if I were you," Conrad called.

Lincoln stiffened. It was all falling apart too quickly. Where was Nikki? He took a deep breath and turned around.

Conrad held Nikki in a headlock, one arm around her neck, a pistol held in the other hand and pressed against her forehead.

For some reason, she didn't look afraid. Her eyes were narrowed, lips pursed as if in annoyance.

"I won't hesitate," Conrad warned.

Nikki kicked him hard in the ankle.

Conrad winced, glaring at her, then to Lincoln.

He had no choice. Lincoln dropped the gun, lifting his hands in surrender.

Nikki stopped struggling, her eye's meeting Lincoln's in obvious disbelief.

Lincoln pressed his lips together and shrugged. She might not fear for her own life, but he couldn't risk finding out if Conrad was bluffing.

Conrad let go, shoving Nikki to the ground, and with a snarl, stormed on to Lincoln.

Hope rose in his chest. Maybe he could grab the gun

again and threaten Conrad now that Nikki was free—

Something rustled through the dead grasses around him. Lincoln froze.

Figures emerged from the shadows. Maybe about five or so, dressed in all shades of dark green, black, and brown, some in a similar uniform to Outown's. They looked pretty rough, like they'd been living off nothing but scraps and fighting off wild animals for months. Many had faint scars marring their skin, their faces so thin that their eyes seemed to bulge out.

More importantly, they were holding guns.

Lincoln's heart sank. He didn't fight as the Defenders marched him silently back to Conrad.

Nikki got her feet, shooting Conrad a dirty look.

Outown continued to watch curiously from Conrad's side.

Conrad looked around. "What are you all standing around for?" he snapped, clapping his hands sharply. "Bind them!"

Lincoln's Defender cuff were removed, crackling as they glitched and sparked. He couldn't help the smallest bit of pride that brought a smirk to his lips. He'd completely ruined a piece of Defender tech. He hadn't even expected it to work. And all with a bit of simple magnetic tech.

Two new cuffs were clamped around his wrists.

What were these ones made of? Were they cheaply made? The officers looked like a mess.

"Outown," Conrad snapped, turning to the young Officer, who stood casually leaning against the side. "I said to wing it!"

"And I didn't. As usual."

Conrad cast her a hateful glare. "Watch them *closer*. Or I'll have you removed."

"Yes, *Sergeant*," she scoffed, her voice riddled with sarcasm as she strode to Lincoln.

Nikki was shoved forward, her cuffs locking together with his.

A toothy grin spread across Conrad's face. "How would you like to go to the base?"

Blindfolded again, Lincoln stumbled down a long trail of steps, almost falling but for the steadying death-grip of one of the Defenders at his elbow. His feet finally hit level ground and the fabric was ripped from his eyes.

Light glared down on them, and he winced, squinting as his eyes adjusted.

They were in a small circular room, the walls a metallic steel, three doorways leading out into various glowing, white hallways lit by bright fluorescent lights. The number 065 was painted in large black letters on the wall, though it was worn and scarred. The place had a damp, unsettling chemical smell to it, though at least it didn't have the earthy smell of the Oquelite's liar.

With the tap of Conrad's wrist band, Lincoln's cuffs clicked free from Nikki's.

Conrad seized him harshly by the back of the neck and dragged him down the hallway. Each loud, thunderous step Conrad took echoed through the halls. He stopped at a door in the wall as it swung open to meet them, revealing a small, dark room within.

Lincoln bit his lip against a flinch as Conrad removed the magnetic cuffs, then shoved him inside the cell. Lincoln barely caught himself from falling, crashing into a metal shelving unit and clutching it for balance. Pain seared his wrists and he staggered upright. The shelving covered the walls on all sides except the door. Was this a closet?

Nikki gave Conrad a glare, but he simply ignored her, turning to Outown, who held Nikki firmly in place.

"You lock 'em up, Outown," Conrad said, throwing her a card and stalking away.

Outown rolled her eyes and mumbled, "You can lock 'em up, Outown," in a mocking impersonation of Conrad's voice.

She grabbed Nikki by the arm and flung her into the room with Lincoln. Nikki stumbled, but caught her breath, glaring at Outown.

The woman smirked, like she was amused. "Gosh, Squirt. I'm not going to kill you," she said, with a small smile.

Lincoln steadied himself, cradling his throbbing wrists against his stomach. "Why didn't you stop me?" he asked, raising his voice to a false confidence.

"I don't know what you mean," she said, her voice so cool, and her smirk so obvious, that it was like she wanted them to think the opposite.

"You let me break the bonds."

"No, really? I could get moved down because that. I wouldn't do such a thing." She slammed the door shut, but it just bounced back open.

"Oh, and don't take everything Conrad does personally," Outown said, fiddling with the knob. "He's just a toddler in a man's body. Sergeant Hunter is the one you got to be careful with. She can and will kill you."

Another mention of this Sergeant.

Lincoln frowned at her. "Why are you telling us this?"

Outown shrugged. "I know you're not working for the Oquelite," she said, turning to Nikki again. "The name's Miriam Outown. Now don't go thinking 'cause I've got a cutesy little name I'm some cute little girl, Squirt. Remember. We are the ones in control now."

Miriam Outown slammed the door again and it clicked shut. A thud followed, and Lincoln guessed Miriam had kicked it just to be sure.

These were the Defenders? The Defending Officers of North Cordell?

It sounded like a cruel joke.

Nikki turned to the shelves and began rummaging through the boxes. She found a sheet of some kind and pulled it free.

What? Was this a linen closet now? Lincoln shook his head.

Nikki found a rip in the fabric and tore two strips away, turning toward Lincoln.

He was tempted to turn way and tell her he was fine. No one needed to take care of him. He wasn't weak, but the innocent glimmer in her wide eyes brought a smile to his lips, and he accepted the makeshift bandaging.

"Thanks, Nik," Lincoln whispered, looking down at his hands. He wiped the red off onto his pants and sighed. Carefully, he wrapped the strips around the open wounds on his wrists.

Nikki relaxed as soon as he tucked the end underneath. She slunk away, tucking herself near the wall and settling her gaze on the ground.

"Nik?" Lincoln asked.

There was no response.

16

LINCOLN DIDN'T EVEN KNOW HOW MUCH TIME HAD PASSED when Ray came crashing through the door, with two annoyed Defenders seeming happy to get him off their hands. They shoved Felicity in quickly after him. She hit the ground with a cry. Ray jumped to his feet and right before he could hurl himself right at them, the shut the door sending him crashing into the door instead.

He groaned. He looked to Lincoln and groaned again. "Well, this just *sucks*."

Lincoln flung the hood of his jacket over his head, though it didn't change much of his view. The dark barely bothered his. Ever since he could remember, it was a trait he found to be strange. He knew Ray couldn't see the scowl, but Lincoln felt he could.

Felicity sat up, taking in a deep breath. "T-they think—"

"Save it for that Sergeant to lecture them about," Ray cut Felicity off, crossing his arms, leaning up against the door.

"The Sergeant?" Nikki's soft voice cut through.

Ray looked to her. "Yeah. Her. She's nothing, really."

"She's terrifying," Felicity said, hugging herself.

That didn't sound good.

"You know what, Black Eyes, we need answers," Ray said, turning on Lincoln.

"Most original taunt ever. Really," Lincoln said.

"I'm not joking."

"That's a first," Felicity muttered.

Ray shot her a glare, and she just shrugged.

"Fine," Lincoln said. "I'll tell you what you *need* to know."

They all came in closer and waited in silence.

Where to start? What was he meant to say that could possibly explain this whole situation? That could take hours. And even then, it couldn't possibly cover it. Would they even believe a *word?*

Nikki spoke first. "Aviduous," she said quietly but loud enough for Lincoln to hear.

He took a deep breath. "Alright, look," he began. "Humanity is made up of eight consecutives 'types', for the lack of a better term. Races. Named the Aviduous, Ewyon, Wingor, Ywondie, Sublinight, Humanic, Oquelite and Agu…Aguarious!" He stumbled over the final pronunciation.

"Like the government's sub-divides?" Felicity put in.

Lincoln frowned. What was she talking about?

"The tests," Felicity said. "At least in Liberty, when you're seven they bring you into the government building for the test. I never thought of it as…supernatural. But there are eight categories, like you said. I thought it might be blood types or numbers or whatever, but it's in the files, too. It sometimes can affect marriages. Maybe for children with the best genetic outcome or something."

Ray chuckled. "For being a little Bentsworth girl, you sure know all this nerdy stuff," he said, nudging her.

Felicity's eyes widened and she spun on Ray and smacked him across the face. But it was too late.

Nikki's eyes flashed with the slightest bit of shock, but Lincoln actually staggered back a pace.

"You're a Bentsworth?" he shouted.

"I guess we're getting all the secrets out here then," she grumbled, shooting a glare at Ray, who just shrugged and flashed her a smirk. "Have any secrets too, Rapheal Mathews?"

"Uh, I'm fifteen. Born on the third month of the year, fifteenth day. I lived in the region of Glorgory, and I'm the best Foundation Field supervisor since Gordon Bentsworth created the system." He crossed his arms. "I've got nothing to hide, Miss Bentsworth."

Felicity scoffed.

Ray turned back to Lincoln. "Do you think the sub-divide tests could have anything to do with it?"

Lincoln shrugged, his feet itching to pace but there was barely enough room, and everyone was too close. The words formed in his mind as he stumbled over a formal response. "Of course. The government has always had an interest in illiah—what most people just call essence."

"The second bloodstream," Felicity said.

"Magic!" Ray pumped his fists.

"The people in the black cloaks," Felicity said, ignoring Ray. "What are they? What is..." She dropped her gaze to the ground, fiddling her fingers together. "What is Silas Idicous?"

The room dropped quiet again, like a little ripple of energy had silenced them, though only for a split moment. Ray didn't blurt out a joke right away, though he did nudge Felicity, and he was lucky he wasn't attacked a third time.

"Yeah, what about that Silas Ridiculous guy?" Ray said.

"Oquelite," Lincoln said, quietly, still feeling the tingling aftermath of Felicity's words in his spine. "Also, Felicity, I'd warn you not to say his full name. Names have power. Their blood and essence are strong. Their power latches onto the spoken words, and they can find you."

Felicity's face paled even in the dim light.

"Explain essence," Ray said.

Lincoln paused. "You're kidding, right? I just did."

Nikki and Felicity glanced at each other and then back to Lincoln.

He sighed. These people really did know nothing. "There are eight races—or there was once. We all have the same blood, but what runs in it is what makes the eight races different. We all have a type of essence, some people have more of one than the others, or multiple. Make sense?"

"Nope. Continue," Ray said.

Felicity elbowed him, shooting him a death glare.

"Like I said, Illiah is another name for essence. Some people have it stronger, less or more, but all in all without it your body would no longer be able to function and, well…you'd die," Lincoln said, looking around for any objections.

None.

"In legend, each type adapted to a certain 'thing' that made up the world. Like emotion, earth, water, sky, and all.

According to these legends, people with this essence could manipulate the matter and things connected to whatever element their race adapted to."

"If that was true, why aren't there more Oquelite people running around?" Ray challenged.

"That's the thing. All other types have lost their abilities through the centuries, but the Oquelite are an abnormality. They still have their powers. That's why they're imprisoned in each region, so the government can keep an eye on them."

"And why are they after *us*?" Felicity asked.

Lincoln grimaced. "Because you freed me, and then got away alive."

"But Silas took me too," Felicity said.

Lincoln looked away. "That would partially be my fault."

"Your fault?" Felicity gasped.

"They heard about a full-blood. Someone with complete essence. Active essence. They thought it was an Ewyon. Full bloods are forbidden by the government. No, I don't know why. But supposedly they were a vile, evil race obsessed with themselves and their appearances. Some say they always had the strongest essence. Pride was everything to them." Lincoln scrunched his face up with distaste, then shook his head."Ewyon are also the natural born enemy to the Aviduous. And...I told them you were one."

Felicity gaped. "Me? I hadn't even met you then!"

"I've been watching."

"Why me?" she shouted, her voice echoing.

Lincoln winced. "A-and, look. I just agreed when they asked me. I knew you weren't, and they wouldn't hurt you when they realized. They would be too angry at me to harm you—"

Felicity cut him off. "It's fine. It's really fine."

Lincoln closed his mouth, and nodded, though his stomach still felt sour.

"Why?" Nikki's small voice piped up. "Why do they want an Ewyon?"

"They have the ability to remove essence," Lincoln said quietly. "All the Oquelite need was exposure to another Impure's blood. That's how the Oquelite can generate their abilities."

When Lincoln looked up, he saw Ray had gone pale, and Felicity's were eyes wide with horror. Nikki's expression hadn't changed.

"Silas was—" Felicity choked, unable to finish her sentence.

"Why are they trying to get essence from people?" Ray asked. "I mean, I get the whole power thing, but like it's not like there's much they can do."

Lincoln shrugged. "Perhaps it has something to do with their immortal lifespans?"

"Immortal lifespans?" Felicity said, her face paling even further, her arms beginning to shake. She balled her fists and clenched her jaw to keep herself still.

Lincoln bit his lip and cleared her throat. This wasn't going to be pleasant for her. "Yes."

"How *old* was…he?"

Lincoln cringed. "They age slower. He could have been hundreds of years old, with the maturity of a young adult."

Felicity's eyes were wide and unblinking. She shook her head and set her face in her hands and stared at the ground.

"You're a full-blooded Aviduous." The words belonged to Nikki.

Lincoln nodded, though he couldn't meet her eyes either. He just clenched his fist and stayed quiet.

Ray pulled back a pace. "Woah! Dude, you're not human?"

"Technically—"

"Don't be all technical," Ray groaned, grabbing him by the shoulders. "Your eyes *are* black."

Lincoln pushed him away. "Yeah, so? Your eyes are yellow."

"Correction, they're amber, Black Eyes," Ray said. "What can you do? Anything cool?"

Lincoln looked at his hands, wishing he would back off. "Nothing, really."

"Nothing?"

He shrugged defensively. "Maybe seeing in the dark?"

"Wow. That's cool. But aren't Aviduous supposed to have adapted abilities or something?"

"So, you were listening to me."

Ray rolled his eyes. "Sooo—"

"Look," Lincoln cut in. "Even if I did. I'd suck at it, because I'm a terrible—"

Felicity cut in. "We don't need you two fighting to the death right now."

"We need to get out," Nikki said, looking up.

Lincoln glanced down to where she was sitting against the shelves. She held her legs close to her chest, her face pale, eyes glancing around, biting her lower lip.

"That is obvious," Ray said, slumping back. "But how? That sergeant lady's not going to let us waltz out."

"Nikki got us out of that O-Oquelite place, didn't she?" Felicity said, gesturing to the other girl.

"I helped," Ray grumbled.

"She figured out how to get the door off and got away from the guards. And not to mention she's the one who got

Lincoln out because you were too chicken to do it." Ray rolled his eyes. Nikki trained her eyes away, her lips pressing together tightly.

"I mean, how much harder can this place be?" Felicity said. "And Lincoln, you're good with tools and stuff, can't you just…bust us out?"

"I can't just do stuff out of thin air," Lincoln said. "And these guys are *Defenders*. Legal law enforcement. We don't need the law after us as well as the Oquelite. We just need to explain to this Sergeant there's been a misunderstanding—"

"Dude, that's not happening." Ray said. "How many times do we have to say this lady won't let us out?"

Lincoln noticed Nikki's hands begin to fidget. "Then what *do* we do?" he said.

"Cole Johnson and Tabitha!" Felicity cried out. "They have proof we aren't working with them. Tabitha was hurt by them."

"Hey Liz, I think you're missing one tiny detail. Tabitha and Cole are lost. They won't even know how to find us or what happened," Ray pointed out.

"No," Felicity insisted. "Tabitha will find us. She'll reach out to legal people. We'll have Liberty on our side."

She had a point. She was a Bentsworth.

"But this could also ruin the Bentsworths. You know how bad it will be if they think the Bentsworths bombed Imperial?" Ray said.

Felicity's mouth gaped in horror. "That isn't—" she cut herself off. Her gaze darted to Nikki, but she didn't accuse the girl again. "Then we should bring the Oquelite to justice."

"Yeah. You know how much the government would freak if the general public knew the Oquelite existed?" Lincoln huffed.

Felicity's face crumpled with defeat.

The room grew quiet.

Nikki moved to the far corner, tapping her foot, pressing her back against the wall. Felicity hid her face in her legs, obviously try to keep herself from panicking.

Ray sat beside her.

The quiet seemed to go on forever.

At one point, Lincoln thought he might get up and actually try to tear the door off. But he kept himself down, tightening his jaw and focusing on deep, steady breaths.

Then the door slammed open.

They all jumped.

Miriam Outown stood in the doorway; her arms crossed over her chest. "Alright Squirt . . . and Conrad's new favorite toy, Sergeant's ready for you."

Conrad stood with his chest puffed out in the hallway.

Lincoln and Nikki's hands were bound again as they were led out into the hall. Conrad grabbed Nikki harshly by the shoulder.

"The Sergeant's heard all 'bout you by now," he said as they walked down the hall, taking a sudden turn. "Don't try anything. She can see through that."

They stopped suddenly in front of a door.

Conrad looked to Nikki, shaking his finger at her. "So, don't you try any tricks, girlie."

She snapped her teeth at him.

Conrad pulled his hand away and scowled.

Nikki and Lincoln were shoved to the door. As they pushed Lincoln through the doorway, Lincoln caught a glimpse of the smudged plaque on the door.

Sergeant Taryn Hunter.

The light inside the office was much dimmer from the lights of the hall. The wall was completely covered in maps and random newspaper articles, thumbtacks pinning paper articles in a collage of black and white. There was a desk pushed up against the wall, also covered in a mess of papers. A pistol lay on a stack as a paper weight, and a full length, sheathed sword leaned against the side of the desk. Swords were a strange and rare sight in those days and were normally only for symbolism and military ceremonies and such. Lincoln's eyes widened at the sight of one.

A woman watched them enter from in the middle of the room, her arms crossed, her large eyes taking in everything. Her dark brown hair was sloppily tied back, pieces here and there had fallen about her face and been tucked behind her ear, but it seemed to have an order to it somehow.

Her eyes seemed to be brown, and green, and grey depending on the way her face moved, dark circles accompanying underneath them. Everything she wore was black, though it wasn't the traditional Defender uniform Lincoln remembered. Her Sergeant jacket was tied loosely around her waist and her shoulders were pulled back in excellent posture.

"So, these were the main sources of trouble you found near the burning sight?" she said, her voice rich. Something about it sent a shiver down Lincoln's spine. She looked over to Conrad, then strode closer to Nikki and Lincoln, studying them.

"The boy's a—" Conrad began.

"An Aviduous. I know, Conrad. I'm not stupid as you might think."

Conrad's face flushed red, his shoulders tensing, but he

nodded obediently.

"So, you're that little Aviduous that has been causing trouble around here lately," the Sergeant said, taking her time to look over Lincoln. She frowned and locked her gaze with his, her eyes sharp. "We haven't seen one like you in…years."

Those eyes seemed to shift, the color rotating around as if they were alive. It sent a shudder through him.

"The little girl was a pain to get over here," Conrad grumbled, then he glared straight at Nikki.

The Sergeant turned to Nikki, whose eyes seemed frozen to the ground.

"She may be just an Unidentified," the woman said looking over to Conrad.

Conrad snickered. "Or an Oquelite."

Nikki frowned, her fists tensing.

Lincoln shook his head at her. They couldn't risk antagonizing these people further.

The Sergeant could do as she liked. He didn't trust the pistol on her desk for a single moment, nor that sword. He returned his attention to the Sergeant and Conrad as their argument ended.

Conrad grunted a semi-respectful "Sergeant", glared at the two prisoners, and marched out. He saluted the Sergeant and closed the door.

The Sergeant turned back to them, her shoulders relaxing a bit, but the solemn, cold expression remained engraved into her face.

"Sergeant Taryn Hunter," she said, her voice cool and professional. "It has been a while since our Defending Base has seen anything in these woods besides Oquelite roaming around like vermin. You aren't a mute, are you?" She addressed this to Nikki.

No response.

"Look at me, kid," the Sergeant said, grabbing Nikki's face and forcing her to look up.

Nikki struggled out of her grasp, pulling back and ramming to the wall behind her. She looked up at the Sergeant for a moment in shock, then shriveled away, shutting her eyes tight.

The Sergeant took a step back and crossed her arms, muttering something to herself and glancing at the maps. "What's your name?" the Sergeant tried again.

Nikki opened her eyes and flashed the sergeant a hateful glance.

The Sergeant waited before turning around again. "I asked you a question."

Still no reply.

The Sergeant's face darkened, and she turned to Lincoln. "What is the girl's name?"

Lincoln swallowed, but didn't say a word.

The Sergeant tensed, her jaw clenching, his eyes narrowing into him. "Why children?" she muttered. She took a step back, closing her eyes. Her shoulders rose with a deep breath.

She looked back at Lincoln, frowning. "You're a bit scrawny for an Aviduous, aren't you?" she said.

Lincoln tensed, looking up. He couldn't explain why he looked like he did. Why he wasn't like a normal Aviduous, he didn't know. But that didn't make him any less a full blood.

The Sergeant's appearance was far more threatening though. She was lean—under-fed, obviously—but she was far more muscular. Her presence seemed to demand respect.

"Well then," she said, clearing her throat. She turned to her desk, banging on a panel on the side. "Send me two officers please. And clear out a holding cell. Obviously, they aren't talking—"

"Wait!" Lincoln said, stepping forward. "We didn't do it."

"Do what?"

"Burn down the Inn."

The Sergeant snorted. "Of course you didn't. The Oquelite got there first."

Lincoln frowned. "Wait. Then, why are we here?"

"That is the question I want to know," the Sergeant said, straightening. "Why *are* you here?"

"I-I don't think I understand."

The Sergeant took a step forward, and Lincoln stepped back.

"Don't you? Where are you from, boy?"

"I-I don't know."

"Lies."

"I'm not—" He bit his tongue, keeping himself from lashing out.

The Sergeant looked to Nikki. "Then explain her."

"What about her?" Lincoln said. Why was everyone so suspicious of Nikki? She was just a girl. Maybe a bit quiet, but that wasn't a crime.

"Explain how she got here from Imperial."

Lincoln's eyes widened, whirling around.

"You're from Imperial?"

Nikki looked equally confused. The girl began to shake her head, but then stopped, looking up in thought. She looked to the Sergeant's map and then back to the Sergeant, her eyes begging for answers.

The Sergeant narrowed her eyes at Lincoln. "We have records of your association with the Oquelite—"

"They were trying to *kill* me!"

"Do not interrupt me," the Sergeant snapped.

Lincoln stumbled back.

She stormed to her desk and tapped a panel more forcefully than necessary. "Send me in two officers to take the prisoners back to the holding cells."

She released the panel and strode back to them. "I will find out what you are," she said, her gaze hard. "I will find out what you've done. And I will not hesitate to kill you."

The door burst open and two Defenders stormed in. The Sergeant nodded to them and they grabbed Lincoln and Nikki.

Pain shot through his arm, and Lincoln barely choked down a cry. He looked over to the Sergeant, who was watching them as they were dragged out. As they reached the doorway, she ripped a newspaper article off the wall and tore it in half.

And the door closed.

17

Nikki peered out from behind the shelf.

The past hours seemed to have slipped by without her knowing. Making time move faster was something she'd mastered.

Lincoln, on the other hand, looked utterly miserable. He slouched against the shelving; head propped in his wounded hands as he muttered hopelessly to himself.

Nikki turned her eyes to the door.

It remained shut.

When they'd been shoved into the empty cell, Ray and Felicity were gone. What had happened to them? Were they in another cell now? Had they somehow escaped?

She carefully moved her hands, which clenched the Stone, from her chest and held it out in front of her. She looked over to Lincoln again, then back to the Stone. The green light of the Stone flickered angrily, flaring at the edges of its stone prison. She ran her thumb over the curious marks carved into the otherwise smooth surface. What did they mean? It didn't look like the written Anglish language. Or any language at all.

Lincoln let out a frustrated shout and kicked the wall.

Nikki's heart lurched and she clasped her hand shut, flinching at the sudden noise and movement. Her head bumped the shelf above her, and something tumbled off with a loud clatter. She winced as the sound echoed through the bare walls. She curled up, covering her ears.

Someone tapped her shoulder.

She jolted up, this time not crashing into the shelf as she jerked away from the grip. The hands! She couldn't let them catch her again.

But no, they weren't here. Lincoln stood above her, frozen, his eyes wide.

She clenched her hand around the Stone. It was okay. He wouldn't hurt her.

"Nik," he said softly.

She couldn't breathe but looked up hesitantly.

"I'm sorry," he said, his lips twisting sideways.

That word again. She just nodded, straightening.

Lincoln's gaze drifted to her hand, but she didn't dare expose the Stone. It hated him for some reason, and maybe he would hate it too.

The door beeped.

Nikki jumped to her feet; her breath tight in her throat again. Lincoln stretched out a hand to her, as if to hold her back, or perhaps shield her from whoever was coming.

The door swung open and the blue-haired woman, the

woman who's greeted her into the Inn, Sinni, was framed in the doorway.

"Oh my gosh!" she gasped, turning to the Sergeant standing just in view.

"These were the ones you're talking about?" the Sergeant asked.

"Yes!" Sinni scowled, her gaze raking over the two of them.

Lincoln's eyes were wide with shock. He shook his head. "Uh…So, you two…know each other?"

Neither of them answered him, but the way they both looked so agitated glaring at each other made it look like a silent "yes." Sinni's arm was in a sling and parts of her short blue hair was singed black. Soot smeared across her face, accompanied by small cuts and burns. Her long sleeve was torn, but the rest of her seemed alright.

"How long have you had them locked up?" Sinni demanded.

"Fourteen hours at least."

Sinni darted a look at Lincoln. "You were at the Inn a few nights ago, weren't you?"

He baulked. "How'd you—"

Sinni laughed. "I know a lot of things, Aviduous."

"Maybe a little too much," the sergeant muttered.

Sinni's eyes widened as she turned to the sergeant. "What did you say?"

"Hutson. Calm down," the sergeant said.

Sinni huffed, turning back to Lincoln and Nikki. "You should come out of here," she said, glaring at her as if daring the sergeant to defy her. "There are some things you might want to know."

Nikki checked the Stone in her pocket with a quick touch,

then followed Lincoln from the dark room into the blinding light of the hall. Sinni gave another angry sigh as the two prisoners paused to adjust to the light.

"I see you've met Sinni Hutson," the Sergeant said dryly.

Sinni rolled her eyes. "You still say it like you've never met me."

The Sergeant bit her lip, her posture seeming to sway. "Fine, then. My good ol' pal Nini Hutson."

Sinni's brow furrowed, and the Sergeant sighed, shaking her head and turning to Lincoln and Nikki again. "We haven't exactly been communicating. For very specific reasons. And now I think she realizes her youthful views on life were wrong. And dangerous. And merely suicidal." She looked at the other woman over her shoulder, the words obviously directed at her more than anyone else.

Nikki bit her lip, shifting uncomfortably.

"And you're talking suicide," Sinni grumbled.

"You worked for the Oquelite," Lincoln said, his eyes widening in realization as he stared at Sinni.

"Clever boy," she snorted.

The Sergeant's eyebrow twitched, a small smile forming on her lips.

Nikki looked at Lincoln. How had he put two and two together so quickly? She had heard Silas and that green haired Oquelite mention Sinni, but this confirmed it.

Sinni sighed. "Things have changed now."

Sinni looked at the Sergeant, whose face was a mask of disapproval. "What has changed?" the Sergeant said, her eyes shifting quickly back to Nikki and Lincoln. "And why did you need to know we had acquired these children?"

"I'll tell you later."

"You will tell me now," the Sergeant snapped.

Sinni's eyes grew wide. "Now? Here? With…" she eyed Nikki and Lincoln, "…them?"

"Don't make me repeat myself."

Sinni seemed to shrivel at the Sergeant's sudden dominance. "Fine," she muttered. She cleared her throat, addressing the empty hall more than her old friend. "When I was younger, I left this…organization" —She glanced at the Sergeant at this— "and the Oquelite seemed more welcoming and rewarding. They stuck me at an Inn and gave me orders to report any high essence full-bloods to them."

Silence settled between them.

The Sergeant's face paled, her eyes narrowing.

"Why?" Lincoln said.

"You're still prisoners. And suspects," the Sergeant said sharply. "None of your concern."

"*Yet,*" Sinni muttered under breath.

The Sergeant jabbed Sinni with her elbow.

"At first it seemed simple, but after a while, after I saw what they did with the people I befriended and lured in, I got scared. Then I ran. They caught me, of course, and gave me something to remember my mistakes." Sinni lifted her torn sleeve, revealing a long, jagged, glowing red mark. It looked as if someone had slashed through her arm, but the blood glowed, shades of magma, constantly flashing to darker shades of red.

"This is what they call a Leech. It starts out small and begins to take over your body, turning you into a pile of essence when it's done. I just live with the pain and the knowledge this will never let me leave the borders of North Cordell alive." She tossed the torn sleeve to the ground, kicking it aside. "Recently, Silas, the younger son, has been acting…different. I assumed it was because he'd been scolded by the Diones Lord, but soon he informed me to watch for an Ewyon, an Aviduous, and something about a curse. That's when I knew I couldn't take it anymore."

The races were probably the thing the Sergeant said was 'none of their concern'. But after Lincoln's earlier explanation, Nikki understood every word all too well.

The sergeant seemed to relax a bit, nodding. She turned to Nikki and Lincoln again. "How much do you know?"

"Quite a bit. If you mean about the races and stuff," Lincoln said.

The sergeant's face went dark, all the tension returning to her frame.

Sinni raised her eyebrow and bit her lip. "Anyone else know? About the Oquelite. Felicity Bentsworth, Cole Johnson, Raphael Matthews, and Tabitha Delorous perhaps?"

The sergeant spun on Sinni. "Six?" she snapped. "Six…*kids*?"

"Felicity Bentsworth's eighteen," Sinni said. She looked like she was trying not to smile, but with no luck.

The Sergeant scowled, crossing her arms.

"I watched all six leave," she said, her eyes glinting as if she'd said something humorous.

The sergeant wasn't amused. "So, this is why you ran off?"

"I was doing you a favor! The Defenders' good cause is long gone and corrupt ever since *their* death. It was an immature thing to do, but I haven't had choice whether I wanted to serve an Oquelite like a slave or not. But this can't be ignored. The Oquelite are going to succeed, and their search will be fulfilled."

The sergeant stared at Sinni, her lips pressed firmly

together. Finally, she let out a frustrated, defeated sigh. "Fine. Call a search for your other adolescents."

18

It was no use.

Lincoln wiped his forehead, looking down at the standard metal bow in his hand. He wasn't sure how to use it, nor did he want to. But of course, it was the only thing slightly familiar the Sergeant had offered.

Lincoln turned behind him, watching the three Defenders assigned to search with them, and keep a close eye, looking cluelessly behind trees and bushes.

The sergeant's decision caught both Nikki and Lincoln off guard. She'd insisted she was sending them because they recognized Cole ad Tabitha, but it didn't add up why she would send her supposed prisoners to search. Perhaps something Sinni had said?

Sergeant Taryn Hunter's Defenders must have been in

hiding for a long time. Their forms were thin, though muscled, and most of their clothes had faded and torn with time. Their faces were long and their eyes constantly twitching in anticipation, fingers clasped tightly on the grips of their guns.

They looked insane.

Lincoln couldn't blame them though. He had no idea what it was like to hide in such a desolate place for so long. But surely not all defenders were like this, were they? He didn't dare ask. They looked like they'd shoot him dead if he did. The Sergeant only permitted Nikki and Lincoln to search for Cole and Tabitha. She didn't explain why, but Lincoln was sure Ray had said *something* that made the Defenders plead for him to be left behind. Probably to spare their sanity.

Nikki had traveled farther up the mountains, much to their Defender supervisor's dismay. She'd ignored any protest, but at least he could still see her from where he was. She stood crouched on top of the hill, just visible between the trees. It seemed the land was always dipping up and down, so if she moved any further, she'd disappear out of sight.

She was still for a moment, then shook her head and rose.

Lincoln glanced back at the Defenders for a moment and ran to catch up with her. She was unarmed, even though the Sergeant had tried to insist she take even something as simple as a pocketknife. Nikki had looked at it hesitantly, then firmly refused.

"Any luck?" Lincoln asked, reaching her side. He scanned the hill and the valley beneath. A river rushed by and the bottom of the slope, rumbling and white with spray over the shallow, rocky bed of stones.

Nikki shook her head.

"Hey! Kids! I said don't you get too far!" one of the Defenders called out as he struggled up the hill. The other two muttered to each other in inaudible voices, their frowns obvious.

"We're fine," Lincoln muttered, watching them struggle. "Right here—"

Lincoln froze, his senses overcoming him.

Something crashed in the distance. Nikki must have heard it too.

Nikki started off before the sound even ended, darting down the hill and across the river, sprinting farther into the woods. She looked over her shoulder for a moment like she expected him to follow.

Lincoln plunged into the river, fighting the current as it tugged around his knees. He stumbled to the far bank and ran after Nikki, shoes squelching with each step. Was it Cole and Tabitha? Who else would be out here to make such a noise?

He caught up with Nikki and stumbled to a stop, breathless as she paused.

Another snap.

Nikki set off again and Lincoln followed. Did that girl ever get tired of running? The sounds led them around in a half circle, then to another steep hill. Tree roots tore from the earth where the land had crumbled away down the slope, and a small rodent peered curiously out from beneath them before scrambling away into a burrow.

Nikki stopped abruptly and looked up at the crest of the hill.

Lincoln caught up, and she gave him a nod.

He managed to find enough breath to holler up toward

the ridge above. "Hello?" he called.

For a moment nothing happened, then a familiar face appeared over the ledge. "Hey!" Tabitha's bright purple hair made an appearance, wildly contrasted to the greens and browns of the forest. Her eyes were wide, but her dirt-streaked face was very much alive.

Cole appeared beside her; his arm tucked under hers to keep her upright. He was equally as dirty but looked an awful lot more tired. He gave a strained smile of relief. "Thank goodness."

Cole began to help Tabitha down the slope down toward them, but she slipped and they both teetered, almost sliding down together. Nikki darted up the hill, grasping Tabitha's other side. Between them, Cole and Nikki guided Tabitha down.

Finally reaching level ground, Tabitha pulled away and steadied herself. "Guys, I'm fine," she said, holding out her arms. It would have been proof if she wasn't shaking.

"How did you find us?" Cole said, glancing between Nikki and Lincoln.

"Let's just say…things happened," Lincoln said.

The three Defenders, panting and jogging, looking more harmless in their obvious exhaustion, ran up behind.

"You're coming back with us to the Defending Base for questioning," one said, pulling his gun from its holster even as he tried to catch his breath.

"Get back!" Cole shouted, shoving Tabitha behind him.

She stumbled and nearly fell but caught herself on his shoulder. "Sorry buddy, but we're not going anywhere," Tabitha said, crossing her arms.

The Defender shifted the gun to aim at her head.

"Calm down!" Lincoln called. "These are the ones we're

looking for!"

The Defenders didn't respond.

"We are Defending Officers of North Cordell and by the orders of Sergeant Taryn Hunter you are required to come with us back to our base," another stated, her words clipped and rough.

Cole's brow furrowed and he stepped forward. "Who-what now?"

"Defenders," Lincoln said.

Tabitha frowned, looking from Lincoln to the defenders. "Huh…you guys aren't exactly what they look like in Liberty. A bit…shabby—"

"Tabs, shut your mouth," Cole cautioned.

"Thank you," the first defender said, though there seemed to be no sincerity in the words. "Do as we say, and no one will be harmed."

"One condition," Cole said. "You put the guns down."

The Defenders hesitated, eyes narrow and suspicious.

"We're a bunch of unarmed youth, for crying out loud!" Cole snapped. "Put the guns down!"

Almost in unison, the guns were back in their holsters. The Defenders glanced nervously at Cole, even as they led the way to the base. The group moved in a cold silence.

No one spoke. There wasn't a reason to.

"So, we're technically prisoners, aren't we?"

The Sergeant shrugged as if Tabitha's words were only minor details.

All six of them were lined up against the wall, the Sergeant eyes flicking to each of them in turn. A quick talk about the races, essence, and the Oquelite, as Lincoln already explained to them, had left Tabitha with only one question.

"Until we have *solid* proof you aren't in any way a threat to our cause. These are fragile times," the Sergeant said, her chin up, through her eyes shifted to Nikki.

Sinni, who sat with her back against the opposite wall, rolled her eyes.

Tabitha stormed forward, glaring at the Sergeant. "You have no right to do that!" she yelled. "That— that's got to be illegal! Holding…mere children against our will, and without a trial too. You don't even have real legal authority!"

A small smile flashed across the Sergeant's face as she shook her head. "You call yourself mere children? Then you must be watched like so," the Sergeant said. "And those who fail basic University exams obviously know nothing about what really goes down in the region of Imperial, besides it's now notorious bombings."

Tabitha flushed red and took a step back into the line they had formed. How did the Sergeant know about her *grades*? She glared at Cole, who heaved a sigh and looked away.

"You, young lady, were attacked by a dangerous organization of Oquelite, who now are out to kill you. Our Medics helped stabilize you after your attack—you should be thankful," said the Sergeant. "You will be required to follow our rules and regulations, obey our officers, and remain in the base at all times unless supervised. It is either that or to be kept in a cell until the matter has been settled."

Conrad looked eager to thrust them all into the tiny room again, as he flashed a yellow smile at each of them.

None of them argued, and Tabitha noticed man's excitement seemed to fall.

"Very good," the Sergeant said. "Any questions?"

Felicity timidly raised her hand, but she cowered away when the Sergeant turned to her. "H-how long exactly?" she asked.

"It won't take too long to find fault, Bentsworth. Then to Imperial."

Felicity's eyes grew wide.

The Sergeant nodded, lips pressed into a grim line. "Your name doesn't give you privilege. For now, you will be held in the restrictive chambers forty-two and thirty-nine. Any tricks, you won't be proving to me."

Ray began to argue again. "Lady. I've been stuck in locked in rooms for hours. And that's enough. You can't just—"

Conrad hit him hard in the back of the head.

Ray's head whirled, gritting his teeth. What gave that man that authority?

"Shut up, kid," he sneered into Ray's ear. "You're lucky you're not dead yet."

Ray winced and clenched his fists. Anger flushed his cheeks, and he clenched his jaw. He started to step forward, but Lincoln and Cole grabbed him from each side.

"Calm down," Cole hissed.

Ray glared at him, but let his shoulders relax. He rubbed the back of his head, dropping his gaze to the ground. The Sergeant ordered them off.

They were separated, the girls taken one way and the boys trudging sullenly after Conrad.

Cole was fiddling with his necklace and Ray eyed him silently. What was so special about that necklace? He didn't dare ask in the echoing hall.

Really, he just wanted to punch Conrad in the back of the head and book it in the opposite direction.

Lincoln seemed to be unusually calm, his face straight and solemn, gaze focused on the ground or occasionally the cuffs around his wrists.

Conrad stopped them in front of a rusted door labeled 42. A sign underneath the number read, "Boiler Room."

Cole frowned. "These still exist?"

Conrad laughed. "We aren't exactly the higher up's favorite region."

Ray had been expecting a barrack at least, but this was nothing of the sort. Within, it was dark and warm, which was only slightly comforting. Pipes and wires lined the walls, and a large metal stove stood in the center of the room, covered in switches and wires and glowing a bright red.

A guy, maybe nineteen, turned away from a control panel, wiping the soot off his face, and hurrying into a salute. He had a soft, warm smile and dirt brown hair that hung over one of his bright green eyes. He was maybe only a couple inches taller than Lincoln and didn't look threatening. Maybe he'd even be a little bearable.

"Sallow," Conrad sneered.

"Officer Conrad, sir."

Conrad stepped aside to gesture the three boys in. "These three will be staying here. I leave them under you and don't mess this up. The Sergeant is a little too merciful with you."

"Yes, sir. I won't disappoint, sir!" Sallow said, beating his fist to his chest in a salute with each "sir."

Conrad scowled and slammed the door as he left. Sallow let out a sigh, a small grin warming up onto his face as his shoulders relaxed. He crossed his arms, looking over them and nodding approvingly.

"Call me Jack," he said. "Jackson Sallow. Defender… maintenance guy. A bit of a downgrade. Really lovely here, though. Still an Officer, but Jack. Just…Jack. I see Miriam got through the job."

Ray blurted out a real intelligent, "Huh."

"Miriam?" Lincoln asked.

"Miriam Outown," Jack Sallow explained. "Not many of us call each other by our last names, like traditional Defenders. And if Miriam is anything, she's not traditional." He laughed, though it had a nervous, jaded edge. "She's an Outown, after all."

"Outown." Cole's eyes grew wide. "Like Aaron Outown?

A member of the Curatrix team?"

"Brilliant." Jack's smile grew. "Very much so. The Outowns tend to have … mysterious qualities.

He then turned and gestured around the room, the ground littered with cords and wires. "I guess make yourselves at home," he said. "Maybe names?" It sounded more like a suggestion than a command.

"Cole Johnson."

"Ray Mathews."

"Lincoln."

He cocked an eyebrow at Lincoln. "No last name?"

Lincoln shook his head, looking away.

But Jack didn't push any harder. "I'll get you guys some things, you know. So, you don't have to live on this mess." He sidestepped around them and opened the door. "Uh…be good." He left quickly, leaving the three alone in the room.

"He seems cool," Cole said, turning to the rest of them.

Ray just scowled, walking up to the furnace. He slid onto the ground, crossing his legs, and covered his head with his arms.

It was hopeless to discuss with others. He was stuck underground, with some kooky officers. He didn't want to be disturbed. The best he could do was be alone.

"Raphael Mathews, follow me."

20

"DAY FOUR. THREE A.M. GROWING LOW ON RESOURCES—"

Felicity groaned. "What the heck are you doing?"

Tabitha sighed, flopping down onto the ground.

Four days of being trapped. Four days of avoiding the Defenders, huddled up alone in their small rooms.

It was horribly boring.

"You think this is going to go on File?" Tabitha asked, blowing at a hair that had landed between her eyes.

"I don't know!" Felicity snapped, as she stretched her arms out from her huddled position. "I didn't know this is what the Defending Offices were."

"Okay, okay. Sorry." Tabitha sighed, pushing herself up and looking around the eerie room they'd been assigned to. It was pretty much a closet, with a serious leakage problem.

It smelled like dirt, and the only light source was emergency lamps in the walls. It seemed this was the place some Defenders went to get away from authority and engrave things into the wall. There were some boxes stacked in the corner, but nothing interesting inside them. Mostly unwearable uniforms and worn-out shoes.

"I wonder where that panel leads," Tabitha said, rolling onto her back again, her hands under her head. There was a mysterious panel with a rusted handle in the ceiling right above her head.

Felicity frowned and shook her head. "You better not be getting any ideas, Ms. Delorous."

Tabitha laughed. "What? You think I could even reach up there?" She climbed to her feet and jumped for the ceiling. Her fingers didn't even come close to the handle. "See? Way too short."

Felicity smiled softly, pulling the blanket closer around her, and Tabitha's grin fell. She knelt next to her friend, head tilted to the side. "Oh, come on, Liz," Tabitha sighed for the hundredth time. "Is this situation bothering you that much? Like everything?"

"This isn't like everything," Felicity snapped back. "Tabitha, what are we even doing right now? Look at where we are. A few weeks ago, if anyone told me about this mess—"

"You would have had a panic attack," Tabitha guessed.

"No!" Felicity groaned. "I wouldn't have believed them! But I guess that isn't far off either."

Tabitha placed her hand on Felicity's shoulder and forced a smile. "Come on. It's okay," she said. "You've been through worse."

"It's not okay," Felicity said, her voice cracking. She buried her face under the blanket.

Nikki looked up suddenly from the other side of the room. Tabitha hadn't taken much note of her, but now her hand was clenched shut, and she was looking curiously at Felicity.

Tabitha caught her gaze. "She's okay," Tabitha said, half to comfort Nikki, mostly to convince herself.

To her surprise, Nikki got up and crawled to Felicity, sitting beside her with her knees drawn up and her arms hugged around them. Felicity sniffled and Nikki's eyes widened for a moment before she turned and looked down at the ground.

"What happened?" she whispered.

Tabitha frowned, watching Nikki curiously. What did she mean?

Felicity's breath caught, and she peered out from the blanket. "Nothing," she choked.

Nikki looked up again. "You were hurt."

Felicity dropped the blanket, tears trickling down her face.

Great, now she was even more upset. Tabitha was ready to tell Nikki to leave Felicity alone, but her friend sat up straighter, meeting Nikki's eyes.

For once, Nikki didn't shy away, keeping her graze steady.

Felicity shook her head. "Just a stupid auto accident and…" Felicity stopped, her voice cracking, and clenched her fist against her chest so tight her knuckles turned white.

"Why?" Nikki asked, suddenly. "Why did it hurt you?"

Felicity's lip trembled. "Because of whom I am."

"Who?"

Felicity glanced at Tabitha for support, but Tabitha just shook her head, uncertain. Felicity took a deep breath. "I don't know," she said.

"Mad?" Nikki said.

Felicity wiped the tears from her face and gritted her teeth. "Angry."

Nikki sat in silence, seeming to ponder the word.

Felicity sat up, her back straight, though her eyes were brimming with tears. "Someone tried to kill my friend. Someone tried to kill me," she said, her voice trailing off. "They ruined my life."

"So, you're scared?" Nikki said. "Scared of everything."

Felicity blinked, tilting her head. "I'm not scar—" She stopped again. "I guess…sometimes. I'm scared. I'm scared they'll come and hurt people."

"The scared…die," Nikki said, her face shifting to a frown.

Felicity's eyes widened. Tabitha expected her to start sobbing again but somehow Felicity held strong. She glared down at her hands. "You don't get it," Felicity said, clenching her jaw. "None of you do!"

Felicity started to get up, but Tabitha quickly grabbed her shoulder and pulled her back down before she could do anything stupid. She stared intensely into Felicity's eyes, and growled, "Felicity. You're going to start falling apart again."

Felicity started and pulled back. She looked at Nikki, but the other girl was glancing away toward the door again. Felicity bit her lip and turned back. "I thought…I could trust him," she said. "But Silas turned out to be just like they said. A total stranger, working for some *shady* business! It makes me scared. Nikki's right, I am afraid."

Nikki slowly turned back to Felicity, shaking her head just the slightest. "Angry," she said, like she'd accepted Felicity's previous words. "You're angry."

Felicity looked at Nikki, then nodded, her fists tightening. "You're right," she said finally. "I am angry."

"You have a right to be," Tabitha said, placing her hand on her friend's shoulder. "You're stronger when you're angry."

Felicity laughed. "Tabs, that's not a good thing."

"I promise you, Bentsworth. It is so much better than you having random panic attacks."

"Are you sure?"

Tabitha grinned. "I'm sure. We just need the real you back. So, you can smack Silas in the face. Real hard. Show him how much you're willing to fight. Show him your rage."

21

"IF I DIE FROM YOU STEPPING ON MY FACE——"

"Cole, I'm not going to step on your face."

Tabitha stood on Cole's uneasy shoulders. How on earth had she talked him into this, again? Something about clearing things up and she would apologize for everything if he helped her reach and search a strange door in the ceiling of the girl's room. "Why do I agree to your ideas?" he grumbled.

"Because they're good ideas. And you had nothing else to do."

A sheet of metal clattered to the ground, just missing Cole's head. "Be careful!" he snapped. "Unless you want me to drop you!"

"You wouldn't let that happen," Tabitha's reply was

muffled as she stuck her head into the shaft. She pulled herself up into the ceiling, her weight lifting from Cole's shoulders. For a moment, she disappeared, then her head popped out again. "You coming?"

Cole raised an eyebrow. "You expect me to go up there? How?"

"Find a way or you don't get an apology."

"You're ridiculous."

"Genius, actually," Tabitha corrected. "I see a chance and I take it."

Cole sighed. "I want to know what the Sergeant's talking about too, but is there another way besides cramming yourself into the ceiling?"

"Bye!" Tabitha called, and she disappeared again as she scuttled away down the shaft.

Cole scowled, shaking his head. This was stupid. He climbed onto one of the shelves and jumped, catching the edge of the shaft's entrance. He pulled himself up with a moment of struggle and rolled out into the cramped shaft. It was oddly warm and just as small as he'd dreaded. Tabitha sat cross legged before the entrance. He raised his eyebrows and she shrugged.

"I wasn't really going to go alone," she said. "I'm not that crazy."

"But you admit to being crazy."

Tabitha shrugged again. "Maybe a little." She turned and crawled along the cramped shaft.

Cole muffled a groan and followed her, the ceiling creaking beneath his hands. The entire way was silent but for their own scuffles, and Cole peered down through the vents as they passed. Every room was full of silent Defenders, staring blankly at the floor or their weapons. A chill went down Cole's spine.

Tabitha paused at the next vent, and twisted to look at him over her shoulder, eyes wide. "What do you think happened to them?" she whispered.

Cole looked down into the room. "Nothing good."

It was the same in every room they passed until the shaft met a dead end, and they were forced to stop. Tabitha groaned. "Seriously? All this way for nothing?" she said, a little too loud. Her voice echoed through the system and Cole shot her a glare and shushed her.

She winced. "Sorry."

Something metallic clicked, like the countdown of a clock. Tabitha flinched back from the dead end, crashing into Cole.

"Ouch. What are you—" he cut off. Pressure tugged at his neck and he glanced down. His medallion had escaped from inside his shirt and was pulling toward something beyond Tabitha. He grabbed it, but even in his hand it was fighting to escape.

"Take it off," Tabitha whispered.

Cole frowned at her. "What?" His heartbeat quickened and he curled his fingers around the medallion. "Never."

He squeezed past her, following the pull of the medallion. When he reached the last panel, the medallion escaped his grip and stuck to the metal like a magnet. An automated voice droned, "*Welcome Aaron Outown.*"

"You're Curatrix Team Member Aaron Outown?" Tabitha's voice was full of confusion behind Cole.

"What? No!" Cole said. "My name is Coleson Johnson, not . . . Aaron." He trailed off as the panel in front of him whirred, then slid back, revealing a dim opening.

"Well, whoever they are, they got us in. Come on!"

Tabitha said. "Go in!"

"I don't think thanks a good—"

Tabitha shoved him from behind and Cole tumbled forward, crashing to the floor with a grunt. He scrambled to his hands and knees again, then shoved sideways in time to avoid being a landing pad for Tabitha as she followed.

Tabitha plopped down beside him but quickly found her feet. Cole stood up, dusting himself off and scanning the room with wide eyes.

Somehow, they'd come out somewhere entirely different from the Defending Base. The walls were polished steel, the lights were hovering just below the ceiling, held in place by some invisible force. This place was entirely high tech.

"Woah," Tabitha muttered, taking a step forward.

The room flickered to life as blue holograms emerged from the ground, whirling out in front of them. The screens were blank, waiting for a passcode to activate them. They must not have been used for a long time.

Tabitha leaped into a hovering chair that had appeared beside the main screen and tapped *Password* into the keyboard. No luck.

Cole turned in a slow circle, taking in the rest of the room as Tabitha continued to try to guess the password, her answers varying from *Defending Department* to finally *thesergeantisajerk*.

"What is this place?" Cole asked finally, his jaw slack as he looked around. As he stepped forward, it was like he had stepped in a puddle, the holograms waving out from under his feet. These were a gold color unlike the blue that had popped up earlier. He reached for the medallion, holding it up in front of his face. He'd had it for so long, but it'd never done anything like this.

He looked over at Tabitha, who was spinning around in the holographic chair like a small child. She didn't seem like she'd be the type of person who thought things out ahead of time. She didn't know about this room any more than he had. But was this really an accident?

Tabitha stopped spinning for a moment and tilted her head, furrowing her brows. "Bring your necklace over here."

Cole sighed, crossing to her. "It's not a necklace."

"I'm sorry. You look very pretty," Tabitha said.

Cole rolled his eyes and held the medallion out in front of the screen.

A message appeared.

Password Correct! Welcome Aaron Outown. Child lock activated.

Tabitha frowned, a smirk forming on her lips. "Child lock?"

Cole shrugged, pushing Tabitha and her rolling chair aside. The screen lit up with a dozen different options, and a thrill went up his spine. He selected "surveillance", and the screens flickered from blue to white as hundreds of video feeds appeared. Cameras in almost every room of the base.

Tabitha squealed with glee. "Find the Sergeant," she said, rolling closer.

"Are you sure that's a good idea?" Cole said, looking across the surveillance feeds for anything familiar.

"We're being held captive. It can't get any worse."

"Spying through technology in a weird, high tech room doesn't make it any less. If that Conrad—"

"That man can't fit through the shaft even if he wanted to," Tabitha said.

She had a point there.

Cole turned back to the screens and started flicking through the feeds. There were a lot of rooms.

A lot.

The chair had expanded to fit the two of them, and Cole scooted it closer. Tabitha, so quickly bored, was leaning back with her eyes half closed only a few minutes into the search. Finally, Cole jumped up, tapping on a box to enlarge it. "Found it!" he shouted. His voice echoed back in the quiet room, but he couldn't care less at this point.

Tabitha straightened, then scowled. "Gosh darn it, she's gone." She slumped back in the chair, groaning.

Cole didn't join her. He clicked the image again and it zoomed in, refining itself. These cameras were amazing quality. He zoomed in on the maps on the Sergeant's office wall, and he could see every detail clearly. He scanned the maps of each region, but there wasn't anything unusual. Then, he found an article.

A newspaper.

Tabitha wrinkled her nose. "Do those still exist?"

"You still use paper," Cole pointed out.

"Yeah, but newspapers haven't been around since the EarthShaker," Tabitha said, scooting closer. "And even then, they'd declined in popularity."

The newspaper title was printed in huge bold letters, '**TITANIC SINKS, 1500 DIE**.' Underneath, the Sergeant had scribbled in red pen 'framed?'

Cole and Tabitha exchanged a glance.

"1912?" Tabitha said. "This lady has a newspaper from *hundreds* of years ago!"

Cole fiddled with his medallion, trying to think. "And she thinks the sinking of a ship…was framed?"

Tabitha zoomed in on another article about the death of a leader of a Northern region country. Apparently, the man was shot, and the man accused of murdering him was shot before trial. the Sergeant had simply written 'Member' on the newspaper.

Members?

Some were more recent printed by the Sergeant herself. Tabitha cringed visibly at the picture beneath '**3 UNKNOWN HUNG DEAD IN TIGIA**', showing the three hanged corpses in a blurred photo.

Cole quickly moved on. Another article was pinned above the Sergeant's desk, this one heavily annotated. The photo was much more pleasant—a black and white image of a group of five figures. A woman with tanned skin, dark hair, and her arms crossed stood on one side, a sly smile on her lips. Beside her, was a light-haired, younger girl, maybe in her late teens. To her side was a boy with darker hair that almost covered his eyes. His freckled face had a smirk to compliment it as well. On his other side was a girl with dark skin, her light hair braided down to her waist. And finally, beside her there was a man with light hair and tanned skin who looked to descend from the Southern Regions.

The title wasn't as pleasant as the photo:

5 OFFICERS MURDERED AT HOME

Tabitha gasped. "Cole," she whispered. "It's the first report of the Curatrix team's assassination."

Cole's eyes widened. Tabitha was right. The date and time were clearly printed beneath the header. The exact day the murder of the famous Defenders went public. 1.25 am.

"Look." Tabitha's voice cracked as she pointed to a smaller article was pinned alongside it:

EVIDENCE FOUND TWO-YEAR-OLD AGUIRRE CHILDREN DIED IN FIRE ALONGSIDE PARENTS.

"Reyna and Lyell Aguirre's children," Cole whispered.

He'd heard about them a few times, but now seeing the article on the Sergeant's wall suddenly made him feel sick. Two Defenders he didn't even know. Some sort of political disagreement cost them their, and their *children's*, lives.

Tabitha stared, unblinking, at the screen, his mouth hanging open, trembling.

Cole placed a hand on her shoulder, trying to steady her though his own stomach was writhing. "We can leave."

Tabitha shook her head, shutting her mouth. "We made it this far," she said. "And Cole, you need to see this. This-this changes everything."

"Tabith, what—"

She pressed her finger against the screen to the small print below the smaller blonde girl in the group.

There was something about her big eyes, the shape of her face. Cole bit his lip and checked the words at Tabitha's fingertip.

The dead girl's name was printed clearly.

Sergeant Jessica Hunter (Age 26)

"T-TABITHA?" FELICITY PEERED INTO THE DARK CLOSET, flicking the light on. She hadn't seen Tabitha in hours. It had to have been around midnight, but Felicity could barely keep track of time in this place. It never really changed since the entire base always seemed to be awake. Felicity stepped into the closet, and nearly tripped on the rusted panel on the floor. Her heart lurched and she glanced up. The hole in the ceiling gaped down at her.

No. Tabitha couldn't be in there. There was no way. Fear threatened to steal her breath, but Felicity forced a deep inhale. Tabitha couldn't go up there. And Felicity definitely couldn't follow. What if she got stuck? This was serious. Someone had to know.

She ran back out into the hallway, her heart racing. The

hallway was silent and eerie, her echoing footsteps only sound in the bright corridors. If only Tabitha would stop being so ambitious. She was going to get herself hurt with behaviors like that.

"The Sergeant said you would be following my orders on this patrol!"

The yell sent a shiver down Felicity's spine and she stumbled to a stop, heart pounding. Conrad stood at a conjunction point, where all the halls met in their quarter. He faced the short brown-haired woman, Miriam Outown.

Her face was flustered, and her fists were clenched, but she somehow still seemed haughty. "You know you say the Sergeant says a lot of things," Miriam sneered.

Conrad eyed her. "You know what's good for you, Outown. Get over your fear of a few meters off the ground, and I might start thinking you more capable."

"I don't take any of your 'wing it' crud any day, Conrad."

"Scat, Outown!"

Miriam huffed and turned away, then paused as her gaze met Felicity's. "Are you okay?"

Conrad shoved past Miriam, his gaze pinning onto Felicity. He cursed, folded his thick arms over his chest, and glared at her. "What do you want?" he snapped, between the heavily applied cursing.

"M-my friend is—is missing," she managed to blurt out.

Conrad let out a hoarse laugh. "I should hope so."

Felicity's face burned, pulse roaring in her ears. "Why? We—we've done nothing to you."

Conrad's brows furrowed and he stormed closer. His eyes were scattered with red veins around his irises, and his face was red and sweaty, crisscrossed with countless scars. His smell hit Felicity with enough power her stomach flopped. "What did you say?" he demanded.

"We've done nothing to you," she gulped.

Colors flashed over her vision, and pain snatched a gasp from her as she toppled back.

It took Felicity a moment to realize she'd been slapped.

Slapped. No one had ever dared lay a finger on her before. She didn't even know how to react.

"You really have no idea, do you?" He chuckled. "You still think you're an innocent little girl, with dreams and a good file, don't you?"

He took a step closer again. "What if I were to tell you that you are none of that? You're a monster. You have already killed us all. All of us are suffering because of you!" His hand went back to strike her again.

Before the blow could land, someone grabbed his arm, twisting his wrist back.

Felicity scrambled to her feet, backing away.

Nikki didn't turn back to Felicity, her gaze locked on Conrad.

"You little—" Conrad's face was growing redder with anger.

"Eh, eh. No cursing in the presence of children. That's a bad example."

Felicity looked behind Conrad, relief and fear jumbling in her chest.

Ray stood, his arms crossed and his golden eyes sparking with anger. Despite the humorous line he'd just dropped, he didn't seem to be in a funny mood. His nostrils flared, and his jaw clenched.

Conrad scowled, clawing at Nikki.

She let go of his arm and ducked out of reach.

Conrad turned on Ray. "Come here!" He caught Ray by

the shoulder and squeezed it till Ray let out a cry.

Ray lunged out, kicking Conrad in the gut. Conrad staggered and tossed Ray to the ground. He kicked the boy in the stomach, and Ray curled up on himself with a groan.

Conrad turned, a wicked smile on his lips, to Nikki. "Wanna fight me too, punk?"

Nikki shook her head, edging closer to Felicity.

"You scared?"

Nikki shook her head again.

Conrad scowled, throwing his hand at her.

Nikki skidded to the ground in a neat, dance-like dodge.

Felicity clamped her hands over her mouth, backing away further.

Nikki rolled her feet and waited for Conrad to swing again. Her face barely changed from its stone expression.

Conrad didn't wait long. He let out a quick blow. Nikki dodged again, but his foot came out and tripped her.

She fell back, catching herself against a small, corner side table. She grabbed the tablet from it right before Conrad took the moment of distraction to ram her back against the wall. He shook her harshly, hands gripping her shoulders. "Come on. Fight me, girl. I know you can do it!" he shouted.

Nikki squeezed her eyes shut, refusing to respond, and finally Conrad thrust her to the ground.

Nikki clenched the glass tablet to her chest and scrambled to her feet.

Conrad snickered, turning to Ray as he struggled to pick himself up. He placed his foot on top of Ray, shoving him back to the floor.

Ray choked for breath but gave the girls a thumbs up. "No- no worries!" he gasped. "I got this!"

Nikki lunged forward, throwing the tablet. It hit Conrad

straight in the eye. He stumbled back, roaring in pain and clasping his hand over his eyes.

Ray struggled up and pumped his fist. "Take that, jerky face!"

Felicity's entire body was frozen. Wouldn't that just make Conrad angrier? They had to get out of here, but she couldn't move.

Nikki tapped her shoulder, and the touch roused her from her shock. Felicity tried to give the other girl a small smile of thanks, but it came out like a grimace.

Conrad moaned, holding his face. "You're hurting people! You've been doing it since the day you were conceived!"

Nikki wiped the blood from her lips, then grabbed Ray's arm and pushed Felicity ahead of them both down the hallway before Conrad could recover.

The man continued to yell as they hurried into the maze of hallways.

Felicity shuddered. "Are you alright?" she asked the others.

Nikki didn't say a word.

"What do you think he meant?" Ray said, his voice low and hoarse.

Felicity couldn't answer. Conrad's words stung with each echo in her ears. How could they be hurting people? She'd never hurt anyone, and even if she wanted to, she probably wouldn't be able to. She looked back over her shoulder, though Conrad was out of sight, and swallowed down the lump in her throat. What were they doing wrong?

23

SHE WAS DONE FOR.

Had she condemned the rest of them? She couldn't have just let Conrad treat Felicity that way. It wasn't fair. She hoped the Stone might provide her an answer, but like the past few days. It was dormant.

It was no help. And now, she would have to face the Sergeant by herself. Miriam had to come and fetch her, which surprised both Felicity and Ray, who argued they should go as well, but Miriam said that the Sergeant just wanted Nikki.

Nikki paced outside of the Sergeant's door. She kept her head low, trying to prepare herself for the Sergeant's rage. Surely, she would be angry that Nikki had thrown a tablet at her assistant's face. She forced her thoughts to the back of her mind, trying to numb her emotions. She tried to straighten herself, trying to stop her fidgeting fingers, and still her tapping foot, her jaw sore from being clenched.

The door creaked open. Nikki froze, her heart racing.

No one emerged.

She crept slowly toward the door, peering through the crack into the office. No one was there. Just the flickering lights and the maps and holographic newsreel playing on the desk.

"Come in."

The words came out of nowhere, and Nikki's heart flinched again, but she refused to show her shock. She pushed the door open enough to slip herself in. Now inside, she spotted the sergeant sitting atop a shelf, her uniform jacket tied around her waist and her dark brown hair pulled into a bun. She held a tack in her hand, a pen behind her ear, and a tablet floating in front of her. That was not a function of the device Nikki had seen before.

Despite appearances, these Defenders did have some quality tech, few and far between though it may be.

The Sergeant looked up from her work, and her brows creased. "When they said one of the new kids started a fight with my assistant commander, I didn't expect this one," she said.

Nikki held her hands behind her back, shifting on her feet, but her expression remained still. The way the Sergeant stared was unsettling.

The Sergeant pushed the tablet aside, casually crossing her legs up on the shelf as she studied her. "Do you have anything to say for yourself?" she said.

Nikki kept her mouth shut.

"I see," the Sergeant said, tapping the tips of her fingers together. "Usually, there is a punishment for this kind of behavior. But from the report of bystanders, you actually resisted the fight my oh-so-bright Conrad gave you, rather than engage in unnecessary combat. And for what? The sake of a fellow comrade below you."

A curious spark lit up the Sergeant's eyes and Nikki took a small step back. That was an unfamiliar right.

The Sergeant jumped down from the shelf, landing comfortably on her feet, her pistol and dagger swinging casually at her side. The Sergeant moved with ease having weapons so close. She strode in a circle around Nikki, her face becoming tighter as she studied her. The Sergeant turned swiftly and stepped to one of the maps, her back to Nikki, seeming to be in deep thought.

Nikki watched the sergeant. What was she thinking?

Then the Sergeant jolted around, pulling the knife from its sheath, and flung the blade at Nikki's head.

Something clicked.

He body moved before her mind. She skidded to her knees, the blade whizzing past her ear and buried behind her. Nikki couldn't breathe. She was alive.

She looked to the Sergeant, who's lip held the faintest draw of a smile, as she looked back to Nikki. Nikki got up slowly, not taking her eyes off the Sergeant for a single moment as she backed to the wall and retrieved the knife. The blade was nothing like she'd ever seen. A pure silver, with a symbol etched into the upper section of the blade. The blade seemed to be scorched by fire, the black streak seeming to have a sheen to it.

Nikki brought it to The Sergeant, offering the knife with her arm outstretched to keep herself as far away as possible.

The Sergeant snatched the knife and examined it, running her fingertips along the symbol before slipping it back into the sheath. "Fine weapon isn't it?" she said.

Nikki didn't move.

The Sergeant laughed softly, shaking her head and making her way back to her desk. She glanced at her holograms before looking back over her shoulder. "A fine weapon that has struck every victim it was sent to kill."

Was the Sergeant trying to kill her? Nikki's lips parted slightly, the question rising to her lips, but she pressed the words back before they could escape.

"I had a feeling you'd be able to avoid its lethal call. A few can. Instinct. Or is it…something else?" The Sergeant raised an eyebrow and turned back to the screens. She brought up a small image in the corner of one screen, too small for Nikki to quite make out. She glanced from the picture to Nikki and back again. "What's your name, kid?"

Nikki's fist tightened again, and she bit the inside of her lip.

"You know if you won't tell me, I know others who will be glad to."

Nikki didn't budge. She didn't care if the Sergeant knew her small, simple name. She just didn't want to have the answer come from her. It felt like giving in to the Sergeant's authority.

The Sergeant gave a sigh. She snatched the pen from her hair, scribbling something on her desk beside the jumble of other notes scratched across her workspace. She looked back to Nikki, tapping the pen against her lips, then jotted another note and stuck it back in her hair.

"I know you can talk, kid," the Sergeant said, crossing her arms. "You're going to have to spill sooner or later."

Today wouldn't be that day. Nikki was determined about that.

"Hit me," the Sergeant suddenly snapped.

Nikki's eyes widened.

The Sergeant smiled, sliding into a fighting stance. "Come on, kid."

The sly smile on her lips was unceasing, but Nikki shoved emotion aside, waiting for some actual instruction.

The Sergeant winked, then swung her leg at Nikki.

Once again, she lost all control over her own body. She let the sergeant's sweeping foot send her tumbling, but she caught herself on her hands and whirled around, knocking Sergeant Hunter over.

The sergeant crashed into the edge of her desk, sending papers flying. Panic rushed through Nikki and she scrambled to collect the papers that had fallen across the floor.

The Sergeant recovered quickly, on her feet in a moment. "Don't look at those!"

It was too late, but Nikki hurriedly handed the papers back to the Sergeant. The bold titles of old news articles glared up from the fading pages, their dates going back hundreds of years.

The Sergeant tore them from her, scooping up the remaining papers. As soon as the articles were returned to a stack on the desk, her anger seemed to dissolve. She straightened, brushing herself off and crossing her arms.

"That...was something," she said, a gleam in her eye. "Your balance...a bit off. But it's familiar, isn't it? The instinct to fight."

Nikki took a shaky step backward. What did the Sergeant mean? What was she implying? Nikki didn't understand. She wasn't sure she wanted to.

She was tired of the Sergeant's mind games. She was more complicated than any other opponent Nikki had ever faced. More complicated than she had seemed at first, even. The Sergeant was trained to deceive. She was messing with her, and Nikki couldn't risk letting her guard down for even a second.

The Sergeant turned back to her desk, pulling a drawer open, and withdrew a small, crisp white envelope. "One more test, kid," the Sergeant said. Her eyes lifted, and Nikki noticed the previously energized spark had faded, replaced with the usual hollow expression. "And then, you'll be free to go, and I'll... have information to calm Conrad."

Evading a knife to calm Conrad down didn't line up. The hesitation in the Sergeant's voice didn't even seem to try to hide the lie. Again, she was messing with Nikki. Why? What did she want?

The Sergeant sat down on a hovering seat. She gently opening the envelope, and let a small, dark item slip out onto the palm of her hand. She held it out to Nikki.

The item was a small metal circle, just big enough to fit your finger through. A... ring. That was the word. It was a dark grey, the surface scratched, and worn. A smaller band ran around the outside, flickering on occasion. A screen perhaps? A tiny little black screen...Like it had once glowed. Red, perhaps. Red? Why had red come to mind?

She realized her hand had drawn closer to it. She looked hesitantly up to the Sergeant, who's gaze was still transfixed on her.

Nikki gently touched the ring. It sent a shiver through her, and she pulled back.

"Do you recognize it?" The Sergeant said, her face a lighting up and for the first time, Nikki saw a small, genuine smile on her hardened face.

Nikki looked up and shook her head.

The Sergeant's face fell. "Oh," she said. She cleared her throat and put the ring back into the envelope. "It belonged to a friend."

Nikki was quite sure the friend was not her. She was far too young to have possibly ever made any sort of connection with the mysterious Sergeant. Unless Nikki was supposed to have a connection with the friend...

"You're free to go now," the Sergeant said, slamming the desk drawer shut. "And tell your little friends to quit calling me 'the Sergeant' as if I'm of some cartoonish villain of theirs. Taryn would be much more suitable. The name has no connection I am fond of."

She took *Taryn*'s statement as a dismissal and ran for the door.

She closed the door behind her, slipping her hand into her pocket and trying to steady her breathing. She glared up at the Sergeant's name, 'Taryn' plaque above the door, and a small chill went down her spine.

How had the Sergeant so quickly gone from angry to...this?

Nikki took a step back, withdrawing the Stone from her pocket. The light surged inside, and a light laugh echoed through her mind.

She tore down the hall, her minding scrambling, her thoughts haunting her The Sergeant, Taryn. *Taryn*. She didn't know that name. Why was she so interested in her?

Who was she? Did that ring have to do anything with it?

Why had she been in Imperial?

She found the door to their closet, and flung it open, gasping for air.

She slammed the door and threw the Stone at the wall

with all her might.

It hit the wall, the clatter echoing through the dark room as it fell to the ground. Nikki turned her head away. She wished it had cracked, but she knew if she looked back, she would just be disappointed. She could hear it spinning on the ground behind her, probably growing furious.

It was far too close with the Serg-Taryn. *Taryn* had come too close. It felt as though the Sergeant knew exactly what was going on. Did Taryn know what the small room Nikki remembered so vividly was? Did she knew know about the piercing pain?

She had too. Right?

But why had Taryn brought her here in the first place? Why mess with her mind constantly? What did she and the others have Taryn wanted?

And only one essence knew and refused to tell her.

The *Stone.*

Nikki kicked the Stone to the other side of the room. It flew in an arc, not even hitting the wall, and flung itself right back toward her, hitting the end of her foot. It flickered again. She drew back, heart pounding.

What are you? she demanded.

The Stone shuddered on the ground. She could feel its anger. Nikki crouched down on her knees, watching the Stone.

What are you? she repeated.

"What? " the Stone laughed coldly. "*Child, I am no 'what.'*"

Nikki turned away, but the Stone's snicker echoed through her mind. She couldn't escape it. Then her mind went silent.

"*You want to know.* "

Of course, she did. She wanted to know what was playing

with her mind.

"I feel the real reason you ask this is in the hope you'll find what you are in turn."

Nikki didn't respond.

The Stone gave a sigh. A small static blot flashed inside the Stone, and it began to shake. The encryption engraved into the Stone was the only part not emitting light. Little bolts began to zap along the edge.

"You have a choice to make."

Nikki stared hard at the Stone. She wanted answers. But did she need them? She wasn't the only one in the mess. Had the others gotten in trouble because of her? She needed to know. And the Stone was the root of this all.

She shut her eyes, breathed in, and reached her hand out. Her fingers barely brushed the surface, but a jolt of pain surged through her, tearing at every inch of her body. Her mind went blank. Her senses gone. All that remained was the static pain.

Then darkness.

24

The scene melted.

Panic devoured Nikki in a cloud of darkness. She couldn't breathe, couldn't think, then everything flew into focus.

A tall, elegant woman peered into the grand ballroom bright with the colorful gowns of ladies dragging across the floor and laughing men in the corners with their swords casually sheathed at their sides.

"Avalon?"

Avalon jumped as a younger woman appeared from the shadows of the curtains. The second woman moved beside Avalon on the balcony overlooking the event. She shared the same stunning violet eyes as her sister, but so did everyone in their race. Avalon always found her sister curious with her button nose, freckles, and dark brown curls, so contrary to her kinds long drawn, sharp features, and blonde ripples. Avalon often was envious of her sister's ability to stand out.

"Carastene, look at them all!" Avalon sighed, tucking a long lock of hair behind her ear.

Carastene giggled as she scanned over the crowd. "It's a shame you're soon to be married to…one of those," Carasten smirked, pointing to one of the black-eyed guests as he dumbly looked around the room, his greasy hair slicked back.

Avalon slapped her sister's hand. "Carastene!" she snapped in a harsh whisper, though she couldn't hold back a smile. "It's rude to point."

Carastene sighed, leaning against the railing, cupping her face in her hands. "I know he's a lord and all," Carastene began, "but I couldn't imagine having to deal with that face every single day."

Avalon watched the small group that had formed around the lord. It was hard to look at his round, childish face and his long-braided hair without cringing at least inwardly. The Wingor that stood beside him, with his majestic glittering wings, was hundreds of times more brilliant to look at.

"That…hair though," Avalon muttered.

"If you can call it hair," Carastene laughed. "I bet he went and saw a faerie just for tonight."

Avalon rolled her eyes. "Those things do tend to play tricks."

"Those hideous black eyes," Carastene sighed.

"They all have black eyes, Carastene."

"But his are big…and ugly and…quite unsettling. Really. He could do without them." Carastene had to cover her mouth from laughing as she spoke. "A troll looks better than that Aviduous."

Avalon laughed softly, nodding in agreement to Carastene's statement.

"But to marry him? Oh, Avalon, that's a disgrace! A disgrace to every Ewyon that ever lived! No wonder we used to stay away from these arrangements," Carastene said, a look of sympathy in her eyes despite her laughter.

Their kind did tend to stay away from the Aviduous for many reasons. Avalon couldn't care less about most political conflicts in the High Court, but the Aviduous' looks really did them no favors.

"Well, at least you're not the one who must speak to him tonight and link arms and pretend to be having a splendid time," Avalon grumbled.

Carastene giggled again. "Don't worry, Avalon," Carastene said, straightening her posture and linking her arm with her sister's. "Your arm is mine."

The two headed for the stairs, and Carastene squeezed Avalon's arm. "You ready?"

"Anything to stop this horrendous war."

The rest of the night seemed to pass in a whirl and simultaneously drag into the longest night Avalon could remember. She was relieved to be able to slip back into her rooms and finally remove the heavy velvet gowns and corsets. Her curls had been smoothed to blond ripples pulled back from her face.

She walked to the window that opened over the peaceful view of the woods, taking in the sweet smell of the ocean. The moon was full, it's shimmering silver light falling among the tall trees, shining through their branches, scattering their shadows across the floor. The stars were spotted across the sky, their multitude shimmering through the sky caught Avalon's breath. A breeze blew through the room. Avalon pulled her rode to her chest with a shiver. She sighed and began to pull the blinds.

Something clattered on the stone windowsill and she paused, frowning out into the nighttime.

A second rock hit the blinds close to her fingers and she screamed, jumping back. What on earth? She frowned and pulled back the blinds a bit to nearly be hit with a rock. She screamed, jumping back, scattering to the ground. She crept back to the window and peered outside, holding her shawl closer to her chest. She nervously clutched an emerald shard that hung from a golden chain around her neck.

"Hullo? Anyone there!" A man's voice drifted up from the foot of the castle.

Avalon leaned out the window, her gaze finding a man waving both of his arms above his head. It was too dark to see his face clearly, but the moonlight shone on his light hair.

"Who might you be?" she called, her long hair falling over her shoulder and trailing out the window.

The strange man looked around for a moment, then redirected his attention back to her. "Come down, m'lady."

Avalon hesitated. This man could be dangerous. Why would he want her to come to him at this time of night? She glanced at him again and sighed. The warmth of her power flowed through her fingers and she pulled herself straighter. He couldn't do anything to her that she couldn't do to him five times worse. She turned toward the door, making up her mind.

"No! Not the door!" the man shouted. "Climb down! Down the tower, my lady."

The man must have been crazy. Any normal person by

this point would have already called the hall guards to take the man away and let her have a well-rested night. But as Avalon slowly tip-toed across the stone floor back to the window, a spark of excitement raced through her chest.

She scanned the wall below, noting a few weak and surely dying vines that had entwined their way into the cracks of the tower.

"I'll kill myself!" she yelled down to the man, though she wasn't quite sure she believed it. Something about that warm thrum of power denied that fear.

The man shook his head. "You underestimate the power stirring within you, my lady."

Avalon sighed. He sure had a way with flattery, and she wasn't going to let some peasant boy think she was a fool. She pulled herself up onto the stone ledge and swung one leg out of the window. Her foot got caught up in the hem of her gown, and she struggled to pull it out. The wind tugged at her. She shrieked, finding a secure support in a crack between the huge stones, then she moved her other leg down. She tucked her gown between her legs in hopes it wouldn't cause any further trouble. With one hand grasping the windowsill, Avalon touched the stone dangling around her neck for reassurance. She took a deep breath.

She could do this.

She carefully moved her right foot from its spot and felt around for another crack. Her toes gripped a crumbling stone, and she began to move her other foot, but her other foot slipped free. Her weight jerked down on one hand still clutching the windowsill.

Avalon let out a cry as her fingers pried from their grip and she tumbled backward. A scream rising in her throat, she grabbed the stone around her neck and squeezed her eyes shut.

Suddenly, her fall slowed.

She nervously opened one eye and realized she was floating slowly toward the ground. The man held out his hand to her, seemingly unphased by her fall. Avalon grasped the man's hand with her own shaking one as her feet gently hit the ground.

"Th-thank you," Avalon stuttered, looking up to meet the man's eyes.

He looked much different up close. He had steel gray eyes, much different from her own race's familiar violet. He had a sand brown tint to his hair to frame the sharp edges of his face.

He wore a simple brown, beaten tunic and worn trousers, with no weapon at his side. He was tanned from the sun and his face was sprinkled with freckles. Despite his obvious lack of wealth, he met her with a warm smile.

"You're a talented tower jumper, ma'am," he said, shoving his hands in his pockets and glancing between Avalon and the tower window.

Avalon couldn't help but smile in return. She carefully opened her fist to show the stone. "All the essence of the fallen spirits has guided me."

The man's eyes grew wide with wonder, but Avalan clasped her hand over the stone again. He shook his head and smiled softly, holding out his hand to show a golden ring on his finger.

"I own something similar," he whispered. "Doesn't contain essence, but the legends say it's the key to the Universe."

Avalon laughed, having to tear her eyes from the enchanting ring. "What's your name?" she asked.

"Orion Idicous."

"Orion," Avalon repeated under her breath. "Like the stars?"

Orion shrugged. "I suppose so."

"Lady Avalon Amara Emberson. As you most likely know," Avalon said, straightening her shoulders. "Why have you asked me down here?"

Orion's smile faded as he fumbled with his fingers. "To speak with you, madam. We need someone to listen. I mean, if you understand. You're an Iso."

Avalon hid her smile at the thought of being needed and thought of so highly. Her father was technically the Iso of the kingdom, but no one had ever considered her as one as well. Instead of mentioning this, she crossed her arms and watched Orion narrowly. What was he hiding?

"You aren't a Shifter? Lyntox?" Avalon said, biting her lip in disgust. "We don't often keep them around here."

Orion laughed softly again, rolling his eyes with obvious amusement. "One can only wish."

Avalon pressed her lips together and paced around him, inspecting him. Orion stood uncomfortably, watching her in turn.

Then it struck her. "Oquelite?" she said, her eyes growing wide.

Orion looked down and nodded.

"Shouldn't you be in your quarters? It's awfully late for one of your kind to be out," Avalon said.

"That is why I'm here. We've gathered. We need someone to…listen," Orion said, taking a shaky step forward.

Some Oquelite worked around the palace grounds, but she rarely saw much of them as they were usually harvesting the fields or preparing a room that her family wasn't present in. And that was only the ones who'd remained. The Oquelite in other farms and kingdoms had suddenly disappeared just a few weeks prior.

Many blamed the Dark Force—a strange mysterious force that had been sweeping through the kingdoms. Where it came nothing remained, but for a few dazed survivors.

Avalon sighed. That was part of the reason this alliance between the Ewyon and Aviduous would be such a good thing. Many speculated it to be the Oquelite. How else would that explain their random disappearances? But Avalon didn't believe it. They were talentless. Only good for farm work. But the thought of an ordinary servant rising and murdering nobles in their sleep was certainly unsettling. Those without abilities couldn't have souls. They didn't deserve them, the rumors said. That's why they could kill without mercy.

"I see you've heard the rumors as well," Orion said, looking into Avalon's eyes.

Avalon grimaced. Was she really that easy to read? "W-well, I've never believed the things people say," she stammered. "I like to think for myself."

Orion smiled sadly and nodded. "I see you are uninterested, madam," he said, turning back towards the hill.

Avalon reached out to Orian, her hand brushing against his arm. He looked around, shocked, and Avalon gave a soft smile. "I can tell you'd never hurt anyone."

Orion put his hand on hers. "I'm glad you can see that my lady."

"Call me Avalon, please."

The scene shifted quickly, faces blurring by too quickly to process, then the image focused again on a different night, dark and glowing red with fire.

"Carastene! You have to get her out of here!" Avalon shouted.

People were pushing past her screaming, torches racing above their heads as they rushed for the harbor.

Carastene stood trembling by Avalon, her shawl clutched to her trembling body. "But I-I can't," Carastene said, tears welling in her violet eyes.

"They're coming for us. They're coming for me. For her," Avalon said, staring down at the restless infant nestled in her arms. "If they get to us both, they will kill everyone."

Carastene looked down at the child, her shaking shoulders settling a bit.

"You have to take her and leave," Avalon urged, her own voice quivering.

"But what about you?" Carastene said, as Avalon passed the child to her.

The ground shook again, sending the crowd into panic as they fled toward the boats rocking and crashing the frantic sea.

Avalon lifted the Stone from around her neck and placed it in the bundle. Tears streamed down her face as she pulled her sister into her arms and squeezed her tight.

The earth trembled again, and Avalon pulled away. "Leave!" she screamed, pushing her sister toward the harbor.

Carastene froze, staring at her sister, the child wailing in her arms. Avalon looked toward the mountains and shouted again for Carastene to go. Carastene nodded and she tore away, running across the sand into the terrified crowd.

The last of the crowd trickled into the ships.

Avalon watched them part from the harbor and grow smaller and smaller as they sailed into the distance. She sank to her knees. This was her place. She deserved this, like every disgusted noble who'd laid eyes on her in the past months would agree.

This was where she belonged.

Only three worn soldiers remained with her, but their violet eyes showed their cowardice.

A shiver went down her spine. The air stirred around her as the presence of a strong essence approached. The ships were almost out of sight now, the glowing light of the torches beginning to dim. She took a deep breath. There was no going back.

She got up to her feet, her gown tattered and ripped, her bare feet exposed, and her elegant features scorched and dirty, but her violet eyes still bold and alive. Something shimmered in the distance and her mind screamed at her to run, but she stood firm.

The shimmers turned to troops storming out of the darkness.

Out of thin air.

All the soldiers looked the same in their black and silver uniforms, every step they took in clear unison, coming at a steady pace toward her. Avalon fought the instinct to cower before them.

Her own soldiers got up from the sand and onto their feet, fumbling to draw their swords. The air wavered in front of the proceeding army, and three generals on horseback stormed out. Out of the thousands they led, only these three wore gold.

They halted a few feet in front of Avalon. All in unison, the three officers dismounted, flawlessly landing on their feet. The left officer stepped toward her.

He removed his hood, a scarf covering the bottom half of his face. His head was bald and swirling tattoos decorated his skull. A scar ran across his nose and it twitched as he looked to the harbor, then to Avalon's soldiers, and then finally to her.

"Where are they?" he growled, closing in on her.

Avalon took a step back, trying to hide her fright, but from her wide eyes and pale face, she knew terror was clear. "They're gone," Avalon said, steadying herself.

The man growled and pulled a knife from his belt, thrusting it into the sand just beside her feet.

Avalon jumped back, tripping on the torn hem of her dress.

"General." The center solider stepped out, pushing the furious man back. The second solider knelt next to Avalon and held out his hand.

Avalon frowned, but accepted his generosity, sliding her fingers into his palm.

He pulled her to her feet, and their touch lingered for a moment longer. She looked up beneath the hood and into the grey eyes of the solider. He didn't need to remove the hood for her to know who he was and what this man had done.

He let the hood fall, pulling down the scarf from the lower half of his face.

"Orion," Avalon breathed.

Orion nodded, giving her a soft smile, but this time Avalon had no answering smile.

"*Lord* Orion Idicous, Avalon," he corrected.

Avalon stared at him. "Lord?" she gasped, her brows furrowing.

"They needed a leader. Someone to lead them out of this treachery we've been forced to live," Orion said, stepping closer and throwing his hand out to the hundreds lined behind him.

At first, Avalon was speechless, her lips trembling and her mind scrambling to piece together his words.

She squeezed her eyes shut, shaking her head. No. This wasn't right. None of this was right. "I helped you!" Avalon screamed, her eyes flying open.

Orion's own gaze drifted downward.

Avalon scowled at him. "So, what's your excuse? Your excuse for murdering hundreds?" she shouted. "Your excuse for not even being there for the birth of *your* child?"

Orion froze, his eyes narrowing, but the moment of softness quickly melted as he forced his eyes back up to meet hers. "Avalon—" he stopped, eyes widening. "Where is it?"

Avalon frowned, her fingers lifting toward her throat, but the Stone was gone, of course.

Orion looked off to the distant ships and growled. He stepped away from Avalon, his gaze darting toward the dying sun. He turned to his assistant general.

"It's gone?" the general shouted, his face turning red with fury. The man turned to Avalon again, his hand moving toward his knife belt. "It's on those ships, isn't it?" he said, pointing toward the sea.

Avalon didn't even need to answer him.

"Where are they going?" Orion said, his brows deepening in an angry scowl as he stepped in front of the general, his tone domineering and strong.

Orion's eyes looked darker than ever, and his face full of a hate and anger she'd never seen before.

Avalon tried to hide her own fear. She couldn't tell them. It would endanger thousands of her people. But she could die. She tried to push the thoughts away, lest they make her resolve crumble.

The assistant general nodded and the first line of the Oquelite unsheathed and unfamiliar sword-like weapon, rigid and curved. The surface of the blades looked like a pool of black water, constantly simmering and rippling.

Avalon almost stumbled back.

The general ordered a few to advance. Avalon's soldiers stepped up to meet them, yet within moments they were weaponless and pleading for their lives. The general flung his arm up and shut his fist, and one of Avalon's soldiers was thrown into the air, sprawling like a helpless child.

"H-How?" Avalon stuttered, stumbling back a pace. What was this power?

"I'll ask you again, where are the ships heading?" Orion said.

Avalon stood speechless.

Orion nodded to the general, who smiled at Avalon as he drew his weapon and slashed it across the arm of the nearest soldier. The soldier released a childish yelp. Orion lifted his hand, and a blue mist began to flow from the soldier's wound.

His face contorted in pain and he screamed and cried for help.

Avalon screamed in horror, clasping her hands over her mouth.

Then the soldier fell, motionless, to the ground.

"What did you do?" Avalon choked.

"What every one of my kind was born to do," Orion said, rolling his shoulders back to a dignified position, blue mist dancing around his fingertips. "Essence isn't just an idea like your philosophers and doctors say. It runs in all our blood and if it's gone…we die."

Avalon could barely breathe, staring at the thousands of

soldiers behind him. The Oquelite. All of them could kill someone that easily. She had so many questions.

"Where did the ships go?" Orion demanded again, swinging the remaining two soldiers into the air.

Avalon looked back at the remaining men's pleading eyes.

They were cowards. Her whole race was made up of cowards. She tightened her fists. They'd thrown her out. She was no longer one of them.

She was strong.

She squeezed her eyes shut, trying to block out the cries. This was for the good of the universe.

Only one soldier remained.

Avalon turned to Orion, her face full of horror and silently pleading for mercy.

"Where did the ships go?" Orion shouted.

The last one fell with a horrifying shriek.

Avalon trembled

"Lady," the general said, stepping toward her again. "Where did the ships go?"

Avalon looked up, fear clutching at her chest.

Orion leaned close to her ear, his voice still rich and soothing as his breath tickled her neck. "You were foolish all those years ago, climbing down for a slave. Be a fool now and bow down for a king."

Avalon couldn't keep herself from trembling, squeezing her eyes shut as tears burned down her cheeks. She could be safe, but then her entire remaining race would suffer even more from her mistakes.

"I am no fool, and you are no king," she said, her voice quivering.

The general growled. A force on her shoulders pulled

Avalon to her knees.

"You have made a mistake," Orion muttered, shaking his head as he leaned above her. One hand cupped her cheek, soft and gentle for a moment, then the tip of his sword sliced down the other side of her face.

Searing pain tore a cry from her. It was as if someone was trying to peel her skin from her flesh. A muffled crackling and buzzing roared in her ears, drowning out her own screams. She didn't see Orion turning away, not able to bear the sight. Bolts of electricity ran up her spine and it felt as though every muscle was pried out of her. She clenched her jaw, trying to bear it.

Finally, Avalon couldn't fight for a moment longer, and she welcomed the strange, soothing darkness.

25

NIKKI'S HEAD SHOT UP, HER HEART RACING AND HER forehead damp with sweat. Her hands shook, her fists clenched. Had she fallen asleep? No, she was still crouched, the Stone cupped in her hand. She stared down at it with new curiosity.

The dream rushed back to her, more vivid and real than any memory. The names, faces, thoughts, feelings—she'd experienced everything.

What are you? Nikki asked again silently.

The Stone gave a shallow laugh. *"You mean* who *am I? I'll let you guess."*

Nikki couldn't process it. No. It wouldn't make sense. "Avalon," she muttered under her breath.

The Stone sighed. *I guess that's what I've been called. Yes, child.*

"Idic—" Nikki couldn't bear to finish the name out loud.

"How?"

"You are thinking of that boy. Aren't you? Silas. And the elder, Matthias. They are the lord's sons, not mine. After I blacked out, as you saw in the memory, I woke up in this...Stone. It's my duty to protect it. It is one of seven artifacts. But you are too young and foolish to understand."

Nikki frowned, sliding down the wall until she sat on the floor. She pushed her bangs from her face and ran her fingers over the engraving on the Stone. Whatever it meant she was going to find out. And what about the Stone itself? It was connected with the races somehow.

"You want to know the race. That knowledge is too dangerous. It's best to keep you oblivious. I already had to resort to a simple child anyhow. Fifteen years is barely any experience in this world. I feel sorry life will never side with you."

A pang of annoyance settled in Nikki's gut at the Stone's words, but she kept it to herself.

"Remember your purpose," Avalon muttered, then the Stone went quiet.

The door swung open, and Nikki jumped to her feet, shoving the Stone in her back pocket with a new sense of urgency. Tabitha burst into the room, followed by Cole, both were covered with soot and dirt, but neither seemed to care.

"Come on!" Tabitha shouted, out of breath. "We're getting out of here!"

The two turned quickly, leaving Nikki only scramble after then as they ran down the halls, dodging a few annoyed Defenders in the process. Tabitha burst through the door labeled "Boiler Room", where Nikki found the other three waiting impatiently.

"Meetings?" Ray said as he sat at the top one of the boxes of plugs and wires. "Those seem to be our kinda thing."

"You say 'our' as if we are a collective unit," Tabitha noted.

Ray shrugged.

"What happened to you?" Lincoln said, frowning at Tabitha and Cole. "You two have been gone alone for a…"

Tabitha shot Lincoln a glare and he trailed off.

"We heard *she* got in a fight with Conrad," Cole said, looking at Nikki.

"Hey, I helped," Ray butted in.

Felicity snickered.

"I did!" Ray protested.

Cole sighed, shaking his head. "I don't doubt you tried, Ray."

"Yes. How could you doubt me? We aren't all as perfect as you."

Tabitha groaned. "Can everyone just shut their freaking mouths for, like, five seconds and stop trying to murder each other?"

Cole raised an eyebrow at Ray, and Ray gave a smile, but neither spoke.

"Taryn's either a zombie or a shapeshifter!" Tabitha shouted, and everyone immediately started paying attention. Tabitha brushed her hair out of her face, still trying to catch her breath, and meeting everyone's gaze with a furious intensity.

"What do you mean?" Felicity said.

"We went into that vent in the ceiling," Cole explained. "It led to a secret hall, and somehow my medallion unlocked it." He held out the medallion pendant that hung around his neck. "I have no idea why. But it led to this super high-tech place and a computer. Long story short, the Sergeant. I don't know why I didn't think of it. I thought Hunter as such a common last name—"

"We think the Sergeant might be part of the Curatrix team. Jessica Hunter."

Nikki stepped back, accidentally sending a room clattering to the ground. She picked it up, avoiding everyone's glances as she straightened it and hid her face behind her hair. *Jessica?* Another vaguely familiar warmth tugged at the back of her mind.

"How?" Ray said, suddenly. "They're all dead."

"I—I don't know," Cole said. "But the photo looked so much like her, just younger. And blonde."

"It's entirely possible she changed her name, and dyed her hair brown," Tabitha said.

The Sergeant Taryn's words replayed in Nikki's mind: *Taryn would be much more suitable. The name has no connection I am fond of.*

Felicity shook her head, massaging the bridge of her nose. "I heard she was friends with members of the Curatix team, but one of them? Don't you think the media would have reported on her? Constantly interviewing her?"

"Unless someone didn't want it to be known," Lincoln said, softly.

"But why? I thought the media loved the Curatrix team." Felicity opened her eyes, looking over their faces.

"They love the drama and controversy," Tabitha said. "But if Taryn...Jessica survived, and they didn't report on it, that would mean she would have to have done something, or offended someone, so big for no one to ever talk about her."

"Whatever it is, she hasn't stopped. She's obviously planning *something*." Lincoln began to tap his foot. "And I'm afraid it has to do with us."

"That fact doesn't change whether she's Jessica or Taryn," Ray grumbled. "And I'm kind of sick of it."

Felicity suddenly gasped. "You said she had tons of articles on deaths?"

Tabitha raised an eyebrow. "Yes?"

Felicity began to take in deep breaths, holding her arms close to her chest. But Nikki saw something new in her. A fierce determination as she bravely looked up, not cowering away to tell them: "What if she killed the Curatrix team?"

"That *would* be a big enough scandal to try and keep her quiet," Lincoln said, his eyes growing wide.

"And to have such terrible Defenders," Ray added.

"No!" Nikki shocked herself, slamming her hand over her mouth.

Everyone's attention turned to her, their eyes wide, and mouths gaped in shock. Nikki's face heated.

"No?" Felicity frowned.

"She—she couldn't have."

"Why is that?" Tabitha's voice demanded.

Nikki pulled her hair over her face.

A hand gently touched her shoulder. "It's okay, Nik."

She heard Avalon groan in disgust, but Nikki ignored her. She glanced to Lincoln. It was okay. She was safe.

"T-taryn couldn't be a killer, if she had an attempt on her own life," she said quietly.

For a moment, the others were quiet.

"She actually has a point," Ray sighed. "Jessica Hunter, who we're assuming is Taryn, was reported to be killed. Somehow miraculously survived. She couldn't kill and be 'killed' at the same time."

"While that is a good point, there is just not a not evidence to prove wither claims," Cole sighed. "The Sergeant

Taryn...Jessica, whatever her name is, can't be trusted. And I think her possibly murdering the Curatrix team has to be considered."

Nikki clenched her fists. She wanted to speak. Defend Taryn somehow. But she couldn't. What further proof did she have besides her gut feeling that Taryn couldn't have killed them? Something about the ring pulled on her.

Was the ring related to Orion's gold ring?

No. Avalon interrupted the thought quickly. *How that blasted Sergeant got a hold of that ring, I have no idea, but it has not connected to Orion's. His has far more consequences.*

You were fast to correct me. Nikki noted.

Avalon gave a frustrated sigh. *Make your assumptions, girl. They might save you.*

The Stone cut the connection.

"I think it's been a given the Sergeant can't be trusted," Lincoln was saying. "But we can't condemn her to a murderer. Not yet."

Tabitha scrubbed at some of the soot on her face. "But this only confirms that the Sergeant's motivations are unstable ground. If she isn't with the law, don't we have a right to leave?"

Before anyone could answer, the air exploded with thunder and the earth shook violently around them, knocking everyone sprawling.

26

"WHAT THE *HECK* WAS THAT?" LINCOLN LIFTED HIS HEAD from the floor, temples throbbing from the impact. All six of them had been sent down by the sudden quake, and someone was lying half on top of him.

Lincoln groaned and shoved the body off, getting up to his hands and knees.

Ray—obviously having fallen from his shelf onto Lincoln—groaned in echo. "That was not an earthquake for sure."

Another blow. The entire room shook. Lincoln rammed into a wall, Ray crashing after him with a yell. Again, it steadied, but Lincoln hesitated, making sure that the world wasn't going to try to shake them up again.

"Well, this is fun," Tabitha said from across the room.

Everything paused for a minute.

Finally, Lincoln sat up, Ray joining him, nursing a bruised elbow.

The hallway suddenly burst to life beyond their boiler room door. The thunder of feet rumbled past, and shouts began echoing through the halls. Lincoln scrambled to the door, tearing it open.

Defenders stormed through the halls in stiff, efficient rows. The shouts came from the speakers overhead.

The earth shook again.

Everyone stumbled to the ground, some catching themselves against the wall. Even the shaking didn't stop them from moving. Some crawled and stumbled against the walls, trying to pull themselves forward. Nothing seemed to stop them.

Speakers blared commands. "Squads four and five assigned to border watch. Proceed quickly. Fire control should be second command and priority."

"Fire," Nikki whispered.

Lincoln hadn't noticed her get up and join them at the door.

"There's a fire?" Ray said.

"They said the fire was a second priority. And those quakes…" Cole didn't finish his sentence.

"Explosions," Tabitha muttered, her eyes growing wide. "You're not saying that—"

Nikki suddenly pushed past them and burst into the hallway, racing through the Defenders.

"Wait!" Ray called after her. "Where are you going?"

Cole jumped out into the hall as well. "What are you all waiting for? They're going to destroy this place! And we wanted to get out, so—"

"Gosh darn you," Ray muttered, standing up. "Okay, everyone! Let's go save this cursed place."

Nikki threw the door open. Sergeant Taryn Hunter was frozen at her desk, her hand gripped on her pistol, her eyes wide. She softened her stance, when she settled on Nikki, continuing to gear herself up, without giving Nikki a second notice.

"Sergeant Hunter," Nikki said.

Taryn raised her eyebrows, crossing her arms. "So, she speaks."

Nikki's didn't falter, her glare demanding an explanation.

Taryn sighed. "They're trying to take down the wall—The advanced border technology that protects each individual region. Anyone can travel through them, but Oquelite essence cannot, excluding a few exceptions. The very fact they are trying to destroy the wall is absurd." Taryn's eyes glimmered with mischief.

"We're going with you," Cole said, stepping forward.

Taryn's lips parted. "You can't. You're under arrest and it is my duty to keep simple citizens out of unauthorized scuffles."

"If this group of Oquelite has the strength to destroy this wall thing of yours, they could do worse once they're out. It's not a matter of whose fight this is. It's all our lives. Even if we are guilty of this 'crime' you claim we are. Maybe we can use this to help prove our innocence to you," Cole said.

Taryn's lip curled, seeming completely unsurprised by Cole's remarks. "Even that little Bentsworth is willing to feel the heat up there? She looks a bit pale."

Felicity straightened her shoulders, her jaw tightening. "I'm not little," she grumbled.

Taryn nodded again, lips pressed into a line. "Perfect. You'll be placed *as far away* as possible. Just helping any citizens who need to evacuate. So, if needed we can get you out as soon as possible."

There was no objection.

Taryn pulled a pistol from her belt and tossed it. Nikki caught it swiftly, staring at the weapon like it was the most disgusting thing she'd ever seen.

"Lesson One. Fighting isn't fun and games," Taryn said. "People get hurt."

The next thing Nikki knew was heat blasting in her face, her heart beating, and Taryn barking inaudible orders at the scattered Defenders.

People were flooding out of shops, some scrambling for their trucks, others running for buckets of water, and some even drawing their own weapons.

There were no Oquelite in sight.

Nikki watched the fire race from tree to tree, crawling up the mountains. She turned back to the chaos that had transformed the streets of North Cordell. The law enforcement of the region walked with the Defenders like it was completely normal. They did give them a few sideways glances, but no one could blame them.

Sergeant Hunter had forced Nikki and the others to wear pistols and axes at their belts, and tattered jackets over bulletproof vests. The Oquelite never seemed to use guns, so why would they need the vests? She wanted to remove it, but every time she tried, Lincoln elbowed her. She wished he'd just ignore her and let her take off the weird thing.

Taryn still managed to look like a leader, even decked out in a helmet, with her pistol in hand. Her jeans seemed out of place paired with the defender jacket. She barked orders at the defenders and enforcement officers, her dark hair tied back firmly, and her face one of steel. She looked ready to kill.

An auto took a turn too fast and rammed through a window of a shop, alarms blaring like mechanical screams. Nikki rushed to the auto, yanking the door open. A middle-aged man rolled out and Tabitha and another Defender were quickly at his side.

"You alright?" Tabitha said, helping the man up as the Defender quickly dabbed at the cut in the man's forehead with a cloth.

"The farms. They need to be warned. The fire's gonna devastate them," he managed to sputter out.

Tabitha looked up to Nikki. "You got that?"

Nikki nodded, running over a group of men and women she'd seen gathered in the shops earlier, now standing with weapons in hand. "Farms!" she shouted.

A woman burst from the crowd. "We're on it!" She flashed Nikki a smile.

Another truck was loaded, barely missing a building as it tore off the road and into the grasses toward the farmland in the distance.

Lincoln and Ray ran from across the street to join Nikki, arguing as they came.

"How can you be hungry?" Ray asked, frowning at Lincoln.

"I didn't say that. I just pointed out that they left that store unsupervised and the food was just there," Lincoln shouted.

Nikki had no idea why the conversation was relevant or needed to be brought up in the middle of this. She didn't even need to interrupt them, however, because the earth rumbled again.

Nikki stumbled, slamming into the asphalt. The roar was louder above ground, and the sound itself felt like it was tearing through her eardrums. Once it finally stopped, Nikki lifted her head from the ground, her vision wobbling into focus.

She could see the wall.

A wall of fire.

Not orange fire, but a strange blue-grey flame.

As far as the eye could see, blue flames had emerged around the border. Of course, the region was too large to see all around, but even on the horizon a small blue smudge blended into the sky itself. Ahead, heat blew in her face as the wall rose higher than the mountains themselves.

Taryn screamed for the forces to advance to the flames. Nikki almost began to run as well, but Ray caught her, and she ripped from his grasp, whirling into a fighting stance before she could stop herself.

He jumped back, his hands up. "Okay! Sorry, but I'd rather not die right now," Ray said. "Also, we can't go. Sergeant Taryn said we should stay here. 'Cause we're children and we have to stay safe."

"This society is very ironic, isn't it?" Lincoln said.

"Don't think too hard about it, Black Eyes." Ray sighed.

"When was the last time you thought about anything?"

Nikki sighed. "You're going to get killed," she said. "Silence."

The two glared at each other but closed their mouths. The earth trembled and Nikki braced herself to be thrown to the ground. But instead, the air rumbled and a breeze swept through the street. The air rippled, sparked, and a black uniformed Oquelite broke free.

Just like in Avalon's flashback.

Behind him, the Oquelite poured out, appearing on the sidewalk, the tops of buildings, and in the flames themselves. Ray, Lincoln, and Nikki stepped toward each other. Nikki could see Taryn in the distance beyond the enemy, frozen in place, her mouth open in surprise.

That wasn't reassuring.

Taryn had meant to keep them from the front of the fighting but the Oquelite had taken a different approach. The Defenders looked sparse compared to the ever-growing numbers of the Oquelite. A Defender ran toward them, dodging an arrow that crashed into the street, exploding into flames.

Nikki recognized Miriam Outown before she reached them.

"We need to get you back!" she called. "There's way more than the Sergeant anticipated."

"Your sergeant said—"

"You've done your part!" Miriam yelled at Ray, sweat trickling down her face.

Suddenly, an Oquelite materialized in front of them. He threw his blade at Miriam. She dodged it but stumbled back. Ray grabbed the pistol from his belt and pulled the trigger. The gun fell to the ground, Ray grasping his shaking a wrist.

The Oquelite fell to the ground, crumbling into dust.

Ray cried out, staring down at the man's remains on the street in horror. "W-what j-just happened? Oh my gosh!" His breath came in short gasps and he staggered back a pace.

Miriam grabbed Ray by the back of his shirt and led them over to the sidewalk, where Tabitha, Cole, and Felicity had taken shelter behind a pile of boxes.

Miriam put her hand on Ray's shoulder. "Calm down,

kid!" she said. "These things are basically immortal unless they're killed directly. The older ones are easier to kill. They just turn to the form their actual age is at. It's okay."

Ray stared at her, his shoulders still heaving.

Nikki paused, looking at Lincoln, who was watching her, entirely clueless. She touched Ray's hand, and he looked up. She just gave him a single nod; not sure what words would manage to calm him. Ray managed a sort of terrified smile.

"Now hide!" Miriam snapped.

"I thought you said—" Lincoln started, but Miriam shoved him down with the others.

"Whatever I say right now is all that matters!" Miriam yelled. "And right now, I say hide! We don't have time."

With that, Miriam ran off, a distant cry of Conrad shouting "Wing it!" for her. She left the group hidden from a deadly supernatural threat behind some cardboard. Nikki felt trapped in the small quarters, trying to hold herself back from bursting out to get space. The others didn't seem so enthusiastic about their situation either.

"Lincoln, you smell like dirt," Ray muttered.

"Well," Lincoln said. "I wonder why."

Ray shoved Lincoln, who rammed into Nikki. Lincoln gave her an apologetic look and moved over to give her space.

"You two need to knock it off," Cole hissed.

Felicity screamed. "Fire! Fire! Move!"

No one hesitated. They scrambled from the hiding spot as the boxes went up in flames. Felicity stared at their shelter, her mouth open in terror. She didn't seem to notice that a piece of her hair had been scorched. Now they were exposed to the world.

And the Oquelite were advancing.

An Oquelite vanished from his place down the street and appeared on the roof above them.

They began to scramble back, but Nikki shouted, "Stay together!"

They froze, exchanging helpless glances.

The Oquelite pulled out a sword, the blade glinting and morphing its size as he swung. He flung the blade out at them and the tip of the sword splintered into small shards, like tiny bullets. Nikki slid to the ground, dodging the projectiles, and reached for the knife in her belt. She ran for the Oquelite, but the sword melted into a shield, and her knife thrust bounced off uselessly.

The shield whipped back into a sword and the Oquelite stepped toward Nikki, slow and confident, his shoulders high.

Someone grabbed Nikki from behind, nearly knocking her off her feet. Then she was running, dragged by one arm behind Lincoln and the others.

Lincoln let go of Nikki as soon as she was running after him. Running wasn't the solution she had in mind—it wasn't a solution at all.

The Oquelite ran after them. Maybe he didn't have enough energy to teleport again, but surely, he would in another moment.

"The bow!" Nikki called out.

Lincoln looked back, frowning for a moment, before his face lit up. "I think I got it, but I'm not sure. Sometimes you have to use more than two words to explain a plan," Lincoln said, taking the bow from his back and removing on his own arrows, which Taryn had allowed him to take back. "And remember, I'm not an expert when it comes to shooting Defender's stupid standard bows."

Nikki nodded. "Trust me."

Lincoln's eyes widened, pausing a moment. "Let's do it."

Nikki took a sudden turn around, seeing the three Oquelite heading for them. The first must have picked up some allies.

Lincoln was shouting some brief directions and soon Cole, Tabitha, and Ray were by her side. Nikki barely had a moment to even consider where Felicity was before a blade whizzed by her face, just grazing across her cheek.

One of the Oquelite disintegrated into dust before them.

Lincoln barely gave the knife that lay in the heart of the dust a second glance before running off.

Nikki ran into the nearby shop. She'd seen the place earlier, full of farming supplies. Now the inside was littered with loose boxes and equipment poured over the floor. She took a deep breath. A thick smell stung her lungs that allowed her to give a relieved breath.

Oil.

This place was flammable.

The others quickly followed. Ray's eyes grew wide as he stepped inside. He looked out the shattered windows at the Oquelite fast approaching. "We're going to kill ourselves!" he said.

An Oquelite materialized behind the desk, another appearing beside him a moment later. The two they'd been previously fighting quickly burst through the door.

The one at the desk laughed coldly. "You're strong little fellows, aren't you?" she said, jumping over the desk. "I say the skinny girl and the frumpy boy are mine."

Nikki lunged, grabbing a shovel. It was pointless, but she had to do something. The Oquelite swung the sword at her, and she met it with the makeshift weapon. The blade clanged against the metal shovel and the Oquelite gave out a terrible, inhuman screech. The next swing split the shovel in half.

"We have to get out!" Cole yelled.

Nikki tossed the end of the shovel at the Oquelite and spun toward the others. Ray looked up to her, his eyes wide and his hands raised, shaking. "Hold on!"

And the building burst into flames.

Nikki toppled onto the ground, out of breath.

One moment, they'd been in a flaming building, and the next instant they were out in the street.

"What just happened?" Lincoln yelled, stumbling to his feet.

Ray pulled himself off the ground, brushing himself off. "Maybe we just went through a portal the Oquelite made to escape or something…hard to tell in the blast." Ray shoved his hands in his pockets, looking toward the burning building.

Nikki frowned, watching Ray's face carefully.

"How'd you do that!" Felicity exclaimed, her eyes wild with excitement as she looked at Lincoln. "You shot the arrow and boom!"

Lincoln shrugged, his smile quickly dissolving as he looked around. The Oquelite seemed to have mostly moved from these streets, but one still limped out of a portal toward them.

Nikki quickly grabbed the other knife from her belt and thrust it into the Oquelite's chest.

It didn't have time to fight, crumbling into dust around the blade.

"Into the shop!" Cole ordered, pointing at another abandoned produce store.

They were barely inside when the ground shook again, sending them all pitching and stumbling to the floor. Nikki grabbed the edge of a shelf, trying to brace herself till the chaos stopped.

She ran to what used to be a window, now shattered by the heat, and looked out toward the border. There were so many black uniforms. Figures sprawled across the ground, but she tried not to look too closely. Where was Taryn? The Sergeant was what was holding their defense together.

"Is that a new reporter?" Ray shouted.

Nikki turned her head to an auto-van that had pulled up near the square in the center of the town. They were close enough to see a well-dressed, fuchsia-haired woman in heels hop out of the auto-van. Nikki wrinkled her nose as a man with a huge camera quickly followed.

"They look like they're soaking in money," Ray whispered as they all crouched behind a stand near the window.

The woman patted her hair and gave a white, toothy smile. Tabitha began to laugh, but Cole shoved her hand over her mouth. His other hand went over Ray's mouth before he could make another sarcastic comment.

"We're here at the Southern Region, North Cordell, the cutest little Preserve Region, where there's been a lot of mysterious reports lately. There seems to have been a brawl breaking out between a new threat to our grand world, which might be the source of North Cordell's latest so-called disasters," the woman went on.

Ray moved Cole's hand for a moment to spit out, "Can she see there is a literal wall of blue fire?!"

Cole shot him a glare, but the pink haired lady didn't seem to hear the sudden interruption. Nikki's fists tensed. How could the fluffy lady not even care what was happening?

Suddenly, their van burst into flames.

The woman screamed as an Oquelite emerged unharmed from the vehicle. The cameraman didn't stop filming, though the woman was only reporting screams.

"We can't let them kill her though," Cole sighed, jumping out the window.

The others quickly followed. Ray jumped in front of the camera, waving his arms. "Hey everyone! It's me!"

The woman blinked.

"Ray!" Lincoln yelled, and Ray winked to the camera and ran to face the Oquelite, who had been joined by another.

"Stop filming!" Ray yelled over his shoulder, but the reporters ignored him.

Nikki was weaponless, so she'd have to rely on her fists. She felt more at ease with them, but not in the least bit confident against the Oquelite.

Cole abandoned the gun as his Oquelite grabbed it from him and simply melted it in their hand.

Cole had managed to punch the Oquelite's hood off. The Oquelite looked at him in astonishment at the panicked teenager fighting off pure adrenaline. He growled, reaching for his sword. Tabitha darted forward and snatched the sword from his side before he could draw it and tossed it as far away as she could. The Oquelite started after it, but Cole slammed himself into the Oquelite, knocking him off into the side of the auto-van. The Oquelite grabbed Cole's shoulders and slammed him to the ground.

Nikki dodged the other Oquelite's blade and ran to help Cole. Her heart pounded into her ears. Behind her, the Oquelite shoved Lincoln to the ground, and he lost his grip on the bow.

The Oquelite, however, had no interest in him. He turned

his bloody, exposed face to Nikki and licked his lips.

"I shall make him proud!" The Oquelite yelled as he moved toward Nikki, drawing his sword and slicing at her.

She dodged back and the blade only cut through the sleeve of her shirt. "Lincoln!" Nikki shouted as she swung a kick at the Oquelite's feet, knocking him over.

The Oquelite vanished before he even hit the ground and rematerialized in front of her.

"The arrow!" she yelled.

Lincoln ran up behind the Oquelite and tossed the arrow to Nikki. He leaped on the man, wrapping his arms around the Oquelite's neck from behind.

Please be old. Please be old, Nikki begged.

She gripped the arrow. It was made of metal, the end more like a blade. She was going to have to ask Lincoln what he did in his free time later. She thrust the arrow in the direction of the Oquelite and jumped back.

A boom cracked through the air, and dust sprayed everywhere, a few small bones following.

Lincoln looked up, shocked, his hair full of dust. He spat, shaking his head and setting off a cascade of grey remains from his hair and shoulders. "That is gross."

Nikki agreed.

Tabitha and Cole stumbled toward them, Cole leaning heavily against Tabitha for support.

"That dude banged him up…a lot," Tabitha grimaced, glancing back at the second Oquelite—or rather, the dust that was left of him.

"I'm fine," Cole said, straightening with obvious effort and wiping the dirt and blood from his face. He pulled his hand away and frowned at it. "Blood."

Tabitha gulped and nodded.

"The reporter person won't go," Felicity said, approaching from by the van. "She's probably from Kennedy with that hair. Like a Golden Region wannabe."

Nikki looked out toward the wall. The blue fire rippled. That couldn't be a good sign. "We need to go to the border," she said, picking up Lincoln's arrow and turning toward the other five.

They exchanged reluctant glances. Cole looked beat up, Tabitha was tired, Ray was still in shock in his vacant gaze, Lincoln was wiping dead Oquelite dust from his eyes, and Felicity had gone even more pale than before.

But they'd survived one attack mostly unscathed, which they had to admit was far better than and if Taryn and her Defenders were going to stop the border from falling and unleashing hundreds—or thousands—more Oquelite, they'd need as many capable hands as they could get.

27

Nikki knew from the look on Taryn's face when she saw them arrive at the border that they were going to be in serious trouble. If they survived this.

Taryn gave Nikki a stern look before disappearing into the commotion, though her voice could still be heard screaming out orders.

Nikki turned to run into the fight, but something stopped her. A tingle brushed her fingertips, then all the way up her spine.

Everything went quiet.

They were back.

The hands slid around her waist, clasping stone fingers over her mouth so she couldn't scream for help. She couldn't move. No matter how much she fought or mentally screamed for Avalon. The commotion around her came in various clips and flashes. She could feel the ground moving beneath her feet, the air growing colder around her.

Then she fell.

The world sprang back to life as she picked herself up from the pine needle floor of the woods. The commotion of the fighting and the flames was distant and dulled by the thick trees. How far had they taken her?

"Hello, little one."

Nikki burst back, whirling around.

Silas stood behind her, his pale face and perfect uniform untouched by the blood of the fight below. His strange sword was drawn, and his lips pulled into a soft smile.

Nikki braced herself, her fists clenching.

"So, this was strange essence I've been feeling," Silas said, examining his sword. "Don't think you're going to get away with continuing to hold us back any longer."

His eyes gleamed with excitement as he stepped forward.

Nikki's heart fell. Silas's eyes looked different. His pupils wider. Crazier, than she had scene from their previous encounters. Something was horribly different in his aura. His steel eyes looked paler, faded blue veins peeked out from his eyelids.

"I can feel your pain. The cuts and burns you're choosing to ignore," he said. "But I know much more than that. I know what you seek and what you wish to know. I know what you are."

She just stared him in the eyes, waiting for him to strike. Was he lying? She narrowed her eyes. There was something unfamiliar flickering in his gaze.

Silas sighed. "I really find this turning out to be a monologue. You should really speak up more. I bet that voice of yours was lovely." He vanished, then reappeared right in her face and swung his sword.

Nikki ducked and scattered away from him.

Silas didn't seem to find her threatening. He sheathed his sword and looked off to the mountains, as if he had all the time in the world. He probably did, but Nikki didn't. She had other plans.

He turned his attention back to her and waved his hand in a circle. A ring began to form around them, sparking, then bursting into a bright blue flame.

Nikki drew her small knife, looking down to it, then back to Silas. She made an instant decision and threw the dagger into the flames.

Silas raised an eyebrow, but her actions didn't slow him. He flicked his wrist and Nikki was tossed to the ground.

She managed to roll aside and jump to her feet. Her shoulder throbbed from the impact, but she dodged most of Silas's invisible blows. He had set his sword down, his hands twisting in their obscure ways. He suddenly disappeared, leaving Nikki alone, waiting in breathless silence.

A voice echoed through her mind, the words inaudible.

Then she thrust her fist out, knuckles connecting with something hard.

Silas appeared in front of her with his sword to her throat, one of his eyes squinted in pain. A piece of his perfect, white hair had fallen into his face and he glared down at her. "I will kill you," he said flatly. "All of you."

The sword pressed against her throat. Then he tossed it aide into the flame, the weapon sizzling and disappearing into smoke.

Nikki threw her fist out, but Silas deflected the blow. He

grabbed her arm, holding her arms against him, his arm pressed firmly against her neck.

"But today's not that day," he said.

Nikki tried to fight him, but the too-familiar hands twisted their way to her lips.

She couldn't move.

She couldn't speak.

She couldn't breathe.

Silas's hand pressed harder into her arm, her skin warming beneath his fingers. Then it began to sting, then burn as if someone was trying to tear the very flesh of her bones. The strangely sweet smell of burning flesh filled the air. She wanted to jerk away or cry out, but she was trapped.

Finally, Silas let go, flinging her to the ground.

Feeling rushed back over her, and she tried to push herself back to her feet, but a flick of Silas's hand sent her head slamming into the ground.

Her vision blurred, but she wouldn't let her eyes close.

Silas' dark figure loomed over her.

She weakly reached to her arm, feeling the sting of the open wound, her head swaying.

Fight it! Avalon's voice thundered through her mind. *He's using you. Manipulating you to feel this way. Don't let his abilities fool you!*

Nikki tried to force herself up, but Silas' foot pressed down onto her shoulder. The hands were crawling all around her now, mocking her. She was in their control now. She couldn't escape.

Avalon's sigh echoed in her mind as the hands crawled to her throat, pulling Nikki down under into their terrible dark dominion.

28

THE FIRE ROARED AROUND THEM, ONLY DISTURBED BY THE jumble of shouts and weapons blurring around them.

Cole found himself entirely alone in the field beside Tabitha, who kept giving him worried glances every so often. He was fine. His head throbbed, though he could still think clearly enough.

A multi-colored flaming ball roared through the air, and Cole grabbed Tabitha and ran. Was he seeing things or was there a legit rainbow bomb? He yelled at Tabitha to get down, flinging himself down onto the ground and throwing his hands over his head.

The ground thundered below them, dirt and debris raining down. Tabitha jumped back up, staring at the scorching earth where the flaming ball had hit. Cole staggered to his feet after her, and Tabitha began shouting at him, her words drowned out by the noise as she pointed urgently into the distance.

"...forward...move...this...!"

"What?" he yelled after her, but Tabitha started running, disappearing around a corner into the smoking commotion. Cole tried to run after her, but he stumbled to a stop again as he rounded the building. She was gone.

There were no Oquelite. No Tabitha.

No one.

It seemed even quieter. He ran back around the corner, the world swinging back into commotion. Why had Tabitha run there? Had she been trying to say something important? Questions raced through his head as he stepped reluctantly into the burning wasteland she'd vanished into. Shattered weapons scattered the ground. Loose fabric fluttered in the wind, singed by the fire. Cole walked slowly. This place didn't feel right.

"Tabitha!" he called.

No response.

Cole walked further, his head beginning to rock, trying to ignore the younger Oquelite spread across the ground, their bodies nothing but bone and dust.

Something caught his ankle and Cole tripped, falling to the ground.

He sat up suddenly, jerking away as he saw a small, uniformed figure with his hand clutched around Cole's ankle. The boy moaned.

Cole froze, his pulse pounding in his ears. "Are you alright?" he managed.

The Oquelite's head jerked up, the hood falling off to

reveal a boy barely older than himself. Cole's throat tightened.

The boy didn't open his eyes, but his pale lips struggled to form words as his fingers dug deeper into Cole's leg.

"Stop…now. Dark times…ahead. Don't…do."

The raspy voice sent a chill through Cole's body. Why did the voice sound so familiar? He tried to pull away.

"I said don't!" the boy screeched, lunging his body forward before sinking back, groaning like it was a terrible mistake. "You'll…regret it! You will! You…idiot!"

The ground shook again, but Cole couldn't move.

"Cole!" Tabitha's voice called in the distance. "Cole!"

Cole's head jerked in the direction of her voice, searching around desperately for her, but the Oquelite jerked his ankle.

"Don't continue. Don't go with her!"

It was just a boy. Should Cole help him? But there was something off about him still. The way his fingers dug into his ankle like claws and the hoarse rasping of his words from his unnaturally pale lips.

"I can't stay," Cole said, trying to jerk away again.

But the Oquelite growled. "Don't do….it! Don't m-make the same mistakes!" The Oquelite's eyes burst open. They were completely white, no pupils or iris, just deadly white.

Cole choked on a scream and jerked free of the boy's grasp, staggering to his feet. The boy collapsed into the earth, quivering as his skin began to melt.

Cole ran. He ran harder than he ever had before.

He couldn't think of what the Oquelite said, and what he shouldn't do. He tried not to think of the warning when Tabitha's cut, dirty face lit up upon seeing him. Suddenly, the flames became something else. The pain in his skull, and the deaths around him.

They were *real*.

All of it.

Lincoln and Ray raced through the battlefield, following Nikki's instructions to reach the gate. They'd been side-tracked once already by a couple Oquelites who wanted to engage in a fight. It was harder to fend them off since they'd been separated.

"So much for sticking together," Ray mumbled.

The pink-haired lady and her camera man literally almost died about twenty-nine times, and Lincoln and Ray kept trying to tell them to leave, but they wanted to move in further. She asked a lot of questions, which they ignored.

The pink-haired lady stomped her heels in delight. "Okay, go!"

The camera zoomed in on Ray. He groaned. "Hi world. Now leave!"

Lincoln walked up to the camera man. "May I see that?" Lincoln asked.

The cameraman eyed him, mouth open to protest, but Lincoln shoved him over and with the click of a few buttons, the blinking red light dimmed.

"Hey, kid! What did you do?" The cameraman snapped, growling and flexing his arms. As if he could intimidate them when there was literally an army of Oquelite out for their demise.

Ray frowned. "Wow, how did—"

"How do *you* think you disable a security camera?" Lincoln shrugged.

"I wouldn't know."

"Good point," Lincoln said, turning to the pink lady and the man. "Now, you guys really have to—"

"Oh, my graciousness!" the woman shrieked.

Lincoln turned around slowly, and his jaw nearly dropped. The Oquelite had stopped. They'd stopped fighting off the Defenders and were disappearing in huge groups at a time.

They'd won. The Oquelite were surrendering.

They must have decided they couldn't win this one. Lincoln looked to Ray, who blinked in equal astonishment.

Then the earth shook again, as violently as it had the first time, knocking them to the ground. Lincoln tried to grab something, but out in the open his hands had nothing to grasp but the dirt beneath him.

When the shaking slowed, Lincoln shoved himself to his feet again, and his stomach dropped.

The Oquelite reappeared, lining themselves around the wall. Some Defenders charged but were blasted away. Taryn—a small figure near the front of the defending line—stepped back. It was pointless.

The blue flames of the protective wall went still, and for a moment the world was quiet.

An Oquelite on the front lines flung off his hood, scanning over the Defenders and townspeople before him with a cruel smile. Matthias Idicous raised his weapon and drove it into the solid flame.

At first nothing happened, then the wall burst into a million pieces, the blast blowing them back. The shards of the wall rained down in flames. Lincoln was shoved to the ground by the force of the explosion and this time he could have cared less to get up.

Lord Matthias Idicous had broken their only safe hold against the greatest force of power of all time. The Oquelite

leader brandished his weapon and shouted three simple
words.

"We are free!"

29

"I THINK SHE'S DEAD."

Nikki jerked up, her breath heavy and her heart racing. She looked around, finding Ray and Lincoln beside the low cot she was lying on. She was in a large hall full of identical cots bearing moaning and wounded people, Defenders and civilians alike.

"So, she's not dead," Ray said, nodding approvingly to himself.

"You feeling alright?" Lincoln said, looking down at Nikki.

Her arm stung with a sharp pain and her head throbbed dully. Snippets of memory pieced themselves together slowly in her fuzzy mind. She wanted to bury her face in her hands, remembering it. She was so helpless against Silas. She reached for her shoulder, wincing as her fingers brushed against the bandage.

"D-did they escape?" she asked, her dry voice cracking.

Lincoln nodded solemnly.

Now the whole world was exposed to the Oquelite. No doubt they were going to free the Oquelite from the other regions too. The memory of Orion made it only worse. They way he'd simply drained Avalon of her essence.

Avalon! Nikki quickly reached for her pocket, panic rising in her throat. Her hand tightened around the familiar surface of the Stone and relief seeped over her again.

At least one thing had gone right.

"Taryn wanted us to let her know when you woke up," Lincoln said.

Nikki turned, swinging her legs off the side of the cot and easing her feet to the floor. Her legs felt numb and tingly under the pressure. "I can find her."

"You sure?" Ray said, frowning.

Nikki nodded, turning away from them and wrapping her arms around herself. The cold floor seemed to burn against her bare feet. Her shoes were missing but she didn't dare ask where they had ended up. Nikki glanced around those lying wounded in the metal cots, thin dividers set up to separate them.

Most of the patients had been well attended to, their wounds cleaned and bandaged, but some lay still, their faces pale, the only sign of life was the harsh rising and falling of their chests.

Many more cots were empty. The place must have been able to hold hundreds when it was full.

Hundreds of Defenders in North Cordell. What had happened to them all?

She spotted Taryn supporting a furious Defender. He nearly collapsed, but Taryn quickly caught him, and medics rushed to help her.

As the fitful patient was carried away, Taryn wiped her forehead. The circles underneath her eyes had grown deeper. Her lip was scabbed, and the dirt and ash smeared on her face told that she hadn't had time to clean herself up after the attack. Taryn suddenly caught sight of Nikki and some of the creases in her forehead relaxed as she rushed over to her.

"It's good to see you came out in one piece and are still good on your feet," she said. "We weren't sure what had happened to you. They spent hours looking for you and how you ended up in the woods…" Taryn shook her head. "I'm just glad you seem alright."

For the first time, Taryn didn't sound so distant and uptight, her voice seemed to be genuine and open instead of echoing back to things Nikki couldn't imagine. Like for a moment, Nikki wasn't her prisoner and Taryn wasn't a stone-faced Sergeant.

Taryn frowned suddenly, her worried creases returning as her gaze settled on Nikki's bandaged shoulder.

Nikki stepped back, covering the bandage with her hand and turning her arm away from Taryn's view.

"Please. I've been trained, I'm not going to kill you," Taryn said as she slowly took a step toward her.

Nikki froze, wincing as Taryn gently moved Nikki's hand away and undid the loose wrapping. Taryn's freezing fingertips gently skimmed over the burned skin.

Taryn bit her lip, studying the wound. "You fought the Oquelite prince, didn't you?" Taryn said, her voice stern and serious now. "The one with the white hair. He never seemed one for combat. I thought he was more reserved."

Nikki nodded, trying to focus on anything but Taryn's hand or her wound.

"It must have hurt," Taryn said, as she gestured for Nikki to follow her. "This burn was inflicted by what ancient Ywondies call Play Fire. It's mostly to put its victim in pain and burn off the skin. Used as a torture mechanism, which is why it heals quickly. So they can inflict again."

Taryn led Nikki to a small white cart set up in an intersection of the makeshift hospital. The Sergeant held the collar of her shirt back for a moment, revealing a scar crawling from under her shirt and across her chest. "I speak from experience," she said.

Nikki's expression softened as Taryn let her jacket fall again and pulled out a small jar. She motioned for Nikki to expose her shoulder. She did so hesitantly.

Taryn dabbed her fingers into the strange metallic paste and brushed it against the wound. Nikki flinched for a moment, then the sting of the fire sparking across her skin eased, like an actual flame had been extinguished and a cool wave had rushed over it. A knot of tension eased from her muscles.

Taryn smiled. "I'm going to guess it's working."

Nikki nodded, struggling to remember the words. "I-I am…Th-thank you. Thank you."

Taryn's eyes widened, but she quickly shook off her shock. She smiled and nodded, though her expression was distant again as she looked at Nikki. "Yes," she said, clearing her throat. "Now that you six *convicts* are settled, I should be going."

Nikki frowned. "You're leaving?" she whispered. She hadn't meant to whisper aloud at all, and the words surprised even her.

Taryn blinked, then heaved a sigh. She took a wet cloth hanging from the cart and wiped her hands clean. "They've summoned me to Imperial. I cannot deny this command," she said reluctantly, a scowl underlying her words. "The Oquelite are moving quickly. It's not ideal. Especially with Conrad." The last part Taryn grumbled under breath.

Nikki pursed her lips. Taryn didn't seem so happy about having to leave North Cordell. Perhaps it had been years since the last time the woman had left.

"I'll settle the legal things there too," she said. "We'll see about your 'innocence'."

Nikki nodded, though that wasn't what she'd been thinking about. She glanced around for Conrad, the second in command. Until Taryn got back, they'd have to be careful.

After the burn had been securely bandaged, Nikki headed back over to the cot she woke up in in search of her boots. No luck there.

She sighed. Her boots had to be somewhere.

She stepped out of the room into an unfamiliar hallway. All the hallways looked almost the same, of course, but this hall was clean and polished. The Defending Officers rushing through it seemed a bit more alive, with polished plaques on the non-rusted doors. How large was this base? Did it run under all of North Cordell? Or was it in a pocket of space and time like the Oquelite's labyrinth?

She turned down the corner, seeing the next hall filled with Defenders too.

They all seemed spread out, moving around and muttering inaudible things to each other. Most stepped away from her, a clear outsider from their society. She moved quickly down the hall away from them.

"You need some help getting back? I think the rest are at

the boiler room."

Nikki jumped back, tensing until she spotted Lincoln as he stepped out from the corner. She relaxed her shoulders.

"I'm going to take that as a yes," Lincoln said, smiling.

Nikki nodded, looking over Lincoln as he led the way. His jacket was tied around his waist, all the scratches and cuts on his arms clearly visible, along with cuffs still secured to his wrists. He'd tied bandages on his wrists under the cuffs to stop them from tearing open the wounds any further, but the awful scabs still peeked out from underneath the bandaging. The only bad wound she could see was a cut across his cheek, but it seemed to be healing nicely. He looked tired though.

"When was the last time you slept?" she asked.

"I could ask the same thing to you," Lincoln countered. "And getting knocked out doesn't count."

That was a fair point. Still, he looked worse than she felt.

Finally, they turned a familiar corner to a beat-up hallway she could immediately recognize.

"Okay," Lincoln said, gesturing to the hall. "We've arrived."

Nikki nodded to him. "Thank you."

"No problem."

There was an awkward silence between the two. Nikki paused, biting her lip.

Lincoln studied her, like he could sense her hesitation. "Is everything…good?"

"Taryn's leaving," she blurted out, her voice small.

Lincoln's eyes widened. "She's leaving? Where? When?"

"To…to…Imperial," Nikki said, the word unfamiliar on her lips. "Today."

"Imperial?" Lincoln said, taking a quick inhale, his eyes shifting around nervously. "That means she's heading to the

Defending Department main base. This can't be good."

"Conrad," Nikki said.

Lincoln cursed under his breath. "That guy is going to kill us. We have to get out."

"She said she—"

"You trust the Sergeant?" Lincoln raised an eyebrow.

Nikki pressed her lips together. *Did* she trust Taryn?

"Nik. The Sergeant's the only reason we're here. Although she's also the only reason we haven't been killed by Conrad, because he hates us so much," Lincoln said.

"What about Miriam?" Nikki asked.

Lincoln's expression softened. "I don't know about her. But the other Defenders…They're just standing around" — his voice lowered— "waiting."

Nikki nodded, both falling silent as a dark uniformed Defender rushed by with a sense of urgency.

Lincoln looked back to her. "Stay low. And *away* from Conrad. We can't trust Sergeant Hunter. We can't trust any of them."

Nikki touched her arm, with a small, firm nod. But she wasn't sure if she believed Lincoln's doubt of the sergeant.

Taryn had healed her. Taryn seemed to be trying to protect them. But then the attacks, and Taryn had to leave, right after they seemed to be on decent terms.

They were on their own now.

PART THREE

THE VOICE

THE SILENCE WAS TOO LOUD TO BE NORMAL.

Nikki lay on top of the empty shelves, holding the Stone close to her chest. She finally had a moment to process what the voice in the Stone had shown her.

The voice had a name…Avalon.

She had so many questions and blank spots in Avalon's flashbacks.

What had happened to her daughter after she fled on the ships? What about Orion? What happened to the alliance between Avalon's race and the Aviduous?

The Aviduous in Avalon's flashbacks looked nothing like Lincoln. Their faces all scrunched up and their bodies bulging awkwardly with muscle.

A roar echoed through the hall.

Nikki jumped up, banging her head on the ceiling. She winced and shoved the Stone into her pocket.

It was like cheering and crashing all at once. Nikki's heart thudded faster as she jumped from the shelf to the ground.

On the floor below, Felicity sat up immediately, but Tabitha just threw a blanket over her head and continued to sleep.

Felicity scrambled for the lantern, the sensor light bursting to life with her touch. Her eyes were wide with horror. "W-what's happening?"

Nikki shook her head, turning to the door.

Something banged against it.

Nikki jumped back. Felicity scrambled away. Footsteps pounded outside. Screaming echoed in the hallway.

"We're being attacked," Felicity squeaked.

It couldn't be possible. Nikki frowned.

Felicity squeezed her eyes shut, taking in a deep breath. Another moment and her eyes burst open, steadier as she rose cautiously to her feet. "What do we need to do?"

The door shook again. Nikki grabbed Felicity's light. They needed to turn it off! How did the thing work anyway?

Felicity snatched it back and the light disappeared.

Good. Nikki ran for the back of the closet, wedging herself in between the wall and a large storage container.

Felicity didn't follow.

Another bang.

Nikki peered out. Felicity was trying to drag Tabitha with her, but the other girl was still—somehow—fast asleep. Nikki ran to help, gripping one of Tabitha's arms and heaving her toward the back of the tight room.

Another bang. Panic swelled through her as a red light flowed from the crack under the door.

She fell to her knees, shaking Tabitha, but the girl simply ignored her.

The door burst open, and Nikki whirled to her feet, fists raised and ready for a large crowd to rush in to kill them.

Miriam burst in, then froze, holding her hands up defensively. "Calm down, Squirt," she said, catching her breath between words. "I'm not going to kill you."

Nikki straightened, but her heart was still crashing to the commotion outside in the halls. What was going on?

Miriam wiped sweat from her forehead, brushing back the loose hairs. Her gaze fell incredulously on Tabitha. "How in the world is she still sleeping?"

"She can sleep through pretty much anything," Felicity said shakily, still recovering from the shock.

"Well, what are you waiting for! Wake her up!" Miriam said, rushing to Nikki. "There is business going down in those halls. Business that's not going to end well for you lot. So, you need to get up and get out."

"What do you mean?" Felicity said as she tore the blanket from Tabitha.

Miriam began to rummage through the shelves, knocking boxes to the ground. "Not sure yet! Squirt, grab that med kit! No! Top shelf!"

Nikki grasped the small white box, tossing it to Miriam.

"Go away," Tabitha groaned.

"Stump! We gotta go!" Miriam shouted, shoving the box into her bag.

"What did she just call me?" Tabitha lifted her head.

"Stump," Miriam repeated firmly. "Let's go!"

Tabitha glared at her.

Felicity hauled her to her feet, shoving Tabitha's bag into her arms.

"Where are—" Tabitha began.

"No time for questions," Miriam cut her off.

"I'm not even wearing shoes!"

Miriam turned to the door and jerked it open again.

At first the corridor seemed empty, only an echo of cheers and screams. It sent a shiver down Nikki's spine. The hall glowed an eerie red, the usual bright white lights had been turned off and the red light glowed from one side of the hall.

Miriam peered out, then ushered them to follow her.

Nikki went out first, Tabitha and Felicity following close behind. Nikki peered down the hall at a dark mass that crowded against the walls at the distant end of the corridor. It took a moment, but when she realized what she was seeing, her stomach tied into a knot. It was a crushing group of people.

The noise grew and the shouts unified into one constant roar.

"Squirt!" Miriam snapped.

Nikki turned around. Felicity, Tabitha, and Miriam were all heading the opposite way down the hall, but the defender was looking over her shoulder and gesturing at her. "Come on!"

Nikki glanced back at the crowd, then ran after them.

"What's going on?" Felicity asked as Miriam quickened their pace to a jog, winding deeper into the dark maze of hallways.

"Uprising."

"Uprising?" Tabitha gasped, a little too loud.

"With the Sergeant gone for the first time, it was bound to happen. It's been coming in this trashy region for as long as I remember being at this Base," Miriam said, taking a sharp turn.

A light flashed up at them.

All four froze. Nikki held her breath.

A group of Defending Officers blocked the hallway ahead. "Outown," the one holding the light said, his voice deep and gruff.

Miriam didn't even flinch as the light shone in her face. "Yes, good day, sir. Fancy seeing you," she said, her voice coated with thick annoyance.

"Why do you have the prisoners?" someone said from behind the light holder.

Miriam raised an eyebrow. "It's not safe to keep them near the commotion, is it?"

"You're up to something, Outown." The light holder stepped forward. "She's always up to something."

Miriam didn't move. "Well then, what do *you* suggest we do with the child prisoners?"

Felicity scoffed under breath, and a few eyes turned.

"I say we take them with us," another said. "Let 'em be a little scared. See what they've done to us."

"We didn't do anything," Tabitha said, crossing her arms.

The group snickered. Miriam's face twisted with distaste.

"You don't really have a choice here, Outown." The light holder's hand slipped toward his holster. "Really, the easy choice is to kill these youngin's while they're still ours."

Nikki held her breath, his fists tensing.

"Fine," Miriam said, turning on her heel. "I hear Conrad is a *brilliant* speaker. Hope he has something good to say."

Felicity's eyes narrowed and she looked at Nikki. They were basically being led, by the threat of death, to see whatever mischief Conrad was brewing. Again, Nikki caught herself wishing Taryn was there.

They moved into the crowd and it morphed around them, swallowing them up, the heat off bodies beating around her. Nikki tried to keep close to Miriam and the others as the angry crowd pushed and heaved on every side.

Nikki tried to keep her distance from the rowdy people ramming around her, but it seemed almost impossible not to get slammed into every five seconds.

"We're leaving! Tonight. We've spent too long under the ground, tortured and in hiding. Our purpose is gone! We've been used!" The thundering voice belonged to none other than Conrad.

Another roar of agreement followed his words and Nikki tensed.

Miriam growled. "He's an idiot."

"Agreed." A young man appeared from the crowd, dark haired and tan faced, goggles pushed up on the top of his head and worry etched into his brows.

Nikki's eyes widened as three familiar male faces followed.

Miriam caught the man's eye and frowned. "All six… together?" she said, glancing at the three boys. "Not smart."

"The plan wasn't to meet here."

"Yeah, well I got thrown off—"

Conrad sent the crowd into another frenzy, and Miriam's voice was drowned out in the noise. A new wave of Defenders pushed through the group, and Nikki was shoved out of the way, slamming into someone behind her. They barely acknowledged her, yelling agreement to whatever Conrad had just said.

Nikki caught herself, looking around. Her heart dropped. Miriam and the others were gone.

She tried to push through, but she was shoved out of the

way. She tripped, falling into the ground into the sea of stomping hooves. Panic rose in her throat and she rolled to avoid a swinging foot, then scrambled to her feet, trying to steady herself among the ramming bodies.

Something crashed against the wall again. Sparks flew from the ceiling.

"Nik!" Lincoln grabbed her wrist, pulling her out from under the light.

She tore away from his grip. "The lights…" she began.

"They're tearing the place apart," Lincoln finished for her.

Nikki looked around. The red light had shifted to blue. In the eerie glow, everything looked fake. Shadows crawled up the wall. Vivid memories of the invisible hands seized her.

Conrad let out a shout. "Leave no surface unturned! We are leaving a message for the Department! We are leaving a message to the world! That from now on, it's gonna be every man for himself!"

Whistling, screams, shouts. Something was tossed over their head.

Lincoln and Nikki ducked.

"We have to find Miriam and Jack!" Lincoln called out over the commotion.

The Defenders began to run in all directions, shoving each other out of the way, laughing. Gunshots rang. Lincoln was nearly caught off his feet. Nikki grabbed him, then flinched at the touch.

The phantom hands still groped for a hold in her memory.

She caught sight of a gap between the pressing crowd and ran for it. Lincoln followed close behind. She slid out of the way of a raving Defender, smashing lanterns against the ground. He glared at them as they passed, but she didn't give him a second glance.

Conrad yelled again, but the chaos all around was too loud to hear the words. A roar of laughter. The smell of smoke.

Nikki's eyes widened. "The injured!" she cried out, spinning back the way they'd come. Lincoln grabbed her arm and she tried to fight against him, but he held her back firmly. She kicked him hard in the ankle and he faltered. She tried to tear past him, but he grabbed her again.

She knocked him off his feet, but his grip on her wrist dragged her down too.

"Nik!" he yelled. "You can't save them all! The medics are with them!"

Nikki stopped struggling. Her stomach dropped, and bile surged in her throat. Her head whirled with the scent of smoke and the screams. What if the medics couldn't protect the injured though? What if these people killed them all? Her eyes burned as she stared up into Lincoln's dark, black eyes that reflected the flashing colors around them.

For a moment, she realized why Avalon despised them.

The reflection.

They scrambled to their feet, running down a hall. The crowd had thinned, but lights and switches were sending out sprays of sparks. Laughter and yelling still roared from the few sprinkled about. Several defenders dragged their knives across the walls, cutting huge, jagged gashes in the plaster.

Lincoln just ran faster. Nikki followed.

They approached another circular conjunction where a crowd was beginning to gather. Nikki clenched her jaw but refused to slow. They burst into the crowd, weaving between the press of bodies.

Her eyes widened. This place was familiar. It was the place her and Lincoln had had their blindfolds removed right when they were first brought in. It was the way to Taryn's office and the door to the outside.

The door out had been torn off.

Nikki hesitated, scanning the hallways, then chose one that looked closest to the direction of Taryn's office and ran for it.

But before she could reach the hallway a strong hand grabbed her shoulder, jerking her back. She stumbled, remained on her feet. Conrad twisted her around, his other hand locking around her throat.

His grip was loose, but the smile on his face seemed to say he had no problem with tightening. It was all for the show.

Nikki grabbed his hand and tried to pry his fingers away, kicking out at him at the same time.

The crowd backed up, leaving Conrad and Nikki in the center of the circle they'd formed. Jeers and shouts surrounded them on every side.

Out of the corner of her eye, Nikki saw Lincoln push through the crowd, his eyes wide with horror. Miriam, Jack, and the other four burst in from the opposite hall, then stopped short in horror.

Conrad shot them a glare. "Back it up or I kill these little vermin," he snapped, spitting into Nikki's face.

She hated him. She never knew what it was like to hate someone so much it burned to breathe like this before.

His cruel, beaten eyes turned to her, and he shoved her to the ground, giving her a crooked smile. "The Sergeant's little pets," he chuckled, but his eyes showed no sign of humor. He stepped forward slowly, intimidating. "Her little prisoners."

Nikki was back on her feet, trying to tell her hands not to clench into fists. She wouldn't fight him. Oh, but how much she wanted to smash his face in and watch him pay.

"Sergeant's made us suffer too long," he sneered. Then he turned his arm to the five in the crowd, but his eyes still glued to Nikki. "And these—these children come along and ruin everything! They're going to tear our world apart!"

"You just called us kids," Ray yelled. "How the heck are we going to ruin anything?"

Conrad ignored Ray, his eyes boring into Nikki's. His cold hand roughly grabbed her shoulder and twisted her toward him further.

"Thought I'd leave this fight unresolved?" he said. "You won't leave until I've killed you and cut that nasty lil' look off your face."

She had no idea why he hated their blood so much, but there was no time for logic. Anger blocked out any thoughts. Everything she'd ever hated echoed through her mind, and the anger and the thoughts she kept to herself in the back of her mind burst free as he reached for her throat.

She fought him back.

Her shoulder cried out in pain, but she ignored it, fending off Conrad's attacks. She was blinded by the red anger across her vision. Deafened by the roar of her own pulse. Only one word rang clearly in her ears, over and over again.

Insane.

Was that Avalon speaking or her own self? She was slammed to the ground on her back and Conrad pulled a knife from his belt, his face bruised and his nose bleeding. The knife raced for her throat.

But then time stopped.

The voices, crackling, and chaos became blurs of sound. The dagger was inches from her throat. Conrad became another blur.

Do it.

Her fingers wrapped around something in her pocket. A familiar voice was yelling for her to stop, but the other voice screamed louder.

Everything rushed back, and Nikki shoved her arms up, and everything exploded.

31

BEFORE SHE EVEN KNEW WHAT HAD HAP-pened, Nikki was on her feet. Conrad and his weapon were thrown back and the roof above them exploded. Dust and plaster rained down, sunlight glinting through in tantalizing hints.

Nikki stared at the crowd of horrified Defenders and her own friends, confused and stunned.

Everything had gone silent.

Conrad scrambled back on the floor. "Ewyon! Ewyon!" he screamed, pointing frantically at Nikki.

Nikki's heart skipped a beat and followed his pointing finger.

The Stone sparked with energy in her hand, glowing between her fingers.

She dropped it to the floor with a clatter.

Everyone was perfectly still.

Nikki scanned the crowd, searching for anyone who didn't have their jaw's gaped or flinch back from her gaze.

Conrad scrambled to his feet, now a safe distance away. "See? See what they've put among us!" he yelled, and his voice cracked. "They put an *Ewyon* in our Base. An Ewyon!"

A roar of agreement went up from the gathered crowd, except for Miriam who looked like she was screaming out curses.

No one listened to her, their cheers drowning her out.

"If the Sergeant wants her prisoners, she can have them! Let whatever dark legacy attached to them be *her* curse. Not ours," Conrad riled.

The answering cheers echoed in Nikki's ears.

The Defenders tore past, barely even giving her a second glance. The exit. That was the only reasonable destination. Everything blurred around Nikki and she crumpled to her knees, trying to catch her breath. She squeezed her eyes shut, forcing out the thoughts that crept upon her.

Insane.

Unstable.

Avalon remained silent.

Darkness seemed to move, creating shapes along the walls. A shadow of Avalon's features darted across her vision, but she blinked it away. The presence of the hands seemed to jeer at her. Had she failed?

She was their prisoner now.

What did it all mean? Pressure built up in her throat, and she clenched her jaw to keep herself from crying out. She fought the thoughts away as the words clawed at her mind.

"Nikki."

Her mind went blank.

She forced her eyes open but didn't dare to look up. She knew Felicity stood above her. Everything was empty around her and inside her. Flickering flames in the rubble, electricity sparking from the torn walls.

You didn't listen. You can only find safety in me.

Nikki tried to block out Avalon's voice. An Ewyon? The race Lincoln had spoken so ill of? That meant the Oquelite had come for *her* essence.

She should have been taken.

Felicity was right.

She had hurt them.

"Nikki," Felicity repeated, tearing through her thoughts.

Nikki raised her head, but still didn't meet her eyes.

"The Sergeant wants to talk to us," Felicity said. She took a deep breath, as if she was going to continue, but turned and walked off without another word.

She could run away. The thought flitted briefly through Nikki's mind. She brushed it off, getting to her feet.

"Don't go with them. Run now."

No, Nikki said. *I can't. Not after what I did to them.*

"You're growing attached." With a growl, Avalon disconnected.

Nikki took a deep breath. She wasn't ready to leave the others behind. Despite her body shaking with every step she took after Felicity, Nikki wouldn't give in.

All she wanted was to be safe.

But the others deserved it too. Everyone deserved safety, and she was determined to help them.

When Felicity finally stopped, Nikki stayed distant. It was impossible to ignore the stares of the others gathered around.

Maybe she should explain, but the words wouldn't come,

and she couldn't even bring herself to raise her eyes. How could she explain? She didn't even know what she was.

All she knew was that she was a threat to their lives now.

Miriam spent an hour at the tele, trying to get a clear connection with Sergeant Taryn Hunter.

Nikki sat to the side, separate from the rest of the group. She fumbled with the Stone, turning it over in her hands again and again. Avalon wouldn't speak to her or explain anything.

All she knew was that Ewyons were bad.

The Ewyon hated the Aviduous, and they seemed so concerned with how they looked. No wonder Avalon had disliked Lincoln. Nikki wanted to bury herself in a hole and never come out.

"MIRIAM OUTOWN, WHAT HAPPENED?" Sergeant Hunter's voice roared into the corridor and brought Nikki from her trance.

Miriam cringed, holding the tele a little further from her. "It was Conrad—"

"I know it was Conrad. Are they still there?"

"The kids?"

"Who else would I be talking about?"

"They're listening," Miriam said, looking up at the group of kids around her.

Taryn's voice lowered. "All of them?"

"Yep," Miriam said, her eyes settling on Nikki. "All of them."

"Outown, what happened?" Taryn's voice had softened, though it still held a stern underlying tone.

"Sergeant…there's been…a complication."

"I haven't noticed," Taryn said, sarcasm lacing her words.

"Sergeant," Miriam hesitated, clearing her throat. "There's a full-blooded…"

"Full-blooded what?"

"Ewyon."

Silence. They all shifted, their eyes turning to Nikki. All but Lincoln, whose dark gaze was set firmly on the ground.

"What?" came Taryn's response.

Miriam gulped. "Yep."

Taryn took a moment of silence. "The lanky, quiet girl. It's her, isn't it."

Miriam nodded. "Yes, Sergeant."

Nikki longed to hide her face, but she resisted the urge. She would be strong. She held her chin up, embracing the humiliation. She deserved it, anyway.

Taryn let out a long breath, then chuckled softly. "An Ewyon! Without violet eyes."

Nikki wished she could disappear like the Oquelite. She itched to run, but something else held her back. A curiosity. She was closer to the answers than she'd ever been. She couldn't run now.

"So that means it's true?" Jack muttered to Miriam, his eyebrows raised.

"What's true?" Tabitha asked, holding her binder close to her chest, looking between the two Defenders, obviously dying for an answer for their mysterious behavior.

"We still don't know where their loyalties lie," Taryn interrupted, ignoring Tabitha.

"Haven't we made it obvious?" Cole said, a hint of annoyance in his voice. "We fought for you!"

"Sometimes our soul's loyalties are different than our minds, Johnson," Taryn said.

"That doesn't make any logical sense."

"Logic's overrated," Taryn replied.

"You can't keep us captive forever. Obviously, you have something else going on," Ray chimed in. He was a little separate from the rest of the group too, though it seemed self-inflicted on his part. His hands were shoved deep into his pockets and he leaned against the wall, but there was something fake and cold about his casual position. "Like Miriam. She's like your secret spy lady or something?"

"Spy. Assistant. A person of considerable ability"— Miriam scoffed— "or whatever you like to call it," Taryn said. "Sallow" —Jack perked up— "and Outown. Tell them."

"Everything, Sergeant?"

"Only the Council information."

Miriam nodded. "Yes, Sergeant."

"And tell them my deal. If they reject, you know what must be done. And for the love of Fate, don't have the kids call me Sergeant."

Miriam nodded. The connection was cut.

"Look," she said, turning to the rest of the group. "We don't have much time to explain, but you've all been collected by Sinni for a very specific reason."

Silence.

Jack met eyes with Miriam, then picked up the thread. "Each of you come from different backgrounds and histories, and somehow you've all ended up in North Cordell. That's exactly as intended. The Sergeant's been planning a reformation."

"Of?" Cole raised an eyebrow.

Miriam sighed. "An ancient Council. Members of this council were predestined from long ago. Apparently one group for each century. Including seven members, each a full-blood from each of the seven Impure races. You know, don't you? I heard the Aviduous explain them to you. The other five are more unique, with different roles."

Miriam looked to Jack, who gave her a nod.

She continued. "The Illuminate and Shadow Holders. Representing Light and Dark, Good and Evil, all that jazz. The so-called Guardian used to represent all Mythics. Creatures." Miriam's voice was not very confident on the last point. "And . . . gosh darn it. What's the last one, Jack?"

"The Keyper. It's a hereditary role, passed down through a few families," Jack explained.

"Council? Wait, wait I'm lost." Cole frowned, his hand going to his medallion. "You think *we're* part of this... Council thing? I thought we were arrested for burning down the Inn?"

Miriam groaned, and tore her fingers through her hair.

Jack, on the other hand, was more patient. "Yes. About the Council. And no. The whole 'arrest them for burning down the Inn' thing was a bit of a cover. Not that she didn't have her suspicions where Nikki came from, or your loyalties."

Tabitha scoffed out a laugh. "That's insane. Obviously, the sergeant's some crazed bozo whose head is stuck in the past—Council?"

Miriam cut Tabitha off. "Why do you think the Oquelite targeted *you*? Why do you think the University of North Cordell so easily accepted a mediocre student such as yourself, Stump?" Her gaze went to Cole next. "Why would they make such a rare exception for a pianist who lived alone with a single father in Sulfur?"

Cole's face burned.

"The Sergeant thought you might be Members, so she had you accepted to keep you closer and to observe you,"

Jack said. "The only one the sergeant didn't expect was the Ewyon."

"The Council has twelve members," Miriam said. "Once united, their power is unspeakable, and, unknown. It's been centuries since they ever really had a complete Council. And definitely not one with a lot of teenagers."

Jack sighed. "A reformation has been forbidden for centuries. The Oquelite get too riled up. They thrive off essence, and Council Members have the strongest, which means they both have the power to give the Oquelite more ability, or to finally give them an equal match. Many people's essence is dormant nowadays," he said. "But something stronger has been stirring in the air. I mean, Taryn's Council almost made—"

Miriam elbowed him in the stomach and glared at him, her brows furrowing.

Jack grabbed his stomach, grimacing and falling silent.

"Taryn was part of a Council?" Felicity asked, standing up.

Jack laughed, but Miriam scowled, looking away. "The Curatrix team" Jack said.

Everyone went quiet. It all clicked together.

Nikki's jaw fell slack. So, Taryn *was* Jessica. A warm tingling feeling ran through her. She blinked. The sensation was strange. She closed her mouth and tensed her fists.

"Why is the Sergeant—Taryn…Jessica…alive?" Cole said slowly.

Miriam looked to Jack and he shook his head. "We aren't authorized to tell you that," Jack said. "Almost everything about this case is secret. No one is allowed to know much about it."

"What *can* you tell us?" Felicity asked.

Miriam closed her eyes, pulling in a deep breath and Jack placed a hand on her shoulder, looking to them, the look in his eyes clearly saying *this-topic-is-touchy*.

"You know the basics. Five Defenders, who stopped a rebellion during their Trial as trainees. They went on to gain tons of popularity, and Reyna Wents began to start a reform in the Department, and all that," Jack said. He shrugged. "People weren't happy when they found out they had potential for a Council." Jack's lips twisted to the side, and he shook his head.

"Of course, the public doesn't know anything about Councils or races. The information is classified. Not to cause uproar or panic. No one knows Officer Zita Klirkpatrick was kept under radar her entire life for being an Aguarious. Agent Lyell Aguirre was a close friend of Taryn's. He had Ewyon blood. Some say he knew about another Council reformation, but he was killed before he had the chance to go public."

Jack looked at Miriam, who finally managed to straighten a little, her shoulders shaking, and her arms wrapped around herself, her eyes never leaving the ground. "Aaron Outown… was you probably guessed, my brother."

Cole and Tabitha looked at each other. Cole dropped the medallion down his shirt.

Tabitha contained a smile behind her pursed lips. "I knew it."

The wind whistled softly through the gaping room, playing around the group and stirring the dust from the floor. Miriam obviously didn't feel like talking about it and no one dared to ask. Miriam would probably take them down if they did.

Jack gave her a quick squeeze.

"And Reyna Wents?" Cole reminded Jack.

Jack bit his lip. "Despite being the media's favorite to pick on, Taryn never talks about her. Whenever someone does bring up Agent Reyna Wents Aguirre, you better hope she's in a good mood. According to the Sergeant, Wents was reckless, ambitious, and ran on instinct."

Nikki could feel the stares as the others glanced her way. She tensed, trying to block out the sound of Jack's voice repeating in her ears.

Miriam shoved to her feet with a growl, looking over the group. "Their team was a warning," she said. "Even though it's unclear who killed them, it is clear Councils are a dangerous business."

"Alright, so what if we want *no* part in the Sergeant Taryn's delusions?" Ray said.

"Well, you're *technically* still under investigation for assisting the enemy in burning down a little, old Inn," Miriam smirked, adding sarcastically.

Ray groaned. "Not this again. You already said those weren't true allegations."

Miriam suppressed a chuckle. "Right, sorry. It must be frustrating to learn the real reasons she was so interested in you was her fascination with what most call practically a forgotten child's tale. And like you said, what if you want no part?"

"Does this have to do the Sergeant's…deal?" Felicity said, her eyes lighting up hopefully.

Miriam looked to Jack, and he took in a deep breath. "Right. You are a group of potentially very dangerous … children. Your abilities and your durability are still unknown. The Sergeant watched you throughout your time here, but she still has a final test."

"She doesn't control us," Cole snapped.

Miriam sighed, shaking her head. "You have no idea what she controls. She's a Defending *Sergeant.*"

"Just get on with it," Lincoln said, crossing his arms, visible frustration rising on his brow.

"The Sergeant Taryn Hunter requests your attendance in Imperial. In a week."

"A week?" Ray frowned.

"Where in Imperial? That region is *huge!*" Tabitha exclaimed. "Not to mention, recently bombed?"

"Imperial. Seven days. Further instructions will be given once you reach reasonable destinations," Jack said. "If what Taryn suspects about you is true, you could be a serious threat. She's keeping you alive because she needs proof that you're willing to fight."

"We fought for North Cordell," Felicity said, her face growing paler by the second.

Miriam smiled. "You survive alone, without help from Defenders, with Oquelite hunting you down, you've proven yourself accountable. You fail and try to run? Don't show up in a week? The Sergeant will find you. And kill you."

32

Departure was a quiet affair.

There wasn't much of a decision to make. Go to Imperial to prove their innocence or die.

Cole was the one who'd made the proposition to go in separate groups, which Felicity personally thought was a terrible idea. But Cole's reasoning made sense. The bigger the group, the bigger the target. And they could move quicker separately, giving some chance for them to make it to Imperial within a week.

The only one who didn't participate in their meeting was Nikki, who had secluded herself off to the side, listening in silence.

Felicity was tempted to say something to the girl, but everything she thought of felt too awkward. *I'm sorry you're an Ewyon! We still sorta think you're cool!'*

At least she wasn't an Oquelite.

Lincoln kept his distance from Nikki. He never said anything about it, but his mood had obviously shifted, and he barely spoke.

Now that there could've been a threat in the girl, Felicity couldn't garner up the disdain she'd had before. Nikki looked harmless and lonely.

Ray gave Felicity his Comm number, as the two of them were the only ones with functioning communication devices. He and Lincoln had finally decided to travel north together, then go separate ways once they reached Isledowle, a region bordering Imperial.

They set off after an awkward farewell. Cole, Tabitha, and Felicity headed east by rail and whatever transport they could rent. Nikki had gone alone. She didn't say where she was going or what she was going to do, but if she decided not to show up to Imperial, it would be her fault when it cost her life. A twist of guilt speared Felicity's stomach at the thought.

Felicity and Tabitha walked side by side along the torn road. Felicity took a deep breath. She'd been trying to ignore Tabitha's complaining, but now it was becoming a little too much.

"Once we get to Midventern, we'll meet Cole, who's there renting a way of transport. We'll take that to Elery, then take a speed rail back to York," Felicity said through her gritted teeth.

Tabitha didn't seem to notice her companion's growing frustration and groaned again. They walked past a sign on the side of the road that was bent and scorched and falling off its supports. Once, it had been brightly glowing, and read, *'Leaving North Cordell! Come back and visit!'*

Tabitha laughed softly, scanning over it. "No one's coming back to visit you anytime soon," she said to the sign.

"Maybe once they get things fixed," Felicity said, holding her head up and trying to hide her uncertainty from Tabitha. Things were going to get better.

"After what Miriam said and everything that's been going on, I doubt it," Tabitha said with a shrug.

Felicity didn't want to believe what Tabitha said. How could she not be worried? The place they'd stayed for over two years had been burned to the ground and half the town was destroyed. Hope was looking scarce.

Loneliness crept over her, no matter how hard Felicity tried to shake it off.

Though Tabitha looked as determined and strong as could be possible, Felicity knew she was worried. She only acted strong when she wasn't. But Tabitha would never admit it. She was too proud. She would never admit defeat.

Felicity tried to smile confidently, but it faded away as soon as her lips attempted. Was this the end?

Tabitha began humming.

Felicity didn't stop her.

Tabitha was thinking. She only hummed aloud when she was nervous and thinking about other things to distract herself. She reached into her bag and grabbed her binder, flipping through as they walked. That binder had survived a lot.

"Got something new, Tab?"

Tabitha didn't respond. "How does 'my inn just blew up and a base just blew up and so did North Cordell' sound?" she asked, finally.

"You might as well just say 'My life blew up,'" Felicity

laughed.

"I like that," Tabitha said, scribbling something into the binder.

She continued to hum, and Felicity caught her from running into a few street signs multiple times and finally Tabitha sighed.

"Today, my life blew up. My room went up in flames. Then outside the window, my region did the same. When I thought things were getting better, a defending base went boom. And now if things stop blowing up, I will be home soon," Tabitha sang to a simple tune Felicity remembered from when she was younger. Maybe a nursery rhyme that Tabitha had made up.

"Do not sing that to your children," Felicity laughed.

Tabitha rolled her eyes but bit her lip to keep from laughing at her own song. "Don't worry, I won't ever have children."

"I don't even see why you can't make money from that, Tabs. Or even go to a University for it either," Felicity said, recovering from her laughter.

Tabitha's grin melted away, a solemn look replacing the familiar spark in her eyes. "Society, Felicity. Society says I can't."

Felicity shifted her eyes away. She sighed, then elbowed Tabitha, grinning. "Do you think it was a good idea to send Cole to Midventern alone?" Felicity said.

Tabitha's trademark smirk reappeared. "We better hurry," Tabitha said, dashing down the road.

Felicity smiled, and ran after her into the east, down the road, and into the region of Midventern.

The bell rang as Felicity pushed open the bright green door

to the Transport Rental.

"Please don't tell me he rented bicycles," Tabitha muttered as she finally slowed.

Both their faces were red from running, and they cast suspicious glances around the shop. Empty bike racks were driven into the wall, holding only a few brightly colored bicycles.

"Don't worry, Tabs. We're not going to make you work that hard," Felicity said, the door clanging shut behind them.

Mr. Owenshawn's, the rental owner, face lit up as they walked through the door. "Good afternoon ladies! And Ms. Delorous," he said, nodding to Tabitha, who gave him a grin.

"I'll pay you back soon, Mr. Owenshawn, once we get back to York," she said.

Felicity raised her eyebrow, and Tabitha shrugged, not wanting to discuss the fact she'd accidently destroyed one of Mr. Owenshawn's electric hover bikes in a complicated incident.

Mr. Owenshawn laughed heartily, but it still managed to send a shiver down Tabitha's spine. Felicity stepped closer to her.

"Going back to Liberty? Need a rental? And I see you're going along with a friend," Mr. Owenshawn said, turning in his chair to Felicity.

"Oh, yeah. This my friend, Felicity Bentsworth," Tabitha said, then clamped her mouth shut, realizing her mistake.

Felicity sighed heavily.

"What!" Mr. Owenshawn exclaimed, leaning over his desk to get a better look at her. "A Bentsworth?"

Felicity glared at Tabitha, sucking on her bottom lip. Tabitha knew she was in for it when they left.

Tabitha gave a slight shrug and mouthed, "Sorry."

She turned back to the stunned Mr. Owenshawn and walked right up to his desk. "Did you have anyone come in here by the name Cole Johnson?" she asked.

Mr. Owenshawn turned to Tabitha, his mouth still hanging. He shut his jar and, after studying her for a moment, he snatched a folded sticky note off his desk. "If you mean a young, blonde fellow, he left this for Rusty and Stump," he said, handing it to her.

Tabitha frowned at the nickname. *Well, thank you, Cole Johnson,* she thought, rolling her eyes. The real question was why he hadn't used their real names or told Mr. Owenshawn his own.

Felicity snatched the note from her and waved to Mr. Owenshawn. "Uh, thank you for the help!" she said, and pulled Tabitha outside of the shop. "Rusty and Stump?" Felicity frowned, looking down at Cole's note.

"Blasted Miriam Outown," Tabitha grumbled.

"And Tabitha! You can't just tell people my last name!" Felicity said.

There it was.

"Look, I'm sorry. Honest. This is the first time ever I've slipped up. It won't happen again. I promise," Tabitha said, placing her hand on Felicity's shoulder. "And Mr. Owenshawn isn't going to call anyone. No one would believe him if he said he saw you here."

Felicity thought about it for a moment, then sighed. "I hope you're right, Stump."

Tabitha frowned.

"What?" Felicity laughed. "You deserve it."

Felicity unfolded the yellow note, frowned, then flipped it over so Tabitha could read.

It read 'Garden Sm, east' in Cole's messy handwriting.

"I'm gonna call him Goldfish when I see him," Tabitha said. "For calling me Stump and literally stumping me by what the heck he wrote."

Felicity checked the back of the note, but there was no further explanation anywhere.

"Where's a garden, Tabs?" Felicity asked, still studying the note.

"There's a garden in your greenhouse in Liberty?" Tabitha said.

Felicity growled under her breath. "What does *Sm* stand for?" she asked.

"A lot of things."

"Do *garden* and *sm* have anything to do with each other? Somewhere nearby?" Felicity asked again.

"I dunno, Sherlock. Maybe." Tabitha snatched the note from Felicity, flipping it upside down and sideways to see if there was some sort of secret message.

Then Tabitha smacked her palm against her forehead. "How could I have been so stupid! That depot!" she shouted, turning to Felicity.

"What?" the other girl said, utterly lost.

"The old depot that closed down for safety reasons a few years ago. It's got graffiti lining the walls, like a solid sheet. I may or may not have contributed to that, but that's not the point. It had a ton of plants before it closed down the same year, we came to North Cordell. Some students called it the Garden Supermarket as a code name," Tabitha said. "I had no idea he knew about that stuff."

"Okay. Great. What's east then?" she said.

"East is a direction, duh!" Tabitha said, racing down the sidewalk. This time Felicity ran after her.

It took them about ten minutes to reach the graffiti-infested depot. Vines and all sorts of weeds had grown on the outside of it. It stood out in the street corner of a modern town.

"Cole Johnson?" Tabitha called out. "Goldfish boy?"

The fair-haired boy stepped out from around the corner, glancing around nervously before he spotted Felicity and Tabitha. "You made it!" Cole said, relief rushing across his face.

"Why was your note so…shady?" Tabitha demanded, holding it out.

"I'm not taking chances," Cole said. "You have a reputation for attracting danger."

Felicity nodded.

Tabitha rolled her eyes.

"So, what did you rent?" Tabitha asked.

"Don't get too excited," Cole said. "The best thing I could get with the money Felicity gave me was a ten-year-old auto that smells like cigars."

Tabitha looked to Felicity, who stood tense, her freckled face pale. Of course—she'd almost forgotten Felicity's fear of autos. Just because she could run without panicking now, didn't mean she still wasn't terrified of what almost killed her.

Tabitha grabbed Felicity's hand. "You got this?"

Felicity nodded, forcing a smile. "J-just don't let me drive. This will be better than walking the whole way. I'll be fine."

Cole placed his hand on Felicity's shoulder. "You need something, just say so and we'll stop," he said. "Even if you're just feeling nervous, we'll stop for you."

Felicity gave a weak smile, but this time it seemed more real. "Th-thanks."

Cole led them down the corner to a small, beaten, five-seater car. It looked ancient, like something the people in the history textbooks would ride in before the EarthShaker.

Felicity sat up front, which surprised Tabitha, since surely being in the front would be more likely to bring on a panic attack. It would feel like it had just before the crash. Except Felicity didn't remember what happened before the crash. She didn't even remember getting into the car.

It was odd, but the crash must have made her forget.

Tabitha brushed the thought aside, leaning back in her seat and burying her hands in the pockets of her coat, and trusted Cole not to kill them.

33

I WARNED YOU.

Nikki glanced down at the bulge of the Stone in her pocket as Avalon spoke in her mind.

"Ewyon are unwelcome in their society. Full-bloods are deemed dangerous, even though that prejudice is ridiculous! You could barely even live up to the potential of a mutant half-breed."

Thanks, Nikki said to Avalon. She trekked up the mountains, hoping to reach a gap in between soon. She walked without a specific goal. The woods were dead and quiet, blackened and ash-clad after the fire. The only green was the specks of vegetation toward the tops of the mountains where the fire hadn't reached.

Her temporary stay in North Cordell was over. Her departure was long overdue.

She looked back down at the destroyed little town, one of the few in North Cordell. Its tiny capital had been squashed and destroyed. She turned and ran, as she had done weeks earlier. This time no hands attempted to stop her. She just ran and tried not to think.

But thinking was all she could do.

"Remember your purpose," Avalon reminded her.

Nikki tried, but she couldn't help but wonder what Avalon was making her do. She thought of the wounded and injured. What if she'd ended their lives? All because of her blood and the essence that ran through her veins.

She wished the essence could just be torn from her like Orion had done to Avalon, but she couldn't die without getting to Imperial. She couldn't let them down again. No, not yet.

She'd have to die later.

A twig snapped somewhere.

Nikki jolted to a stop. She looked around cautiously. Nothing stirred the dead forest. Only the burnt trees standing lifeless in the dirt and smoking brush. Then she saw something glint in the corner of her eye. The air wavered, smoke not passing through a portion of the air, leaving a strange transparent figure.

Nikki turned and ran.

The Oquelite obviously saw no point in hiding anymore. They charged after her, the debris of the woods crunching beneath their feet.

Nikki reached for her pocket but scolded herself. She wasn't going to be stupid again.

The trees around her were becoming greener the farther up she ran. She just needed them to be denser so she could vanish into them and shake the Oquelite from her trail. She ran with all her might, not looking back. She took a sharp turn, and jumped down a slope, rolling to her feet in an instant and fitting herself in a gap in a tangle of tree roots.

She heard the Oquelite walk to the edge of the slope. They were still for a moment, then turned and ran off. But her heart continued to race. She didn't dare move yet.

"The faster we reach Isledowle the better."

Nikki froze. Of course, she was going to have a run in with Lincoln and Ray. This day just couldn't seem to let her go.

Ray did an epic failure of a cartwheel and plodded along the mountain road. Lincoln followed a way behind, paying more attention to Ray's Comm than Ray.

Nikki stayed put in her hiding place, but a glint of shadow in sunlight in the middle of the path brought her to her feet. She heard the Oquelite rustle through the bushes, but it stopped nearby.

Ray spun to Nikki as she jumped out from the wall of dirt and roots, his eyes wide. He relaxed when he saw who she was. "Couldn't resist coming back to us, could you?" Ray said.

Nikki ignored him, standing perfectly still, head cocked.

Lincoln looked up, frowning when he noticed her, but suddenly he went still too.

"What are you—"

Lincoln and Nikki shushed him in unison. Ray shut his mouth and waited.

Movement rustled again, and the Oquelite burst from its invisibility running at them.

Lincoln whirled around, kicking the Oquelites legs from under him. He knocked Ray and Nikki out of the way in the same motion.

The Oquelite recovered easily from the ground. He laughed and rolled his shoulders like he was just warming up.

"Where do you think you're going, kids? Traveling alone in the dangerous woods?" he asked in a teasing tone.

This Oquelite's voice sounded almost normal, like he could just be an annoying older brother. He dropped his hood back, revealing his thick, curly red hair, and pulled down his mask. It would have been welcoming enough, except for the disturbing curl in his smile, like the mischief of a Cheshire cat.

Nikki clenched her fists. She felt Avalon move in her pocket. She didn't have time to think about what Avalon wanted done, she just wanted to make sure no one else died.

"Hi, I'm Zach and I'll be your escort today," the Oquelite said, his smile widening. "Or not. Depending on who you are and how much you struggle. So, if I could get you to come with me—"

"Yeah, not a chance," Lincoln interjected, tossing the Communicator into his bag, and grabbing onto his bow.

Zach examined his nails, then whipped his finger upward, and Lincoln's bow was tossed to the ground. He looked at the bow and nodded approvingly.

Then he watched them carelessly.

Lincoln took a step back and Ray stepped toward him. Ray had gone abnormally pale, his jaw clenched, his eyes shifting nervously.

Nikki stood firm, refusing to be cowed by Zach's confidence.

The Oquelite studied them, then just shrugged and disappeared again.

Ray sighed with relief.

But the next thing Nikki knew was someone had grabbed

her. She thrust out her fist, managing to hit her attacker, and he jumped back. A ball of flames appeared in the air, headed for them. All three dove away and the flame smashed into the ground, leaving an unnatural dark streak across the road.

The wind picked up, thrashing through the trees.

This guy was no Matthias or Silas Idicous, but he proved to be quite strong in his powers.

Zach shed his invisible form again and threw his hands up, tearing a pine tree from the ground, sending it tumbling for the road. Nikki shoved Ray out of the way, sliding to the ground to avoid the trunk at the last minute as the tree slammed down behind them.

The wind whirled faster.

Lincoln, Nikki, and Ray scrambled up quickly. The wind whipped Nikki's hair into her face.

"So you are Impure!" Zach yelled, his smile only becoming bigger as he held his hands out. He looked at Ray. "Aren't you?"

"You could say that," Lincoln yelled back, his sand-brown hair whipping against his forehead in the wind as he jumped in front of Ray.

Nikki frowned and glanced between Lincoln and Ray.

Ray was looking down at himself in horror. His feet stayed latched to the ground, without a single struggle against the harsh winds, his barely even flying.

Ray frowned, looked at Lincoln, jerking his head the opposite way. Lincoln widened his eyes, like he understood what Ray had communicated, and shrugged.

Nikki looked desperately between the two of them. What were they doing?

Lincoln turned to Zach again, spreading his hands wide. "Well, aren't you gonna get us?" he said, a small smirk framing the teasing in his voice.

Was he crazy? He'd get himself killed.

Nikki's mind was racing. How could they defeat him? Zach wasn't focused on her or Ray any longer as he watched Lincoln.

"I mean come on, dude, if you can't catch some kids, what's the point of all those powers anyway?" Lincoln shouted.

"I see what you're doing, Aviduous," Zach said, with a snort, turning away from Lincoln and narrowing his eyes at the other two.

The wind whipped around harder.

Lincoln pulled his bow out, which he must have picked up in the commotion with the tree falling. He grabbed one of his intricate arrows and shot it at Zach.

The arrow turned to dust as soon as Zach yawned.

Zach seemed to find the entire affair to be just a game to show off, but he was also completely distracted. The Stone was vibrating viciously in Nikki's pocket, trying to draw her attention. She ignored it. For now.

Ray jumped up, pulling a knife from his pocket. Ray was a natural at acting like an idiot.

Zach seemed to enjoy the newfound entertainment, with a small laugh, and a small taunting applause.

Nikki looked to Lincoln and he gave a small nod. It was time to attack together.

The Oquelite seemed to sense their plan. He vanished, then slammed straight into her.

Nikki could feel his presence as he moved around her and she followed that instinct, blocking and dodging and throwing punches of her own as she tried not to die.

Ray threw the dagger, but it just fell to the ground,

melting into a mess of hot metal. Lincoln had grabbed the bow again, and let another arrow fly.

The Oquelite suddenly called out, flashing back into view with the arrow in his ankle.

Lincoln seemed a little surprised but shot an icy stare at the man.

Zach finally seemed to get the hint this wasn't fun and games. "You little—" Zach didn't finish his own sentence as he limped forward, the storm growing stronger around him.

Use me. Touch Me.

Nikki reached for her pocket.

Ray tried to attack Zach, but he was simply slammed aside by a gust of wind.

Lincoln fumbled with the bow as the storm grew. Another lucky shot might not be possible.

Zach advanced on him slowly, lip curled into a snarl.

Nikki finally gave in. She grabbed the Stone and thrust it to the ground.

The earth shook.

Zach whirled around, noticing the Stone immediately. He snarled, gaze meeting Nikki's for a moment.

Something rumbled beneath them.

"Run!" Nikki yelled, diving for cover in the brush as far as she could.

The world exploded, dirt flying into the air, trees rattling with the *whoosh* of the blast.

Nikki clenched her hands over her head.

The wind settled and everything went quiet.

Nikki peeked through her hands. Zach was nowhere to be seen and the Stone lay perfectly unharmed on the path. She got up slowly, listening for the Oquelite, but nothing moved.

Lincoln and Ray also got up, both unharmed.

Raindrops began to speckle the road with dark spots of moisture.

Nikki picked up the Stone, examining it. The shard showed no chips, burns, or smudges. It seemed perfectly fine. Avalon glinted inside. She didn't scold or begin to lecture. That had to be a good sign.

"Are you crazy?" Nikki said, spinning on Lincoln.

"You used one of the most powerful objects on earth right now. Twice! Who's crazy?" Lincoln said. "What are you, anyway? You can fight. I've seen it. Legendary Ewyon don't usually do that."

Nikki looked down. Fighting wasn't the word she'd use. She was insane. She didn't understand exactly what it meant, but she didn't like how it felt.

"Like you said, we have to stick together," Ray said. "That's how we work best. Ewyon or not."

Nikki nodded. They would have either been dead or on their way to the Oquelite Labyrinth if it wasn't for Lincoln's distraction that gave her time.

"Thanks," Nikki said, softly.

"No problem," Ray said, placing his hand on her shoulder.

"So, we're traveling in a group?" Lincoln said. "Until we reach Isedowle."

Nikki looked to Lincoln. He kept his distance from her, and she noticed she was leaning away from him too. She waited for Avalon, but the voice never came. So, Nikki slowly nodded, unsure.

"Well, then, we better go," Lincoln said. "But I have to warn. Bad things happen. Aviduous and Ewyon—it's bad luck. Always has been and always will be. It's not my fault. The Ewyon's really like to mess things up."

Nikki nodded, not daring to argue. Ewyon. That didn't sound right. The word didn't seem to fit with her at all.

Thunder rumbled in the distance and the wind began to pick up. Lincoln looked up into the cloudy sky and then back at Nikki, scowling.

"I-I'll separate…sooner than Isledowle," Nikki said.

Lincoln nodded and began to continue into the woods. Ray raised an eyebrow at her and glanced between the two of them.

Nikki ignored him. She could fend for herself, but she wasn't so sure if she could take an Oquelite attack single-handedly. The Ewyon Stone was too dangerous though, and until they reached a safer destination they'd have to part. That was the final deal.

BEING STUCK IN THE RAIN, AT NIGHT, IN A FOREST WITH someone your blood rejects, is exactly as terrible as anyone might think.

At some point they must have left North Cordell, and the trees were a thriving green around them, even in the dark of night. Lincoln wasn't sure what region they'd ended up in, but he'd check in the next town they approached. It was a preservation region for sure, though, as not many regions kept the trees so plentiful.

The four mountains were still a smudge in the distance.

Lincoln was attempting to keep a small fire from burning out in the rain. Ray crouched with his denim jacket thrown over his head as he typed on the Communicator. Nikki was a little farther out, pacing in the mud and pouring rain, out of the protection of the trees. Her gaze kept darting around, like she was waiting for something to jump out and attack them.

They'd been running and walking for hours in the storming terrain. They were only stopping briefly, till the storm let up a bit and until it was easier to tell which direction they should be heading.

The frost was biting at Lincoln's face, and the small flame didn't seem to help. It didn't seem right for it to be raining. It felt like it should have snowed, it was so cold. The dew on the trees had frozen into small icicles.

Lincoln had grown used to the harsh weather of the small mountainside town, yet it still surprised him that it never snowed. It hadn't snowed in North Cordell in years. Some said it was bad luck for snow to fall on the grounds of North Cordell. He remembered two elderly friends speaking of it when he was younger, trying to warm up by the burning furnace inside a shop.

"Snow. Nature's cushion for the dead. I tell you every time the white cushion spreads across the ground, someone breathes their last and falls," one of the women had commented.

"It never snows here in North Cordell. Never has and never will!" the other snapped.

Now, Lincoln looked back to Nikki. She moved closer to the fire, still walking back and forth in a worrisome fashion, keeping her distance. He felt awkward.

"You cold?" he asked, desperately trying to fix the silence.

She shook her head, though he didn't believe her. She was tense and her jaw was clenched, her arms crossed.

Ray switched the Communicator off and sighed. "Felicity says they're still alive. Which I guess is a good thing. Living's great."

Lincoln looked down at the arrow he was working on. It had been chipped in multiple places, but it had served its purpose well. He wiped away the mud with his sleeve and held it up to the fire.

"So, how'd you build those arrows?" Ray asked, watching. "Out here?"

Lincoln put it back in the bag. "It's not as hard as it looks. Scraps are frequent. Connecting. The hard part is ignition on impact, and not wanting it to explode at bad times. Adding the sensory system was complicated. I had to work out the speeds and impact pressure so I could get it just right. It's based off an automatic heater in the grocer. But on a smaller, more destructive scale—" Lincoln stopped, realizing that wasn't the answer Ray was looking for.

Ray blinked and shrugged, pretending to know what Lincoln had just said. "How do you know all this...stuff?" he asked. "Did you go to a university when you were younger or something?"

Lincoln looked away into the rain falling through the trees.

Nikki sat down, folding her hands together. "Where did you come from?" she asked quietly. Her gaze pierced him, like it had when they first met, like she was trying to decide who he was.

Lincoln took a deep breath, as thunder rumbled across the sky. "I don't remember."

Ray frowned. "Y-you don't remember the name of where you came from? Or—"

"I was found half frozen in a river when I was ten," Lincoln interrupted.

Ray went silent.

Lincoln ran his fingers through his wet hair, touching the back of his head. "I must have banged my head or something. The only clear thing I remembered was my name."

"But…you know so much," Ray said.

"That's why I ran from the foster organization that took me in," Lincoln said. "I started getting these random thoughts and pieces of information. One day, it all pieced together, and I couldn't be there anymore, or I would have been killed."

Lincoln looked down at his hands. They'd done the wrong things for as long as he could remember. Instead of using weapons, he made them. He thought too much, and he knew too much. It was like one day waking up and realizing that you were a mistake. Some messed up creature. Maybe that's why he'd been in a river.

Because someone couldn't deal with a mu-tant Aviduous.

"It doesn't matter though," Lincoln said, quickly breaking through the silence. "I'm hopeful that one day I'll maybe get it back. Who knows?"

Ray laughed. "You legit just said you're amnesiac, and for some reason have all this knowledge about things that could kill you, and all you have to say is 'it's fine'?"

"I don't think about it much," Lincoln said, looking into the dying flames. "Seriously, it's extremely frustrating trying to think about things I've lost."

It was much more than that. Sometimes, when he was younger, he'd get furious about it. He tried to remember who he was and where he came from. He could feel it inside, but it was so distant at the same time. He felt like somehow it was his fault he couldn't remember and that he didn't even know who or what he was. Was he different before he lost his memories? Mostly, he forced himself not to think of it.

Ray nodded. "It must be frustrating."

"What about you?" Lincoln said, deflecting the attention.

Nikki turned to Ray, nodding.

Ray shrugged. "I'm from Glorgory. Nothing too exciting. My mother's a doctor." He twisted his hands together awkwardly. "My father went missing when I was five, but I don't remember too much. It's…life. Fun. Yeah."

"That's how you know how to heal," Nikki said, looking up with wide eyes.

Ray smiled softly, nodding. "Yeah. I'd much rather be saving people's lives with my mom than being stuck in a stupid Foundation Field."

"Why do you work in a Foundation Field?" Lincoln asked.

Ray shrugged. "I-I wanted to."

Lincoln didn't believe him. Ray liked to do things in the medic field, not in digging ditches to create a job system and the fields meant to help solve unemployment rates.

"And you?" Ray said to Nikki. "Where do you come from?"

Nikki shrugged.

"What about the Stone?" Lincoln asked. It seemed less invasive.

Nikki reached into her pocket and pulled the brilliant object out. The fire went cold. "I had it," she said simply. "It found me."

"You're brave to still be carrying that thing around," Lincoln said.

Nikki shook her head. "Not brave," she whispered, putting it into her pocket, muttering another word under her breath that Lincoln didn't quite catch.

"What happens if the Oquelite get their hands on that Stone?" Ray said.

"Bad things, I guess," Lincoln said. "It's part of a Key, like Miriam said. But from what I've seen, that thing is freaking powerful all on its own."

That's why Lincoln knew he couldn't get too close. The Stone was made by a race that hated him, even if Nikki herself didn't. It seemed so alive. And its power already proved deadly.

Lighting flashed above them, and the rain pounded down relentlessly.

"I guess we're to blame for this storm too, just like everything else," Ray grumbled. "Wake me up when it's not raining. And maybe when we're given free food and a SpeedRail ticket back home. But when it stops raining works too, I guess." He covered his face in the jacket and went quiet.

Lincoln went back to the fire and tried to restart it, but the flames seemed to hate him so he put the lighter away, sitting down in the wet, storming darkness. Nikki crouched, the space between them still so obvious and gaping. She took a deep breath and leaned back, though her eyes were wild and awake.

"You okay?" Lincoln asked.

Nikki nodded.

He should apologize to her. Tell her he didn't mean to avoid her. But the truth was he did.

She was an *Ewyon*. It sent a sick feeling through him.

Lincoln ran his hands around the cuffs on his wrists and looked up toward the clouded sky. His eyes were unaffected by the dark, like they'd always been.

He wasn't weak. He was an Aviduous. He wouldn't show

her even a flinch. He gripped an arrow and took a deep breath. He was ready for anything.

35

THEY'D BEEN DRIVING THROUGHOUT THE NIGHT. COLE couldn't blame Tabitha's bored groan. Her and Felicity switched places, so Felicity could get a decent sleep, and that meant he was directly next to Tabitha and could clearly hear each of her clear complaints.

He admitted he was equally as agitated with the journey so far. After a while, conversation always fell flat after a few minutes. The silence was mind numbing, but the only thing Cole really wanted to talk about seemed to be the only thing they couldn't.

The reason they were on this insane trip.

"Look!" Tabitha cried out, sitting straight up in the seat and pointing out the window, her face coming alive with color.

Cole jumped, looking to where she pointed. Felicity leaned in between the two seats; her frizzy red locks tucked away in a bun that crowned her head.

A cluster of buildings had come into sight.

"A town!" Tabitha gasped. "We *have* to stop there. Please, Cole. I'm dying."

"Maybe we should take a walk or something. Clear our minds," Felicity suggested, glancing at Cole.

"Why are you asking me? I'm not in charge," Cole said.

Tabitha scoffed.

Felicity shook her head. "Well, then. Looks like we're taking a small detour."

Tabitha gave a triumphant shout.

They steered the auto in the direction of the town. The buildings were the grey steel of small, quickly constructed towns. A few people roamed the streets, balconies shading the sidewalks. Several shops even had the classy upgrade of a moving ground entrance.

A bot or two stood guard at their assigned store, blurting automated advertisements and greetings to uninterested customers.

As soon as Cole stopped the auto, Tabitha had swung the door open and jumped out.

Felicity carefully stepped out of the car and followed. "This is a nice little place."

"Better than Liberty?" Cole asked, locking the auto and slipping the card into his pocket.

Felicity's face hardened at the mention of the region. "Anything's better," she said coolly, taking a steady step to the sidewalk.

Cole looked to Tabitha.

"None of your concern," Tabitha said, crossing her arms

with a smirk.

It had been a while since Cole even laid eyes on functioning tech that wasn't falling-apart Defender heaters and Comms.

Cole ignored stares whenever they passed, or adults looking up momentarily from their work to frown. Tabitha kept making weird faces at any who dared to scrunch up their nose. Felicity grabbed Tabitha's arm and moved her faster.

It surprised Cole how Felicity ignored them completely. She just pushed past them, her head up. No one would have never recognized the rich man's daughter, her freckled face scraped and bruised, her tangled mass of bright red hair pulled back. She strode confidently down the sidewalk.

"Where are we going exactly?" Tabitha asked finally.

"The post office," Felicity said.

"A post office?" Tabitha said, frowning. "Do those even exist anymore?"

Felicity laughed. "Of course they do. Where else do you think they take all the business down for packaging and transporting? In Liberty?"

It was part of her family's profession to ship packages and other things around the world from their large factories. It made sense why she'd know more about post offices than Tabitha and himself.

When Felicity stopped in front of an emerald-colored glass building, Cole stared in shock. For some reason, he'd thought of a small building in an old field, with a board nailed to the porch with *"Post Office"* scrawled out in red paint.

They walked up to the doors, and Cole reached out to push them open. Suddenly, the doors glittered away and both him and Tabitha jumped back. Felicity casually walked inside.

"Forgot about the 'screw normal doors when you're

a Bentsworth' thing," Tabitha said to Cole, laughing nervously.

He shrugged.

Tabitha and Cole walked into the building after Felicity. The entire place was large and spacious, with palm tree plants, paintings of abstract objects along the walls, and stools with stripes and checkered patterns. Felicity waltzed right up to the window in the wall, where a dark-haired boy sorted through some enveloped packages.

He looked up and jumped back. "Well, that is a surprise," he chuckled, with a faint remainder of an accent. "Felicity Bentsworth, is it?"

He held out his hand. Felicity shook it and nodded.

"Turner. Rico Turner," the boy said, clearing his throat and wiping his shaking palms on his pants. "Two deliveries for you."

"Two?" Felicity frowned.

"Yeah. One from your father up there—he was planning on sending out searches to North Cordell. He'll be glad you're safe," he said, snatching a Scroll from his desk. "Sent one of these to every major Post Office in the North West regions."

Felicity took the Scroll. "And the other one?"

Turner handed Felicity a small piece of paper. She frowned, taking it into her hands.

Tabitha's face fell in horror. That wasn't just any paper. "That's from *my* binder," she hissed, too low for anyone but Cole to hear.

"Dropped off earlier this morning," Turner said, leaning forward in his chair. He snatched an envelope off the desk and handed it to Felicity.

Felicity gave a forced smile, turning toward a bench, but

Rico blurted out, "Were you in North Cordell? I heard it was nearly burned to the ground."

"Was it that obvious?" Felicity said, laughing and looking at herself.

Rico laughed in return. "Well, that's all that anyone has been talking about. Some say that the place is…" Rico leaned over to her, shading his hand over his mouth, though it wasn't quiet. "*Cursed.*"

"That's ridiculous!" Felicity said, with a laugh that was obviously forced.

Tabitha looked to Cole, her eyes darting to Felicity. Cole shrugged. Felicity seemed to be handling it fine.

"It's got plenty of evidence," Rico said, leaning closer. "It hasn't snowed there in a century. It doesn't get much funding except for its now out of business university. The four ridged mountains, and the way they curve. It's gotten cursed written all over it."

Felicity laughed nervously again. "Yes, uh, definitely. You must be very observant." She straightened and thanked him politely, then walked away from the window, back to Tabitha and Cole.

Felicity immediately tossed aside her father's message, grabbing the paper. Tabitha eagerly ripped it from her hands. Felicity and Cole crowded around her.

In messy, blue handwriting, the note read simply, "Regal Road. 5516. S.H"

"Directions," Tabitha whispered. "To where? And S.H?"

"Sinni Hutson," Felicity said, her forehead wrinkling. "It has to be the address in Imperial. But where? They're way too vague."

"Probably the Imperial City," Tabitha said. "Almost everyone who lives in Imperial lives in the Imperial City, unless you're boring. And let me tell you, sergeants who send their blue haired friends out to do things can't be boring."

"And it's also the host of the Defending Department central base. Top floor of the Tower," Cole said, offering a more logical answer.

Felicity took the note from Tabitha. "Regal. 5516," she muttered. "Sorry."

"Sorry for taking my paper?" Tabitha said.

Cole elbowed her.

Felicity folded up the note and put in her pocket, worry still etched in her features as she unrolled her father's Scroll.

She scanned over it and sighed, disappointed. She handed the Scroll to Tabitha, who let Cole read from over her shoulder.

To Felicity Alexandria Bentsworth,

I hope this has reached you in a state of good health and safety. If you've opened this letter, please inform one of my agents to escort you and Ms. Tabitha Delorous back to Liberty, where you can continue your studies in a guarded, safe environment. You are to inform us immediately once you receive this message.

Gordon W. Bentsworth.

Tabitha had gone pale, not a sarcastic remark escaping her lips. She looked up to Felicity. "We *can't* disobey your dad."

"We also can't disobey Taryn," Felicity said with an agitated sigh. "Or we'll…you know, die?"

"Disobeying your dad is just about as bad as that."

"Tabitha!" Felicity shushed herself, as turner looked from his desk. "Be serious."

Cole butted in before Tabitha could suggest anything else. "Look, Felicity, you know your dad. And I'm with you. As much as it would suck to have one of the biggest men on the planet on your bad side, being dead and having the Oquelite destroy everything would be much worse."

Tabitha gave a low groan. "Fine. I guess someone's going to have to protect Mr. Coleson here anyway."

Felicity smiled, her eyes glittering. "Good." She rolled the Scroll back up, returned to the desk, and slid the note to Rico.

Felicity looked at Tabitha and Cole, then back to Rico. "Could you please forward a message to my father?" Felicity asked.

Rico nodded, turning in his chair, to the keyboard. "Go right ahead."

"Tell him we won't be needing an escort. We're heading to the Imperial City and we will check in with him there," she said.

"Alrighty, Miss Bentsworth," Rico said, typing in her message. "Have a great day!"

Felicity walked back to Tabitha and Cole. "Let's go." Felicity gave Tabitha a small smile. "And don't forget, we do need to protect Cole," she said, nudging him.

Cole rolled his eyes, though he couldn't keep from smiling as they walked out the emerald doors.

Felicity could breathe.

Anxiety tried to claw at her mind. She'd defied her father. She was going to Imperial, where a strange Sergeant waited, and could kill them. She'd been given a vague note. She could possibly be part of a Council…just like the infamous Curatrix team.

And yet, she was able to breathe.

That was a positive. She could *breathe*. A grin crept up on her face, as she straightened herself a little higher and walked down the sidewalk.

A friendly waiter from a sidewalk cafe gave her a small wave.

Felicity's stomach suddenly dropped, and a bot rammed into her ankle. She nearly cried out, the floor rushing for her. She was caught by her arm and jerked to her feet.

She looked to Cole, and mumbled, "Thanks."

So much for being confident.

She didn't dare look back at the waiter, and kept her place between Tabitha and Cole, out of the way of any sudden eye contact.

"Don't get all worried over it, Liz." Tabitha tossed a stray hair from her face and shrugged.

It was easy for her to say. Felicity sighed. "I'm not."

"I've tripped over so many bots back in Liberty. Seriously. Why are they manufactured so small? They have such noisy speakers though. And very annoying advertisements." Tabitha gave her a big smile.

Felicity gave her an awkward grin back, and then shifted her gaze back down to her feet.

"She is coming."

Felicity jerked her head up. She looked around. No one in the trickle of people in the streets had stopped walking. They were all engaged in conversation or their eyes down to their teles and comms. Where had the voice come from? "Hello?"

"Hi?" Cole frowned at her.

"You didn't hear that?" Felicity said, looking from Tabitha to Cole. They both looked at her in bewil-derment.

She was going crazy.

Felicity cleared her throat. "N-never mind. I just thought I heard something."

"There are quite a few people around here," Tabitha said.

But it wasn't like that, Felicity thought. The voice had been loud, and distinct. Speaking directly to her.

"Follow me."

Felicity stopped in her tracks. Cole and Tabitha paused and looked over their shoulders back at her. She opened her mouth, her lip quivering. "I heard—"

She couldn't speak. She was frozen. She tried to cry out. Scream. Anything, but her body remained planted perfectly still.

"Liz?" Tabitha's brow slowly creased into a frown, as she turned on her heal.

"Leave them. I have something to show you." The voice was sweet with a slight sing-song accent, with a cold, ominous edge. Felicity's heard whirred.

"I have to go." The words spilled from her mouth. Calm and confident.

Her mind panicked. No, no, no! She didn't want to leave! She wanted to cry, but tears wouldn't come. Her gaze was still, and her eyes dry.

Tabitha's mouth fell. "Liz? Are you serious? I promise tripping wasn't that—"

"I shall meet you in Imperial." Shall? Why was she using the word shall?

Felicity's heart rose seeing Tabitha's face darken. Could she tell it wasn't her? Could she save her?

"Felicity, this isn't like you."

Yes. Yes. It wasn't like her at all.

Felicity's mouth spoke on its own again. "It must be done, dear friend."

No. No. No. *NO.*

Tabitha hesitated. "If you say so, Liz."

No! I don't say so! Felicity's mind cried. Of course, Tabitha wouldn't try to defy her. Yes, Tabitha loved to tease, and poke fun every now and then, but when it really came down to it Tabitha *obeyed* Felicity. She was a Bentsworth after all.

Tabitha hesitated, and Felicity screamed into her mind.

"Leave her. I need to show you something."

No! Felicity cried. *Tabitha!*

Felicity's feet suddenly turned, her body betraying her mind, and began to walk down the sidewalk, awkwardly against the current of people.

She begged to look back. She needed to see Tabitha. She couldn't leave. She would die. She couldn't be alone.

But her body kept moving and forcing her to breathe.

36

She hadn't meant to fall asleep.

She couldn't believe she'd given in so easily. And the dreams were terrifying. Three words flashing over and over in her mind and she couldn't escape. *I couldn't escape.*

Lincoln gently shook her awake and she tried to hide her humiliation as they set off again.

The rain had finally let up for a few hours as they walked down the roads. Eventually, after catching a bus, they were standing back in the drenching rain.

Nikki avoided speaking to her two companions the entire time. What say did she have in their decisions anyway? She was just a burden. A danger.

"Stop beating yourself up." Avalon laughed. *"Sleeping through the night is natural. You need to get outside of that negative mindset,*

child, or you're going to be dead before you know it."

Nikki folded her arms, looking to the storming clouds above her.

"What is it?" Avalon asked. *"Something is bothering you besides your ridiculous self-degrading over sleep."*

I want to go to Imperial.

Avalon broke out into laughter. *And why would you do that? There is nothing for you in Imperial. Death is inevitable.*

Nikki glanced quickly to Ray and Lincoln, who continued to quarrel. *They need help.*

"And what makes you think they want yours? It's true, you're the strangest case of an Ewyon I've ever seen. Truly the strangest looking, and your attitude. Child, you need to shape up, but your race is hated."

Then why can't I prove them wrong? Nikki replied.

Avalon went dead quiet for a moment. *"You're doing this because of those other children and…that sergeant."*

You said earlier they had potential.

"That was before I knew all the pieces. A Council reformation is dangerous. The sergeant should be able to tell you that."

Nikki wished she could see Avalon's face and see what she meant. *You've seen Taryn before.*

Avalon laughed, again. *"Jessica, or 'Taryn', as she calls herself, is an interesting case."*

I'm going to Imperial, Nikki said again.

Avalon sighed. *"I can't stop you, child."*

Lightning flashed and thunder rumbled, Avalon's presence quickly disappearing. Lincoln ran up to Nikki, his hood over his head, though it didn't seem to help much. Ray ran quickly behind him.

"Looks like we've made it," Lincoln said, looking up to the weather-battered sign.

Welcome to Isledowle! the sun-scorched, flashing sign

blinked.

It had been hard to see the dim sign in the storm. It seemed like the sky would never stop sending down rain. Nikki stood in the open, completely drenched, looking nervously toward the town. Once Isledowle had been a booming electrical base. The evidence was clear from the rusted buildings that soared above them and once richly dressed houses vacant and chipped away at. There were a few roadside charging stations and fast-food stores, but besides that the town looked almost lifeless.

Lincoln took his attention away from the sign and to Nikki and Ray. "We'd better get inside somewhere," he suggested.

Nikki had no objections to the idea, following Lincoln and looking around in fascination as they walked. Lincoln had said the entire place was a ghost town. It seemed strange how a once rich, booming region could turn into such a sad, gloomy place. Only people wanting to get away from society lived here. Mostly drunks or rebels who wanted to hide their face from the world.

Lincoln led them to the doors of an old, run down diner. The lights glowed from inside the clouded windows. He opened the door.

They were greeted by a glum, bland voice, "Hello and welcome to Isledowle Burger. What can I get you today?"

Lincoln shook his head. "Nothing, thank you."

The man at the counter didn't seem to care, like he knew that they were coming in for refuge from the rain like all the others, who sat in the booths, staring at their devices.

Nikki came in cautiously, her eyes constantly twitching to the others in the room. Ray swept his dripping hair from his face. They moved to a corner, as far away from other people as possible, though they were still close enough to hear a news broadcast blast through some tropical-shirted guy's headphones.

"Today, another anonymous attack was recorded in Court Illegia, destroying nearly half of the west territory in the region's supplies and factories. Officials are…"

Lincoln glanced at Nikki. Her muscles tensed. Soon every single region's Oquelite would break free.

The idea scared her. This was the opposite of safety.

But what were they after? The Oquelite weren't going around blindly. Nikki's hand slipped to her pocket. A reformation. Was that what they feared? Or is that exactly what they wanted?

The door of the diner chimed open again, and the man at the front desk recited his lines, but the newcomer ignored him. They wore a long cloak, which made everyone inch away. It floated outward at the sides as if there was something underneath and a deep hood covered the wearer's face. No one wore cloaks except…Oquelite.

Lincoln and Ray saw it too. Nikki began to inch away, her fists clenched as the figure came closer to them. Lincoln's hand hovered over his bag. The figure rushed towards them and pushed their hood back, shaking the rain from her short, wet hair.

Miriam Outown gave them a sharp smile, glancing behind her. "I'm pretty sure I'm not going to kill you."

Nikki fists relaxed.

Ray frowned, opening his mouth, but Miriam brought her finger to her lips, signaling him to be quiet. "I'm glad I caught you." Miriam scanned the room again as she spoke, visibly tense.

Nikki looked behind her, noticing the man who had been

listening to the news report on the Oquelite was peering over his tablet at them. Her brows furrowed. The man adjusted his sunglasses and looked at his tablet again.

"Lovely weather we have today." Miriam grabbed a napkin off the nearby table and scribbled something down.

"Yes," Lincoln said, clearing his throat. "Lovely."

Miriam shoved the note to Nikki. She put on a fake smile. "Yes. Very nice to see you again. Have a nice day!" she said, in a fake, high-pitched friendliness. Her face darkened and she winked at them. She threw the hood over her head and ran out the door.

The oddly dressed man dropped his hand and scowled, walking to the door, peering out, then frowning back at Lincoln, Nikki, and Ray.

Nikki's heart dropped.

She shoved the note in her pocket and grabbed Lincoln and Ray's arms. She ran through the "Employees Only" door.

The room was full of unused kitchen supplies and janitor carts, and a lot of other useless junk. The large metal cupboards caught her eye. She swung the door open and slipped inside. Ray and Lincoln jammed in behind her.

Ray slammed the door shut, holding his breath.

Nikki's back was to Lincoln's chest and her face was in Ray's dripping hair. She felt Lincoln go stiff when the door to the kitchen swung open.

A crash.

A cabinet door was torn off its hinges. The footsteps came closer.

Lincoln tapped Nikki's shoulder. He held out an arrow. She frowned, but then she remembered the battle. He's blown up a shop, of course there had to be a way to blow through the thin diner wall. Ray turned as much as he could to see the arrow. His eyes grew wide, but he nodded anyway.

Another door clattered to the ground. The man was getting closer.

Lincoln jammed the arrow into the wall, making a screeching sound. The footsteps went quiet. Ray turned his head and held Lincoln's eyes.

Then burst from the hiding spot, charging at their pursuer.

Nikki shoved her hand over her mouth to keep herself from screaming.

Lincoln jammed the arrow deeper.

Nikki turned to run after Ray, but Lincoln grabbed her and yelled at her not to move. Nikki froze, her mind going wild as she squeezed her eyes shut. Someone called out in pain, and she could feel the warm energy around her, the echoes of blow flowing around her. She opened her eyes to see a glowing hot, uneven circle in the wall.

Nikki didn't hesitate. She kicked her feet up against the wall. It broke beneath the force, crumbling outward, and Lincoln shoved her through.

Nikki fell out into the rainy street.

"Ray!" Lincoln called out.

Nikki turned, trying to get back into the diner, but Lincoln was shoved out, the wall suddenly sealing itself behind them. Lincoln lay in the mud, staring at the wall, his breaths rapid. Lincoln fell back into the mud, throwing his hands over his face. "What have I done?" he muttered through his hands.

Nikki walked slowly to the wall, running the tips of her fingers over it.

Ray could get himself out. He wasn't gone forever. They

could just run through the front doors of the diner. They had to save him. They had to.

But she knew it was too late for that. The Oquelite were too fast. They couldn't kill Ray. They wouldn't kill him. She tried telling herself over and over again.

Dead.

Dead. Avalon taunted her thoughts.

Lincoln stayed on the ground, and Nikki walked over to him, waiting for him to stand up.

"It's pointless," Lincoln said, his arms falling from his face.

"They can't kill him."

Lincoln shot up, fists clenched. "You've seen what the Oquelite can do," he said. "And you just think they can't kill him?"

"They won't."

"And why not?"

Nikki reached into her pocket for the note, unfolding it. "They think he has information."

Lincoln went quiet, thinking for a moment. Then he shook his head. "What—what does it say?"

Nikki scanned over it, then handed it to Lincoln, but he shook his head and handed it back. Nikki frowned.

"I...I can't read," he said, reddening.

Nikki nodded and took the letter back. Of course, not many people could write or read. Then how could she? Being able to identify the letters was one of the few things she found some sort of relief in.

"Imperial City Regal Rd. 5516. Don't be startled," Nikki said softly, as if someone might be listening to them. She tore the note into tiny shreds, letting the pieces scatter in the wind. No one could find the address.

"Don't be startled," Lincoln sighed. "I do *not* like the sound of that."

329

37

"WHAT DO YOU MEAN, WE CAN'T BOARD?" TABITHA YELLED, fighting against Cole's restraining grip. She wanted to punch the ticket seller in the face.

The seller turned up his nose. "It costs fourteen for two to board. You only inserted ten," he said, agitation building in his voice.

Tabitha growled, but Cole shoved his hand over her mouth. "We're sorry. Thank you for your time. We'll go now."

He pulled her away from the booth and out of the station.

"Only ten? He didn't even refund us! If he knew what we were doing—" Tabitha yelled. "If Felicity was here, we would show him!"

"But Felicity's not here. And he might not let her on either. We don't have any money, Tabs. That's the real reason. Not to mention the fact we look like—" Cole said, gesturing to himself, mud splatters and all.

Tabitha huffed.

Felicity had disappeared with the bag with the money for the tickets. Then later, they'd gotten a message on Felicity's Comm saying she was on her way with Sinni.

Tabitha couldn't help but feel a little betrayed.

It was spontaneous. Like something in Felicity had just snapped, and she had run off. Tabitha knew she should have followed her. She scolded herself.

Then of course the auto broke down and they had to *walk* a mile to the SpeedRail station.

Cole placed his hand on her shoulder. Tabitha looked up to him. She tried to give a small smile, but she was too tired. She wanted to go kick a wall and burn a building down. This was pointless. She was stupid to think they would be able to get to Imperial.

"Maybe we will have to become…street rats. If we can even survive," Tabitha's voice became quiet. "That's the… happiest outlook."

Cole brows furrowed. "Tabs, don't think like that. We're going to get to Imperial. We *need* to get to Imperial." Cole squeezed her shoulder encouragingly.

Tabitha managed a weak smile, pulling away. "Yeah, thanks," she said, looking down and walking off in front of Cole.

Tabitha wandered down the streets, a little distance ahead of Cole, her hands in the pockets of her battered jacket. The city was large and grand but could never compete with her Liberty. Liberty was the finest of its kind. The familiar sounds of giggling friends kept their distance from her here. Even the music inside her head made her feel sicker and more lost in despair.

Felicity's backpack was slung over Tabitha's shoulder. The stupid freckled, red-headed girl haunted her mind.

She thought of Felicity as almost family. Did Felicity feel the same way? She knew their friendship was a bit forced, but she always felt safer in the Bentsworths manor than at home. At least no one yelled at her there.

She wasn't being constantly reminded that she was always going to be below Clarence.

They'd first met when Felicity gave her hand when Tabitha was lost at a conference. Tabitha didn't know it was a Bentswoth at first. The girl was older than her, but she treated Tabitha as though they were equals. She led Tabitha through the halls. Tabitha remembered stopping in front of the large music room. It was the first time she saw an instrument. She always sang to herself, but she never knew an instrument made music too.

Felicity had always led the way, unafraid and welcoming and then, of course, the crash happened.

"Help! Someone! Help!"

Tabitha snapped out of her trail of thought.

The voice. It sounded strangely familiar.

No one around her seemed to notice. She looked over her shoulder. Where was Cole? There was no time to wait for him. She pushed past them, looking for the source of the plea.

"Help!" it called out again.

Tabitha darted in between a couple and down a rural street. The smell of manure and rotting food stung her nose. The windows looked like cells with rags as curtains. Each door was numbered. She wanted to get out of this place as soon as possible.

"Help me! Please!" the voice cried out again.

"I'm here!" Tabitha yelled back. She hurried down the empty street, searching for the source of the cry.

Curtains ruffled and lifted as people peered out at her.

"Help!"

Tabitha looked down and to her shock the screams were coming from a vent into the ground. The sewer, most likely. She jerked the vent open and dust exploded from inside of it like a rumbling storm. The dirt whirled around the entire street, obscuring everything.

"Help me! Hurry!" the victim called out again.

Tabitha coughed into her sleeve, squinting into the darkness. "I'm coming!" She shouted, jumping down into the shadows. Tabitha fell a couple feet before slamming into the ground. Above her, the lid shut itself, everything going pitch black.

Fire burst to life, flickering in the torches along the stone walls, and a cold draft ran past her. This was no sewer.

Tabitha scrambled to her feet. She gasped, whirling around in awe. "Hello?" she called out.

There was no reply.

She walked down the corridor, scanning over the engravings in the wall. There were strange pictures and words in a language she couldn't understand. The images varied from great celebration to mountains of dead in a battlefield. One image showed someone being burned at the stake. Tabitha shivered.

At the end of the hall, there was a huge mural, far more detailed than all the other engravings. It could almost have been a photograph. It showed a blood red mountain towering into the smoking clouds above the smoldering world below it. Tabitha eyes went as wide, taking in the immensity of it. All the images seemed to be pieces of a terrible story, but this…this was how it ended.

With a red mountain.

She brushed her hand against it and the wall rose. An opening appeared behind it. She stepped back, and a gust of cold air pushed against her.

In front of her was an empty room, glowing a dim blue though there was no real light source. The walls were empty, and the ceiling reached so high Tabitha couldn't believe it was underground. Then she saw her.

In the middle of the room was a girl wrapped in a blanket, her red hair damp and fallen across her streaked face.

"L-liz?" Tabitha whispered, approaching her gently.

The girl smiled. She stood, letting her blanket fall into the dust. The smile morphed in a smirk. "Welcome, Humanic, to the Hall of Heroes," she said, her voice booming off the walls, far deeper than it should have been.

Tabitha frowned.

The girl began to twist and grow, her face becoming so wrinkled and distorted it wasn't even a human face at all. The skin became dry and cracked and it looked green in the blue light. Suddenly branches and vines sprouted from the cracks, lifting the creature high above Tabitha, as the living vines swarmed around her.

"This age's Council will not survive. You and the other eleven will die!" it spat out at her.

Council. Not this again.

Tabitha shot a glare at the creature. "Hate to break it to you, but I'm not Impure!" she yelled, trying to hide her panic.

The creature just gave her a satisfied smile. The branches lunged on Tabitha.

She yelled and struggled, but they tangled around her wrists and ankles, and finally her neck. Tabitha kicked wildly at them, but every movement made them squeeze tighter around her neck.

"Tabitha!"

Tabitha tried to turn around and see him. It was Cole's voice. It had to be.

"Cole! Co—!" she yelled out desperately, but the vines tightened around her neck.

The serpent laughed. The vines turned her around, and she spotted Cole as he ran through the doorway.

"Two in one day? That is a lovely surprise," the creature hissed, but Cole didn't flinch.

He stood unafraid, with a fierce intensity in his eyes. The branches lunged for him, but when they got close, they wilted away.

Cole's eyes grew wide.

Tabitha tried calling out again, but she couldn't. She was helpless and forced to watch and wait for the creature to choke the life out of her.

Cole stepped out of her view, but she could feel the branches retracting away from him.

"Kill him!" the serpent screamed, but nothing moved. It growled and hissed, "Kill the female Humanic! "

All the vines and branches rushed toward her. Tabitha struggled against the firm hold. Soon she was so encompassed by branches she could no longer see. The pressure would crush her in a moment. She was going to die. She fell limp, darkness creeping over her despite her struggles.

"Tabs!" Cole came into sight, the branches rotting away as he ran toward her.

She could barely hear his words, but she thrashed again, trying to free herself. Something sharp dug into her skin. The branches were growing thorns. The room had transformed into a jungle, but Tabitha could still see Cole clearly as the branches and vines bounced away from him. She winced as the thorns started digging into her skin, and she stopped struggling or she would only hurt herself more.

Cole was still forging his way forward as the vines jerked her farther and farther from his reach. He growled and flung his pack off and drew out the knife Taryn had given him for the battle. He looked Tabitha in her eyes and ran to her. The knife slashed through the vines imprisoning her, though they seemed to fall away at his touch.

"I'm going to get you out!" he shouted.

Tabitha could barely hear him. Cole was still screaming something at her, and Tabitha thought she saw tears in his eyes.

Finally, he rammed himself into the vines, which barely melted away from him before touching his skin. The entire room shook, and the vines fell away, dropping Tabitha onto the ground.

Cole caught her, steadying her in his arms.

Tabitha tried to stand up, her head still light, but as soon as Cole let go of her the vines rushed back. Tabitha fought off a few, but there were too many to keep track of. A small vine crawled up her neck, entangling itself in her blonde and purple hair. Tabitha tried to jerk away, but it pulled her back.

Cole's eyes flashed with panic, darting around for a solution. He grabbed the knife, dripping with the steaming sap of the plants, and ran to her, but stopped, hesitating at the last second. But they didn't have time for hesitations.

"Do it!" Tabitha screamed.

Cole glanced at her for a moment, then lunged.

Tabitha fell free, whirling around and watching her locks fall prisoner to the killer shrubbery. She looked up at Cole, breathing heavily, but managed to smile. "I've never been so glad to see you in my whole life," she gasped.

Cole gave her a small smile. "Me too, Tabs."

The vines were growing closer to her again. Cole grabbed Tabitha and pulled her close to him. "Sorry," he muttered under his breath.

Tabitha clung to him because her life literally depended on it. He kept his arms around her as they began to back out of the room. His plan seemed to work—the vines wouldn't touch him or Tabitha.

"You cannot escape!" the serpent screamed. "You were warned. Let go of her!"

Cole flinched, tightening his grip around her. Finally, they backed out of the plant-filled room and collapsed onto the floor, the wall slamming shut. They both just lay there for a minute, trying to catch their breath.

Cole suddenly rolled over, grabbing her shoulders. "Tabitha. What were you thinking?" he yelled. "You just ran off without warning me! That— that was stupid! Dangerous!"

Tabitha turned her face away, blinking back the tears that stung her eyes.

Cole looked at her hair and cringed. It now reached to right above her chin and was all jagged and uneven. Cole must have noticed she was still shaking and covered in bruises and scratches from the thorns. His anger eased to concern. "I don't think I'm going to have a future in cutting hair at all," he said.

Tabitha laughed softly, still lying down, tears stinging her eyes. "If that's what you want to call saving my life," she whispered.

Cole sat up, and Tabitha struggled to follow. She looked up. Cole gently cupped her cheek in his hand. "Tabitha, are you okay?"

Tabitha nodded. "Yeah. How'd you do that? Fight like that? And why did those things not attack you?" Tabitha turned her brown eyes to him, though they still stung with tears.

"Fighting? I guess you haven't been in Sulfur. If you don't defend yourself, you're as good as dead." He shrugged as if it should have been obvious. "And I don't know about the tree things."

Tabitha sighed. "That thing said this was the Hall of Heroes, whatever that means. But Cole, it spoke about the Council." She frowned at him.

"Like what Miriam said. Being part of the Council is dangerous. They're killed immediately because they can open the door to the Realm…" Cole trailed off, his eyes growing wide. "Tabs, you don't think—"

"I do think it, Cole," Tabitha said, biting her lip.

Were *they* really destined to be the next members on this Council? Taryn *wasn't* crazy.

They left the conversation off there, not daring to say the words aloud yet. Once Tabitha stopped shaking, Cole stood up.

"Come on, let's get out of here," Cole said.

Tabitha nodded, standing up and adjusting Felicity's backpack, which was torn by the thorns. She took a deep breath.

"Are you sure nothing's wrong?" Cole said.

Tabitha looked up to him. "Is it weird if I ask…can I have a hug or something?"

Cole gave her a side hug.

It sent a wave of relief through her. Though it was awkward, and somewhat forced affection, it was still reassuring.

Cole let go of her, smiling hesitantly. "Okay, now let's really get out."

Tabitha followed Cole out of the Hall of Heroes with one final backward glance at the red mountain, hoping to never return.

Felicity groaned.

Her head throbbed, her ears ringing. She could barely put a thought together as she pried her eyes open, light blaring down onto her face. Her vision cleared, and she frowned up…into branches. The leaves went endlessly upward, and only cracks of sun spilled through on her.

She gasped and scrambled up to sit. She was sitting on a thick matt of braided branches, grasses, and foliage, trees going on around her.

She couldn't breathe.

She tried to stand up. Something snapped beneath her and a few seconds later, the crash echoed far below. Felicity carefully sank back down, making as little movement as possible.

She was in a *tree?*

She had to be hundreds of feet above ground.

How had she even gotten up there?

Her heart raced as she tried to recollect the last moments of her memory.

A chilling roar rang through the air and sent the sick feeling back to her stomach.

She looked down to her arms. They were covered in new bruises and cuts. She tried to keep herself from shaking the mat of branches was the only thing keeping her from plummeting to her death. The tree began to sway, and a soft buzzing ascended toward her.

Felicity's stomach flipped, but she told herself to knock it off and try to stand up. She needed to get back to her friends.

Something ripped through the bark of the tree. She could hear it tearing and crashing, a humming rustling toward her lair in the trees, hissing in a raspy voice. The thing crawled into the thicket of branches above her, circling.

Felicity gripped a branch to steady herself. What was that creature? She focused on where the creature was, preparing to defend herself as she pushed her fear down her throat. The scattering went quiet, till the only sound was the soft humming and swaying of the decaying foliage hanging from the trees.

Then, Felicity was slammed down onto the mat, the entire hammock of branches swinging back and forth wildly. A scream caught in her throat before it could escape. Long, scaly fingers pressed her head against the branches, but she lay frozen. If she resisted, she might fall right through.

The creature pulled her out from under it, holding her by her neck, leaving Felicity grabbing onto their hand for her life. The creature's skin—

No. It wasn't skin.

It was scales. Blue shimmering scales. It had two teeth escaping through the cracks of its lips, and its head possessed no hair or ears, only two small holes in the side of its head. The legs were bent in a fashion like the back legs of a goat and the feet curved out unnaturally with three toes and long talon-like nails. Rags of rotting foliage seemed to hang off the creature. As it breathed, a strange humming sound vibrated from its lips.

"L-let…" Felicity gasped, gaping at the creature.

The creature, towering a good foot above her, licked its long, snake-like lip. "Humanz?" it hissed. It shoved its face into her stomach, sniffing like an animal, then pulled back and frowned, licking her face with its long tongue. "No. Pup. Stale pup."

Felicity nodded rapidly. "Yes! Pup! Ch-child! I still need— need to graduate before I die!" she said.

The creature released her, letting her fall helplessly to the mat of branches. "Simple meat. Worth nothing." The creature sighed.

For some reason it made her blood boil at being called 'worth nothing', even by a weird monster. She was fed up with people saying that to her.

"Probably not taste good too. Fire hair."

Felicity almost fell through a crack.

Did that thing just say taste? As in eating her?

"I don't taste good! I promise!" she said, though it sounded pretty pathetic.

"Talk too much," the creature said.

Did she really talk too much? Her face was as red as her hair. The creature made a strange, wistful smile, and its humming grew louder.

The rhythmic hisses seemed to leak through Felicity's ears and into her body, making her feel as though she was being pulled toward the creature.

This was *not* how she imagined she would die. Being manipulated by a stupid creature? She had to fight it. She'd had enough people fighting her battles her whole life. It was time for that to change.

The humming music had the same laughter and joy in it as Tabitha's and the warm smile of the friend she'd left behind. Then something else flashed past her. The fires of North Cordell swarming through Liberty, the faces of those she couldn't recognize, but felt so attached to, falling before her. The earth overturning, with a small, sly smile on a hooded face that struck fear into her heart. But the last image was of two eyes full of fear, despair, and pain. Violet, and unknown.

But they spoke to her.

Like she knew them all too well.

Wake up, Felicity.

What was going on? She shook her head and twisted to looked below her and then back at the creature that was trying even harder to bring her to the bait. Felicity gave a fierce smile.

"This is long from over," she said, scrambling up and jumping through one of the torn holes, landing on a branch and grasping it for support.

What in the world had just come over her?

Felicity rolled onto the forest floor, looking up only briefly for the hissing monster, wildly racing down the trunk of the tree after her.

She scrambled to her feet, tore off her jacket, which was

in burned shreds, and threw it to the ground. She ran through the woods. She had only seen it outside of the auto window before but being in the middle of it now was completely different.

From the road, it seemed beautiful.

But now, it was a waking nightmare.

Huge trees. Giant spider webs draping from the branches. A musty, rotting smell hung in the air, and strange screeching noises cut through the rustling trees.

Her mind seemed a little sharper than it had been, and she tried not to let the anxiety build up in her. Every movement she made could get her killed. The faster she ran, the louder the heavy, enraged breathing of the creature could be heard, howling at her to return, sending creatures scuttling off in every direction.

Felicity skidded and tumbled to the forest floor, catching her breath, but didn't spare any moment to rest. She was at a dead end. The dark forest trees were braided together and all that was available for escape was the cracks in between the trees, that were dark and gloomy, and guarded by a curtain of moss and web.

Felicity stopped in her tracks, looking around desperately for a single crack, or any way to escape. Something dashed out of one of the cracks, sending Felicity back in fright. She picked up a fallen branch, and held it in front of her, ready to whack anything that dared approach.

The creature came out of the shadows and into a faint patch of light in front of her. It looked like a small dog, with the large ears and frisky red fur of a fox. Its eyes were an abnormal yellow and black color as if they belonged to a cat, not a dog. It stared at her curiously, but held its ground, ready to pounce if Felicity gave it any reason.

Felicity wasn't sure whether to wave the stick or take the chance at whacking the dog creature on the head and then run for it. She surely couldn't run anywhere now, except into the claws of another monster that was hunting her down.

She placed the branch down slowly and got down on her knees.

It sure wasn't a dog, but it was the only shot she had. She'd be eaten either way.

"Hey, boy," she said, in the friendliest voice she could muster, patting her knee and cooing the creature over.

The dog-like animal tilted its head in confusion and sat down, still looking at her as if saying "What are you trying to do?"

Felicity growled under her breath. She didn't have time.

"Hey, Buddy!" she said in a harsh, more pressing tone.

The animal growled.

"Oh. Fine. You don't like that?" she said, sitting down and crossing her arms. "What are you?" Felicity asked, leaning closer.

The animal leaned back and barked. It was a young, deep bark. It was a pleasant sound ringing in her ears.

"I don't understand, dog—"

"PUUUUUUPPPZZZ!"

Felicity bolted up. "Oh snap," she muttered, looking back at the dog, who had also jumped up.

It snarled, teeth bared, and rose into a threatening stance.

Felicity picked up her stick and braced herself.

The creature burst through the trees, screaming like it had gone mad, its sharp claws out and ready to pounce on the nearest prey—Felicity.

The dog snarled and prowled forward.

"Buddy! No!" Felicity called out. It would surely get

clawed to death by the monster.

But the little guy didn't back down. It bared its teeth and moved forward. The monster made an inhumane crackling noise, which enraged the little dog even further. The monster jumped out at it, but Felicity darted forward and whacked it so hard that her stick broke.

The beast turned to her, its scaly skin growing tight, and melted into a different shape, until another monstrous creature stood in front of her.

A lizard.

A *giant* lizard, with claws and fangs.

Felicity stepped back slowly, but the lizard had enough. It pounced, slamming her back against the ground. It would have ripped her into pieces, but the tiny dog jumped up and slashed at its exposed belly. The dog rolled, its fur disappearing and human skin replacing it. A boy morphed into view, with thick reddish-brown hair, blue curved marks down his cheek and collar bones, and his teeth that of a canine animal.

Felicity couldn't stop a gasp. He could *shift?*

But more importantly, why had this thing made himself more vulnerable!?

"Watch out! You idiot!" she yelled, trying to run to his aid, but the boy again made the strange bark at her and she staggered back again.

The dog boy jumped onto the lizard, shifting into a dog again and lashing out with his claws as the lizard did the same.

Finally, the lizard melted back into its hideous monster form and ran off, limping and screeching. Felicity ran over to the little dog, who was panting and lying on the ground, scratched but not mortally wounded.

She picked it up and hugged it. "You're sure something different," she gasped, and the little dog licked her. She put him back down, then looked around again. There was…a person behind its unusual eyes.

"Well done, Felicity." The young voice sent a shiver down Felicity's spine. *"Your friends will be glad to know of your findings, but you will find its meaning to yourself soon. I will come for you."*

And then it was gone. Felicity found herself gasping for air, her mind free and thrust back into reality.

The little dog sat staring up at her.

She cleared her throat. "I need to get out of these woods."

The dog nudged at her leg. *Where to?* it seemed to ask.

"The Imperial City," she said, frowning. "I mean, I don't know which way to go or if these woods can even get us there."

Why was she talking to a dog?

Yet the little canine seemed to understand and ran off through the trees. Felicity scrambled to her feet and ran after it. It must be leading her to safety, and for the first time in ages, she wasn't sure if she could be afraid.

LINCOLN TIGHTENED HIS GRIP ON THE LEATHER BAG SLUNG over his shoulder.

Something wasn't right.

The borders were nicknamed "wastelands" for a reason. The land was no longer fertile, dug up and dry due to the warfare of the EarthShaker. North Cordell didn't have a wasteland, but now that he'd crossed into the north regions, they were more common. His mind flitted through random scraps of knowledge.

United States of America. The place had been a war ground like the southern regions couldn't even relate. But that had left the earth dead.

Nikki stopped, tensing.

Lincoln halted as suddenly as Nikki did, reaching for his

bow. Something was moving.

No, not something.

Somethings.

The earth began to vibrate. Lincoln braced himself, pulling out an arrow.

Suddenly, roots began to tear free from under the earth and twisted into the air, small leaves sprouting from the branches that erupted from the bark. The trees began to age, moss crawling quickly around the trunks. The dirt below their feet turned and rolled like an ocean wave.

In almost moments, the part of the wasteland they'd stood in was alive.

Nikki inched closer to Lincoln, scanning across the new scenery.

Something scattered off in the distance, and a pair of yellow eyes blinked through the leaves, like creatures had been living here for ages.

Then, there was a blood-curdling roar.

Not a roar for any human or person at all. A roar so loud it hurt your head just to listen.

All the creatures scattered away through the trees. Lincoln was blown to the ground, covering his head.

"Get down!" he shouted, though he couldn't tell if Nikki had followed his instructions.

Whatever was making that sound wasn't letting up.

The roar gave a final blow, then echoed into silence for an eerie moment.

Lincoln looked up. Nikki had been thrown to the ground by the force, her eyes wide in both horror and amazement. A creature flashed across the sky and out of sight into the thundering clouds. Wings? Scales, that shimmered green in the sunlight.

Lincoln was ripped off his feet. An invisible force grabbed him by the neck and dragged him into the darkness of the still-growing wood.

"Lincoln!" Nikki yelled.

Through his gasps for air, Lincoln attempted to fight his opponent off. They disarmed him, throwing the bow and arrows into the woods and slamming him against the ground, pinning him down.

"Stop struggling or I'll kill you now."

Lincoln stopped instantly, not because of the threat, but because of the voice. That wasn't…no, it couldn't be.

His captor, still invisible, grabbed him by the shoulders and hauled him to his feet. The Oquelite shimmered into view, his hood covering his face. He was close to Lincoln's height, though Lincoln considered himself a little taller.

Another Oquelite burst into view.

"I have the Aviduous!" Lincoln's captor snapped at the newcomer. "Track down that girl!"

The other Oquelite dashed off as quickly as he could.

Anger burned through him. Lincoln lashed around, catching the Oquelite off guard and smashing him in the face with his fist.

The Oquelite stumbled back, his hood flying off. He jerked his head up, snarling like a wild beast, amber eyes burning with hate and anger.

Lincoln stepped back in shock, though some distant part of him had almost expected it already.

Ray smirked, not his usual playful smirk, but a deadly one as he wiped the blood from his nose.

Lincoln was slammed to the ground by the curve of a finger, pain bursting though his side, as the air was caught from his lungs. He caught the smell of smoke, his shirt beginning to dampen with blood.

"You're embarrassing," the Oquelite said, his voice cracking.

Raphael Mathews towered above him, a deadly energy swelling in his palm.

The truth fully took form in Lincoln's whirling mind, sickening him to the stomach.

Ray was an Oquelite.

40

NIKKI TORE THROUGH THE WOODS THAT WERE BURSTING TO life around her with every step she took. Hissing surrounded her and the stares of the little yellow eyes of creatures staring at her through the brush prickled down the back of her neck. The branches tore at her skin and face, but she kept running.

A part of her mind was screaming for her to go back to help Lincoln, but her instinct had taken over her body and forced her to run. They couldn't do much to him…besides torturing him, doing worse than rubbing the skin from his wrists, killing him, or draining the essence out of him like Avalon. She tried to ignore the swelling guilt.

Suddenly, the hands ran over her. They pulled against her waist, dragging her back. She pushed herself faster, struggling against the grasp. The hands crawled along her body, groping and scraping at her.

She continued to fight. She didn't have time to be manipulated by supernatural forces.

Run and don't look back. Don't let them touch you. The raspy words of the dead ran through her mind.

She'd given in. She'd gotten too comfortable and now look what had become of it.

She jumped over a fallen branch, but the hands threw her off balance and she slipped into the mud. She scrambled up again and ran. They would pounce on her if she even hesitated.

Now she could see Oquelites glinting in and out of invisibility, running through the trees. They glided through the trees in perfect balance, keeping up with her without the slightest struggle or noise.

Panic heated inside of her and she was tempted to reach into her pocket for the Stone. She fought that urge too.

No matter how powerful the Stone was, if the Oquelite saw it, she'd expose herself, and an Ewyon in Oquelite power could endanger everyone she knew.

The sound of rushing water caught her attention.

The landscape was growing steeper, and the hands were pulling harder. The crashing waves became louder as she began running higher and higher.

She was running straight for a cliff.

Nikki jolted to a stop, whirling around. The small pack of black-uniformed Oquelite shimmered into view, making their way toward her. She looked over her shoulder to the rushing river below. The Oquelite held their strange swords and some slick handguns.

One wrong move and she'd be blown to bloody bits.

Silas tore off his hood, tossing his flawless hair to the

side. He hadn't even broken a sweat. "What are you running from, little girl?" he asked, annoyed. He pulled out his sword.

Nikki began to back up, but the ground crumbled dangerously beneath her, stones and dirt crashing into the water below.

"You don't have anywhere to go, kiddo. Come with us, and everything will be…alright," he said smoothly. He stepped closer, and Nikki's heart quickened.

She needed to escape, but there was nowhere left to run.

Silas lunged out at her, but she ducked, sliding beneath his outstretched arm. The hands gripped her tighter, pressing her wrists into the ground. She jumped back up. The hands dragged her toward Silas. They dug their fingers into her, but she fought to maintain control of her own body.

Silas smiled, his companions chuckling a bit. "Come closer. Just let go."

Don't let them touch you.

Her brows furrowed, and she clenched her teeth. There was only one way of escape left. She took a painful step back.

Silas' smile melted away, his eyes flickering with fear. "You wouldn't," he sneered, though he didn't seem so sure.

Nikki's eyes flickered.

Silas lunged out to grab her, but it was too late.

Nikki looked into his eyes and jumped.

The water enveloped her, cold pierced into her skin and swirling darkness pushed the breath out of her as the current and waves of the river pulled her through the water.

The hands twisted her arms behind her back.

They were trying to kill her, but she couldn't think about that now.

With her hands bound, she could barely swim. Nikki clawed at the bonds, but she was thrashed by wave after wave.

No matter how hard she kicked, she kept sinking further below the rushing water.

Her lungs were screaming for breath. It was a lost cause, but she had to try.

A dark red stain flowed through the water around her, and panic stuck through her chest. Blood. It was coming from her.

The pressure was gaining on her. The swirling rush of water raced onward, pulling her helplessly with it.

Her head was going light. She forced herself to bring her hands under her feet and jammed her heels against the invisible bonds, straining to break them. The water swirled and tumbled around her, buffeting her even farther into the darkness.

Then something snapped. Nikki felt her wrists split apart.

She kicked upward, finally able to use her hands, but her lungs were burning and the higher she pushed herself, the more vicious and cruel the water was.

She was going to die.

Suddenly, her head burst over the waves. She gasped for breath, trying to take in as much of the precious oxygen as possible. Her head dipped back under. Her limbs ached, but she fought the water.

It seemed like an eternity when her foot caught up against something solid. She twisted her body, her arms breaking free, her hands grabbing onto a stone that sliced through her skin.

She cried out but inhaled a mouthful of water.

She pulled herself up above the water, threw her weight onto the muddy banks and dragged herself out of the rushing river. She coughed up water and crumpled onto the warm ground in the sun. For a moment, she refused to move. She wanted to stay there and die.

Her entire body was shaking. She reached up, brushing the blood from her nose, but smeared the blood from her hand against it.

She pulled her hand away to a smeared bloody mess.

Finally, she forced herself to sit up, her back against one of the trees. She looked back to the rushing river, the white rapids, crashing and carving through the land like it has been there for ages. She crawled hesitantly to the shore and dipped her hand in the water.

The blood washed away, but as soon as she removed it from the water, it began to flow again.

The cliff had appeared out of nowhere. The entire woods had appeared out of nowhere. How was she meant to keep track of directions when the land kept changing?

She noticed that one of the buckles on her left boot had been torn off in the rapids, and the top of the boot hung loosely around her leg now. Nikki looked back up to the cliff.

The Oquelite were gone now. Maybe Silas thought she was dead, and her body was at the bottom of the river now.

The trees rose high above her, their trunks twisted in glorious age, moss beginning to crawl along their bark, wild grass growing along the roots.

Nikki frowned.

Not just grass.

Pheomonea Fleux. The genetically modified healing plant Ray had suggested. Perhaps it could relieve at least the pain.

She ran, falling to her knees, tearing the plant from the

ground. It had the familiar forked leaves, and minty smell as she ground it between her fingers.

Nikki applied the paste to her cut.

Her crimson blood seeping into the paste. A tickling sensation ran down her palm. And then her mind went blank.

"Her vitals are low!"

"But she's survived, hasn't she?"

The world rushed back. She shook her head. Had Avalon spoken to her? The voices didn't sound like her at all. They had sounded so distant...and familiar.

She dipped her hand back in the water, letting the rapids wash away the paste and the blood. She pulled her hand back out, and gasped.

The cut was gone.

The only trace was a tiny thin white line in her palm.

Nikki sat back, staring. Was that normal? Was the paste that effective?

Maybe Ray hadn't been using it right before, and that's why it had never been very effective in the past.

But when *she* used it, it did wonders.

It had to be a coincidence.

What else could it be?

She dragged herself to her feet, leaning against the tree for support, and took a deep breath.

The strange forest was still growing, and it was growing fast. Maybe Avalon belonged in this supernatural phenomenon. Nikki looked behind her, hoping that maybe Lincoln would appear through the trees, unharmed, and the Oquelite defeated.

Nothing.

She sighed, turning back toward the wood. The Oquelite

were tearing apart the world. Despite the world trying to tear *her* apart in return, she had to stop them and whatever might be brewing below.

Even the darkest corners of her mind couldn't change her decision now.

41

THEY ALL MOVED AT A QUICK PACE, SORTING THROUGH THE supplies and preparing for their next attack, their black uniforms shimmering every so often as if the very fabric had its own soul. The young figure crouched in the shadows of campgrounds, watching each one cautiously for any suspicious movements. He'd been there for hours, his senses still heightened and crisp. He seemed to feel everything that could breathe around him. No one had dared interfere with him.

Ray looked down at his clenched, bruised fist. He felt so lost and angry. Cheated and lied to. He didn't know who needed to be smashed in the face. How come no one had warned him? Ever since he pulled that trigger and shot the Oquelite in the battle of North Cordell, new blood seemed to flow through him. Somehow, he could move from place to place.

Teleport.

He'd saved their lives out of the burning building, but now he wished he would have let them all die. He leaned his head back, closing his eyes.

He had been searching for Nikki after the battle, through the burning, decaying wilderness. He'd gone alone. He'd wanted to. He needed to sort things out with himself. He pulled out the knife Taryn had gifted him. Its silver blade felt wrong. Its hilt didn't seem to fit right in his hands.

Something whirled around him.

Ray jerked his head up, the knife cutting his palm. He winced, clenching his hand shut, and threw the knife into the ashes. The wind whistled through the bare, scrawny trees, blowing the ash and dust around the ground. A crow scampered around the ground, only stopping to stare at Ray, who growled at it. The crow flew off, cawing and screeching.

"Welcome, little hybrid." A cloaked and hooded figure shimmered into view, leaning against a tree.

Ray approached him with no fear. He caught sight of a sly smile from under the hood. Ray gave no reply, just a cold glare, hiding his wound in his hand.

"You know what you are, don't you?"

Ray glared at the Oquelite. "It's just stories."

The figure held his hands up. "This is quite a lovely story, isn't it?"

Ray scowled.

"You must fix what your father broke," the Oquelite said, crossing his arms under the cape. "You must fix what this universe has destroyed."

"I can't go through with this."

The figure gave an unsettling chuckle, as if what Ray had said was clearly foolish and stupid, and he stepped out from the shadow of the tree. "Not like you have a choice, hybrid boy. Not like they need you nor want you."

"My mother needs me."

"Silence! Those of your blood will be fine without you. It's your essence that separates you from them. You can't keep them safe anymore."

Ray frowned, stepping back, his heart beating hard in his chest.

"We're willing to spare you," the man said, stepping closer.

"And if I don't—"

Ray's arm suddenly pulled itself forward and his first opened. A blue mist escaped the wound and into the fingertips of the figure's outstretched hand, pain shooting through his arm.

"It's your choice."

Ray clasped his hand shut. He'd made his decision.

Now, he looked down to the blade they'd made him fight for. It was a curious thing. At first, he thought he was going to be killed when the man dragged him out. He yelled and begged, telling him he was an Oquelite too. The man in sunglasses sneered and muttered, "Mere hybrid."

He'd woke at the feet of Matthias Idicous. He'd talked a lot and Ray mostly ignored him, until Matthias pulled out the wicked blade. He wrapped a towel around the hilt, holding it up to Ray. He looked over to the other Oquelite in the room.

"Do you understand?" he said.

"Wait, what are—"

Matthias didn't wait. He raised the blade and plunged it through Ray's chest. Ray shut his eyes, bracing himself for death. Nothing happened. He slowly opened his eyes and looked down. He nearly screamed. The blade was impaled into his chest. There wasn't any blood, or pain, but it was terrifying. He couldn't speak.

The room went silent.

Matthias pulled the blade out and set it on his desk. "What are you waiting for?" he shouted. "Untie him!"

The soldiers scrambled to undo his bonds. Ray stood, bewildered, staring down at the blade.

"The Blade has chosen its champion," Matthias said, turning his eyes to Ray. "Now the champion must prove the Blade."

Apparently, attacking Lincoln in the woods was proof enough. The blade itself was curious. Matthias hadn't bothered to explain…or maybe he had and Ray hadn't paid attention. It had a glassy, liquid-like shimmer to it, the point of the blade stained with silver. If he pressed it against the ground, the grass would go up in smoke. He put the blade away.

"Hey, Mathews!" the red headed Oquelite called to him as he walked to Ray's hiding spot.

"Get lost, Zach," Ray growled at him, standing up.

"Matthias Idicous wants to speak to you. You can't just ignore an Idicous," Zach said, his tone becoming less playful, his eyes shifting around.

Ray scowled, pushing past Zach and into the light of the day. He threw the hood over his face to avoid the blinding sun that seemed to shine too bright today, and block out the sound of any potential conversation Zach tried to start. Ray followed Zach at a distance to a large tent, which was sheeted with metal and lit with the eerie grey glow of the Play Fire.

Ray pushed his way in, not going through the trouble to bow as Zach did. Matthias didn't seem to mind. "Thank you, Kendrick. You're no longer needed," he said.

Zach nodded and vanished into the air. Matthias's face automatically switched to a frown and looked at Ray. "What were you thinking?" He spat at him.

Ray shrugged. "Doing what was most important."

Matthias rolled his eyes. "I forgot you're still a young, and an unreliable hybrid. But how…how could you let the Aviduous get away?" Matthias said, his wispy greying hair flickering like a flame. "I thought you said he was weak."

"You failed to keep him in your control too," Ray said, unthreatened and partially annoyed, examining his nails.

"That's because of that girl, who Silas finally dealt with," Matthias said.

That caught Ray's attention. He jerked his head up so fast his hood flew off. "What do you mean?" he said, moving closer to the desk. Had they caught her?

"Silas says she went off a cliff into a rushing river. She jumped. Ignorant of her, but it is one off our list," Matthias said, his mood and hair calming a bit.

Ray bit the inside of his lip. He hadn't told Matthias or Silas that Nikki was an Ewyon. Possibly the only full-blooded one that was left. They'd have to search the globe to find another. He didn't know why he hadn't shared that information with them, but somehow, he felt it would be betrayal. But who was there left to betray anymore?

"Does that bother you?" Matthias said, leaning over the table and sniffing as if trying to sense Ray's emotions.

Ray jerked his head up, his face slipped back into his

solid, stone expression. "No. No, it doesn't," he said, clenching his fist.

"Then kill the Aviduous." The voice came from behind him.

Ray looked over his shoulder to see a face he despised.

Silas walked in, removing his gloves and shoving them into his pocket. He acted far different from his brother. In a more terrifying and intimidating way that Ray had been trying to reject for four long years.

"If the Aviduous is part of the Council, he needs to go," Silas continued, his eyes darkening as he towered above Ray.

"And if he's not, you still want him dead?" Ray guessed.

Silas gritted his teeth.

"Back to the point, Mathews," Matthias said, standing up from his desk. With the flick of a wrist, the desk was gone and now nothing was between the Idicous brothers and Ray. "You're being spared for one reason. Don't make us go back on it and have to slit the throat of one of our own. You're to go with a troop early, and don't mess this one up."

Ray gave a reluctant, obedient nod. He pulled his hood back over his face and turned for the flap of the tent.

"Hey kid."

Ray didn't turn to look at Silas, but he could feel the presence behind him as he left the tent.

"What do you want?" Ray said, finally stopping and turning on his heel to Silas Idicous, who seemed pleased with getting his attention.

"Just to give you a grant of luck," Silas said, breaking into a grin, leading Ray through the camp.

"Really? After all those times you tried to kill me?" Ray muttered, his mind flashing back to the wall of glass shattering into a million pieces and the fires that burnt down the place that was a second home to him. "Or is this about that sword thing?"

Silas gave a hoarse laugh. "Its proper name is the Shadow Blade."

"Stupid," Ray grumbled.

"You want control," Silas said, his voice dropping to a whisper like someone was watching his every move.

"Control? I want control over my fate, not over other people," Ray said. He gagged, a horrible shudder overcoming him.

Silas smirked. "You're still new to having new essence in your blood."

Ray shot him a glare, breaking into a coughing fit.

"I could tell you your fate, Mathews," Silas offered, his eyes lighting up, almost begging Ray to agree.

"If that's a temptation, I'm not falling for it," Ray said, moving on and trying to ignore the awful jolting of his stomach.

Silas followed. "It's a shame really," he said, looking over to Ray as he leaned over in pain, trying to catch his breath. "You really would be quite powerful, if you weren't too blind to see it."

42

As they left the alley, the streets were less crowded, and somehow the sun was rising.

Cole had gone in after Tabitha in the afternoon, but now the sun was rising Employees were arriving at their offices, and small shops doors were opening automatically on the eight o'clock call. Tabitha noticed it too, but she stayed quiet, though her eyes darted around and a frown creased her brow.

There was no way they'd been in the hall for an entire night. Cole tried not to think too hard about it, but it still disturbed him. Anything was possible now, wasn't it?

They'd reached the crosswalk when Cole saw a person out of place. A man, tall and sturdy, with hair dyed half black, and the other side pure white, dressed in leather. He ran across the road, without a sign blinking to let him cross. The tech simply ignored the man. When Cole was younger, he once tried to run across the street without the blinker telling him to go and everything seemed to go off, blaring alarms at him.

The strange man leapt onto the sidewalk and turned toward Cole and Tabitha. He studied them, and it struck Cole one of his eyes was *metal.* The man seemed to wait for them to follow. Cole just moved along like nothing was wrong, ready to run if the man attacked. They passed him, hoping he'd just lose interest and leave.

When they were finally far enough away, Cole looked back and noticed the man was dashing off. Tabitha let out a shout and wriggled out of Cole's grip, running after the man.

"Tabitha!" Cole yelled after her. Not again.

Then he noticed what had happened. The backpack, holding all their belongings, and Tabitha's precious binder, was no longer on Tabitha's back.

"Oh, come on!" he yelled. He ran after Tabitha.

She was surprisingly fast for her height. The man looked over his shoulder and scowled, picking up his speed and taking a sharp turn.

Cole skidded around the corner to find the man gone.

Tabitha waved at him. "Over here!" she shouted.

When Cole reached her, he found her pointing at a slim crack in between two walls.

"He went through there!" she said, trying to squeeze force herself through the crack.

"He couldn't have," Cole said.

Tabitha ignored him.

Cole pried her out from in between the walls. He leaned against the wall and peered into the dark crack. "You have to be sensible about—" Cole nearly fell over.

Part of the wall moved apart. He stared wide-eyed and unable to speak. Tabitha grabbed him and ran through the walls, not even questioning why the walls had begun to move.

But as soon as they opened, the walls began to close around them.

"Run!" Tabitha yelled.

Cole snapped out of his daze and broke into a sprint. The light of the exit was coming closer. The walls brushed up against Cole's shoulders. They would be crushed if they didn't do something fast.

"Tabs! Brace yourself!"

Cole ran faster, grabbed Tabitha and skidded out of the closing walls into the open air.

Tabitha jumped to her feet. "Second time you've saved me in less than an hour in my sane mind," she said, holding out a hand to him.

He took it gratefully. "Where is that thief?" he said, scanning around.

It seemed like another city behind here. Stalls were set up on all sides, their owners broadcasting advertisements, and little bots rolling around with directions to their owners' shops taped onto them.

Tabitha asked Cole if they could get one of the little robots. He said no, which left her disappointed, but only for a moment until she found something new.

The market was full of queer looking figures. Many had scars, tattoos, strange hair or none, or missing limbs. They were all dirty and rough looking, and no one seemed to take notice of Tabitha and Cole, who seemed to fit in fine, with Tabitha's roughly cut hair.

"We shouldn't be here," Cole muttered, leaning over to Tabitha.

"That's what makes it all the better," she said gleefully. "And besides, we need that bag. If he dares—"

"Yeah, I know. If he lays a finger on your binder, you'll kill him and punch him three times over. But after that we need to get to the Imperial City," Cole said with a low sigh.

"Authentic dragon scales! Back in stock!"

Tabitha jerked her head over to the stand. "Dragons?" She looked up to Cole. "Why didn't I think of this before?"

"They're clearly cheap fakes, Tabs," Cole said. "Dragons don't exist."

Tabitha glared at him. "Do you think other creatures exist too?" She turned to run to the stand, but Cole kept his grip on her wrist.

"Keep your cool. I can't have you running off again."

Tabitha grumbled something under her breath and slumped her shoulders.

"Hello young man."

Cole jerked his head around in shock, his instincts ready to fight, yet instead he was faced with a woman whose face was so wrinkled he could barely make out her features. Her hair was white and thinning and her tent looked like it was ready to collapse at any moment. Scrap metal hung from poles and piled across the ground.

He looked around, hoping to see another younger male walking by. "Me?" he asked.

"Yes, you," the old woman snapped.

Cole walked cautiously over to her stand. He couldn't disobey an old woman. He was never able to, even when he was young.

Tabitha, still in his grip, followed him reluctantly, heaving a groan.

The woman squinted — though it was hard to tell through all her wrinkles — at Cole. Then she spun around in her chair and leaned over, sorting through a pile of her metals.

She brought out a twisted knife and put it on the table. "Will it do?" she said.

"Uh. Ma'am, I—"

"No. You're right. It won't do." The old woman threw the knife right over Tabitha's head, and turned back to search.

Tabitha looked to Cole, her eyes wide. "I thought you said we had to hurry," she said through her gritted teeth.

"I know. We will," Cole said, though he could feel Tabitha's wrist tensing again like she was going to try to run.

The old woman spun back to them, her arms full of weaponry. She took out a mace, which sparked like a broken circuit, and she threw it out like she had done the knife. She laid out the pile in front of her. "Alright. Now search, child," she said.

Cole frowned. "Ma'am, I'm afraid you might—"

"You're here aren't you?"

Cole gulped. "Yes." He looked down at the pile laid out before him.

What was the harm?

This little old lady just wanted someone to check out her stuff. He didn't have to buy any of it. He let go of Tabitha slowly. She didn't run, just watched him. He moved over to the table.

"Choose wisely," the woman breathed.

Cole reached out for a curved, rusted knife, hoping to get things over with, but it jerked away, throwing itself off the table. He jumped a bit in surprise, but considering all the weird stuff they'd already seen, he wasn't too startled.

Tabitha noticed the jump and started to walk closer.

"The vines," she muttered under her breath.

He reached for a small pistol, and like the knife, it flew off the table and into the dirt. He looked over his shoulder at Tabitha, who was watching in fascination.

"Keep going," she said, giving him a small smile.

Cole gave her a nod, then closed his eyes, letting his hand scan over the table.

He could hear everything clatter to the ground. He felt around the table, about to open his eyes, knowing nothing had remained, when his hand brushed against something. It didn't fly off the table. He slid his hand onto the hilt.

He opened his eyes in astonishment to see a rusted broadsword sword in his hand. The hilt was made of tarnished silver, and wrapped in a tight, sturdy leather.

What *was* this place?

The old woman laughed with joy. "He did it. Yes. He did it," she crackled to herself.

Tabitha looked at him, her eyes wide. "What?" she said. "That's—" she didn't finish her sentence, just kept staring at him.

Cole continued to study the hilt. Something was below the dust on the guard. He blew onto it.

The dust was suddenly absorbed into the silver.

The entire sword seemed to polish itself, revealing the pure white blade.

"Now that's awesome," Tabitha said quietly.

But Cole wasn't listening to her. He was mesmerized by the sword's silver hilt, decorated with golden rays. "How much do you want for it?" he asked suddenly.

Tabitha frowned at him.

The woman laughed again. "It's yours," she said.

"Mine?" Cole said, looking wide eyed at the woman, then back at the sword.

"It's yours," she whispered again, placing a sheath onto the folding table.

It wasn't made for the sword; it was made only of cheap metal and was roughly welded to most swords. "Choose wisely," she whispered, again, pushing the sheath toward him.

Cole slid the sword into the sheath and slung it over his shoulder. He nodded, though he still wasn't sure what any of this meant.

The woman smiled, the corners of her eyes crinkling.

Cole found it hard to pull away, but Tabitha suddenly shouted, pulling at his arm. "It's him!"

Cole broke out of his trance, catching sight of the thief heading for a podium in the center of the market. Tabitha didn't even hesitate, running after him in full speed into the growing crowd around the stage.

Cole jolted around to thank the woman, but all he saw was an abandoned tent, empty, like no one had been there at all. The sword was still over his shoulder, but the amazement seemed to fade. Why couldn't she have given him something useful? Like a pistol?

He brushed it off and ran into the crowd, ripping past people, and shouting out Tabitha's name. "Tabitha! Where are you? Tabitha!"

People were closing in around him, limiting his movement. They all seemed determined to get as close as they possibly could to the podium.

"Cole!"

Cole saw Tabitha burst through the crowd in front of

him, her face breaking out into a grin with relief. "There you are!" she yelled.

He wanted to tell her to quiet down, but he could barely hear a thing with all the other conversations and yelling blasting around them. "Did you get the bag?" he asked.

Tabitha rolled her eyes, holding out her hands. "Obviously not, genius," she said, pointing up to the stage. "He went through the back entrance. He has to be performing or something. Maybe he's a clown. We just need to get the bag from him when he gets off."

It seemed straight forward. Just wait for the guy to show up on the stage then ambush him when he exits. Something like that. The details were definitely not finalized.

At least this time he was armed with something more than a dagger, which was an improvement to their previous circumstances. Cole grabbed Tabitha's wrist, making sure she wouldn't try to run off again.

The podium, a giant mechanical stage, rusted and worn from the weather, began to rise a few feet before a man erupted from the floor of the stage.

He was stout and looked shorter than average for his age. His hair was a thick, unnatural purple fluff that seemed to just sit on his head, and his leg was completely mechanical, decorated in magnets and paint.

He strode to the edge of the stage with a large grin, showing the gap between his teeth. The crowd went wild, screaming things, both cruel and supportive, or just plain screaming at the top of their lungs.

"This is a historic day!" he shouted to the crowd, his voice lisping slightly. "The Defending Department have finally taken a blow. One which it is hard to tear from the eyes of the public."

Defending Department? Cole looked to Tabitha who had the same look of confusion on her face.

"Defenders?" she said, looking up at him.

Cole shrugged.

Cole kept his eyes on the man on the podium. Something about him made Cole feel strangely uncomfortable. Maybe it was because he was up there bashing the Defenders, a group he mostly thought to be on the right side of the conflicts. But the more he thought about it, he knew that he never fully trusted Taryn, Conrad, or any other Defender.

The only two that stood out to him that earned the title of a Defending Officer were Miriam and Jack. They didn't revolt. They fought with bravery, and they were loyal. They were the only two loyal left now in North Cordell.

Maybe they'd been onto something about a Council. Someone needed to get the world back in shape before it tore apart.

The man continued to yell. "We now have control! We no longer have to fight! We are—"

"Tony, don't bore them."

The one-eyed man, a circlet now placed on his black and white hair, strode onto the stage. He winked to the crowd and the entire crowd cheered and screamed. He was clearly the favorite among them.

"Ah, Cecileo. You decided to show up after all," Tony said, holding his hands up to the man. "Here we have the Pater Cecileo Reuder!"

"Just had to pick up a few things," Cecileo replied casually, crossing his arms.

That comment made Tabitha wild. To Cole's relief she didn't try to straight out attack him, or pry out of Cole's grip again. She just gritted her teeth and squeezed Cole's arm hard to make sure he could feel her rage.

Cecileo walked to the end of the podium, scanning over the crowd. Everyone cheered wildly again.

Cole ducked, pulling Tabitha with him. "He knows we're here," he muttered.

Tabitha frowned.

Cecileo finally turned back, looking reassured. "As my fellow said in a long complicated fashion, we've come one step closer! The Defenders had their grip too long. Look what they've done to us. They took my eye. They took Deena's hand!"

A woman in the crowd cheered, holding up a stump of an arm.

"They took our homes. They took everything! That's why we call these markets home. Isn't it time we take away what true purpose they stand for? We've waited too long, standing around and waiting. We have power in our midst. The new age is coming! The government thinks they can make us happy with those petty defending officers, agents, and sergeants? The defenders' sole purpose is to destroy anything that stands in the Joined World's way. To destroy us. To destroy everything we hold dear to our hearts. What do we say to that?"

The crowd went crazy in agreement, throwing things and chanting.

"No! That isn't true!" a familiar voice yelled out.

Cole looked down at his empty fist. Tabitha was gone. How had he not noticed?

He groaned.

The short, dirty, scraped and bruised figure of Tabitha Delorous marched up to Cecileo.

He looked at her a little surprised, his eyebrows raised.

"Who are you?" he said slowly, enunciating each of his words.

"Tabitha Alyssa Delorous. And who do you think you are?" she said.

Cecileo laughed, but it was a nervous, thin laugh. He grabbed her by the collar, pulling her face toward his. "Where is the other one?" he snapped harshly.

Cole ducked, hoping none of the others would notice him, but Cecileo had seen him already.

"Nowhere, you idiot!" she said, struggling to get out of his grip.

Cecileo turned to the crowd. "The boy who so very kindly escorted Tabitha Alyssa Delorous into the Market, please let your presence be known," he said. "Or she and your belongings will not be seeing the outside world in a very long time."

Without thinking, Cole raised his hand, and ran forward to the podium. He said nothing, just glared Cecileo in his one eye.

Tony looked from Cole to Cecileo, genuinely confused.

The crowd was quiet for a moment, murmuring and shuffling nervously.

"Who are they?" one yelled out to Cecileo.

Cecileo didn't respond.

"Well, I don't like no undeservin' in my market!" came another voice.

Someone charged toward Cole. Cole ducked from the man's blade, pulling out his sword.

"He's armed!" another shouted from the crowd.

The man, who had only one functioning leg, and the other robotic, looked at Cole with a natural look of excitement and joy. He seemed eager to crush his face, like he'd done so many times before, Cole guessed.

"You know how to use your weapon lad?" he asked.

The real answer was no but saying that sounded like giving into an enemy. "Uh, yeees…" he said. He awkwardly straightened the blade.

The crowd grew excited by the presence of his blade. The man frowned at Cole's grip. Cole must have been holding it wrong.

"Now fight, boy," the man said, charging at him.

Cole tried to dodge him, but the balance of the sword's movement threw him off. The man gave a laugh. He dropped his own weapon and walked to Cole.

Cole tried thrusting his sword out in front of him, but the man just shooed it away.

"Stand up straight, boy," he said, pulling Cole's shoulders back.

He took Cole's hand and pulled his thumb onto the blade right above the hilt. "Grip it with ease, don't tighten so much," he said, adjusting Cole's fingers and turning the sword to the side.

The man backed up, his hands on his hips. "Now that's more like it. Try again," he said, grabbing his own blade from the ground.

Cole looked to his hands then back at his opponent. Why had he helped him? But right now wasn't the best time to contemplate.

The man charged, and Cole felt sure he was going to die, yet this time when he dodged, he didn't completely fall apart.

"Quit running, boy, or nothing's ever going to get done!" the man snapped.

Cole ran at him, clashing into his blade without even thinking clearly about it.

He didn't have time to think. Rely on instinct. How much did he trust his own body to keep him alive? Trust was something that didn't come easy with himself. He couldn't win this fight, but somehow every time his blade collided with the other, even though he hadn't won, it felt like a surge of new hope.

Like maybe he wasn't such a disappointment after all.

"Stop!" the voice of a woman erupted from the crowd.

The gathering parted to let a short woman, probably in her late thirties, make her way through. She had hair as black as night itself and large green eyes that seem to bulge out of her head.

"Cecileo! I called for entertainment, and boy, look here was you brought! Get that darn girl down here!" she said.

Cecileo growled, but reluctantly dropped Tabitha off the podium.

She was fine, but outraged, giving Cecileo a nasty glare.

"Cecileo is the finest swordsman in this age. If you can beat Doran and Cecileo together, you might have some entertainment," she said, glancing between Cole and Tabitha.

Doran, the man who'd already been fighting Cole, looked at her in surprise.

"I prefer the pistol," Cecileo muttered, jumping down from the podium.

"An inexperienced swordsman and a scrawny little girl, versus me and Cecileo? They deserve a little more than that," Doran said.

The woman looked over to Cole and Tabitha. "Do you have any other friends?" she said.

Cole shook his head. "Not here."

Tabitha snarled. "If they were here, we could rip your

face off before you had the chance to say a single word!"

The whole crowd gasped, some laughing.

"Really now?" the woman said, smiling, quite into Tabitha's proposition.

"Tabs, shut it," Cole said, under his breath.

She ignored him. "Of course, we could!" she said, folding her arms. "We're on our way to the Imperial City to meet them now actually."

Cecileo and Tony exchanged glances. "The Imperial City?" they said in unison.

Tabitha nodded.

"Then we'll have a showdown there!" Tony said, like a small child jumping up and down, clapping.

"No! That's not what I mean!" Cecileo shouted.

Tony looked down, disappointed.

Cole frowned. "What do you mean by a showdown?" he said. The word had a childish feel.

"The one we just experienced. Between you and Doran. It's what we've been waiting for," Tony said, dropping down from the podium. "But now, it's the blonde kid versus the Pater."

"Nice blade, by the way," Cecileo said with a slim smirk, grabbing Doran's sword. He thrust it at Cole, who blocked him almost instinctively.

The crowd cheered.

Doran ran to pull Tabitha away from the commotion.

"Can't we do anything?" she yelled at him.

"Can't mess with fate," Doran said.

"Stupid fate," Tabitha grumbled.

Cecileo seemed to fight with ease yet showed no mercy on his young opponent. "Tired yet?" he shouted.

Cole gave no reply, his heart beating in his ears. He

wanted to cut Cecileo's head off so badly. The fact that Cecileo was purposefully taunting him made him burn. Cecileo hit his shoulder with the blade and flung Cole off his feet.

He heard the sword scatter off somewhere and the world rocked back and forth, the sounds muffling into murmurs around him.

A little voice told him not to get up. Admitting defeat was easier. What was the point anyway? Just let Cecileo have him.

No future awaited him beyond this moment.

"Cole. Get up!"

He could see a blurry figure of Tabitha pulling at his arm. He couldn't back down.

No. They had gone this far. It would be selfish to die now, when so many lives depended on his right now.

He stood up and everything zoomed into focus. The crowd wasn't too pleased with Tabitha's interruption as they screamed for her to leave.

"Stay together. Remember?" she said, holding out her hand.

Of course, he remembered. That's how they stayed alive in North Cordell and that's how they intended to stay alive here.

Suddenly, the sword came flying back to his hand. His eyes were wide, but he tried to remember what Doran had said. Tabitha stood beside him.

To his shock, Cecileo dropped his sword. "You win," he said.

Tabitha and Cole looked at each other, confused. So did the entire crowd.

"Wait, how?" Cole said.

Cecileo laughed. "Us Marketeers fight for honor and

glory, not for winning. Though we bend our rules for many of our other hobbies," he said.

"Stealing," Tabitha coughed.

"And I think you both proved that as well," Doran said.

To Tabitha's delight, a Marketeer came out holding her bag. She ran and hugged it like it was her own child, pulling out the binder counting every page. The crowd was overjoyed with the show. They began swarming around, talking to each other and around Cecileo, who looked Cole hard in the eyes before disappearing into the crowd.

Doran strode to Cole, a grin on his face. "I knew you could do it," he said.

"Do what?" Cole said.

Doran looked to the blade. "You don't know what you're holding, don't you?"

"I'd like to."

"The Illuminate," Doran laughed. "Boy, you're a Council member. Perhaps I ought to sit you down in explain it all to you."

Cole opened his mouth to protest, his heart racing. "I know—"

"You better clean your wound though," Doran said.

Cole looked over to his arm where Cecileo had cut his shoulder.

"One question," Tabitha said, grabbing Cole's other arm.

"Ask away, little lady."

"What is this place?"

"The Market. Perhaps we're a bit of a rebel group, hidden away in the shadows of the cities," Doran said. "Our lesser-known purpose is to hold the Illuminate, until the Member comes to retrieve it. The sword decides its owner. Cecileo is the Pater, our leader. He helps the Illuminate decide."

Cole looked down to the sword.

"The fight is a life-or-death thing. If the holder is worthy, they can live. If not, Cecileo would have killed you. We stand for three purposes. Defeating the Defenders, selling illegal splendors, and finding the holder of the Illuminate."

Doran broke out of his serious tone and smiled. "Now, let's really do something about that arm. And maybe a little help to Imperial."

43

IF THE SIDEWALKS WEREN'T AS WET AND MUDDY, AND THE air wasn't as humid, and every inch of Lincoln's body didn't want to die, it might have been a bearable day.

He used the last of his money for a bus as far as it would take him, but he would have to walk from here. He didn't know what region he was in or what time of day it was or what day it was at all.

Standing upright was even a painful struggle.

The only good thing that had happened he guessed was that the wound in his side wasn't bleeding anymore. Or at least not through his jacket. His shirt was now permanently stained dark red. Every so often he'd have to remind himself where he was going.

He finally stopped and looked down the road. There

were only a few autos, and all of them sped by quickly not noticing him. The sidewalks were empty in the little neighborhood of houses. He should have expected it.

"Are you alright?"

Lincoln spun around, snapping alert.

A woman watched him, worry streaked across her face, and her hands full of grocery bags.

Lincoln blinked a few times. "Do…do you need help with that?" he asked, reaching his hands out for the bags and wincing slightly as his side pierced with pain.

The woman raised her eyebrows, but burst out into a smile and thanked him. She handed him a few bags, a small smile forming on her lips. "Thank you, child," she said, her voice soft and comforting. "Are you okay? You look… well…more than awful."

Lincoln released a small, tired laugh. "I'll be fine," he said. He looked up into her eyes, which had a flicker of warmth he'd never seen before. Then she nearly dropped her bags. Lincoln flinched. She must have seen his eyes.

But instead of trying to pass him quickly, as most did, she collected herself and smiled again, then hugged him with her arms full of bags. Lincoln wasn't sure how to react.

The woman backed up, her face beaming, with a mysterious joy. "I can't believe you've finally come. I don't live far from here—oh goodness. Your parents most likely don't want you associating with strangers," she said.

"I never knew my parents, ma'am."

The woman frowned for a moment. "Oh," she said, her eyes softening. "I'm sorry."

Lincoln hadn't expected the apology. He wasn't even sure how to respond.

The woman sighed. "You must come with me. My home's

not far, and you can just drop off the bags. Then maybe we can make sure you don't starve to death and I can give you directions to anywhere, if you need them."

Lincoln thanked her. It might be nice just to relax for a moment, rather than struggling to keep awake while walking to a city he barely knew the way to.

"Dr. Blythe," she introduced herself. "What do they call you?"

Lincoln walked alongside her feeling his energy returning to him. "Just Lincoln," he said.

"Well, then Just Lincoln, where might you be from?" Dr. Blythe asked him.

"I came here from North Cordell," Lincoln said, wincing again as his arm brushed against his side.

Dr. Blythe's eyes widened, and her face darkened as she turned to him. "We must hurry, young Aviduous," she muttered.

Shock grabbed Lincoln's breath away.

Dr. Blythe and Lincoln snuck through the neighborhood, her head constantly whipping around making sure no one was watching them. She opened a little white gate to the front of the house, and the two slipped in. The small suburb house looked so homey and welcoming. The gardens were well tended and made its ugly gray surrounding look somewhat bearable. The outside walls of the house were covered in vines crawling through the brick.

A little face peeked out from the bright red front door. The little boy's face lit up and he swung the door open the rest of the way. He ran up to Lincoln, a childish grin on his face as he jumped up and down. He had bright eyes and dark brown hair, like his mother's.

"Adam, don't pester him," Dr. Blythe scolded softly.

Lincoln followed her into the house, placing the bags on the counter of the small kitchen. Adam followed close behind.

As soon as Dr. Blythe shut the door, she called out for some help. A tall, lean girl made her way down the stairs and smiled at Lincoln cheerfully, brushing her bushy, black bangs out of her amber eyes. She quietly walked over to her mother and began unloading the bags. Lincoln turned to help her, but Dr. Blythe grabbed him gently by the shoulder.

"They warned me this day would come," she whispered, looking so angry and upset she might begin to cry.

"Jenna, please help him. He's wounded. I'll be back." She patted Lincoln on the shoulder and forced him into a chair before she hurried down the hall.

Lincoln watched her go, brow furrowed.

The girl, who must have been Jenna, walked over to Lincoln, but Adam jumped up onto his leg before she reached him, squealing. "You got black eyes! Like in mam's stories!"

Lincoln laughed nervously, a little stunned at the little boy's reaction. "Yeah. I-I guess I do."

This answer only made the little boy more excited. "How old are you? A million?"

Before Lincoln even had a chance to answer, Adam chattered away with more questions.

"Can you lift a truck?"

"Do you really talk to animals?"

"Are you awesome with swords and stuff?"

Finally, his older sister interrupted him. "Adam! Calm down and stop annoying him. You're going to hurt him!" she said, giving Lincoln another nervous smile.

"He's fine," Lincoln said, looking back to Adam, who was

now sitting on a stool turning round and round.

"I'm afraid he's a little obsessed with Mam's tales. Especially of your race," she said, placing her delicate hands behind her.

"Well, that's sure something new," Lincoln said.

Jenna gave a small laugh. "You're not what the legends say Aviduous should…look like," Jenna said, as she began to fold up the bags.

Lincoln got up to help her. "I get that a lot," he replied, clenching his fists. *Breathe.*

Exhaustion sapped at his strength, the pain in his side hitting him again.

Another boy came in through the front door. He looked at Lincoln for a moment before giving a small smile. He couldn't have been any older than fourteen. "Mam said she found an Aviduous." He laughed, holding out his hand. "Noah, Fourteen, Glorgory."

"Lincoln, Fifteen."

Noah shook Lincoln's trembling, sweating hand. Lincoln took his hand away and wiped it against his shirt. He could barely function. Stupid sleep. Stupid pain. Fresh blood had seeped through his shirt, and now his hand was sticky.

Jenna gasped. "Oh goodness, you *are* hurt!" she shouted, running to steady him.

"How long have you been out there?" Noah asked.

"Three days or something like that," Lincoln admitted drowsily.

The last time he had rested was the night in the woods. Since then, surviving was the only thing on his mind. Lincoln awkwardly removed the jacket, as he was guided back to a chair.

"It can't be too deep. Adam! Get the HCS kit!" Jenna

yelled to her brother.

His eyelids were heavy. His mind screamed for him to keep them open, but he was weak, and he hated that. The pull was too strong, and he shut his eyes, letting the world sink away into darkness.

Early morning sun was shining in the window when he awoke. It took Lincoln a moment to remember where he was.

A stranger's home. A stranger that knew about the Impure. A stranger who'd been expecting him.

He pulled himself up and winced, grabbing his side. His fingers met a neat bandage, wrapped tightly around his middle.

He stared at the ugly cuffs still around his wrists. The bandages from the defenders had been replaced with clean ones too.

Jenna was right.

He had been exhausted.

The room was small yet seemed to be organized enough to make it livable. The bare walls were gray, with the paint chipped off in certain parts, like someone had been picking at it. The closet doors had been removed and on the inside was a desk made of wooden packaging crates and a stool from the kitchen that was missing part of a leg but held up by a stack of crushed cardboard boxes.

Lincoln looked over the desk, obviously occupied by someone semi-recently.

A crumpled piece of paper teetered on the edge of the desk like it was about to fall. Though he knew he probably should respect whoever it belonged to, his curiosity got the better of him and he unfolded it.

Congratulations! You have been accepted into the University of North Cordell.

Lincoln frowned.

North Cordell?

The rest of the form was ripped and scribbled out in rage.

Whoever it belonged to had obviously not accepted the invitation. He crumpled it back up and returned it to where he'd found it. He turned to leave when his hand hit the mug of pencils off the corner of the desk. He scrambled to catch it, but the pencils scattered onto the floor, and the stack of papers under the mug fell to the ground.

Great job, genius.

He collected all of the styluses and pencils as fast as he could and began stacking up all the papers again. Most of them were blank or with little notes in Anglish. He finally put the mug back on top, satisfied. He back away, but something crinkled under his foot.

He jumped back. A small, wrinkled photo lay face up on the ground. Lincoln kneeled to pick it up.

It was a photo of the entire family. Jenna, Noah, and Adam.

And another boy in the photo. A happy one. Amber eyes, sly smile, and black hair.

The boy was undeniably Rapheal Mathews.

Lincoln's heart skipped a beat, holding the photo closer. It was Ray, for sure. His mind began to scramble. Coincidence?

No. It couldn't be. Why was the stupid boy showing up everywhere?

He was going crazy.

He dropped the photo, shooting to his feet.

Jenna, Noah, and Adam were Ray's siblings. This couldn't have been a coincidence. Dr. Blythe knew something he didn't.

It didn't make sense.

Ray was an Oquelite. So how could he be related to these people? He grabbed his jacket and ran out into the hallway.

He burst into the kitchen to see Dr. Blythe—or Dr. Mathews, whoever she was—standing in the kitchen, staring into her mug.

She looked up at Lincoln, who stared at her, trying to catch his breath. He didn't even have time to think. "Rapheal Mathews is your son?"

Dr. Blythe gave a weak smile. "You're clever for an Aviduous," she said, motioning for him to come sit down.

"You lied about your name?"

Dr. Blythe gave a soft smile. "You may call me Mrs. Mathews if that suits you better, boy."

Lincoln walked to her cautiously. "You—you're an Oquelite?"

Dr. Blythe gave a tired laugh. "No. Far from it," she said.

"Then what are you?"

"I'm an Unidentified," she sighed. "Not a hybrid. Not close to a full-blood. Lincoln, you have no idea how long I've been waiting for you."

Lincoln was still tense. "Why? How do you know what I am?" He frowned. "How do you know *who* I am?"

Dr. Blythe stared at her reflection in the drink, laughing softly to herself. "Child, the human races aren't much of a secret. Before the EarthShaker, they used to openly address the races. And of course, you must know what happened after the war in the Dark times."

Lincoln nodded; the knowledge had always been present

in his mind. "They tried to erase all previous history to join all the previous countries, wanting no separation or inequality. So, it's just not in the public anymore, unless you decide to become a Defender, right?"

Dr. Blythe nodded, leaning against the counter, taking in a deep breath. "There are still are common people who wish to educate themselves properly. I know perfectly well who and what you are," she said, sipping from the mug then setting it back down on the table, both her hands clasped around it. "I knew I'd have to find an Aviduous. He would be the one I would tell."

"Tell what?" Lincoln asked. He felt as if this conversation was getting him nowhere.

"Tell you the story that will destroy the Council," Dr. Blyth said calmly. She turned to look at him, so he could see the sorrow and regret glinting in her amber eyes.

Lincoln couldn't bear to be angry at her. "What is it?" he said, walking closer, and standing right in front of Dr. Mathews' hunched figure.

She looked up at him with a small smile in the corner of her lip. "A simple explanation really," she said. She immediately turned, straightened herself, and began. "The children already knew some of the Impure history. That's how Adam took a fancy to you, because he finds the Aviduous like a superhero race. I had told Ray some of it, hoping it might be able to save him, yet he refused to believe any of the rubbish." She hesitated, shaking her head sadly. "I didn't want to press the truth onto him when he kept denying it."

That would be dangerous, Lincoln knew.

"He was the only one who inherited Oquelite blood," Dr. Matthews said softly, confirming Lincoln's suspicion.

"Why?" Lincoln asked. "His father?"

Mrs. Mathews nodded. "I am a doctor. Years ago, during Glorgory's last little rebellious outbreak. A soldier came to me with a child barely older than a year—"

"Ray?" Lincoln interrupted.

Dr. Mathews raised an eyebrow. "No. This child was not *my* son. The child was dying, and the man couldn't heal him. That was the first time I had ever laid eyes on an Oquelite in uniform. Beat, wounded, and feared by everyone. I healed the child and wed the soldier a year later."

Mrs. Mathews stopped, seemed hesitant to continue, but she kept her face calm and her posture strong, and managed to move on.

"He educated me on the Impure, folklore and legend, and most of all, the truth. All the things the EarthShaker had erased. The Oquelite came looking for him a few times. He was miserable, hated the order. Then, one day, they just stopped coming. Until *my* son was born. The Oquelite were furious.

"They attempted to kill me and my son. We first understood when the child opened his eyes. They sparked like a flame when they first opened. So alive. When an Impure child first opens its eyes, it shows their power, and my son was beyond anything my husband had ever seen. He was Oquelite, and no ordinary one. He was a Hybrid. Not a full Oquelite, but the power could compete with any fullblood.

"That was the night my son's destiny was doomed. The child I healed—now my step-son— was an offense to the Oquelite. He wasn't a threat, no Impure in him, but like my son he was against the Oquelites orders. I couldn't understand why they hated the older boy so much.

"Yet when an Oquelite son was born, the Oquelite saw this as a threat. His essence was too powerful, another stain on the Oquelite souls. The Oquelite claimed that my son would fall in line with them to accept a destiny. One they said about Ray...killing the older boy. A curse some might say.

My husband moved away with the older son to be raised separately to keep them apart, so the Oquelite couldn't target us all. He came back occasionally for periods of time, until he couldn't. And he didn't."

"Your son was Rapheal Mathews," Lincoln said, in a low whisper, his eyes trailing away from her face. "He's an Oquelite."

He shot his head back to her. "What does this have to do with me?" he asked.

Dr. Blythe stood up, putting her hands on Lincoln's shoulders. "You're part of the Council, my boy. Isn't that clear yet?" she said, laughing and pulling him into an unexpected embrace.

Lincoln tried to process what she was saying. Part of the Council?

Dr. Blythe finally released him, the childlike excitement shaking in her hands.

"How?" Lincoln said, looking down at himself. "That can't be true."

Dr. Blythe noticed his doubt, and lifted his chin. "How can it not be?" she said, with a small smile. "The world's heroes cannot all be the same, that's how we got into this mess."

"So, you think I'm in the Council...and Ray?"

"Ray and his brother."

"Noah? Adam?"

Dr. Blythe laughed. "His older brother. I think you might

know him as Coleson Johnson."

Lincoln's jaw dropped. It couldn't have been possible. Everything around them was planned by fate. He wasn't sure if he liked that fact. Cole? Ray's brother? "But how?"

"Fate has its ways. So do the Shadow and Illuminate," Dr. Blythe said, taking a sip from her mug. "And I have kept in touch with his father. I hoped they might come across one another, especially when the peculiar Sergeant reached out."

Lincoln was speechless.

"What did I say about heroes not all being the same?" Dr. Blythe laughed, standing. "You have no idea how many people have been preparing for this reformation. People who know about your past, Lincoln."

"Y-you know about…my past?" Lincoln's throat had gone dry, his head whirling. "H-how?"

"The time will come for you to learn that infor-mation."

Lincoln held his head. "B-but why? Why *us?*"

"Because I think the world's ready to get a little banged back in shape. There are forces far worse than the Oquelite coming for us. And it might just take something new to withstand them."

A warmth spread across his chest, despite the confusion. He was beginning to like Ray's mother. She was a determinedly cheerful, sturdy woman. A little like he imagined his own mother might be.

"Alright then. You said you needed to get to the Imperial City?" she asked.

"Yes," Lincoln said, nodding and steadying himself as his head whirled.

He was beginning to see why they had to go on this crazy quest after all. If there were all on the council…

"Good. We'll get you there."

Lincoln dreaded his departure.

He'd spent the morning with the Ray's siblings, who were thrilled to hear that he knew their brother. They flooded him with questions, and he ended up telling them a summary of what happened, leaving out a few parts, like Conrad blowing the base up, and other gory details.

The first thing Adam yelled when Lincoln finished was, "Did my brother hurt you?"

Lincoln scrambled to answer him, not wanting the little boy to lose faith in his older brother. "No! No…He's saved us. A lot," Lincoln said, patting Adam on the head, and the little guy broke into a grin.

Now he stood outside the door of the house, Mrs. Mathews' written directions in his hand on how to get to the nearest SpeedRail. She gave him one last squeeze, muttering, "I'm counting on you, Aviduous. Make sure my son is safe."

He wasn't the best at protecting people, especially if they were Ray, but he agreed anyway. There was no way he could say no to someone with the love of a mother.

Mrs. Mathews squeezed his shoulders, a shimmer of tears in her eyes. "And remember, Coincidence is always Fate," she whispered. "Do not ever forget this."

Adam ran up to him, his eyes wild with excitement as he handed him a stack of hand drawings and notes. "Some are for you, and some for Ray. Give them to him when you see him!" he said.

Lincoln put the stack of sticky, colorful paper into his bag. "I will," he said. He gave Adam a pat on the head, which made him squeal.

Jenna, who had spent the entire morning pouring out stories about her brother whom she adored so much, brushed her hair from her eyes again.

"Good luck," she said. "And if you ever need a Medic better than Ray, let me know." She kissed him on the cheek and made her way back to the house.

Lincoln finally walked out of the gate, and it slammed behind him, automatically locking. He continued his path, now knowing where he was going, and fully awake, yet he couldn't get his mind off the Mathews family and Ray and Ray's...brother.

Maybe he had underestimated Ray's origins, and his own.

44

THE SKYSCRAPERS SOARED ABOVE THE TRUCK SO HIGH INTO the sky she couldn't even see where they ended.

Tabitha stuck her head out of the window, her short hair flying around her face, and let out a cry of relief. "We made it!"

She looked back at Cole, sitting in the middle of the truck, his sheathed sword across his lap, and his arm bandaged. He sat with his chin in his hands, quiet and exhausted.

Tony had turned on the most terrible music, following along to every screeching word. Doran sat in the other seat, looking around the Imperial City, gripping a pistol casually in his hand.

The gun made Tabitha a little nervous. When someone

was holding a weapon it meant trouble. What was Doran expecting to find? The city looked completely safe to her. It looked very similar to Liberty.

Tabitha plopped back down next to Cole. "Isn't it great?" she said, elbowing him.

"Uh-huh."

"It's amazing. Just like Liberty, but way better."

Cole looked up. "Liberty? What's it like there anyway? A big city with fancy hotels lining the streets?" he said.

Tabitha laughed. "Where have you been all this time? North Cordell?".

"Sulfur, actually," Cole corrected her.

That was the first time she heard him mention his home region. All she knew was that Sulfur was a populous region full of mines for the Foundation Field Project. Many less fortunate families flooded there for work.

"So, you were a working kid?" she said.

Cole shook his head. "Nope. I got kicked out a week after I turned eleven."

"Why? What did you do?"

"Nothing that I remember."

Tabitha frowned. "Then how did you get into a university?"

Cole bit his lip, shifting in his seat to turn toward her. "My father was promoted in the Fields to a supervisor," he said, keeping his voice low, like it was some sort of sin to mention it. "I was teaching myself to read, and had been playing the piano ever since we found one in the alley way when I was six."

Tabitha felt guilt hit her in the gut. "There's no way for you to get back into the university?"

Cole shook his head, then shrugged. "Where things are

heading, it wouldn't matter anyway."

Tony's groan interrupted them. The music finally took an advertisement break, much to Tony's disappointment, and Doran turned around in his seat to them.

"What's that number again?" he asked.

"5516," Tabitha said.

Doran nodded, repeating the number to Tony.

There was a moment of silence. Tabitha hummed under her breath, tapping her knees. She clenched her jaw, looking back to Cole. "I'm sorry for punching you."

Cole frowned.

Tabitha could feel herself growing warm. "Two years ago?"

Cole tilted his head, his frown growing deeper, then his eyes widened. "That was you?"

Tabitha bit her lip and nodded.

Cole's lips parted, studying her, then he burst out laughing. "So, there is a reason you hate me so much."

Tabitha flushed red again. "I don't hate you anymore," she stammered. "I just mildly dislike you in some aspects of your personality."

"That's not what it was."

Tabitha pulled her legs up to her chest, shaking her head. "Someone took my binder," she muttered, looking away from him. "It was stupid. They dared me to talk to you. And I guess...I got...slightly carried away and..."

"Hold up, your binder?"

Tabitha scowled. "That's not related! Those girls were pathetic. So immature."

"Says the person who freaked out over a binder," Cole muttered.

Tabitha punched him in the shoulder. "The point is I've

been unnecessarily holding a grudge over nothing. And I'm sorry. I have no real reason to be angry at you besides the fact that people like you and you seem to just … have it easy." She buried her face in her arms.

Cole placed a hand on her shoulder. "Hey, I'm sorry too, Tabs."

"You didn't do anything wrong," Tabitha said, squeezing her fists. She'd been pointlessly using him as some sort of emotional punching bag. Her pride got the best of her, and she never imagined it to be so hard to admit it.

"Tabitha?" Cole said, moving closer. "Is there anything else?"

Tabitha looked up to Cole, his eyes full of concern, a worried crease forming on his forehead. She gulped, pulling him down to her height, and whispered into his ear. "I'm a third child," she said.

"Liberty. The two-child thing. For each of the five capitol regions," he whispered. He squeezed his eyes shut like he was trying to figure it all out. They burst back open. "And this makes you wrong?"

"Embarrassing," Tabitha said, biting her lip, her heart beating faster against her chest. "Please, don't tell anyone else about this."

Cole pressed his lips together and nodded. Tabitha forced a small smile.

The car suddenly swerved, causing other shining cars honk at him and yell out their windows.

"Gosh, these snobs. Think they own the road!" Tony yelled.

They approached a section of the city where the skyscrapers were replaced by huge houses. Tabitha had seen mansions, but these houses were better than the ones she dreamed of. Some floated above the ground, and others were over ten stories high.

"5516. Here we are," Doran announced.

The truck bit the brakes abruptly in front of a house, its walls painted with whitewash, and the ceiling curved up to form a U-shape. Tabitha pushed the door open and jumped out onto the pavement.

Out of the huge, white front doors, Miriam Outown burst out in full speed. She stopped in her tracks, her jaw dropping.

"You're alive!" Her lip curled into a smile.

She jogged to Tabitha and ruffled her hair. "Nice cut, Stump."

Tabitha couldn't be mad at Miriam. She was so happy to finally be able to let down her guard and relax that she could barely speak. *They made it.*

"Thanks for the ride!" Cole yelled to Doran.

"Anytime! We'll be around, kid. Call us whenever you need a hand!" Doran shouted back, the truck zooming away down the street.

Cole turned and barely had a moment to take in the surroundings before Miriam was hugging him as well. "Good to see you too, Miriam," he gasped.

As soon as she let go of him, she overflowed with questions. "How'd you get a ride? And from a Marketeer?"

"Long story. Sword fights, and stuff—"

"And why are you so late?"

"Because—"

"What did you do to your arm?"

Cole gave up trying to answer her flood of questions.

"Well, it's good that you made it here at all. Welcome to the…er…my parent's house," she said, biting her lip as her face went red.

"It's awesome," Tabitha said. "You live here?"

Miriam shrugged. "I used to. I'm a Defender, I do things for myself now."

She led them into the house, which was even more stunning than the outside. The walls soared high above them, the ceiling decorated with silver designs. The floor was marble, and so clean Tabitha could see her grimy reflection looking back at her. The chandelier hovered above them, sending light dancing across the walls through its dozens of crystal shards.

"There they are," a voice came from behind them. A familiar one.

Tabitha and Cole turned around to see Taryn. Tabitha wasn't sure whether to be relieved to see her or yell in her face for how much trouble she had put them through to get there.

Taryn looked like she could be a casual, normal woman, in jeans and tennis shoes, but in Tabitha's opinion Taryn was neither casual nor normal. Taryn looked the two of them over and raised her eyebrows. "You might want to freshen up. We have a lot to discuss," she said.

Tabitha raised her eyebrows in return.

Freshen up? That was an understatement. Right now, a shower sounded like heaven.

PART FOUR

THE FRIEND

45

IT HAD BEEN NEARLY TWO IN THE MORNING WHEN LINCOLN heard the main door of the Outown manor thrust open, and Felicity's voice immediately begin to rattle on, in a panicked, breathless pace, Miriam trying to calm her down.

He only arrived a half an hour previously, and still hadn't met with Taryn. He'd taken a quick shower and followed Dr. Blythe's directions to properly tend to his wound. He'd left the washroom and was quickly greeted by Felicity's voice.

"No! No! Miriam! You don't understand—"

"Felicity, you're going into hysterics. Calm down!"

Lincoln threw on his jacket and ran down the hall to the main entry way. He pulled the jacket down over his head and stopped in his tracks.

It wasn't just Felicity and Miriam who stood in the dim

light of the chandelier.

"Nik!"

Nikki's small figure jumped, startled, from behind Felicity. Her clothes were spattered with mud, her hair tangled and frizzy, a buckle on her boot torn clean off, and her arms covered in scratches.

But she was alive.

Felicity had fallen silent, and both her and Miriam had turned to look at him.

"You made it as well," Miriam said, flashing him a smile. "I didn't see you come in."

Lincoln shrugged. "Jack let me in."

Nikki still stood staring at him, like she couldn't believe her eyes, and in a moment, if she blinked, he might not be there. Then, she shook herself off, blinking a few times, and gave him a shy wave.

He waved back.

"Gears," Miriam looked to Lincoln. "Show Squirt to an empty guest room. Down the hall and to the left—" She turned to Felicity "—and you, come with me."

Felicity frantically brushed her matted hair from her face as she followed Miriam out the opposite door of the room, leaving Nikki and Lincoln alone.

She walked slowly to him, her every step on the marble floor echoing off the towering walls. "You're alive," she said.

"And so are you." He stepped aside letting her through to the dark hallway.

She followed closely to his side as they made their way into the darkness. She smelled of dirt, and...blood?

"Nikki, are you okay?"

"Yes."

"What happened?"

She hesitated. "I saw Silas. I got caught in a river."

Silas? The Oquelite had pursued her? Chased her? If Ray was an Oquelite, they must have known *she* was the Ewyon. Lincoln's mind went wild. He contained his panic. He wasn't about to freak out in front of her. "A river?" he said coolly.

"Yes." Her eyes stayed glued on the floor.

She was alive.

Light poured out from under a door, the soft sound of muffled music, coming from the room. A fork then came in the hallway. Lincoln turned them left. As they stepped into the hall, gently lights burst on, hanging from the hallway ceiling, revealing a row of doors against a magenta wall.

The manor had sensors that triggered lights? Lincoln was astonished. That was beyond the tech he'd ever seen in North Cordell.

"Whichever one you like I guess," Lincoln said, holding his hand out.

Nikki didn't turn to choose a door, only watched his face tentatively. The dim lights cast shadows across his face, her hair fallen uncared for across her muddy face. Then she looked away quickly. "Thank you?" she said quietly.

Lincoln smiled. "Yes, thank you. And I say, you're welcome."

She nodded, glancing at him before turning to the nearest door, and with her touch on the knob, the door opened. She jumped, then shook of her startle and walked inside. She peered out, back at him. "Talk later?"

"Tomorrow. Yes," Lincoln said, nodding.

She nodded in return and closed the door behind her.

She was alive. And why should he care? She was simply an Ewyon. An adorably ignorant girl to the world. He was a full-blooded Aviduous who was better at creating weapons than using them. He was here because his life depended on it, not because he'd grown soft.

He began to walk out of the hall, the lights falling dark.

But he *was* soft, wasn't he? The whole reason he was in this mess was because he'd helped some kids escape the Oquelite.

But his life wasn't worth them. His entire life was based on survival, and being alone, and he wasn't going to stop now.

Bang!

"Wake up!"

Lincoln's eyes fluttered open, cringing, light blinding him.

"Oh Fate, are you up yet?"

Lincoln jerked up. Panicking for a moment at the unfamiliar room. It was huge, the ceiling towering above him, a fireplace empty at one wall, the baseboards tainted with gold. A huge window looked out over the court-yard; the green drapes pulled back by golden rope.

The Outown's manor.

"I'm awake!" His voice cracked. He cringed, stumbling out of the huge bed.

"Good," Miriam called. "Dinner is in five hours sharp. You're expected by Taryn to attend."

"Five hours?"

"It's 13.00" Miriam sighed, her footsteps turning and walking down the life.

It was *afternoon*? He'd slept in that late? He jumped up, immediately alert.

He spotted his bag set on the oak dresser by the wall. He found the drawers filled with clothing his size, though most of it was Imperial finery that he could never imagine wearing. He managed to find one pair of pants that wasn't tight fit, or laced with silver, and covered the fine button up shirt with his jacket, to keep it from being ruined.

He left his room, and explored the long twisting, empty hallways, stopping when he found two slim, tall, windowed doors. Through them he saw a parlor, decorated with white, and gold, sofas, a ceiling reached farther than he could see from the door, and tiny golden feathers painted along the lower halves of the walls. A stature of golden wings sat on a stack of tablets on a side table, and another on the mantel of the ginormous fireplace.

He sensed a theme. Perhaps "wing" was an Outown thing, though it still didn't quite explain why yelling "wing it" at Miriam was quite helpful, other than to agitate her, which worked quite well.

He pushed against the doors. They opened easily, and he stepped inside.

Lincoln paced across the floor of the giant parlor. He was alone, for five hours. He knew he should have felt relieved. He was alive, and in Imperial, but he couldn't stop the dozens of questions and possibilities that plagued his mind.

Ray was bound to show up. And if he didn't? What about Cole? What was Lincoln supposed to say? Was he even supposed to say anything? What was—

"Lincoln?"

Nikki.

Lincoln stopped in his tracks, turning to see her standing in the doorway.

He had to take a double take. For a moment he barely recognized her. This was the first time he'd seen her so put together, not dirty, or bloody, her clothes free of earth stains, and her hair no longer frizzy and tangled from her constant neglect.

He could actually see the true color of Nikki's skin, a soft light brown that he didn't remember well from when he first encountered her. Her hair seemed to be softer and wavier too, with the smallest copper tint. She wore almost the same outfit she had when she first arrived, except more fitted to her frail frame.

"Good morning. Or should I say afternoon?" Lincoln said, taking a step toward her.

She nodded.

They walked toward each other. Nikki seemed to study him too, her brows furrowing. "Who came after you?" she asked. "W-when we got separated?"

Lincoln was barely able to form a response before the answer strode in.

"Hey! Look at that! There you two are!" Ray leaned against the doorway, a smile forming on his lips.

Lincoln's fists clenched. He kept his face relaxed, trying to keep his breathing even. Act like nothing had happened.

Nikki seemed to notice his tension anyway, and her frown didn't disappear. "Hello," she said quietly.

"I thought I wouldn't see you two again," Ray said, with his playful smirk, that rubbed off much differently now. "Good thing I got out."

"Definitely," Lincoln muttered under his breath.

"Anyway, I'll see you two around," Ray said, turning to the door. "Oh, and Miriam wanted me to let you know that dinner's in the main dining room."

Lincoln waited a solid ten seconds before jolting around to Nikki. "Ray's an Oquelite."

"Oh," she said calmly, as if she suspected it.

"Well, then how about Cole being Ray's brother?"

Now Nikki's eyes widened and her lips parted. "How do you know all of this?"

"Long story. Ray's mother found me…guess I ended up in Glorgory after we were attacked."

"Ray…attacked you," Nikki whispered, looking toward the door.

"What if he's here to take down whatever Taryn was planning?" Lincoln said. "He could be conspiring to kill everyone. The plan is fragile—"

"He wouldn't," Nikki said, her face becoming firm. She stepped back. "He couldn't."

"Nik. Please—"

She shook her head. "He can't. He's not Silas."

"But Oquelite are all the same," Lincoln said, his words falling faster than his own mind could comprehend them. "It's like they're instinct to be savage and cruel. They're *insane.*"

Nikki flinched at the last word. She muttered something under breath and turned to the door, hurrying out.

Lincoln watched her go, taking everything in him not to follow.

The Outown's main dining room was the size of a field, and the room was illuminated with chandeliers decorated with delicate gold and silver feathered patterns. A large table ran down the center of the room. One side sat a few adults, their eyes lifted, a few watching him intently. Many were dressed in dark, tight, crisp black uniform, their posture pristine, and they few who spoke, who confident and steady, worn with authority.

Defenders.

But these Defenders were nothing like Taryn. They were far more put together. Stronger and more noble. It sent a small shiver down his spine.

Lincoln turned his attention back to the table, where on one side, little cards were set up, decorated with swirling designs. From the other side of the table, he clearly saw a Defender read the card.

It was a type of print.

He held back a groan. It was worse than trying reading in Anglish. There were too many swirls to even make out a thing. Not that he knew what his name looked like in a plain print. So, he just stood aside, hoping to get a clue from where the others sat.

Most of the others took their seats at the far-right side of the table, yet there were places set at the far-left side still.

Felicity dropped into a seat on the left, then twisted around toward him. She motioned him over, a grin breaking out on her face.

"Could you not find your own name?" she said, laughing a little.

He shook his head, scanning over her. She looked well. Alive. Much more alive than last time he saw her. She was smiling a real smile.

"Use the process of elimination, Lincoln. You're the only person with an 'L' at the beginning of their name." She drew a shape with her finger. A line, then another line from the bottom of it. "And I promise you, you will not find it on the other side of the table," she said, leaning forward in intrigue.

As she had described, one of the signs had a large shape of an 'L' was in front of the other chicken scratch. He sat down, pushing down the anxiety. It seemed like all the eyes from the other side of the table were waiting for him to make a wrong move.

Felicity sat at ease. She probably had been through this so many times it was an instinct for her. She looked so natural and confident compared to all the times he'd seen her in North Cordell.

"You look good," Lincoln said finally.

Felicity laughed. "It's been an interesting week, that's for sure."

"We had an incident, and we weren't able to communicate," Lincoln explained.

"The woods near this place are like none other," Felicity said. "Supernatural."

"We actually need to talk about supernatural shrubbery."

One of the many doors leading to the room flew open. Tabitha waltzed in like it was nobody's business. Her short, choppy blonde hair spilled out of a red beanie, and Cole followed close behind her.

Lincoln tensed on seeing him, his mind frantic when the older boy's light green eyes met his with a welcoming nod. Lincoln held himself firm, returning the nod.

Tell him.

"You're alive!" Tabitha cried, engulfing Felicity in a hug. She got a couple disapproving stares from the opposite side of the table, but Tabitha didn't seem to care, rambling off about how dare Felicity leave them.

Lincoln noticed Felicity pale, her face falling to a frown, but she didn't respond.

Tabitha was placed to the right of Lincoln, with Cole to his left. Lincoln tried to keep himself form fidgeting with Cole right next to him. It felt wrong to just blurt out important details, but it was equally wrong to hide it, surely.

Tabitha seemed thrilled to see Lincoln too, hugging him

awkwardly from the side. She seemed unable to keep her mouth shut, and she spilled out her entire account of what had happened. Felicity, however, remained deadly quiet.

The last of the guests trickled in, along with one more familiar face who sat, her face down toward the table, across from Lincoln.

Whoever made this seating chart knew them a little too well. It wasn't a good thing.

Nikki only looked up when someone rang a bell and the room went silent. Her eyes went straight for the empty seat next to her and then looked back to them as the entire room rose in unison from their seats.

Ray was gone.

From the other side of the table, Lincoln eyed Taryn, who seemed to be watching them with her stern, dark eyes, like trying to say 'don't mess this up or you really won't live to see tomorrow.' She turned her head back to the front of the room.

From the two giant doors at the head of the table, an elderly couple emerged in exquisite clothing that shimmered in the chandelier light. They both had warming smiles and unexpectedly soft eyes. As they sat at the head of the table, the entire room sank back into their chairs.

Then the side doors slammed open. Ray stood in the doorway, looked around for a second, then darted for his seat. "Sorry I'm late," he said as he plopped down.

He was greeted with a harsh shushing.

Lincoln saw Taryn get a few glances from the other guests.

After that, there was a moment of silence until the other side of the table began conversing in at a low volume of conversation.

"What were you doing?" Cole whispered.

"Why are you whispering?" Ray said, a little louder than needed.

Nikki nudged, and he finally seemed to lower his volume.

"I kinda lost my way. That's all," Ray said, in a whisper now. "Big house. It happens."

The food brought out was almost overwhelming. Lincoln didn't remember seeing so much rich food in the same place.

All six of them couldn't help but look over at the other side of the table every ten seconds. The head of the table, the elderly man, was watching them closely, which made Lincoln's stomach knot uncomfortably. Despite them all making it to Imperial, the trial wasn't over.

By the end of the dinner, only Felicity had touched her plate. She seemed quite comfortable and did everything with a graceful motion, as the rest of them relented to awkward silence and staring, except for when Tabitha found out Cole couldn't eat nuts. And she kept asking if anything had nuts in it for a solid five minutes.

The entire room rose in unison, and the head couple left without a word. The crowd went back to chattering and slowly made their way out. The six could finally relax.

Lincoln watched Nikki carefully. She was frowning at something on the table, squinting like it didn't seem right to her.

Ray walked to the table and picked up a vibrantly yellow fruit. "It's a lemon," Ray said, tossing it to her.

Nikki stared at it, still confused, then her face relaxed a bit, studying it closely. "Yellow," she noted.

"It's for you," Ray said with a grin, then disappeared through the crowd.

Lincoln watched him go.

Nikki looked at Lincoln still frowning, running her thumb across the skin of the fruit. Her gaze seemed to pierce him, then she turned around and disappeared once more.

46

Finally, the six of them were led back to one of the Outowns' many extravagant parlors, with Miriam, Jack, and Taryn.

This was the moment they all had been waiting for. A moment to dispel all the confusion, and finally get things clear with Taryn and with themselves.

Awkward silence lingered in the room as everyone waited for everyone else to speak.

Tabitha cleared her throat. "So...you believe us now?"

"I'll tell you my opinion once you tell me what happened on your journey," Taryn said, putting her hands on her hips. She was still the one with the authority.

Felicity, Cole, and Tabitha explained what had happened to them, but when they got to Felicity leaving, Felicity fell quiet.

Tabitha noticed. "Liz?"

Felicity looked up. She parted her lips, but no words formed for a moment. She cleared her throat. "I didn't leave. I don't remember leaving."

Cole and Tabitha frowned.

"You said something about meeting Sinni," Cole began, then glanced around. "Where is she?"

"She couldn't attend today," Taryn said simply.

A confused crease formed against Felicity's forehead. "Could she have…gone back?"

Taryn didn't seem phased by Felicity's suggestion of it. "Then tell us what you *do* remember, Felicity Bents-worth."

Felicity branched out into her own story about the fox boy and snake creature. Jack jumped at the chance to tell her the fox boy she had encountered a Lyntox, a member of the Shifter races, and a Repitox, another Shifter.

They were just myths. Supposedly long extinct.

"About the woods," Nikki piped up. "They're moving." She instantly wished she didn't say anything. Forests aren't supposed to move, right? Everyone would think she was crazy.

Lincoln nodded. "It is. And it's coming fast."

"Woods don't just grow," Jack said. "Unless they're—" he paused. "Felicity saw a Lyntox and was attacked by a Repitox in those woods."

Jack's eyes lit up. "That's where they've been hiding all this time!" he exclaimed.

Miriam ignored Jack, who began to ramble. "The woods? Growing?" she repeated, glancing at Taryn.

The sergeant frowned. "Breaking out of North Cordell did a lot more than just let the Oquelite loose," Taryn said, her jaw clenching.

"What Felicity saw were Mythics. Mythical creatures. They are waking up and coming back into the world. Do you know what this means?" Jack shouted, turning to Taryn.

"It's not just a reformation, it's a reawakening! The government has made full-blooded Ewyons illegal for centuries, but here we are," he said, gesturing to Nikki who stood awkwardly in the corner. "Ewyon! A full blooded Aguarious is *bound* to follow."

Nikki looked up, her chest growing tense. "That means the Oquelite aren't killing the Ewyon," she whispered.

Jack nodded. "The government exterminates full-bloods from conception, keeping the race from coming back."

"Then why do they keep the Oquelite?" Nikki asked, moving closer as she tried to ignore the question of why she wasn't dead.

"Because they can't control everything. The Oquelite are powerful and will try to wipe out their fellow Impure. That's why they need the Defenders, to maintain order, and keep the Oquelite secure in their separate regions."

"And what about the Aguarious?" Ray said.

"Their race had violent tendencies…" Jack said. "Sunk a big ship a long time ago. During the EarthShaker, the full-bloods would use their abilities in…horrific ways."

Miriam finally butted in. "Enough with the lesson, Sallow. The point is we now know Mythics are coming back. Full-bloods are coming back. A *Council* is reforming. What's next?" she said. "Now it's their turn to make an earth changing discovery."

Jack huffed.

Though Miriam had said to move on, Nikki had so many questions.

She was *illegal.* Find an Aguarious? A forest full of weird creatures waking up?

What was happening right now?

When asked for their story, Lincoln gave a brief explanation up until they split up, simply saying they were ambushed. Ray claimed to have escaped and jumped onto a SpeedRail.

Cole and Tabitha, on the other hand, had quite a tale to tell.

Miriam had a couple comments on the Marketeers, who she obviously disliked, but Jack was more interested in the Hall of Heroes. He had never heard of it before, and Cole's immunity to the power of the killer's shrubbery also seemed to stump him.

"Do you have the sword with you?" Jack asked.

Cole nodded.

"Why wouldn't I?" he said, pulling it out from under the couch where he had hidden it in between a board and the cushions. He pulled off the sheath to reveal the clean, white blade.

Jack held out his hand, and Cole offered it to him, but Jack suddenly pulled away.

Ray stumbled as if he'd just been shoved. They all looked at him and he stood up awkwardly. "Is this a bad time to mention…this?" he said, pulling out a black blade that had been hidden by his jacket.

Jack's eyes grew wide.

"Where did you get that?" Taryn snapped, taking a step back.

"Places," Ray said quickly.

"That confirms it," Jack said, turning to Taryn.

Taryn sighed then nodded. "I guess it is," she said in a

small voice. Taryn brushed the hair from her bangs out of her eyes. "This is—" she said, struggling to get her words out straight. "They *are* the Council."

The whole room fell silent. It seemed as if even the wind had stopped to pay its respect.

"So, we're innocent? We're not going to die?" Tabitha said, her face lighting up with relief.

"I figured out the innocent part quickly. The death part…was to find if you were a Council, and a reasonable, responsible one at that. If you were dedicated enough to get here, and give us some time to decide if a reformation would be too dangerous—"

"So, are we going to die or not?" Ray said.

Tarn smiled. "I think you'll be happy to know we've decided against it."

"How? How is that possible?" Felicity asked, her eyes wide in a daze. "A-a council? I— me, Tabitha, and— and Cole. We don't—"

"Yes. You do," Taryn said. "It has been confirmed now. Those Blades are a force I've never been able to see with my own eyes, but it represents one of the twelve components of the Council. Light and Shadow. The Seven Impure, One Pure, the Guardian of Mythic, Light, Shadow, and the Holder. You *are* all one of these."

"But then what am I?" Felicity said. "We have an Aviduous, Ewyon, Dark and Light people, but me and Tabitha—"

"Humanic," Tabitha said, suddenly jumping up from the floor where she'd been sitting. "The serpent in the Hall of Heroes called me a Humanic. Is that Impure?"

"Pure," Taryn corrected.

Nikki began to wonder if Taryn had known all along. If

she knew now, what each of them were.

Tabitha's eyes lit up, but Felicity's seemed to grow wild with panic. "Then…who am I?" she gasped.

"I'm not permitted to give you that information," Taryn said.

"Why? Why can't you tell me what I am? How do you even know I'm part of all of this?" Felicity stood up, her fists tightening.

"There was a reason for the attack on your life in Liberty, Felicity Bentsworth. And a reason you were sent to North Cordell. My cousin had you sent to this region specifically to watch you. If we tell you what you are, you won't be able to awake the essence inside of you naturally. Do you understand?"

Nikki could see Felicity was on the verge of tears. She didn't understand why. She'd seemed so much stronger than before when they were at dinner, but now she looked like she was about to crumble.

Felicity finally nodded. "I…I understand," she said, backing up.

Nikki met her eyes with an anxious frown.

"I'm fine," Felicity whispered, standing straight to hear what Taryn had to say next.

"As the Council, you will either be destroyed or created. Once completed you are an unstoppable weapon. Right now, you have six of the twelve needed. Once the Council is complete, it's a weapon that can travel to the Forbidden Realm. Forces are coming. They've been crawling from their graves for ages. This Council will either destroy or save this world. The Oquelite, along with many political thinkers, think a Council independent from their control is dangerous and shouldn't be formed. They have been tearing apart

Councils for millennia," Taryn said.

"Did they destroy yours?" Ray asked.

Taryn froze. She looked to Miriam and Jack, who stood with their eyes shifted downward. Taryn released a hard sigh and looked to the kids again. She shook her head.

Everyone remained silent, though Nikki wanted Taryn to continue. She wanted her to explain. She wanted Taryn to stop pacing, relax the creases between her brows, look them in the eye, and tell them the truth of her experience with the Curatrix Team.

Taryn's gaze met hers. Her eyes seemed to be mixed with color, like they'd been forced to align themselves around her pupil. "You can stop glaring now," Taryn said, a small smile forming on her lips. A sad smile, but it seemed genuine.

The attention shifted to Nikki.

She kept her attention away from the stares. "W-what happened?" she said.

"To me?" Taryn asked.

Nikki stood silent, her lips parted, afraid of saying the wrong thing.

"I think we've all been wondering," Cole said, looking back to Nikki for a moment, then to Taryn. "If we are this 'Council', I think we should know what happened to you and... the Curatrix team."

To Nikki's surprise, Taryn crossed her arms and nodded, looking off toward the window at the lights shining brightly in the darkness of the city. "Outown and Sallow didn't spill this to you?" she said, looking over her shoulder at Miriam and Jack, who both tensed again.

Cole shook his head, answering for all of them.

"It's short and simple, really," Taryn said, clearing her throat. "Around two years after the Trials, I was given the position of Sergeant at the age of eighteen. One of the youngest…"

"She was *the* youngest," Jack said, seeming proud to say it. "The only close second was that twenty-seven-year-old guy from Manifest thirty years ago."

"Thank you, Sallow," Taryn said. "I was given the position, anyhow, and people weren't happy about it. Especially Cadissa Dean, an Executive. Seven years later, a team of trained fugitives came and beat me half to death… and buried me alive."

Her voice trailed off, and her gaze drifted back to the window. She took a deep breath and placed her hands on her hips. "I woke up, everyone in the Base is dead, and I find out that I've been proclaimed dead as well along with my fellow council members. All murdered. I tried to figure it out. I still am. I don't know who came after us, and why the other's died and *I* didn't."

The names of Taryn's teammates ran through Nikki's head and she flinched. *Reyna Wents. Lyell Aguirre. Zita Klirkpatrick. Aaron Outown*

"All the newspapers," Tabitha said, in realization. "You were trying to figure out how and why they died."

Taryn nodded. "Then after that, funding for our Base was suddenly cut short, the Offices said I'd gone mad."

She paused, entranced by the window.

"I haven't done great things in the past," Taryn said. "But we didn't come here to sulk over me. We're here to talk about your future. This time, I'm determined not to mess it up."

This didn't seem to make things better for Felicity, who stood by Nikki. She wasn't bawling, but she was blinking rapidly, liquid shimmering in her eyes.

"I know it's big to ask, but right now the Imperial City is

in danger. An early move of attack by the Oquelite. The Glass Tower contains something they want. The Oquelite are coming for Imperial, and we must find what they're looking for before they do," Taryn said.

"Why us? And why now?" Lincoln said.

Taryn sighed again, the sound almost like a growl.

"Because I don't have anyone else, and you're smaller. And a *Council*," she said. Then her face softened a bit. "Right now, you are the only hope we have. The only determined strength we have left at all. Everyone else is too caught up in their own worlds to notice the real world they live in is falling apart at the seams. It's up to you now, even if you're young. A lot younger than I hoped for anyone to have to accept this burden."

It seemed hard for Taryn to say those words, like she was letting go of something she had treasured for such a long time. Taryn was giving up her control. She was accepting the fact she couldn't put things right, and now some young amateurs seemed to be her only choice of action.

Maybe there was something else, but at that moment, Nikki couldn't detect exactly what that was.

"Enough talk. What do we have to do?" Ray asked. He perked up, his bored gaze lifting from the ground.

"We're going to need a team to get into the tower to retrieve the item of power, or whatever it is, and get out before the Oquelite finds you," Miriam said.

Nikki glanced at her, then back at the sergeant. It seemed like Miriam had the whole process a little more planned out than Taryn did.

Cole started, "Cool. So, I guess we—"

"Woah. Not you, Goldfish," Miriam laughed. "The girls will actually be doing the going into the building part. More vulnerable looking, and less suspicious apparently. They'll be in for a real surprise when I intend to prove that otherwise.

Gears and Emo will be with Jack, at the City's main power panel, and getting the information we need. You will be staying here for backup."

Both Lincoln and Ray frowned.

"Yes," Taryn said. "Of course, it's your choice. I'm not going to force you into this. Miriam will be leading the girls and will 'wing it' if necessary.

Miriam growled.

Ray raised his hand. "Excuse me…Emo?"

"Quit wearing black and maybe I'll change my mind," Miriam said, her lips curled into a smirk.

Ray rolled his eyes.

Nikki looked over to Felicity, who had been watching her. Felicity would do fine sneaking into a giant building, but her, not so well. Felicity grabbed Nikki's arm and squeezed as if she could sense her fear. "I'm in if you are," she said.

Nikki nodded. And this time she didn't flinch.

47

Felicity had tried to sleep, but she had no luck.

She'd been up for hours, trying to make herself look as normal and helpless as possible. She had assembled over ten different outfits from the giant closet the Outowns provided and had redone her hair too many times to count. She found herself becoming clumsy at her makeup. It was true she hadn't worn any in weeks, but now it felt like her very life depended on it.

Maybe it did. Sometimes it felt better not knowing.

The door flung open.

Tabitha collapsed onto Felicity's bed, in the most ridiculous outfit Felicity had ever seen. She was wearing a bright red shirt lined in silver fluff, and her pants were checkered and reached to her knees. As usual, she wore bright red converse, which seemed like the only thing normal about her outfit.

"Uh, Tabitha. You're not really going to go like that, are you?" Felicity said.

Tabitha looked down at herself, then growled. "This is like the only half not weird thing I was given. I know today's styles are weird, but this is stuff not even the weird people wear."

Felicity burst out laughing, releasing some of the knotted tension in her chest.

Tabitha stood up, tapping her finger on her chin. "But then I thought, Taryn said we're different. So why not embrace it?"

Felicity turned around in her chair to face the mirror again. "Don't remind me," she grumbled.

She saw Tabitha's shoulders slump in the reflection. Felicity knew she was trying to make her feel better. It wasn't every day you were told you would either save the world, destroy it, or die. If that's even what Tayn meant at all.

The truth was she wanted no part in any of this. All she wanted was to disappear and curl up in her own bed, knowing everyone was alive, and forget everything. But she knew she couldn't do that.

There were people who cared about her.

After the meeting, she'd burst out crying in the hallway for no reason, and Lincoln had brought her to her room and tried to comfort her. Tabitha never left her side. Tabitha of all people was the one she couldn't let down.

Ray and Cole had both saved her life countless times. Ray had been there for her, even if he was a pain in her side. It felt strange to think how much she had distrusted Nikki. She still didn't feel right around her, but somehow the girl had managed to save her life countless times over and over. And Silas...Felicity chut her eyes and took a deep breath. He'd given her some sort of hope, and now she'd have to use it to destroy him.

Felicity swerved back over and tossed her a jacket. "Put this on, Hippie Stump. Maybe you'll look less strange," she said.

Tabitha smiled, pulling the jacket on.

The door creaked open. Nikki peered in before opening it all the way.

"Oh, hey!' Tabitha said, which seemed like the most awkward thing to say at that moment, but Nikki waved to acknowledge her.

Nikki hadn't changed a bit since the last time she saw her. "Nikki. Hate to break it to you, but I'm not sure anyone is going to be fooled by that outfit," Felicity said. She never usually judged people's clothes this much. No, that was a lie. That's how she had met Nikki, while judging her. Felicity tried to rub that feeling away.

Nikki looked down at herself. She tilted her head and frowned. She didn't seem to get the fact she looked...like Nikki, and Nikki wasn't someone you want to look like when you're sneaking into a building and doing things Felicity was nearly one hundred percent sure were illegal.

Tabitha looked at Nikki, but with a sly smile as the gears seemed to be turning in her head. "You know maybe if we changed your outfit, and did your—"

"No... thank you," Nikki said, biting her lip.

Tabitha laughed a bit.

Nikki gave a somewhat neutral look, which seemed to be the closest thing she could get to a smile.

Then Felicity thought of something. "Come here," she

said.

Nikki looked unsure. "What are you—"

But before Nikki could even finish, Felicity pulled her over and plopped her down in the chair. Nikki froze in the chair, but hopefully that meant she wouldn't attack Felicity at any moment.

"Calm down!" Felicity laughed. "I'm not going to hurt you!"

Nikki seemed to relax, but as soon as Felicity even touched her hair, Nikki winced.

"This is for your own good," Felicity muttered.

Nikki sighed, then slumped back in the chair, crossing her arms like she'd finally given in.

Felicity laughed under her breath and got to work.

Nikki tried to restrain herself from slapping Felicity's hands from her head. Felicity fingers running her through her hair and twisting it every which way made her feel like someone had a hold of her and could kill her at any moment.

Do not be afraid.

Nikki frowned. The voices. They were back. She looked up to the mirror and to her shock instead of a reflection, a younger child looked at her out of the mirror.

The child was squirming and having a difficult time sitting still, but a woman, probably the child's mother, held her arm down.

The child looked up at her mother. "When will it be over?"

The mother laughed, not a cruel laugh, but a soft, amused one. "Settle down. Soon. I promise," she said.

A shiver went down Nikki's back.

The child seemed to become a little more content, then

the entire scene froze. The woman's gaze rose to meet Nikki's. "It will be over very soon," she said.

Suddenly Nikki recognized the face. She was older, her eyes ancient, but the same, cold edge to her voice could only belong to one person.

Avalon.

The Lady of the Universe is Coming.

Nikki nearly toppled over in her chair.

The normal reflection burst back into view, but this reflection also looked strange. In the background, Felicity looked quite satisfied with herself. Nikki walked closer to the mirror, running her finger along her hair that was expertly tied up at the back. She had never seen it put this way.

She looked over her shoulder at Felicity. "It's—it's…" She couldn't even fathom the word.

Felicity broke out in a smile, her shoulders relaxing a bit. "You should keep it up more often," she said, walking up beside Nikki and adjusting her work quickly, curling Nikki's hair with her finger.

Tabitha nodded in agreement.

"I can't do anything with my hair now," she said, sticking her hair up, and her tongue out. "Too short"

Nikki couldn't help but feel a little more comfortable, Tabitha's comment lightening the mood, though her heart was still beating like crazy. She shot a look back at the mirror to make sure Avalon hadn't reappeared.

How was that even possible?

Tabitha shook her by the shoulders, snapping her out of her thoughts. "You okay?" she said.

Nikki nodded.

Tabitha just looked at Nikki as if something was missing. "Maybe try smiling?" she suggested.

Felicity agreed enthusiastically. "That would make the act perfect!"

They were obviously being a little over dramatic on purpose, like they'd been waiting for a while for this. She raised an eyebrow.

"Seriously?" Tabitha frowned. "You seriously just lift your lip up."

Nikki looked to Felicity then back to Tabitha, then gave Tabitha an exaggerated frown.

Tabitha sighed. "Think…happy thoughts," she suggested.

Nikki took a deep breath, but no thought gave her enough joy to physically affect her.

Positive. Fifty-three times positive.

Nikki looked around. Who said that?

Felicity must have heard the voice too and she stumbled back, but Tabitha sat on the bed seeming perfectly normal and content.

You'll do it right this time.

Felicity yelped, covering her hands with her mouth.

The voice was somehow in both of their heads.

Nikki looked to Tabitha, who stared at Felicity with a frown.

I'll make your skin run with blood.

Nikki felt her face grow hot. A voice not from her mind… but from Felicity's now?

Felicity looked around, covering her ears, looking bewildered at Nikki.

Tabitha looked at them, back and forth. "You two okay?" she asked.

Felicity managed to stutter, "Y-yes. Everything's fine."

This is the last time you will ever see him again.

Felicity immediately blushed hard, looking to the ground. That also came from Felicity's mind, Nikki was sure of it.

"What is it?" Tabitha shouted standing up and pushing between them.

"Voices," Nikki said, looking to Felicity in disbelief. "Hear voices."

Tabitha frowned.

"Are you crazy?" she said. "I thought you two had something wrong with you, but now—"

"No. She's right. I can hear them," Felicity said. "This place is strange."

I told you. I'm never going to let you go.

Felicity went red again. "Why won't they shut up?" she mumbled under her breath, smacking her head.

She looked up to Nikki, who was genuinely confused, yet a little interested in whatever was erupting from Felicity's mind. She was tempted to ask.

Then her mind decided to strike back.

Run. Run and never look back. Never let them touch you!

Nikki's heart was crushed in her chest. For a second, her vision blurred out before focusing back on Felicity, who stared in horror at her. It was Nikki's turn for her face to flame. Who was in her head? Sharing *personal* words from the past not even she understood.

Felicity stared at Nikki. "That was—"

"Nothing. We should get going," Nikki said, trudging past the other two.

She felt betrayed, but it wasn't Felicity's fault she'd heard what she did. Those words meant much more to her then they did to anyone else. Why was her mind betraying her like this?

Felicity was trustworthy. But how much could Nikki really

trust her with things she could barely handle herself?

As she walked down the hallway, acting like she was distracted by the art on the walls, she heard Felicity and Tabitha walking behind her, but keeping their distance.

Felicity was dead quiet too. Maybe she felt the same way. Maybe whatever Nikki had heard was something Felicity didn't want shared from her past too.

The voices had stopped, but where had they come from in the first place? She knew for certain one was an echo of the past. Were they connected to the vision in the mirror? She needed answers, or it'd drive her insane.

"Keep running," Avalon's voice struck her again.

Leave me alone, and keep Felicity out of this. Nikki yelled to Avalon, wherever her essence lay.

"Keep running", Avalon repeated. *"I've had nothing to do with those voices, child. I don't like it. Someone else has breached the realm of the mind..."*

She squeezed her eyes shut and tried to focus. Tune out what Avalon was saying. But she couldn't.

Nikki collided with someone, and they caught her shoulders, steadying her.

"Nik?" It was Lincoln. Somehow, she almost wished it wasn't.

"Woah. What did Felicity do to you?" he said, his eyes growing wide.

She ignored his gaze.

He definitely wasn't sneaking into the Imperial Tower. He was decked out in the forest green hooded jacket, denim pants covered in buckles and different pockets, with gears, wires, and other random things poking out from within. On his back, he had a radio-like machine with two speakers on the side, a screen in the middle, and about a hundred little outlets below the screen, some already with wires plugged into them. She had to admit he looked ready to take down the Oquelite, but in more of a Lincoln-style.

Ray appeared behind Lincoln.

Nikki didn't doubt he might have just literally appeared out of thin air. He seemed relaxed, a sly smile on his lips and a flicker in his eyes.

Unlike Lincoln, he seemed to have quite a light load—just a backpack that seemed to be empty. Had they just given Lincoln everything to carry?

"Lookin' good, Princess," Ray said.

Nikki gave him a glare.

Avalon snickered.

Nikki began to think her race was more of a drag and a curse than a gift and a privilege of power she didn't even have. She just shook her head in disapproval, but she suspected Ray wouldn't back down.

"Good luck up there," Ray said. "Don't let Liz boss you around too much."

"Hey! I do not," Felicity said, bursting into the conversation.

"Not even a little bit?" Ray teased.

"No!" she said playfully, but she smacked Ray hard in the back of the head.

"What is up with you and smacking me?" Ray said, laughing a bit.

"Maybe Felicity's just trying to prepare you. Just in case you insult an Oquelite, and they decide they wanna kill you?" Cole suggested.

Ray rolled his eyes.

Nikki hadn't noticed Cole there before. He was awfully quiet. All six of them were together again, maybe for the last time in a while.

The only one who wasn't in high spirits was Lincoln. His silent gaze was fixed on Ray. Nikki looked away from him. Ray was an Oquelite, yes, but why did that make him untrustworthy? She was an Ewyon, and their reputation was less than great.

Miriam burst out from the opposite hallway, wearing clothes that Nikki never would have even imagined Miriam even owning. She had white jeans, a bright green oversized t-shirt, a sideways baseball cap, and the most expensive, and complimentary white boots. Surprising functional for being a disguise.

"Ready?" she said, a sly smile on her unnaturally red lips.

Jack looked more normal, but that was to be expected. "See you back here, Mir?" he said.

"If we live."

"Knowing you, most likely," Jack said, elbowing her and beckoning Lincoln and Ray to him.

"Good luck," Cole said. They'd decided he would stay behind in case anything was needed back at the manor. Though he seemed upbeat and in good spirits, Nikki couldn't help but notice his subtle disappointment.

Felicity grabbed Nikki's arm and pulled her toward Miriam. They stepped out the door and into the dawn's air. One final voice whispered in Nikki's mind.

"The Lady of the Universe is coming and would like to know your name."

48

Tabitha burst out onto the street from the Outown's long, expensive vehicle. Looking up, her stomach tightened as she searched for the top of the tower.

The Glass Tower. The landmark of Imperial.

Miriam glided up the front steps like she owned the place. Tabitha wished she had that confidence. Miriam probably had been doing jobs like this for a while, being a Defender and everything.

Tabitha, Felicity, and Nikki made their way up the steps in a nervous manner. Even Felicity seemed to be a little angsty, though faking things seemed to be her specialty.

Tabitha couldn't help the rising frustration at the glances Nikki and Felicity kept exchanging. She knew it had to do with that silent pocket of time in Felicity's room. What exactly had happened?

Before they entered, Miriam stopped them in their tracks to run through the plan one more time.

They were some rich kids whose father had sent them to tour the Glass Tower. Jack probably already was in the online system and had scheduled their tour. They would go through the Tower like tourists, and under no circumstances would they break their cover.

Miriam didn't explain past that point. The more oblivious they acted, the easier it would be to not get caught.

Tabitha had questioned her a few times, but the answer remained the same. They would be told nothing more.

Miriam turned, swung the glass door open, and flipped her hair, putting a disgusted look on her face like this was the last place on earth she wanted to be right now. Tabitha straightened and strode into the lobby after her, Felicity and Nikki following. To Tabitha's relief, Nikki was acting natural enough.

The woman at the front desk looked up and blinked a couple times behind her glasses. "We aren't expecting any visitors," she said.

Miriam gave an over dramatic gasp. "Seriously? Papa made sure to schedule! Don't you recognize us? The Wisconsin's?" Miriam said, holding her hands out to the others. Her high-pitched speech made Tabitha cringe, but she managed to keep a cool face and not smile too suspiciously.

The woman at the desk had a right to be confused. They looked nothing like each other.

None of their hair was the same color, Nikki's skin was darker, Tabitha was pale, and Felicity had a face full of freckles and a head of red hair. But Miriam didn't care.

"Lady! Check your device," Miriam demanded. "Papa is never wrong!"

The woman scrambled to the hologram monitor, nervously typing. "Oh! I guess I do have you here."

Jack's skills were paying off nicely.

"Now can I get some names," the woman said.

Miriam replied without hesitation," Cornelia Anastasia Wisconsin."

Felicity seemed to have already been thinking. "Elizabeth Wisconsin. Friends call me Liz."

Tabitha fumbled over her words, pushing past her brain's instinct for something ridiculous. "Mir ... abla Wisconsin."

The woman frowned but wrote it down anyway.

Nikki was now in the spotlight as she stared dumbly at the receptionist. Tabitha was sure their cover was over.

Felicity jumped in. "She has a speech deformity," she said quickly. "Her name's Veronica Wisconsin."

Tabitha tried to keep from laughing.

Nikki frowned, but kept her mouth shut with the act.

After the front desk woman handed them IDs. She offered a guide, but Miriam yelled about how rude she was to think they needed something as silly as a guide, and probably scared her so much she forgot she hadn't checked their bags.

Once they were out of hearing distance, Felicity shot Tabitha a look. "Nice job, Mirabla."

Tabitha shrugged. "Hey, what can I say?" she said. "Veronica? I thought you weren't speaking to your sister."

"We aren't," Felicity said, her eyes shifting away. "She was just the first person I thought of."

"Your younger sister?" Nikki's eyes widened.

Felicity shushed her. "Speech deformity, remember?"

Nikki opened her mouth, but Felicity shushed her again.

"You don't sound like us at all. It might have given us away. It's not a bad thing. Just would be a longer story."

Nikki glared.

Tabitha had almost forgotten. She had been surrounded by accents in North Cordell. Nikki's wasn't North Cordellian though; it seemed more slurred and with a longer drawl on her a's in a way Tabitha couldn't place. Where was it from? Most higher regions shared the same speech patterns, like Liberty and Imperial. Nikki would have definitely stuck out.

Miriam stopped in the middle of the hall, causing them all to collide behind her.

"Miria— I mean Cornelia, why'd you stop?" Tabitha asked.

Miriam turned to a small door. "This is it. The room that will change our lives. The answer lies here."

"The janitor closet?"

Miriam shot Tabitha a look and turned the knob. The door opened smoothly.

"It's not locked," Felicity said, frowning and glancing over her shoulder.

Miriam didn't seem to care. Apparently, it was fate to walk into this closet full of cleaning supplies. The room was about the size of a small bedroom at the Inn and was full of automatic cleaning carts, little sweeper bots, and walls full of extra paper towels, mops, soap, and all sorts of other things. But from Tabitha could tell, it was still just a huge janitor closet.

What was the big deal?

"Squirt, the bag," Miriam snapped.

Nikki zipped open the bag slung around her shoulder, to reveal a bunch of strange looking tools and mechanisms.

Miriam pulled out a machine that had a metal rod

connected to an iron plate. Miriam clicked the button on top, and let the handle go, and to their surprise the mechanism floated in place above the ground.

"What is it?" Felicity asked, turning her head sideways like she was trying to get a better angle.

"I'm not actually sure. Outdated tech Taryn had. I have no idea how it works. She said to just—"

The machine made a whirring sound and began to move. They all jumped back.

"Okay," Tabitha said. "Got it. It's like a magical stick that seeks out what you seek most."

Miriam chuckled and shook her head, "I wish, Stump. But you have to do more techy stuff to make this kabobber do its stuff. The concept of magic would be cooler though."

With that, Miriam began following the stick.

"What are we looking for exactly?" Felicity said, looking around.

Miriam gave no answer.

Felicity looked to Nikki and Tabitha.

Tabitha shrugged. They had been given little to no information on what exactly they were looking for.

"Something Oquelite. Maybe."

"Something they hid here," Nikki added in a mutter. Then she looked up, clearing her throat.

The stick ran out to the wall, a loud beeping going off. The girls jumped.

Miriam growled. "That was my fault!" she called out, picked the device up pressing a few buttons and set it back on the ground.

Tabitha sighed, turning back to Nikki. "But what Oquelite would want to hide something here? Who?"

Felicity shook her head, picking up a box of discarded

scrubbers, so the stick should search underneath. "No. There's no way it has to do with the Oquelite, right, Miriam?"

Miriam only rolled her eyes, and followed the stick as it scanned up the wall.

Tabitha frowned. There was no way. They were after the Oquelite. They were plotting a rebellion, and Imperial? It was a huge region. What kind of Oquelite were kept here?

"This is a Defender thing," Felicity continued. "They called us here…"

"Okay. But if we encounter any Oquelite, you're in serious debt," Tabitha said.

"Aha!" Miriam shouted in triumph. Pushing the stick to the side as she squeezed past a pile of mops and cart to reach a shelf.

"A little help here!" she yelled, beginning to push the shelf to the right.

All three ran to help her, shoving the large shelf out of the way.

Behind the shelf was a door, about the size of a small window.

Miriam rubbed her chin. "Step back. I've had experience with things like this. The door is a device, obviously. Look at its mechanical structure. It will need—"

Tabitha grabbed the handle of the small door. "Got it," she said, the small door swinging open.

Miriam's jaw dropped, then she cleared her throat. "Alright then."

The passage was dark, and crowded with shadows, but Tabitha was able to make out small steps descending into the darkness. "There is a little baby sized stepped staircase," Tabitha said, sticking her head into the door.

Miriam pushed her aside, getting down onto her knees. She looked up the small shaft. "It's too small for all of us to fit. Especially me." She sighed, pulling her head out.

"This is where being short and small comes in handy," Tabitha said, breaking out in an excited grin and crossing her arms.

"You are definitely not going alone," Miriam huffed. She looked to Felicity and Nikki, the last to two possible candidates.

Felicity shoved Nikki to the door. "Nikki's going. She's the one who's less likely to die, and she's slim enough," Felicity said, giving Nikki a reassuring nod.

Nikki looked to Miriam then Felicity with uncertainty.

Miriam took the bag from her. "Well Squirt and Stump are in then," Miriam said. "Me and Rusty will stay out and be your cover. And keep guard. There are some things I'd like to…get done."

"So, what do we do?" Tabitha said.

Miriam handed Nikki a Comm. "Once you reach where the staircase leads, tell me what you find," Miriam said. "I'll give you further directions then."

Tabitha did a small salute and began crawling up the shaft.

The door slammed shut.

Tabitha was surprisingly quiet the entire way, except for the occasional nervous humming sessions.

Nikki hated the feeling of this place. It smelled like mold and dust, and she could feel the dampness on her knees and hands, and she made her way through. If someone found them here, they would be trapped, with no way to run.

The thought was still bothering her.

Why would the Oquelite hide something in the Glass Tower? Why not Capital North, the leading region, as Felicity had called it when she gave Nikki a brief lesson on the regions on the way there? It seemed like a much better hiding place for whatever 'it' was.

The echo still haunted her thoughts.

The Lady of the Universe.

She was coming.

Nikki didn't have any more time to continue pondering, as Tabitha yelled out to her, "We're here!"

'Here' was a door like the one they had entered. Square and low, with a little metal latch for a handle. Tabitha reached the latch and tried to pull it back. She frowned, looking back at Nikki and wiping her hand on her shirt. "I think it's rusted shut or something."

Nikki squeezed past her to the door. She ran her fingers over the latch, finding it rusted as Tabitha said, and damp. She tried to pull it, but it wouldn't budge. Nikki slumped back, staring hard at the eroding door. Maybe she could kick it out.

She tapped Tabitha's shoulder. "Sit back," she said.

Tabitha crawled further back without a single word. Nikki glanced back at her and then the door, then twisted around so her feet were against the door. She braced herself and kicked both heels into the door. The door ripped from its hinges, flying back.

Tabitha looked to Nikki, fear filling her eyes in the dim light that spilled from the door. "Should we really go—"

Nikki grabbed Tabitha's sweaty palm and crawled out.

The room was full of fog, and as cold as a winter's storm, but there was no movement. Even the fog was still.

Tabitha's hand dropped from Nikki's, and she stepped

deeper into the room. "How is this even in the Tower?" she gasped, spinning around, her face full of marvel at the place.

Nikki's chest tightened, her heart beating faster. This place gave her the instant signal to run. It didn't even feel like there was a solid floor below her feet, like she was at the mercy of some unknown power. One wrong move, and like the door said, they would die.

"I don't think we're in the Tower anymore," she muttered.

Tabitha stopped spinning and frowned. "Why not?" she asked.

Nikki walked toward Tabitha, trying not to think about falling. "There isn't even a solid room."

Tabitha nodded. "Maybe some anti-gravity tech. Some cool new thing." But Tabitha didn't seem to be convinced by her own words.

Nikki hoped she was right. She pulled out the Communicator and found Miriam's identification number already dialed.

"You made it?" came Miriam's fuzzy, choppy voice.

"Yep," Tabitha said. "It's a giant room…floating and stuff. Kinda dark, lots of shelves."

Nikki looked up, seeing the fog beginning to thin, hundreds of shelves reaching farther than Nikki could see. Fluorescent lights floated above them.

Miriam was quiet for a moment. "Our target is codenamed 'Key Ring'."

Ring.

"Which is?"

"I can't tell you everything, Stump."

"Key," Nikki said. "Like…the Council."

Miriam was quiet again. "You were brought here for a

reason," she said. "If we needed some random adolescents, I think we could have found a few disposable kids willing to do jobs for a few bucks. You are not disposable. We can't risk losing…again. We need to find this…thing. Do you understand?"

"You can trust us," Nikki said.

"I know I can trust you," Miriam said. "But we can't lose you. Not now. Don't die, but find that thing and get out."

"How long do we have?" Tabitha asked.

"Let's say two hours. We're expecting company," Miriam said.

"On it, Sergeant."

"Officer," Miriam corrected.

"Sorry, Officer. You Defenders and your names."

Miriam disconnected.

"They're expecting Oquelite," Nikki said immediately.

"Do you think they're looking for 'Key Ring' too?" Tabitha said as she handed the Communicator back.

"Probably."

"Well then, what are we waiting for? We don't have much time. Come on!" Tabitha yelled, her voice echoing as she set off into the files.

Nikki followed her uneasily.

The magical file cabinets of doom were kept in alphabetical order and, as far as Nikki could tell, there were billions of files. Maybe beyond what the human races could even count. How could they find the 'Key Ring'?

They still had to try. Then she could go. Once everything was okay, she would leave.

She started down a random row, beginning to sort through. Only birth dates, death dates, occupations and such of normal people, some from the EarthShaker, and others only a few years from the present.

Her thoughts began to stray as she searched. Avalon. Who was she? And why and how was she still in her head?

They said the Glass Tower held files for every citizen of the world of all time. This was her best shot and finding out who the voice in the Stone really was.

There had to be millions of people who had the name Avalon. But the name 'Avalon' was all she really knew about her. What about a last name? Was it Avalon Idicous? Or was that not how it worked? Avalon was royalty, so did she have a title? Was she too old to even be filed?

Nikki barely knew anything about the Impure History. If she got out alive, she'd learn as much as she could.

Time seemed to stand still in this place. Nikki wasn't sure if it had been hours or only a few seconds since they entered. Should she go find Tabitha and get out? But then again it felt perfectly safe here. No, she felt entirely *un*safe.

She didn't trust Tabitha on her own, but since she had been so confident on finding the 'Key Ring' on her own it felt weak to try to find her now.

Avalon Gotubic.

Avalon Jacaquaro.

Avalon Wilson.

The names went on. No luck.

"Avalon," Nikki said out loud. She looked around, hoping maybe the Stone would appear. "I don't know you, but you know me. I know you can hear me. I know you're listening. Whatever you're hiding, reveal it."

Talking to a dead person in a rock seemed a little weird, but Avalon's presence was real. She could still feel it in her mind.

At first, nothing happened.

Then a slip of paper floated slowly to the ground.

Nikki's eyes grew wide, and she stepped toward the strange paper file. The paper folder was worn brown with age. She picked up the folder, running her fingers through the dust. She hesitated to open it—it felt wrong—but she'd come this far. She couldn't go back. She pulled back the cover.

AVALON EMBERSON

The words were bold on the page, blaring at Nikki.

"Emberson," she whispered.

She turned to a new page; Avalon's name printed at the top again. The writing was in a strange language, yet the letters seemed to form together in Nikki's mind as she stared at them.

Avalon Emberson, Ewyon Race, Deceased

"You *are* dead," Nikki said under breath.

She had the voice of a dead person echoing in her head.

Born the Twenty-Second of June on the year of Giles, the Age of Locomote

Date and Cause of Death Unknown

Nikki had never heard of the year or the age. She'd only heard Taryn refer to this time as the Age of Steel.

Only known child, Kathryn Adrienne Emberson Idicous, Daughter of Orion Idicous; Deceased.

So, the baby had a name—Kathryn—and like her mother, she was dead.

The rest of the page was blank. Nikki turned the page again, finding the new page blank. Words began to form in front of her.

Avalon Emberson's essence is trapped under the Order of the Realm in the abyss of Pulcheremii [The Stone of the Ewyon], though has been deemed lawfully unfit to do many unlawful decisions, including one case of mind control, strictly forbidden.

Cursed to the Stone by the Oquelite Lord, Orion Idicous, the Pulcheremii is the only counteracting match against the Idicous legacy. Orion Idicous's actions were equally unlawful.

If you are you concerned this dangerous Holder has an influence on your mind, the following will remove the essence of the Stone and deem Pulcheremii dormant…

She could get the voice out of her head. By banishing Avalon.

Nikki dropped the file and took a step back.

They still drove her insane, but whether it was Avalon or her own mind that drove her, she pushed the file aside, and watched it disappear.

She couldn't do that to Avalon.

Avalon wasn't the one who needed to be punished.

Nikki's heart quickened.

Orion.

This wasn't good.

She ran down the shelves, repeating his name over and over in his mind. Key Ring wasn't just a codename.

It was Orion's gold ring.

And if his gold ring was here, so was Orion.

Cole was slouched on one of the Outown's many couches, bored out of his mind. Since he was alone, he preferred to sit upside down, with his feet up against the back of the couch, and his head hanging over the bottom, feeling the blood rushing to his head.

The sword lay across his stomach, sheathed of course.

It was called the Illuminate Blade, Jack had said, but it sounded like such a weird name for a sword. From most of the books he'd read, the heroes would name their own sword, but he didn't know what to do when the weapon was already named.

He wished he could be out there, doing something useful with his life.

Even Tabitha, the impulsive, though short person she

was, got to at least do something.

"Oh! Hello Coleson!"

Cole flipped off the couch in surprise, knocking a probably priceless vase off the table. He caught it in one hand and picked up his sword with the other. "Uh. Sorr—"

He looked up and lost all ability to speak.

The elderly couple who sat at the head of the table last night stood before him, the woman smiling brightly like he hadn't almost broken her precious vase. She was dressed in a long white dress, trimmed with lace, the color reaching to her chin, golden button lined down her chest. Feathers decorated her sleeves.

"Oh, it's fine. Just put it there, Coleson," she said.

He did as she said, placing the vase back on the table as slowly and carefully as he could.

No one called him Coleson. Not many people even knew that was his real name. In fact, until he was six, he thought his name was just plain Cole. He was too stunned to correct her.

The man eyed him, not disapprovingly, but untrustful, dark shadows under his eyes. He looked at him like Cole hadn't shown him his worth yet and he wasn't to be trusted.

The woman sat down. "Oh, you two sit down!" she said, pulling her husband's arm, sitting him down unwillingly next to her.

Cole sat down out of fear that the man might kill him if he made a wrong move.

"Aw, it's so nice having children back in these halls. Makes everything so much more lifelike. Don't you think, Ludwik?" she asked, turning to her husband, who grunted in reply.

"I'm Anne and this is Ludwik Outown," she said in a cheerful upbeat manner.

"Outown?" he said, but then clasped his hands over his

mouth.

"Of course!" Anne laughed.

"Miriam's parents?" he asked. He kept his mouth shut on the topic of Aaron. If even Miriam got emotional about the death of her brother, it was no doubt her parents would be worse.

Mrs. Outown nodded. "Is it that hard to believe? I didn't think our daughter was too different from us. She does tend to wear those awful overcoats. The black ones. You know what I mean, right Ludwik?" She turned to her husband again and he nodded.

Cole would have guessed they were Miriam's grand-parents, not her literal parents.

They had to have been in their late seventies or something. Miriam was what…twenty-four?

Mrs. Outown just smiled at him. "Surprised, are you?"

"Ye- I mean no. A little—"

Mrs. Outown just laughed. "Don't worry, Coleson. We're far older than you think."

"If it's not rude to ask, how old exactly?" Cole said.

"Two hundred and fourteen *thousand* years old," Ludwik grumbled, speaking for the first time.

Cole just stared, which was probably rude, but he couldn't stop himself. Two hundred and fourteen *thousand* years old? That couldn't be possible.

"Oh, don't be startled. We're Diones," Mrs. Outown said, like Cole was supposed to have gotten an answer from that, but he still sat utterly confused.

The woman seemed to realize his confusion. "A Diones. The immortal protectors of each of the Seven Impure Kin, and the One Pure Kin. Each race has two. Like the rules of immortality, they live until they are slain." She said it so carefree, like it was an everyday thing for immortal guardians to just show up.

Oquelites were immortal if they were full-blooded, so did they have Diones? Did that make them different? He didn't dare ask any more questions on the topic.

Mrs. Outown laughed again, but as her laughter slowed, her deep copper eyes stared at him, begging to ease his uncomfortable state.

Ludwik pulled her closer and whispered something in her ear, and she perked up a bit.

"Right," she muttered, sitting back up. "We have questions, Coleson. Too many in fact."

"I might not be the right person."

Mrs. Outown laughed, but a little more sadness trembled in it then before. "You of all people are the right person," she said. "Why Jessica Taryn chose you is still a mystery to me, but I trust her."

"Why?" Cole asked, relaxing a little.

"You know nothing of Jessica. Who she used to be," Mrs. Outown said, glancing at Ludwik. "That doesn't matter. All that does matter is that you have passed the test."

Cole shouldn't have been surprised. "It's about the Council thing, isn't it?"

"We needed proof," Mrs. Outown chirped, her face rosy and smiling as ever. "When Jessica Hunter came with the news she finally found potential council members, after her years of her obsessive fascination with it, we needed to see for ourselves."

"Were you going to kill us if we…didn't make it?"

"The point is that you're alive!" Mrs. Outown said, rushing past the subject.

Cole tried to smile. Yes, he was alive. That was a good

thing. "You had questions?" he asked.

"Oh, right!" Mrs. Outown said, throwing her hands in the air. "My boy, how do you plan on wielding that sword?"

Ludwik suddenly had the sword in his hands, inspecting it. "It's one of the most powerful blades ever created," he said. "From the very sun itself."

"Of course. That makes sense," Cole muttered.

Ludwik looked to his wife and raised an eyebrow.

"Your position is very high in the Council, Coleson," Mrs. Outown said gravely. "Not all will survive. Not all twelve can live. Their death is a sacrifice."

Cole's eyes widened. Mrs. Outown sounded like she spoke from experience. Some of them would die. Maybe all of them. There were six left to find. He couldn't get stressed now.

"I see you have the Medallion," Mrs. Outown said.

Cole noticed that he was twirling the Medallion in between his fingers, and clasped his hand shut.

"My son had that too, you know," Mrs. Outown said, her eyes growing teary.

"He did?" Cole asked, opening his hand and looking down at the medallion. *Aaron.* That did make sense…

"He loved that thing so much. He wore it everywhere. Made him feel important," she said, looking away.

"I'm sorry," Cole said, holding the Medallion to his chest.

"I warned him of his fate if carried through with his dream of being a Defender. He got what was coming. Murdered," Ludwik said.

Cole pressed his lips together.

Mrs. Outown quickly changed the mood. "Aaron is not completely gone. He left a legacy. A small, delicate one in his son."

"H-he had a son?" Cole said, his eyes widening.

"Yes," Mrs. Outown said, with pride in her voice. "Eleazar's only ten, but he's a fine young man. He and his mother live here most of the time, but they're currently residing in a safe region till this all blows over. Hopefully soon you might meet him."

Cole grasped the Medallion. "Then wouldn't this belong to him?"

Ludwik shook his head. "The Illuminate Medallion does not run through families. It chooses who it sees fit to hold it."

Cole didn't know how to respond.

"That is why we are volunteering to be your patrons," Ludwik said.

"A Patron?" Cole said, frowning. "Like supporting me?"

"Of course. Whatever you need," Ludwik said, handing Cole back the sword.

Cole just stared at it. The Outowns were rich. And immortal. And now they were his patrons? At first, he thought this whole being part of a Council thing was going to suck, but now it seemed it could be turning out for the better.

"Th-thanks," Cole said, trying to keep himself from giving a stupid grin.

The Outowns stood and gave a slight bow.

Cole bowed awkwardly in return.

"Remember, you all have passed the test," Mrs. Outown said. "Everything happens for a reason. Good or bad. You and your young companions' destiny is just a long series of unanswered questions, and they're questions you all must answer."

50

"Rusty. Act sane, for crying out loud. And would you stop doing that with your hands?"

Felicity stuck her hands behind her back and tried to keep a calm face as she followed close behind Miriam.

Miriam had saved them from about six close calls, so far. Felicity didn't work well under pressure. Actually, that wasn't true. She *used* to work her best under pressure and making lies sound natural had come so easily. That's how she survived back in York.

Each day she had a different backstory. She could pull off any lie. Why she didn't do her homework, why she ran a block to school because she didn't want anyone seeing her jumping out of one of her father's company cars. She cut up her jeans and messed up her hair, and came up with a story for that too. She'd draw little stars all over her shoulders and tell the other kids that she got tattoos from her uncle in the Southern Regions who had a dancing tiger as a pet.

Yes, in those days pressure had been much easier to handle. It confused her how she could tell such lies yet struggle to believe what was happening right now. Her eleven-year-old self would have been disappointed. All those years she'd spent trying to cover up the name Bentsworth hadn't prepared her for this.

Miriam walked purpose, not saying a word, her shoulders straight and her head held high with an air of importance.

"Where are we going?" Felicity whispered.

"Kordin's office." Miriam didn't even keep her voice low.

The name sounded familiar. "The leader, big up top guy? Of the Defending Officers? Mir-Cornelia, why are we going *there?*"

"Because."

"Taryn didn't say anything about this," Felicity said, quickening her pace to match Miriam's.

"What the Sergeant doesn't know won't kill her," Miriam said, though the twitch in her brows revealed that she wasn't totally convinced of her own words. "Look, Rusty. Kordin will have answers. And he's the sergeant's uncle, so that's a plus."

"He won't just let you in."

"I'm an *Outown*, remember," Miriam said with a sigh. "I can get into a lot of places. We just have to watch out for Cadissa Dean and we'll be fine. She'll recognize us in a second." Miriam spoke of her with hate in her voice, lowering to a wispy whisper when she spoke her name.

Cadissa Dean? The Executive of the Officers?

Something crashed.

The lights flickered, and the entire hallway went dark. Sirens began to wail, and dim red lights flashed.

"Rusty! Run!"

Felicity was torn from her feet by Miriam's harsh grip. She stumbled into a run, bolting after Miriam's shadowed figure.

They stumbled to the top of the stairs. Felicity was out of breath, panting and brushing the sweat off her forehead.

Miriam seemed completely untouched. She was frowning, her fist and jaw clenched, her gaze fixed on the lone door before them. "Ready?" she said.

Felicity nodded, though Miriam didn't look to her. Miriam ran to the door and flung it open, barging in without hesitation.

Felicity ran in after her.

The door slammed so hard it echoed out into the stairs. A man with bright gray blue eyes, his dark brown hair slicked back, stood at the desk, his face hard and solemn as he met Miriam's furious eyes, not even taking notice of Felicity's entrance.

Papers were strewn on the floor, and the chair the man had been sitting in was on the floor as he stood behind the desk.

"Miriam Outown, what in Azar's name are you doing here?" he said calmly, moving to the other side of his desk with urgency in his step.

"Where is it?" Miriam said, storming to his desk, and pounding her fists down.

"Talk clearly, Outown. I can barely understand a word you're saying."

"Where is it?"

This time Kordin had to have heard what Miriam said, but he shook his head silently.

Miriam growled. "The Key Ring has to have been hidden here. It has to be."

Kordin only raised an eyebrow. "If there was something the Oquelite could use here, I'm sure I would have heard of it," he said.

He looked beyond Miriam and his gaze fell on Felicity. Fear shot into his eyes, though he kept his composure. "You found the Council, didn't you?" he said, the slightest hint of awe in his voice. "And a Bentsworth is part of it?"

Felicity grew hot from his remark. A Bentsworth. She had been a fool to think the head of the Defenders wouldn't recognize the daughter of one of the biggest business men in the world.

"Taryn warned you. It's happening So stop lying and tell me!" Miriam demanded.

Kordin just stared at her, then back to Felicity. His lips formed a hard, straight line, his eyes shifting up, like he was trying to tell them something.

Felicity frowned, suddenly uneasy, but Miriam took no note of Kordin's subtle movement.

The only sound was her enraged breathing. "You've been hiding and waiting ten years for this Kordin."

Kordin shot her a glare, his brows furrowing. "I'm afraid you've misunderstood."

Miriam looked ready to attack him, but a tear trickled down her cheek. "You killed them, Kordin. You gave those orders to kill them and now you're preparing for the last swing," Miriam choked.

The Curatrix Team? Kordin had killed them?

Felicity grew wide-eyed.

Kordin shook his head, sighing. "Is this all you wanted Miss Outown?"

Miriam this time had no mercy. She lunged at Kordin, but Felicity jumped and grabbed her, dragging Miriam down.

"You little—" Miriam hissed, tearing from her grip.

Felicity ended up at Kordin's feet. She looked up at the man above her. "Did you kill them or not?" she asked.

Kordin didn't reply.

Felicity shoved to her feet, rage burning in her chest now. "Did you order them to be killed or not?" she yelled.

Kordin pursed his lips.

"You did," Miriam gasped. "You did give that order!" Miriam stared wide-eyed even though she'd suspected it. Now that the confirmation was given, she received it like a blow.

"We don't have time to worry about past mistakes," Kordin said, looking up at the ceiling hurriedly. He rushed behind his desk, flipping a computer open.

Miriam slammed her fists down on the desk. "Those past freaking mistakes are why this is happening!" Miriam yelled. "The Oquelite are coming."

Felicity frowned. "Why don't they just barge right in? Can't they turn invisible or teleport or whatever?"

"Why don't you ask the *genius* leader!" Miriam snapped, her arms crossed over her chest still fuming.

"They have an impressive range. They are power holders. Some, mostly their lords, have the largest amount of essence in existence," Kordin informed, shutting off his hologram screen, looking up at them, a cold, hard expression frozen in his features.

"But why? What's even driving them? Yes, they've been locked up, but why a hidden attack?"

Miriam rolled her eyes like it was oh-so-obvious. "Revenge of course. It's always revenge," she said in a more stable, clear voice.

Felicity was about to ask another question before Kordin spat out. "You need to leave now."

Miriam frowned. "I don't think so."

Kordin's eyes went wild, and he yanked his hand from the drawer, pulling out a pistol. "Get out!"

But it was too late. A chilling laugh shot a shiver down Felicity's spine.

"Thank you for keeping our guests' company, Kordin. Things are just going so well today, don't you think?" Silas said with a deadly smile as he stepped around to face Miriam and Felicity, pulling out his blade.

And the next moment, she learned what 'wing it' meant.

51

THE WALLS WERE COVERED IN WIRES, SCREENS, CIRCUITS, holograms and numbers. It was hard to understand how the mess all connected to the entire Tower. Jack, however, sent his fingers across buttons and knobs like it was his heartbeat.

Lincoln watched Jack with his complete attention.

Ray was leaning against the frame of the door, looking out at the stairs leading back up to the ground, his eyes bored.

Lincoln had found the perfect distraction from Ray in Jack, watching him closely and quietly. This place wasn't much different small security panels in the back of the supermarket that Lincoln had investigated before. He used to help them fix their panels in exchange for food, when he was younger, before people began to grow suspicious of a teenaged boy roaming around the town without work. It just was huge, and more expensive, which an obnoxious number of wires.

Jack scowled, pulling one of his ear buds out and running his fingers through his hair with a low growl. He looked over his shoulder at Lincoln, and gave a small, forced smile.

"Need help?" Lincoln asked.

Jack shook his head. "Nah. This stuff's a little too complex," Jack said, though Lincoln could tell by his solemn expression the statement wasn't meant to offend. "Downloading Kordin's files onto a disc is a job the Sergeant's tried before but failed. So, I don't suspect you could get through these firewalls."

"So, you've worked with tech before?" Lincoln asked, eyeing the disc that was pulled into a holographic wire. It was circular, little lines running all around it, glowing a soft blue light.

"Being the Defender's janitor and mechanic requires more skill than a mop." Jack laughed. Then he sighed. "But mostly a mop."

Lincoln walked over to one of the many screens hooked up on the wall. "What's the problem?" he asked.

Jack shrugged, letting out another frustrated sigh. "Something in the security. Miriam's heading up to the top floor now," Jack said. He slipped the headphones over Lincoln's ears and a sudden flood of noise filled his head. Every footstep and whisper became audible. Lincoln curiously turned the knob on the side of the headphones and found himself tuned into some staff break room.

"Can you override the system?" Lincoln asked.

"Tried that. Miriam supposed to have gotten us in by now.

I *knew* she would get distracted."

Lincoln got up from the chair. *Think supermarket.* He looked across the gigantic panels and handed Jack the buds.

The shopkeepers always inserted his chip into the device to load all the files and connect it to his hologram in the back. It was often small, and easily bought on the web. It provided as a source of security to block out hackers, but it was one for constantly malfunctioning. That's where Lincoln came in.

But why would such a giant corporation have the chip? Actually, why wouldn't they? They had to have upgraded tech that didn't fail as often. But it still had the same basic functions.

You couldn't hack a chip, but it had to be manually removed.

And Lincoln knew how to do it. "How do you identify the room you're looking for?"

"W.W 505," Jack said, getting up. "That's the technical identification, at least."

It fit in with the little label above some of the panels. *N.W 313. E.W 405.* Lincoln ran down the wall, scanning over the labels. Numbers he could identify. He jolted to a stop. *505.*

"Lincoln. There isn't anything you can do—"

Lincoln pulled out the wires plugged into the panel, cutting off the circuits.

Jack ran to him. "What are you doing?" he said.

"You're trying to get to the top," Lincoln said. "And if there's something stopping you, it's connected to the room. If you take that away, there is nothing to go off."

"But then the room's security doesn't work!"

"This is Imperial," Lincoln said, pointing to the screen as

it flickered to life. "It doesn't need circuits. The top level is Kordin's office. He has the highest tech in the world. Wires are just a precaution."

Jack frowned. "How'd you know this stuff?"

"Supermarket," Lincoln said. "It didn't make sense why the Imperial tower would have its top room working like a little shop in North Cordell."

Jack shook his head, smiling. "Kid, how the heck does that brain of yours work?"

Lincoln had no idea. He shrugged.

"We better get back to work," Jack said, patting Lincoln shoulder then running back to the screen.

His moment of praise was quickly shattered by Ray shouting, "Hurry it up!"

Lincoln joined Ray by the door. Ray didn't meet his eye as he nervously shuffled around, looking through the crack of the door.

"What do you want, Black Eyes?" Ray muttered.

Lincoln glanced at Jack, then looked back at Ray. "What are you planning?" Lincoln whispered.

The unspoken implications of betrayal took immediate effect, and a glower settled across Ray's face. "Nothing much, Black Eyes."

Black Eyes. He was resorting back to childish taunts. "Look, Mathews. I know what you are, and as much as I'd like to see every Oquelite dead, I made a deal with your mother—"

Ray spun around, his eyes wide and his face pale. "You—you saw her? Is she okay?"

Lincoln nodded, a bit of the anger falling away for a moment.

"How? When?"

"Coincidence, I guess." Lincoln had his chance. Ray was

malleable. Desperate almost. He still cared.

"Jenna's quite fond of you. All your siblings are," Lincoln said. "Do you think they'd like to know…what you're doing?"

The split second of compassion fell away, and Ray turned away. "They don't really care."

"She talked about—"

"The Oquelite coming for me? I'd go crazy? A curse?" Ray scowled, not leaving a moment for Lincoln to respond. "That's a stupid lie! Made up stories for children. Lies! I'm sick of being lied to. This is what I *am*. Okay?"

Lincoln held up his chin, frustration burning as he clenched his jaw. "How do you explain Cole Johnson?"

Ray went quiet, but his glare only darkened. "What does this have to do with Cole?"

Ray didn't know. Or was he just playing with his mind?

"Your…brother?"

Ray's eyes grew wide. "My mother's gone insane," he muttered, stepping back. "You're trying to get to me, Black Eyes!"

"So that's your explanation? You have no *idea* what's at risk, do you? You tried to kill us."

Ray grabbed the collar of Lincoln's shirt and shoved him into the door. He brought his face close enough that Lincoln could see the burning flame overtaking his eyes.

"It runs in my blood, Black Eyes. Like stupidity and dullness runs in yours," Ray said, his breath growing uneven and raspy. "And don't bring the Ewyon into this. We all know what happens with Aviduous and Ewyon. If you know your Lore so well, you should know they're cursed."

With that, Ray released Lincoln and walked into the rows of electrical circuits, acting interested, though his frown didn't leave his face.

Lincoln scowled, and the burning didn't leave his veins. When he got the chance, he wasn't going to let Ray get away without teaching him a lesson.

It only took an hour before Lincoln thought Ray was trying to kill them again.

First, Jack's monitor burst into flames, then floor above them. Then, the entire room exploded into flames and Lincoln, Jack, and Ray were in the middle of it all. Ray ran into the flames as more machinery exploded around them.

Jack remained surprisingly calm until the fire began to crawl farther. "Ray?" he yelled, the beginning of panic edging his tone.

No response.

"He's trapped," Jack said, beginning to run for the flames, but Lincoln grabbed his arm.

"Leave him!" Lincoln gasped.

Jack pushed past Lincoln and ran into the fire, shouting Ray's name.

"Jack!" Lincoln yelled. Lincoln tried to move through the growing smoke. Another circuit burst, and Lincoln dodged the exploded bits.

"Lincoln! Move out of the way!' Ray's voice ripped through the air.

Lincoln jumped back, covering his head as another explosion rang through his ears. He scrambled to his feet again and Ray ran to him, coughing and trying to catch his breath.

Ray's face was scorched, his coat a little singed, but overall, he seemed fine. He gripped Jack's arm, half dragging the man from the flames. "We have to get out!" Ray said.

Jack's eyes suddenly lit up. "No, the disc!" he yelled. "You two get out! Run. Warn Taryn. Get your Council! Do whatever you can." He pulled free of Ray's grip and ran back through the flames.

Ray grabbed Lincoln's arm and dragged him out of the basement. He slammed the door behind them and kept running.

"We have to go back!" Lincoln yelled.

Ray didn't say a word.

The ground trembled and exploded from under their feet. Dirt, metal, and glass flew everywhere.

When Lincoln could feel his senses again, he was lying in the rubble of what would have been the Glass Tower's power panel.

That just blew up. With Jack Sallow inside.

Lincoln got to his feet, and pain shot through his head. The ground rocked a bit, though he thought it was just his balance now, not another explosion. He steadied himself, though the pain in the right side of his head only seemed to grow worse and rang louder.

The place just…exploded.

Someone blew it up. It was the most stable place in the world; there was no way it would've exploded without someone doing it on purpose. It made him feel sick.

He looked down at his hands, scraped and blistered, then back at the flames.

Maybe an Aviduous shouldn't have dealt with tech, no matter how natural it felt. *Do whatever you can.* Jack's words echoed in his mind. Lincoln took a deep breath trying to ignore the throbbing pain. "Ray. We have to—" He turned and stopped. A groan slipped from him.

Ray was gone. Again.

52

ALL TABITHA KNEW WAS THAT SHE WAS RUNNING AND tumbling down the small tunnel behind Nikki, who didn't even stop to explain why they were running. She said she knew what they were looking for and they needed to leave right away.

Something about an Oquelite?

As soon as they reached the end, Nikki swung the door open and both tumbled out, Tabitha on top of Nikki.

Tabitha jumped up, looking around. This was not the janitor's closet.

"Uh. Nikki," she said. "Where are we?"

Nikki got up, her eyes wild in confusion. They now stood in the middle of a sparkling hallway, with marble floor and chandeliers all the way down the corridor, the door at the end decorated with so many gleaming gems it hurt to look at it.

"What is this place?" Tabitha said.

Nikki shrugged. Her hair had fallen out of its neat updo, and all that remained were worn ripples, and her face was smeared with some black soot from that small hallway. How did she manage to get like that every time? Then again, Tabitha probably didn't look in top shape either. She wasn't rocking her new haircut, and in this sparkly hallway, they probably looked like trash.

Stupid hallway.

"We have to get out of here," Nikki said quickly.

"Why?" Tabitha asked.

"Hey! Are you ladies lost?"

Tabitha froze and the hair stood up on the back of her neck. She turned slowly to see a security guard in his perfect white uniform and his gelled, hot pink hair partly hidden underneath his hat. He looked like he could be one of the decorations.

Tabitha straightened and gave the man a big, stupid grin. "Nope, we're good," she said, grabbing Nikki's arm.

The pink-haired man made his way forward, letting Tabitha get a whiff of his overly strong aroma of…roses? "Little lady. Do you have a pass?" He grabbed her shoulder before she could slip past.

Tabitha patted her pocket, but her stomach dropped. Her ID was gone.

Nikki gave Tabitha a glance, seeming to say, *"If you want me to attack his face, just give the word."* But instead, Tabitha screamed, turned around, and smacked the guy right in the face.

"Who do you think you are?" she yelled, continuing to make disgusted noises in her throat.

Even Nikki moved away, her eyes wide in horror. The man backed up a bit, blinking in astonishment.

"I'll have my uncle sue you for this! How dare you lay a hand on me!" she yelled, ready to smack the guard again, but he bowed his head and shook with fear.

"I'm sorry! I didn't know!" he whimpered.

That went a lot better than Tabitha expected.

The man looked up and straightened his hat. "Is this your friend?" he said awkwardly, like making small talk would clear the tension.

Tabitha huffed. She grabbed Nikki's hand again, though Nikki squirmed. "She's my sister, you idiot! Now tell me where the main office is so I can file a complaint!" she demanded.

The man nodded and pointed down the hall to the left. "Take a turn and go to the second elevator to the right. It'll take you there," he said, turning and walking off so fast he stumbled over himself a bit.

Tabitha let go of Nikki's hand and scurried down the hall the man had directed them to.

"Why'd you say that?" Nikki asked behind her.

"Say what?"

"That I was your sister. It's just a cover."

Tabitha looked over her shoulder and shrugged. "Are we not?"

Nikki didn't protest.

Then the lights shut off. Sirens started wailing, and for a split-second Tabitha was afraid they'd been caught.

"Please evacuate the building immediately. This is no drill. Security Systems have failed. The Tower is now under attack."

Nikki shot a look at Tabitha, whose face was gripped with

fear in the flashing red lights.

"The Oquelite are here!" Tabitha said, voice shrill.

"We need to get to the lobby. Now," Nikki snapped.

She looked around for something other than an elevator. A door labeled '*Staff Only*' caught her eye. It stood in the middle of the two elevators, and—to her relief—was not decorated in flowers and pink glitter. She thrust the door open to the stairs. Stairs that had to lead down to the lobby.

She looked back at Tabitha, who was still frozen in her place.

"We can't take the Oquelite on by ourselves," Tabitha said, throwing her arms up. "You said we had to work together, and we aren't all together!"

Nikki looked back to the stairs. "What other choice do we have?" she snapped back at Tabitha.

Tabitha didn't answer, just scowled and headed for the elevator despite the warnings over the speakers. Nikki frowned.

"Yeah. I heard the announcement. I don't see a reason not to though. Meet you on the first floor!" Tabitha said as the door of the elevator shut.

Nikki took this as a challenge and dashed down the steps.

To her surprise the winding, dust coated steps were extremely quick, and almost satisfying. Her speed and strength made it easy to navigate in the narrow hallway, sliding, running, or jumping. It was dark and quiet, the way she liked it. She tried not thinking about where she was heading.

Her end.

Facing the Oquelite.

The people with magical abilities who could use a special flame to burn the flesh off her arm, or her whole body if they wanted to make it more painful. She approached the door and burst through it, landing on her feet.

She heard the elevator click only a moment after. So, the elevator was slower. But that wasn't important right now. All previous pleasure was erased as she took in the situation in the lobby.

The woman who ran the front desk sat stiffly at the mercy of the blade at her throat. The glint of her tag caught Nikki's eye.

Saniya. That was the woman's name. Another name that was now in danger because of the Oquelite.

The Oquelite threatening her had thick, fluffy red hair, just a shade off orange.

"Professor Kendrick?" Tabitha yelled in horror from the doorway of the elevator. "You're an Oquelite?"

The woman scowled. "Glad to see you're still alive, Ms. Delorous."

"Wow. You are not an old lady anymore," Tabitha said with a chuckle.

Another Oquelite snickered behind her. "One of your students, Zamara?" he said, laughing and pulling down his hood, revealing another head of red hair.

Zach. The Oquelite who had so proudly given them his first name in the forest, when, of course, he intended to take them.

Nikki wanted to run right back up the steps. This guy nearly killed her. And now he had a sister, and a couple hundred others waiting around the lobby.

Tabitha started laughing. "Wow. No wonder I hated you so much. Also, Cole would like to tell you that he didn't like being kicked out," Tabitha said.

How could she act so calm and crack stupid jokes right

now?

Zach finally caught sight of Nikki and his smile faded. "You—" he said, teeth gritted.

Saniya frantically tried to take this as an opportunity to escape, but Zamara held her down. "Zach, please get rid of them," she said.

Zach nodded and said something in a language Nikki couldn't understand. Apparently the other Oquelite could, and several of them vanished.

Nikki looked around frantically. She knew what they were doing.

Zach was sending them through the building. Looking for the Key Ring. They'd slaughter anyone in their path, even that pink haired guy. Tabitha shuffled toward Nikki as the Oquelite closed in. Saniya watched with terror in her eyes. The security guards called for the Oquelite to stop, but a wicked smile spread across Zach's lips.

Commotion erupted before Nikki's eyes. A masked Oquelite threw something at her, but Nikki's mind was hard-wired to survive. She wished it wasn't. She didn't have time for this right now, but the attacks kept coming and she kept avoiding them.

Tabitha cried out in pain somewhere in the crowd of security guards and Oquelites.

"Tabitha?" Nikki called out. Some sort of purple flame caught the end of her boot, and she ran, trying to stamp it out.

Tabitha was running through the crowd, her face white and blood staining the side of her neck.

"Tabitha!" Nikki yelled again.

Tabitha looked at her, her eyes wide. She was suddenly knocked over. Zach smiled at Nikki and raised his hand, fingers twisted in a shape Nikki had seen somewhere else.

Nothing happened.

Zach frowned, kicking Tabitha. "Are you even Impure?" he yelled at her.

Tabitha pulled herself up, forcing a weak smile.

Nikki ran toward Tabitha and pulled her aside.

Zach laughed. "You're a fool. Pure's Essense is strange. They are better off dead, but you. Your scent. It's quite—" Zach didn't finish his sentence. He just slammed Nikki to the ground.

"Get the front office woman out of here!" Nikki yelled at Tabitha, who nodded and ran.

Nikki pulled herself up. This was going to be the third time she was bashed by an Oquelite.

Zach's smile made her boil. He used magic, she used force, or running away. Both proved only to call for temporary success. She saw Tabitha get up and rush away. Zach looked to Tabitha then back at Nikki and shrugged. In an instant, his sword was in his hand and he stuck.

She ducked, but his blade nicked her cheek.

Even from that small cut, it felt like her own veins were being ripped from her as the smallest, faded ripple of blue mist shot from her into Zach.

Her mind was screaming at her to run. If he cut her deep enough, he could tear the life out of her.

There was only time to run and try to not die. She had no weapon, not even the Stone. Then she realized the one thing she hadn't thought of yet. The reason she wasn't going to win this. The reason why none of this was working.

She was in this *alone*.

Jack tossed his cape gracefully. It shimmered, and in an instant he disappeared.

A favorite trick of his apparently.

She barely had time to process before he rammed into her shoulder, throwing her off balance. She spun catching herself against the desk. Zach jumped back into view.

She grabbed a stylus from the desk.

A stylus?

That was the best she could come up with? With a cry, she threw it, and it harmlessly bounced off his chest. She scrambled up into the desk, as he slowly glided to her, a hint of amusement sparkling in his eyes.

Energy swelled in his palm.

She was done for. Avalon was right. She was only safe with Avalon. She shouldn't have come.

"Nikki!"

Tabitha.

Zach dropped his hand, with an irritated scowl. "Why is that brat back?"

Why *was* she back? Why didn't she leave?

Tabitha burst out from the commotion. Her neck still bloodied, her hair frizzy, a piece scorched. And she was armed with a traffic cone.

"Get away from her!" Tabitha shouted.

Zach groaned, and with a flick of his wrist, Tabitha was tossed off her feet, and sent sliding across the ground.

Zach turned on his heal. "Seriously, I see why my sister found you annoying…"

Nikki's blood boiled. In the moment, she picked up a tablet, aimed and tossed, hitting Zach right in the temple.

Zach cried out. He turned.

Nikki jumped, down on the opposite side of the table. She braced herself. Zach stormed toward her, his uniform beginning to shimmer to disappear.

Then, with all her might, she threw her weight against the desk. The desk came toppling over, taking Nikki with it over. The contents crashed at Zach's feet. The large hologram projector cracking sparking. Zach's cape began to smoke, small flames began to dance.

Zach cried out.

The projector burst out into flames. Nikki scrambled out of the way.

The rest of the tech fallen around it caught fire, the flames swallowing up the desk.

Nikki rushed to Tabitha, who was still lying on the ground groaning.

Zach stomped out the fire in his cap, his hands swelling with blue flames. Nikki fasted her arms on the end of the cone and swung it.

Zach turned too late, throwing out a fireball, that missed Nikki's head by inches, but the cone met its target perfectly.

Zach collapsed onto the ground, twitching and his cape smoking.

Tabitha had saved her. She'd enacted Zach's pride as a distraction. And who else would've known a heavy traffic cone would work so well to knock someone out?

She knelt and shook Tabitha. "Come on," she whispered.

Tabitha's eyes opened slowly. "My head," she groaned.

Nikki looked over her shoulder to the dying commotion in the main lobby. The Oquelite were easily overpowering the young guards. One Oquelite held their victim midair, leaving them sprawling and screaming before they sent them flailing into the window of a window of an upper office. None of them seemed to care about nor notice the fire.

They were playing with them.

Nikki helped Tabitha sit up, slipping her arm under Tabitha's. Tabitha wavered on her feet. "I'm fine," Tabitha grumbled.

"Good." Now they needed to get through the fight without being noticed, or attacked, and out the doors alive.

Nikki tightened her grip around Tabitha. She glanced over her shoulder. The exit to the stairs wasn't entirely blocked by the raging fire. If they went around the combusting front desk circle, and avoided the newly flaming carpet, they could make it. They would be out.

She braced herself, turned, and began to run.

Tabitha slowly came to her senses, her feet catching their balance, running with Nikki, only tipping over her own feet two times, and cursing under her breath over and over again.

Then Nikki stopped.

The room fell still.

A sensation creeped down her neck and down her spine, the hair on her arms rising.

Lone footsteps echoed behind her.

The fighting had ceased to silence.

Nikki snapped out of it. She grabbed Tabitha and thrust her forward. "Leave!" she shouted.

Tabitha stared at her for a moment, dazed.

Nikki pointed for the door, and willed everything in her voice to scream, "*Go!*"

Tabitha jumped. Nikki had never yelled, not ever quite like that, before. And it had its effect. Tabitha gave a quick nod, and slipped through the flameless pass, between the flaming desk and the wall, and after the doors.

Hopefully, she would listen this time.

"The Ewyon girl, is it not?"

The deep voice crept into her mind, slowly at first, and

sent another shiver down her spine, and goosebumps along her arms. The person's presence had an effect. A powerful one.

She didn't look.

The voice lingered directly behind her. She could hear loud, rhythmic breaths, and the nervous shuffling of the boots of the others in the room. The air was stiff. She didn't breathe.

Don't turn around, she warned herself. This is your chance.

"A child," he said. His voice sounded lost, as if he wasn't even speaking to anyone in particular. A mere observation, but a sort of lonely fascination.

She flexed her hand. Just another moment.

Then she jumped, twirling around, throwing her arm out. In an instant her wrist was caught.

Glazed over gray eyes met hers.

A young face etched with an ancient fragility. Blond hair drawn back into a small ponytail, a golden circlet fixed perfectly along his crown, against the deathly pale of his skin.

Orion.

Nikki had recognized his voice from the first instance, but now he stood in front of her, his wrist in his grip. The lover and killer of Avalon, a millennia later, glared at her blankly, as he towered above her.

She tore her eyes from his and looked to his hand.

It was bare. No gloves, like the other Oquelite. Which should've been a good thing.

Nikki's heart felt like it hit her stomach. Her head grew light. Her entire body tensed.

The ring wasn't there.

Her only lead, as crazy as it was, was wrong.

And now, she was stuck in Orion's grip.

She kicked Orion with all her might, though he didn't react. He let go of her, letting her stumble back.

Orion glanced to her, and then back to the Oquelite. "She's not her."

53

Cole couldn't stop looking at the Medallion.

Where had this thing been? Apparently on the neck of Aaron Outown, who was murdered. What about the other Council members?

Were they killed the same way? Was that how *he* would die? He didn't want to die. There was still so much to do.

He had wanted to ask more questions about Aaron. How much did the media not talk about the Curatrix Team? He had a son after all. He'd had a life.

That made Cole sick. Who had killed him?

It finally made sense why Taryn was the way she was. Or Jessica, rather. That was her real name. She must have changed it after the incident.

Without warning, the front doors of the mansion

banged. Cole went to open them, but hesitated. The sword began to glow brighter, it's light seeping out of the crevices of the sheath. The medallion pulled at his neck, until Cole finally unclipped it. He'd never taken it off before, but he carefully let it slip through his fingers now.

The medallion flew right to the sword's hilt, fitting into a groove on the crosspiece.

The doors burst open. Cole's eyes widened.

Oquelite. There were at least three of them in the doorway. This time they wore deep navy-blue uniforms, outlined in gold.

A tall, sturdy Oquelite stood at the front, his sword at one side and a gun at the other, with a bow slung over his back. The leader scanned the main hall.

Cole stood frozen in the middle of the room.

The man stepped forward till he was practically breathing on Cole, but never quite met his eyes. Then the Oquelite took a step forward. Cole braced himself for the impact, or even a stab of some dark magic.

The Oquelite walked right through him.

Cole looked down at himself. His body was pale, like a faded photograph, and the air seemed to ripple around him just faintly. Was he...invisible?

This hadn't happened before. Maybe it had been the combination of the Medallion and blade. It was like when the vines couldn't touch him, and the other weapons that bounced away from him, but this time the Oquelite couldn't see nor affect him.

This could come in handy.

He drew the Illuminate blade and looked over it, then turned and ran down the hall, searching for Taryn. He found her room at the end of the first hall.

She sat alone looking out the window. Cole burst in, grabbing the medallion from the groove in the sword. "Uh, Sergeant Taryn! We have Oquelite in the building!" he finished the sentence in a yell.

Taryn jumped up, pistol in hand. She grabbed her knife from the windowsill and slid it into the sheath on her belt, cocking the pistol.

"What kind?" she asked, pushing past him into the hall.

"They had gold—"

"Oh no," Taryn cut him off, her lips pressing into a thin line. "This is going to be the end of us."

The two burst into the parlor, where Mr. and Mrs. Outown sat.

"They're here!" Taryn shouted.

Mr. Outown looked at Cole and nodded. "We know," he said solemnly.

Taryn frowned. "You know? Why haven't you done anything about it?"

Mrs. Outown shushed her. "Jessica, calm yourself," she said.

Her words seemed to have no effect on Taryn, who cast a nervous glance around the room and began to pace.

Even in a calm situation Taryn didn't stand still. Her hands were always fidgeting, tapping against a table. But now, it had a panicked, unorderly edge to it. No rhythm.

"He's going to kill us!" she snapped, then she looked to Cole. "He's a mad man. This compromises the entire mission." She spun on the old couple, glaring. "You're Diones. You should *know*."

Mrs. Outown patted the seat next to her, and Taryn slumped down, though her feet continued tapping. So, Mrs. Outown had just invited Taryn to wait for her death?

Whoever the new Oquelite, they must have been dangerous to worry Taryn so much.

Something crashed in the hallway and the medallion shot for the sword again. Cole twisted toward the doorway, invisible again.

Ludwik gave a cracked smile in Cole's direction, and Cole nodded back though the man couldn't actually see him.

The doors burst open, and Cole held his breath. The leading Oquelite stepped in slowly and turned his hooded head to Taryn, Anne, and Ludwik.

Anne Outown rose and smirked. "Oh, I never thought I'd live to see the day you'd show your face again."

Cole found the statement amusing coming from an immortal guardian.

The leader turned to an Oquelite to his side. "Retrieve your team and search the manor. Lock the doors to this room," he said.

Something pushed him backward and Cole stumbled a few paces until he hit the wall. Energy pulsed through him— the Oquelite man's presence was beating on him and leaking through his skin.

The Oquelite finally tossed off his hood. He had flowing sand-blond hair pulled back in a small ponytail, silver hairs laced throughout. His face was young and ancient all at the same time. His jaw line was sharp, and his brows thin and knitted together as he watched, with his eyes were large and misty grey, distant and cloudy like he was trying to focus on something too far away. He pulled the mask down from his mouth and looked straight at Taryn.

Cole could tell she was struggling to stay confident and fearless. Her hand twitched on her lap, clenching into a fist.

The man stared at her with a blank gaze before his lips

curled into a sly smile. "Don't you remember me, child?" he said, chilling whatever fire burned in Cole's blood.

Taryn gave a small, stiff nod. "Lord Orion Idicous."

54

Names have power.

And the Idicous lord's name had energy that pulsed through Cole like nothing he'd ever felt before. Like someone had set off a spark in his veins. Was he the only person that felt this? If not, everyone else seemed to be hiding it, except maybe for Taryn, whose entire body was shaking.

She took a step back and clenched her fist. Orion's face was still empty and hollow, seeing no pleasure in Taryn's fear. He just stared coldly.

That wasn't the weirdest thing.

The weirdest thing was Ludwik and Anne Outown.

Suddenly, their skin became tighter, their hair darkening, the streaks of white and grey disappearing. Mrs. Outown seemed taller, and Ludwik stood broader. Then a pair of flickering…wings folded out from behind first Ludwik, then his wife.

Cole's jaw dropped. Mrs. Outown's wings were made of a shimmering white colored energy, glistening and flickering in the sunlight like a hologram, and Mr. Outown's were dark and black, the surface glistening.

They looked a lot fiercer than a little old lady that laughed a lot, and her grumpy husband. When Ludwik scowled, Cole couldn't help but notice how similar he was to Miriam.

Orion gave a hollow smile.

"What business do you have returning?" Ludwik asked, his voice hard.

Orion tucked a stray hair behind his ear. He didn't answer the question, just looked to Taryn, his eyes seeming to focus for a second. He stepped closer to her, running his hand across her cheek.

Though she met Orion's gaze with her own, cold and fierce, Cole guessed Taryn was freaking out internally.

"How quickly they grow old, and yet how well they keep their secrets," Orion said, backing away from Taryn.

Taryn's eyes flashed, and for a moment Cole could have sworn they were not hazel, but some sort of electric blue. It was gone too quickly for him to be sure.

She pushed ahead of Ludwik and Anne to face Orion. This time, she wasn't trembling. "I don't have to keep secrets," she hissed.

"Councils are not to be trusted. They are dangerous and out of control. You have no idea what really happened to yours do you? And you've been spending the last ten years trying to find out."

Taryn's eyes widened.

"I thought you looked different. Their death really took an influence on you," Orion rasped. He snapped out of his trance, turning to the man standing next to him. "Bind the Ywondie. Then properly dispose of her. Diones need to be taken alive."

Orion looked around the room until his eyes locked exactly on Cole's location. Cole held his breath and clutched the hilt of his sword. Orion looked away, but Cole drew the sword anyway, remembering the little Doran had taught him.

But going against this immortal, super-powerful, creep of an Oquelite seemed impossible.

The Oquelite General grabbed Taryn, who seemed to freeze as he touched her. She suddenly burst back to life, kicking at her attacker, but these Oquelites were ordered and stern. The cuffs snapped together on her wrists.

An Oquelite grabbed their dagger and pushed Taryn to her knees. She fought blindly, and even without a weapon she managed to bash the Oquelite's face with her bound hands.

"Get out!" Ludwik snapped to Mrs. Outown. She gave a heavy sigh, pursed her lips, and in a swift crouch, she leapt., launching herself into the air, her wings catching the air, laughing up toward the dome ceiling's window.

Cole lost the ability to breathe. Wings? He almost laughed. Of course.

*Wing*or.

"Anne!" Ludwik's cry threw Cole back to his senses. An Oquelite had begun to run up the wall, defying gravity. A few realized what was happening and rushed away from Ludwik to help their comrade, gracefully leaping from the ground, gravity holding them against the walls.

Ludwik dove out of the way of a swinging blade, jumped

onto a table. It tipped under his weight, and he threw himself into the air.

The vase fell of the table and shattered.

An Oquelite came crashing down, snapping the table into shambles.

Cole ripped the medallion out of the hilt, looped it back over his head, and raised his weapon.

Orion glanced at him with interest, but no surprise.

Cole pulled his gaze from Orion with an effort. He ran to Taryn and slashed through the cuffs. Almost immediately, the metal melted off her wrists.

The Oquelite general's glossy sword clashed with his. Cole wasn't the best at this whole sword fighting thing yet. Seriously, he'd only been practicing for about three days, but he had to try.

Taryn gripped her knife and the pistol in her other hand. Her eyes changed to blue for a flash, then her eyes flickered back to hazel.

Orion gave another sad smile.

Cole grabbed Taryn's arm and tried to pull her away.

An Oquelite drew his knife and slashed at him. Cole ducked, the blade crazing across his cheek. His heart hammered against his chest. With a cry, he swiped his sword. The Oquelite dove out of the way, the sword only catching his shoulder. Red began to seep through the cloth, though the Oquelite so no harm.

Cole's fingers went numb in cold sweat. *Breathe.*

The Oquelite came back for Cole with his dagger. Cole skidded to the ground, catching the Oquelite ankle with the blade.

The Oquelite stumbled.

Cole nearly fell forward, but Taryn caught him. Her eyes

were back to normal, with a familiar fierce, authoritative glare. She grabbed his arm and ran. He stumbled after her. "Ser—Taryn! We can't leave! What about the Out—"

"Coleson!" Taryn shouted, slamming the glass doors of the parlor, leading to the gardens open. "We don't have *time*."

Orion nodded slowly, his lip curling. "You better listen to your little Sergeant. You wouldn't want to miss watching your Imperial City burn down in flames."

55

Felicity's mind was having trouble on deciding what to be shocked by.

Silas' arrival or the two huge wings that had sprouted from Miriam's back. To say they were just wings wasn't enough. They definitely had the shape, but they were made of a glassy, gray energy. They looked almost like a hologram, that moved and breathed with Miriam's movement.

But they were *wings*. Wings! How many times could they have easily avoided a problem if Miriam just revealed that important fact?

No one else in the room was fazed by it.

Silas stepped over to Kordin and with a flick of his wrist, Kordin's pistol was nothing but blasted parts across the floor.

"How those 'Defenders' fall when they realize they aren't the top of the food chain anymore," Silas said, tracing the tip of his blade across the silver defender identification pin on Kordin's chest.

He glanced toward Miriam. "Outown Junior, please don't try anything extravagant. You'll only make things harder for yourself. We have been given orders to kill you," Silas said, his eyes shifting to Felicity. "We know all about your petty little Council."

Felicity clenched her jaw. It wasn't a surprise. They seemed to know everything.

"At one point, I knew you. I trusted you," she said, her heart aching. "You can't kill, Silas."

Silas looked at her, and she thought maybe for a moment his eyes held a glimmer of shame. He hardened again before she could be sure. "Felicity. Our past wasn't real. You never knew me. Now silence!" Silas spat.

Felicity shook her head furiously. "Say all you like," she said, crossing her arms and turning away.

Silas's face flushed red in fury, and he lifted his blade closer to Kordin's neck. His eyes glowed. "Can someone kill her already?"

Felicity huffed. "Why don't you just kill me with your own hands? Or are you too afraid?"

Silas grabbed Kordin and pulled him harshly into Felicity's view. "I am not afraid!" he yelled. In one quick motion, he cut Kordin, dropped the knife, and with a flick of his hand, a blue essence was pulled from the wound.

The defender slumped to the ground, choking on a cry.

Felicity covered her mouth with her hand, staring down at the man, then back to Silas, who's hands were trembling, seeming to try to catch his breath.

"Do you want to be next?" he asked.

Tears welled in her eyes.

Kordin wasn't dead yet, but from the spreading stain on the floor and the shuddering of each breath it wouldn't be too long. He pulled himself up, but Silas shoved him back with his boot.

Miriam's wings suddenly spread out in front of Felicity.

"Miriam, get out of the way!" Felicity cried.

A force slammed into her and Felicity was knocked to the ground. When would the being knocked to the ground thing end?

The room filled with smoke. Felicity sat up, coughing into her elbow as her eyes stung. Someone's strong grip pulled her up and a long stick-like weapon was shoved into her hand. As the smoke began to clear, Felicity saw what it was.

A spear.

And the one who had jumped in also came into view. Jack. He was sweaty, his face smeared with black oil, and he smelled like burning debris. A light shot through the smoke, parting to create a visible path for Silas and his other companions.

Silas scowled.

Miram, Jack, and Felicity began to back up. Felicity's shoulders hit the wall. She looked over her shoulder.

Not a wall, glass.

She looked back at Silas and the spear.

The idea was stupid, and they would most likely die, but weren't they going to die anyway? She gripped the spear awkwardly and hit the glass. At first it only made a small crack, and then a small crack began to grow.

Jack burst out in a nervous, excited laugh.

The Oquelite lowered their bows. Felicity smiled. Of

course. If they shot, they'd complete her plan themselves.

"Come on Silas! Shoot!" Jack said, his voice shaky with excitement. "What? Did some mortal girl just foil your precious little plan?"

Silas growled again. "Foil my plans? The real question is what are yours?" he said.

Did they really have a plan? Miriam had wings.

Felicity looked to Miriam to make sure her eyes had not deceived her. Sure enough, Miriam's glistening wings were still there. That was enough confirmation for Felicity.

Felicity held the spear with both of her hands and ran at Silas. His eyes grew wide. Just as she was close enough to touch him with the tip of the spear, she jumped and whirled around and threw the spear with all her might at the glass. It hit the glass and bounced back.

Felicity gasped. They were dead.

Then the wall of glass shattered into a million pieces. She screamed, half in shock and half in celebration. Silas tried to grab her, but she ran, grabbed Jack and Miriam's arms, and jumped out of the tallest building in the world.

Felicity never thought she'd be flying through the air, falling from the Glass Tower.

To her surprise, Miriam wasn't flying, but falling just as fast as the others, her eyes squeezed shut.

"Miriam!" Felicity yelled, watching the ground rushing to greet them. "Fly!"

Miriam just scrunched up in a ball. She awkwardly began to spread her wings but scrunched them back around her in another moment.

"I've seen you do it before! Come on!" Jack yelled at her.

Miriam spread her wings out, though she was still in a ball. She stopped mid-air, her wings catching the wind.

"Miriam!" Felicity screamed as she and Jack continued to tumble.

Miriam opened one eye and gave a scream.

"Miriam! Open your eyes!" Jack yelled.

Miriam gulped and dove for them.

"Slow it!" Jack instructed.

Miriam lunged for Felicity first, and Jack grabbed hold of her as she dove past him.

"Miriam! Land! Land! Land!" Jack and Felicity yelled.

The ground raced for them way too fast. Felicity shut her eyes. The rush stopped with a jerk, and her feet slowly touched the ground.

She opened her eyes and backed up. She was standing on the safe, hard ground. "Miriam! You did it!" Felicity said, hugging Miriam so tight she heard Miriam gasp for air.

Miriam pulled away. The two giant wings had torn from her back, reaching taller than Miriam when they were folded, their black sheen shimmering in the sun.

"A-and you have wings," Felicity added.

"Yeah, I guess I did Rusty," Miriam said, a tear of terror trickling down her face. "I-it's a Wing—wingor Diones thing. N-never again." Then she turned to Jack, still catching her breath. "And mister, you need to lose some weight."

"I'll take that into consideration."

Ignore it. Ignore it. Find Tabitha. Ignore it.

Nikki felt hopelessly lost. The crowds of panicked people, all armed with cell phones, big cameras, or some sort of weapon rushed through the streets. Many were carrying large suitcases, rushing families into cars. None seemed to notice her, which was a relief.

But she was still lost in one of the most influential cities in the Joined World.

Getting out of the Glass Tower was a fight she didn't want to remember. Every bone in her body ached, and she was surprised she hadn't broken anything.

Orion's pained smile still stared cold into her eyes.

She wished she could yell and kick a wall and sink back into the empty void, ignorant of space, time, and sanity. For a moment, she wished she was back before Avalon had found her, where she didn't have to think or feel anything. Just numb and blind all the time.

Find Tabitha.

Nikki was sure she would have spotted a bouncy, red capped girl bouncing around somewhere, but no luck. Had she made it out alive?

Fear and panic flushed through Nikki.

The cut on Tabitha's neck. Had it been deep? Was it fatal?

Nikki ran faster.

Were Lincoln and Ray alright? What about Cole? How had the Oquelite gotten into the Tower? Where were Silas and Matthias? Where was Felicity?

"Nikki!"

Tabitha collided with her from behind, hugging her so tight Nikki could barely breathe and had to restrain herself from punching Tabitha.

Tabitha's eyes were teary. "Oh gosh, I thought that Zachary guy would have had the best of you," she said.

Nikki shook her head, though Tabitha was definitely right. "Your neck," Nikki said.

Tabitha looked down to her wound. "Ah, he just grazed me," she said, brushing it off as if it was no big deal, but Nikki led Tabitha into an alley. It was surprisingly neat and orderly, all the trash bins lined up perfectly; only a few stray cats roamed, their large beady eyes watching the girls fearlessly.

Nikki made Tabitha sit down and she began to inspect the wound.

"Do you have any water?" Nikki asked.

Tabitha nodded, gesturing to her bag. Nikki pulled out a water bottle and squirted it onto Tabitha's neck, beginning to wash away the drying blood. To her relief, Tabitha was right. Zach had just grazed her.

"You alright?" Tabitha asked, frowning. "You seem tired."

Nikki looked up to Tabitha. "I'm okay," she said, getting up and tossing Tabitha the water bottle. "Do you always overpack?" Nikki asked.

Tabitha broke out into a smile. "Always."

Nikki wished she could replicate Tabitha's emotion. That smile, particularly. Maybe once she could have. It just felt like a piece that was missing or a spark blown out and unlightable.

"And Nikki, you're allowed to be tired," Tabitha said.

Nikki shook her head. "I'm not tired," she insisted.

Tabitha shrugged. "Alright, fine. I get it. Come on," she said, her words riddled with sarcasm.

A flash of movement caught her eye and Nikki spun around, her jaw dropping. Felicity was plummeting from the Glass Tower.

How much trouble could people get themselves into these days?

She broke out into a run toward the Tower.

Tabitha yelled after her, but Nikki didn't stop.

Felicity would kill herself.

Nikki pushed past the crowds, blindly shoving people out of her way. The Imperial Tower was still being evacuated when she approached, but Felicity was no longer falling. As a matter of fact, Felicity was nowhere.

Nikki ran faster and farther along the building. For the first time, she noticed how enormous it was. She couldn't even see the top from here. She nearly tripped on a piece of rubble. The side of the building was a black, smoldering hole. Was this because of Felicity's fall?

Did she explode? No, that was absurd, but so did a lot of things that kept happening to them.

"Squirt?" Miriam's voice came out of nowhere.

Nikki jumped and looked around. Nothing.

"Squirt! Right here!" Miriam shouted again. Miriam collided with her, giving Nikki a face full of...dust?

Nikki coughed, scrambling back in shock, and clenching her fists to pounce. Then she stared at Miriam. The dust was from wings? Miriam's wings. Glittering wings of essence shimmered in the dying sun, flecks of supernatural flying upwards. Nikki dropped her hands to her sides and just gaped cluelessly at Miriam.

Miriam glanced over her shoulder. "Oh, yeah," she said, clearing her throat. "Like Taryn said, it's an Outown thing."

Felicity and Jack ran out from the blasted hole in the ground. Jack looked awful. Parts of his thick brown hair were singed, his face smeared with soot and drying blood. But his smile was still on his lips.

Felicity seemed a little more distraught, her fists clenched around a spear. "Nikki!" she said, her face lighting up. She ran to hug her but stopped herself. "Where's Tabitha?" she said.

Nikki looked over her shoulder. Had she lost Tabitha

already? Suddenly, a bobbing head with a bright cap pushed through the crowd.

"Wait for me!" she called out.

Felicity let out a sigh of relief, then gasped as soon as she caught sight of Tabitha's neck. "Tabitha! Your neck! You got—"

"Felicity. We're not in Liberty anymore. I got my first red badge," Tabitha said, crossing her arms. Then her jaw dropped.

Felicity pressed her lips together. Nikki could see she was trying to hold herself back, but Tabitha was clearly annoyed. Until she turned to Miriam, and her jaw dropped "What the heck is on your back?"

"Wing...things. Made of essence." Miriam grimaced. "I'm the daughter of full-bloods. Surprise? Now, back on track. Where are Emo and Gears?"

Felicity burst out suddenly. "Jack! You were with them!"

Jack gestured toward the debris. "They got out before it exploded. Don't know where they ended up."

Nikki felt a flutter of panic inside of her. She didn't know where it came from. She pushed the sick feeling away. "We have to look for them!" she insisted.

"We will," Miriam said, looking back up at the Glass Tower. "But the Oquelite are here. Kordin's dead. And...Silas is up there."

Tabitha's eyes widened in horror, a strangled gasp escaping her lips.

"Uh huh," Jack said. "We better get out of here."

"We have to get back to my house!" Miriam gasped. "Who knows what's going on there!"

She twisted away, but Jack caught her. "Miriam. Calm down. If you run in like that, you're practically committing suicide!"

"No, Jack! My only family is in my home!" she pleaded, then jerked from his grip.

She ignored her own wings, sprinting through the uneasy crowd. She didn't even bother to cover her wings. People gasped, some just stared, trying to take a photo as she ran.

Jack, Tabitha, Felicity, and Nikki ran after her. For once, they didn't try to hide themselves either.

The entire world was about to find out anyway.

56

Nikki had never seen someone crack as hard as Miriam did that night.

They barely caught up with Miriam as they reached her house. The windows had been shattered; the door torn off. A cry tore from Miriam, but Jack grabbed her before she could run inside. She kicked and screamed against him to let her go. His grip was firm around her.

Nikki stepped forward to help, but something held her back. A lump formed in her throat, her chest aching. Suddenly, she couldn't bear watching Miriam It hurt to watch her like that. Jack had to physically drag her back into an alley. Miriam grabbed her ears and squeezed her eyes shut, falling limp, no longer resisting. Jack caught her. She sobbed, her body trembling uncontrollably.

Tabitha stared at the mansion from the alleyway.

Nikki watched her as Felicity walked up to Tabitha, murmuring something Nikki couldn't hear. Tabitha turned her back, pushing her friend's sympathetic hand away. As she moved past Nikki, she saw the other girl's eyes were glassy. Tabitha was on the verge of tears.

Felicity sighed and turned her eyes to Nikki. "She's worried," Felicity said, nervously tucking a stray piece of hair behind her ear.

Nikki glanced back at Tabitha. The girl had unpacked her beloved binder and hidden her face in it. Nikki wanted to comfort her somehow, but what did she know?

Tabitha was rejecting Felicity, and clearly wanted to be left alone. Nikki left her.

Nikki retreated to a rooftop of a manor that had been evacuated. She couldn't take Miriam's cries. It hurt too much.

The sky had gotten darker, and the faded smudge of the moon had appeared in the sky behind the smog. City lights shown against the heavy clouds, beacons moving in slow rhythmic circles. The streets were alive. The sirens blended into the buzz of city noises in the background, but the flashing lights never seemed to dim.

Nikki pulled her legs up to her chest and rested her chin on her knees, watching the sky. She couldn't remember the last time she could just look at that night sky, alone. A thought crept through her mind sending a sick feeling to her stomach. Hadn't all she wanted was safety? That's what the Stone had promised her. And now, she was just waiting for the morning, and the inevitable horror that would follow. Had she made a mistake?

Not now, she urged herself. Why couldn't she just have a

peaceful mind? One that would leave her alone and let her feel okay?

"Miriam's calmed down." Felicity slid down next to her.

Nikki nodded.

That was good. Miriam was their best shot at surviving tomorrow. But at the same time Nikki felt she might be able to understand her pain. Somehow, she felt like she understood Miriam's cries, and the panic rising inside her.

Miriam needed time.

Felicity took a deep breath. "She said something about voices. *Voices* telling her she needed to go to Kordin."

Nikki looked up. Felicity's eyes had drifted away.

"How's Tabitha?" Nikki asked, steering the subject away.

Felicity looked down at her fidgeting hands. "She's…quiet," she managed. "I think she's afraid of what happened at the mansion."

"Because Cole was in there?"

Felicity shot her a look, but Nikki didn't see what there was to be mad at about that. "I guess so," Felicity said, sighing. "And Taryn. Don't you care about Taryn?"

"Who said I cared?" Nikki said, feeling suddenly defensive. She didn't want to argue with Felicity. Her mind was in shambles.

Felicity gave another heavy sigh. "You know that's not true," she said. "That you don't care about anyone."

Nikki didn't say a word. She'd known Felicity for barely a month. What did she know?

"Sometime before this," Felicity said, "you had to have cared about someone."

Nikki shook her head stubbornly.

Felicity pressed her lips together in a line and looked down into the streets. "I won't force you."

Nikki looked at Felicity's eyes, which were silently begging for a response. "Maybe," she managed.

Felicity nodded, looking away, disappointed. As she turned to leave, Nikki flashed around.

"I hope you all don't die," Nikki said.

Felicity laughed and gave Nikki a small smile. "Hey, I hope you don't die either." She squeezed Nikki's shoulder.

Nikki flinched still, but the support felt good. "If I don't make it—" Nikki began, but Felicity cut her off.

"Please don't finish that sentence."

Nikki pushed through. "I want to tell you…thanks."

Felicity's eyes widened. "For what?"

"Everything."

A small smile crept across Felicity's lips. "I-I don't know what you mean—"

Nikki looked away, and Felicity didn't finish her sentence. She turned back around and laughed softly to herself.

Nikki turned back to the skyline. She still felt sick inside. Why hadn't she said something to Lincoln before they'd left? He'd been trying to warn her.

But the word he'd used.

Insane.

It stung her.

She hoped he was alright. She hoped they were all okay. She didn't know what had become of her, but she knew one thing for certain. She wished she didn't care.

The cold shot right through Lincoln's throbbing head.

He hadn't been able to find Ray, even after tireless hours of looking. The sun was disappearing.

Lincoln knew he was going to die tomorrow.

The ground had shaken so lightly that Lincoln could

barely feel it. But it was a sign. Something or *someone* would die. He felt superstitious for worrying, but he couldn't help it.

He slid to the ground, helpless. The sidewalk of the evacuated neighborhood was lonely. The air was filled with distant siren, and the creaking of a door someone hadn't bothered to close while leaving, letting it swing in the soft wind. He pulled his jacket tighter.

No matter what he tried, their fate would find them. What was he thinking when he'd tried to leave North Cordell? Who was he to think he could *change* things?

He should have stayed in those woods. He rested his head in his arms. He slid his hood over his face.

The hatred toward Ray in his gut had dissolved into a twisting knot. It hurt. *Guilt.* He hated it.

Something brushed against his leg.

Lincoln jumped back, but two glowing yellow and black eyes stared up at him. He relaxed and reached out his head to rub the cat's head.

"I guess it's just you and me now bud. Bad luck," he said, though his voice was drained, and the sarcasm fell flat.

The cat seemed to sense his mood and jumped up into his lap. It purred and rubbed against his chest. Lincoln sighed.

The cat just stared innocently into Lincoln's eyes.

"You don't understand. There are people out there who are going to get hurt," Lincoln said, not even questioning why he was talking to a cat. "People. People I care about. I mean, I think I care about them. I hope I do."

Lincoln released a frustrated sigh and buried his face into the cat's fur.

The cat gave a meow and licked a tear off Lincoln's face.

"Thanks, bud." Lincoln closed his eyes, trying to settle his whirling head.

Maybe he would be granted with a new memory. Nothing changed. Nope. He sighed again. Just stuck with the stupid jumble of random facts.

Jack was dead and it was Lincoln's fault. He could have saved him.

Nikki and the others could probably also be dead. And Ray was gone.

He didn't want to think past that. He wanted to fix things. He did. But how?

The realization hit him harder than he wanted to admit. The only way to fix things, was to try and find the humanity in Ray.

Lincoln wasn't a normal Aviduous. No strength, just brains. He wasn't fearless, he was utterly terrified.

The cat meowed again. Lincoln opened his eyes. The cat looked up at the Glass Tower in the distance and meowed again.

"I can't go there buddy," Lincoln said.

The streets were clearer now. The sirens of police vehicles and security evacuations were the only sounds. The cat gave a disappointed meow. Lincoln patted it on the head and looked up again.

He stood up, gave the cat one more scratch, and pulled his hood tighter. He looked up at the Tower again.

He was the first to notice that it was beginning to lean.

"Great, we're in a mall," Taryn grumbled, getting to her feet.

Cole picked himself up, his eyes growing wide. One moment they were in the Outown Manor fighting Orion Idicous and now they were in a…mall? Orion had teleported them.

Some stunned customers riding on a moving sidewalk, stared at them curiously. This must have been a farther side of the City. The entire ceiling of the mall was made of glass, and it rose several floors, with halls, and railings looking over the floor ground. In the center was a hovering box, its side built with screens, flashing news about upcoming sales and new vendors. On a normal occasion, Cole might have been a little embarrassed, but right now he wanted to yell at all the shoppers to get out of the Imperial City as fast as they could. He didn't need to.

The ground gave a gurgling sound. A loud one. Then a screech pierced through the air. He gasped and flinched back, but the sound seemed to come from everywhere at once. Some of the shoppers pressed their hands over their ears and fell to the ground, yelling. A giant wall of semi-transparent blue shot into the red sky and met in the middle like a giant dome.

How long had the sky looked like it had been dipped in blood?

That's when people started to panic.

"What is that thing?" Cole shouted.

Taryn just stared. "The protective barrier around the Imperial City. Put in place after the EarthShaker like the one in North Cordell."

Cole frowned. That was not a good answer. They were initiating a wall used in the most brutal war of all time in this attack?

Taryn snapped from her daze and ran for the ladder leading to the announcement box hovering over the mall. Cole followed her closely, his sword drawn. Taryn climbed up into the box and shoved the man inside aside. A holographic screen appeared in front of her, reflecting them, like a giant camera. The image appeared in multiple places in the mall.

Taryn showed no weakness, her face as unreadable and fierce as usual. "My name is Jessica Taryn Hunter, leading Defending Sergeant of the Region of North Cordell, niece of James Roland Kordin. I am warning you, today the forces of a human race known as the Oquelite have broken from the bonds the Defending Officers were responsible for protecting." She paused for a moment. "I am the surviving member of the Curatrix team."

The Oquelite were confidential, but there was Taryn throwing it out there like it was everyone's business. And now it was. The very seams of what the world knew was falling apart before his eyes.

"Today they are attacking your city. They will leave no survivors. You must fight or evacuate. They will kill you, no matter who you are."

Cole winced. Her words were a little harsh. He stepped to the screen, trying to control his stage fright. This was why he'd never be in the Performing Arts.

"I am Cole Johnson," he said, glancing to Taryn.

She didn't interrupt, which probably meant she wanted him to go on.

"I am a member a … team. Something like that…But as Taryn said, your city is in danger. The Oquelite are trying to take back the Earth for something we can't even comprehend. We have a Council who can stop them."

Taryn stepped forward entering something into the computer as Cole continued to speak.

"We can't back down now. I know you're probably freaking out. The sky's red, we're trapped in a dome, and yes, we are in danger. But we can't hide anymore. I don't care who you are, but if you care for your country, your family, or your own life, you have to stand up and protect what is yours."

Cole steadied himself with a deep breath. "We currently have six members," he said, catching a glimpse of his reflection. "We're just a bunch of…kids. But we've survived these Oquelite before. And if some random kids can, you can too."

The screen went black, and Taryn gave him a smile. "The whole Imperial City and neighboring regions have received our message."

Cole's jaw dropped. *The whole city heard that?* "I sounded like an idiot!" he yelled.

Taryn laughed, putting her hand on his shoulder. "Johnson, those words coming from a stuttering teenager, holding one of the most powerful weapons in the world will be enough to convince anyone. Sometimes that's all it takes. I'm beginning to see why Fate elected such strange members. The world is going to recognize you. All of you."

"Wait? How?"

"I broadcasted images of each of you as you spoke.:

"How'd you get those photos?" Cole said. "Why?"

"Are you up for this, Johnson, or not? I just got you a rep," Taryn growled. "Come on! Orion and his sons are attacking the Imperial City!" She jumped out of the box, landing on her feet on the ground below.

Cole didn't want to die, so he took the floating ladder.

The people of the mall were in chaos.

The guards tried to calm them; one man stood up on a stand and demanded that the government give them answers. Some younger men and women rallied around him, until a guard dragged him down. Cole expected them to come for them next. But instead, the guards moved out of his way. One guard met Cole's eyes, shaking his head like he was sorry for him. The guard picked up his security pistol into his hands and began to follow a group of angry people out the doors.

"Do you think they'll fight?" Cole said.

"The cowards will run. But their enthusiasm is enough," Taryn responded. "Hurry. We have to find Orion. He has the Diones of the Wingor Race. Not a good thing."

Taryn began to run for a wall and leaped onto a table,

then grabbed the railing to the second floor, swinging herself up. "Coming?" she asked.

Cole took a deep breath, gripping the blade in his hands. "I'm going to search for my Council."

Taryn flashed him a smile of approval and was gone.

Cole took every ounce of energy, dumbing any source of fear, and ran out the doors into the chaotic city.

This was war.

The bloody sun shone down on the chaos.

It turned the dome from its blue to a gruesome red. The reflection on the Imperial Tower was enough to make the hairs stand out on someone's neck just with a glance.

Guns did nothing to the Oquelite, so civilians and government guards either ran from them or resorted to other means. They were treading through the streets, the few daring to try and stop them were quickly dealt with.

"We go with Squirt's usual tactic of sticking together," Miriam said, watching from the shadows of the alley. "They're heading for the wall. They came to free their leader. Who knows what will happen if they get him out?"

Nikki's mind was anywhere but there.

Taryn had broadcasted Nikki's face to who knew where. What if someone saw her and recognized her? That was stupid. Of course, they'd seen her. She stopped her quivering hands.

"Right, Squirt?"

Nikki looked up, nodding.

Felicity raised an eyebrow, eyes creased with worry.

"I agree with Miriam." Cole shimmered into existence in front of them, his medallion in his hand.

Tabitha's eyes lit up. "You're here!" she cried.

Cole smiled. "I'm hanging in there."

Miriam's eyes were widest of all. "Goldfish!" she said.

Cole wrinkled his nose at the nickname.

"Are my parents…?" Miriam began.

Cole hesitated, and Miriam hung her head. "They're strong," Cole said, trying to reassure her. "That Orion guy can't do much to them."

Nikki whipped her head up. Orion? "Orion Idicous?" she said, trying to control her fidgeting hands.

Cole frowned and nodded. "How did you know?"

Nikki shook her head. "This is bad," she muttered. "He wiped out races. He started this all. H-he had the Key Ring."

"Yes," Miriam said, solemnly. She took a sharp inhale, and clenched her jaw,

"We can deal with it," Cole said. "Our priority is the Tower. It's going to collapse and that will be the Oquelite's biggest win, but finding Ray and Lincoln is also—"

"I'll find them." Nikki said, standing up. "I'll find you when I find them."

Cole nodded. "Good idea. And then we'll face Orion."

Boom. There went another building.

No one needed to say another word.

Nikki burst out of the alley, running through the chaotic streets once more. She blended in with the chaos around her, letting her impulse lead her. She had no idea where Lincoln or Ray were in this city. If only Lincoln would just show up. He'd probably have a plan right off the bat.

A good, working plan.

Nikki dodged an auto whizzing down the street. She wanted to call after them and warn them that running away in that auto was only going to get them in more danger.

58

NIKKI RAN DOWN THE STREETS WITH EASE. SHE JUMPED UP onto an auto that had smashed into a store window. Where was he?

She jumped down and continued to search. The street was blocked off, a small squad of Defenders guarding a sad barricade of autos and hologram broadcasters. Citizens were rushing for the subway tunnel. A few stopped for a moment and stared at her. She gave a small girl a half wave as she ran past.

She took a turn finding another cleared street, littered with debris, and flaming windows, and a few other crashed autos.

The Oquelite had been here.

"Nik!"

Lincoln nearly rammed into, bursting from an alley. She nearly stumbled back, but he caught her hand. She steadied herself, relief swelling in her chest. "You're alive."

He gave her a tiny smile, and then it melted into a cold glare as she spilled to him the news about the Key Ring, and Orion, He turned to the sky, and decided to go on a factual tangent of their odds...which, by the way, weren't looking up.

The two burst out into a run toward the wall.

"We've only got security agents from over twenty regions, and only half of a legion of Defenders and a bunch of untrained citizens. Not to mention only half a Council!"

Nikki guessed by their direction they were heading for the entrance to the Imperial City, another fact Felicity had given her a lecture about during their auto ride. It was mostly for show, since you could get in through many other entrances without going through the main gate, but the rumbling was growing louder as they neared it.

It was faint, yes, but the ground seemed to shake, and energy was rushing through Nikki's body like it only had when faced with the Defenders and the Oquelite in North Cordell.

"Hey! You kids!" an officer called out to them as Lincoln skidded under a defense set up.

"Sorry!" Lincoln called out, Nikki following close behind him.

The officer blinked and turned back to a crowd of angry citizens.

"Did you see the broadcast?" Lincoln yelled to Nikki.

"Clear and loud."

Lincoln's face twitched with a smile. "Loud and clear," he corrected.

The sound of yelling, explosions, and sirens zoned out

around her.

The gate was in view.

The red force field trapping them inside the city was transparent enough to see a blur of black heading for them. No, not a blur.

People. Hundreds, maybe thousands of them.

Then silence.

Even the wind even seemed to take a break to honor the approaching.

Nikki and Lincoln stopped in their tracks in front of the gate. The gate, beaten green by time and weather, began to pull open.

Nikki stared as Sinni Hutson, holding a long, colorful knife studded with jewels like she'd never seen, a rifle slung over her back, walked through the force field, followed by Defenders.

Defenders of all kinds, uniforms, and weapons.

Lincoln seemed to be unable to look away. The Defenders all rushed past them into the grounds, but Sinni approached them confidently with a sly smile on her face, tearing off her helmet. Both of her arms were exposed, revealing the red mark along the arm she usually hid. The Oquelite had left their mark on her.

"Seems you might be in need of a bit of assistance," she said, laughing a bit. "I got a signal from Jess finally admitting that she can't do this by herself. We have Defenders from over forty different regions." Sinni laughed.

Forty Regions? That was about half of the entire Joined World.

Sinni's face became serious. "Where's Jess? Taryn?" she asked.

"Probably with the others, heading for Orion and Silas,"

Lincoln said.

Nikki had caught him up on the others' situation on the way.

Sinni's eyes widened in horror. She handed the knife to Nikki. It was strange and flashy, but she held onto the hilt.

A defender handed Lincoln a pistol and gave them an encouraging smile. It sent a strange feeling into her stomach.

"Stay safe," Sinni said with a small salute. "Save this wretched place." She dashed off into the crowd of other Defenders.

"Cool knife. Definitely made for Sublinight. They love color," Lincoln said.

"Thanks for the fact," Nikki muttered, causing Lincoln to smirk despite the chaos. "We need to get the Oquelite out of here."

"Agreed. Meet you at the tower," Lincoln said, turning to dash off.

"Wait!" Nikki called out. "Together?"

Lincoln shrugged, a smile crossing his face. "Why not?"

Lincoln and she ran down the streets.

One Defending Sergeant heard they were heading for the tower and led his entire regiment with them.

Nikki pushed herself to run faster. She had to get to the Tower. A crowd was buzzing near, some people gathering to stare, others running. Nikki pushed through, Sinni's knife slipping from her grasp. There were so many here. How could they ever protect them all?

"You made it!" Tabitha called out from down the sidewalk as they approached the Tower. "With Defenders…a lot of them."

Nikki couldn't make herself think positive. The Oquelite

were tearing down the Imperial City, no matter if they got what they wanted or not. Like Miriam said, it was always revenge. They were holding a centuries-long grudge against the world.

"We need to evacuate the city!" Miriam shouted. "Get the civilians out of here! And if this all fails, I want you to get out too!"

Nikki nodded. The others followed behind. All but Ray. Where *was* he?

The Oquelite had finally met their match—an opponent their size and their strength. The new Defenders seemed a lot more official than the ones they'd encountered in North Cordell, and their experience with handling Oquelite was undeniable. They seemed to recognize the group of kids, moving their battles out of the way to help the people out of the city.

A group of Oquelite's quickly turned their attentions to the new Defenders. An auto was lifted into the air and thrown. A Sergeant called out an order, and his ground leapt out of the way. Two took it as a distraction leaping forward, and toward the Oquelite. A Defender was launched into the air. Another Defender knocked the Oquelite with a baton, and the flying Defender landed flawlessly on the roof.

Nikki was speechless.

"We need to get to the Tower!" Cole shouted.

"Why—" Felicity's jaw fell, her lip beginning to tremble.

Cole frowned and pointed to the Tower leaning dangerously. Below stood a small figure, adorned in a black cape, absorbing the light around it. His hand rose above his head, holding a tiny, golden sparkling ring.

"It's going to fall!"

Lincoln pulled through the crowd of fleeing civilians. Not a single guard tried to stop him. "Clear the area!" he shouted.

No one hesitated to question him. Lincoln began showing people to safe exits and directing them to Defenders. The Oquelites seemed to be retreating, now that a new legion of Defenders had arrived.

Someone screamed, "There! A boy!"

"He's going to be crushed!"

Lincoln whirled around, his eyes meeting Ray's. His eyes glowed gold, his pupil constricted to the point it was only a tiny speck, but he made it very clear his eyes were set on Lincoln.

Ray stood beneath the leaning building, his eyes flickering with an abnormal light and the sly smile curled on his lips. He was outfitted in a black and gold Oquelite uniform Lincoln had never seen before. He tossed the ring playfully and caught it again in the opposite hand.

"Wanna call it a curse again, Black Eyes?"

People began swarming away from the Tower faster than ever now.

Lincoln ran for Ray. "Ray! Get out of there! The Tower is going to fall!"

Ray snickered, walking closer, showing no concern as he flicked his hair back. "Why don't you prove it? Fight me! If I get crushed, you lose your Council Key Ring. Isn't that right?"

"Ray. You're crazy!"

Lincoln slammed hard into the ground, by the invisible force. He caught himself before his face hit the caught, the rough asphalt cutting into his palms.

Ray crossed his arms. "Make me move, Black Eyes."

Lincoln raised his head. "You are going to get yourself killed! I'm not going to fight you."

Ray growled in frustration. Lincoln was flung to the side. Ray looked at him, scowling with disgust, and flung him down closer to the Glass Tower.

The crowd screamed, some trying to move forward, but they were pressed back.

Lincoln wanted to tell them to evacuate, but his voice choked in his throat.

"Aviduous. Powerful, but weak."

"Ray! I don't need a lecture," Lincoln gasped. "You need to go. Snap out of it!"

Ray didn't look the least bit concerned, drawing out the curved Blade, dark as the darkest night, the tip shimmering with a silver substance.

Ray laughed, clasping his hand shut. "I'm saving our world. For people like me. Have fun—ah!"

Ray whirled around, clenching his head. Nikki jumped out. Ray drew his sword. She caught his foot. Ray spun out of her trip but stumbled over rubble. He sliced at her. Her eyes widened with fear, but her arms flew up. The blade crashed against the knife.

Shadows began to spin around the blade, Ray forcing himself down harder. Nikki held steadfast.

Lincoln pulled out the gun from the holster, aimed for the hilt of the Shadow Blade, and in a quick pull, he shot.

And missed. He grazed Ray's shoulder instead.

Ray cried out in pain.

The light flashed from his eyes. He dropped the blade, his eyes growing wide in horror. Nikki took the moment to ram, the hilt of the knife against his chest, knocking him over. The ring bouncing out from his cloak, rolling across the rubble.

Nikki threw the knife aside and ran after the ring.

Ray's eyes flashed back to their glow. He jumped to his feet, grabbed the blade and ran for Nikki.

Lincoln's heart dropped. He threw himself in front of Ray.

The blade slicked through his jacket and into his arm. Hot pain seared up Lincoln's arm and he cried out.

A blue mist rushed from the wound into Ray's palm. *Essence.*

"You're insane," Lincoln choked again.

Ray smirked. "Better than dead."

He vanished, though his words lingered in the air.

Lincoln had only a split second to process what was happening. Everything was going too fast.

"Lincoln!" Nikki's voice screamed.

He didn't have a moment to respond before the Glass Tower crashed on top of him.

59

ONCE THE TOWER FELL, SOME OQUELITE VANISHED, AND THE rest were taken captive by the Defenders.

The force field vanished, and the Defenders had begun evacuating as many civilians as possible. News reporters were all over the place, examining the remains of the Glass Tower. Much of the tower remained intact, but many of the top floors had fallen taking out an entire street.

But no one took note of the dirty girl searching desperately through the rubble and glass of the fallen tower. Everything inside her wanted to yell and scream. Most people steered clear of the remains of the upper levels of the Tower that had crashed down, but Nikki was searching right through, her hands cut and scraped from remnants of the glass staircase and windows. Her wounds left their trace on everything she touched, a trail of red behind her. Her skin was torn, her face covered in ash, and Sinni's knife long misplaced.

The pain was a good distraction as she tried to dodge every painful thought her mind threw at her. Only one person had believed in her. Thought she was worth it. And she wasn't about to let him die like this.

She had been at it for hours. Questions and doubts were flooding in. At first, she thought Ray was coming back for the ring. The tower was falling. Lincoln had frozen. But Ray had grabbed her and, in a moment,, she was thrust out of a portal into an empty street.

Ray was nowhere to be found.

The Oquelite had been put under control, but she didn't feel like they'd won.

A sinking, sickening feeling had settled inside her. Another emotion she couldn't name. She brushed her sweaty bangs aside as they plastered themselves to her forehead.

She pushed away a piece of torn drywall, and tore away a large, thick door with her aching fingers to the most relieving and heart wrenching sight.

"Lincoln!" she called, her voice ripping through her raw throat, her heart skipping a beat.

He should have been crushed, but he wasn't. His face was cut and bloody, so were his arms, but he was still intact.

She wrapped her arms around his chest, dragging his body from the rubble. She stumbled free and collapsed, his head in her lap. She hugged her arms around him.

His heart was still beating. She could feel it beneath her fingers. He groaned ever so slightly.

"Lincoln," she choked out.

He didn't respond.

"Don't die. You're not allowed to die."

She felt him tense ever so slightly. He was still conscious. He shouldn't even be alive. She hauled him up again, further out of the wreckage.

Nikki dragged him as far out of the rubble as possible, staggering beneath his weight and the exhaustion that clung to her.

"Squirt!" Miriam came running toward Nikki, her face pale. She dropped on her knees next to them.

Jack ran after them, followed by Cole and Tabitha.

"H-he was—" Nikki couldn't form the words.

"Caught under the Tower. We know, Squirt," Miriam said gently.

Jack went for help, returning a minute later with a few Defenders.

Nikki couldn't bear to look anywhere but the ground. Guilt choked her throat, like somehow, she could have stopped this. She brushed a lock of Lincoln's hair from his bloodied face before the Defenders took him up into a stretcher.

Tabitha looked to her; her eyes wide with sorrow.

"We need to get to the Outown Manor," Jack directed them.

The manor was swarmed with Defenders. They smiled at Nikki when she passed by. She tried to follow wherever they were taking Lincoln, but Miriam blocked her way with raised eyebrows, and Cole told her that they should probably find Felicity and Tabitha.

Eventually they gathered in one of the smaller parlors at the end of the house, alone. Nikki opened the door, and Felicity gasped.

She ran up to Nikki, nearly hugging her, but stopped herself at the last moment. "You're crying," she whispered.

Nikki shot Felicity a look, brushing away the soot and tears from her face with her scabbing hands. She knew she was a mess, but she didn't care. She didn't want to get any of the Outown's fancy things dirty, so she confined herself to a corner and collapsed, burying her face in her hands. She felt Felicity's gaze, but she didn't dare look up.

The Stone's familiar presence crept into her mind. *"Do not cry."*

Leave me alone.

Avalon was quiet for a moment. The Stone still lingered in her room, but their link was strong. Strong enough for Avalon to show her the File. *"I have left you alone."*

And I failed.

"Far from it. You got Orion's Key Ring."

Nikki wished she could thrust the golden ring into a raging fire, and watch it melt. She squeezed her eyes tighter. *Leave.*

"Child—"

She built energy in her mind, crowding together her thoughts. The words Lincoln had taught her, the feelings she couldn't name, and her pain. She refused to be weak. She could be safe, but she needed to protect others too. She couldn't be happy with the torment clawing at her gut.

With that, Avalon was thrust from her mind. She wanted answers for herself.

And her mind went blank.

Her eyes adjusted to the light...hovering right above her. Her mind was foggy, her entire body numb, her wrists and ankles strapped down by cold metal restraints. She was too tired to move, out of breath, and sweaty.

The struggle wasn't worth it.

Dots sprinkled across her vision.

"Its vitals are faltering." A deep female voice cut through the static.

"This happened last injection." This time male. A head appeared over her. A blue, rubber cap covered his hair, thick lensed goggles were strapped over his eyes, and a mask drawn up over his nose.

Nikki's mind longed to jump up, and reach for his throat, but she was too tired. And last time she'd tried, it hadn't gone so well.

"It'll come back strong in a few minutes. Just watch." He flicked her shoulder. "No physical response."

"She was fighting the restraints for a good two hours before we could get her to settle down enough," the female said.

The man waved his hand in front of Nikki's face, then slowly reached down, and placed his fingers on her eyelids, pulling them upward. Cold air sung her eyes. Her mind screamed for her to jump. He was so close.

"Sclera is reddening." He let go, wiping his hand off on his coat.

"Its vitals are dropping again." That woman's breathing had begun to pick up, her voice trembling slightly.

The man coughed casually. "I told you. It's normal."

"Sir, it's only ten years of age."

The man laughed. "Exactly why Nano Keys chose it. So many more years left in it."

Feeling began to creep back into her fingers.

"Sir..."

The man gave an agitated grunt. "What is it?"

The pain in her arm slowly crept back to her.

"Her vitals—"

"I know! I know! They're going down I heard you!"

The dots vanished, and the weight was torn from her chest. She gasped for air, and shot up, the bonds slamming her back down. She tried to kick, and scream, but her throat was already raw and only a shriveled cry escaped.

"Hold her down!" the man thundered.

"She's already being held down! We can knock her out—"

"Don't be stupid! That will mess with her blood purity!" The man turned and grabbed Nikki's shoulders and held her down against the table. His dark eyes stared down at hers through the fogged lenses. She saw her own reflection snarling back at her. A tiny, malnourished child, nostrils flared, and jaw clenched.

She tried to knee him in the gut, but the restraint kept her leg down.

"We tried the neck restraint, but she nearly choked herself last time," the woman shouted.

"What about the Exil Libium?"

"Her allergic reactions only grow more severe, and they're messing with her mental state."

The man sighed. "Get 88 then!"

The woman's footsteps ran off, followed by the swinging of doors. Almost instantly, they rushed back in... followed by another pair.

"Hold her down, 88!"

"Hold her—"

"Do it!"

88's voice was familiar. Tension loosened in her body. 88 wouldn't let them touch her. Nikki was sure of it.

The man eased away from Nikki, and warm, gentle fingers pressed against her temples. A face appeared briefly above her. A young woman, her skin dark, her eyes large and kind, her hair cut short and close to her face, curled into delicate ringlets. "It's okay. Just be still."

88 disappeared, though her warm hands were still on Nikki's face. Nikki listened. 88 would keep her safe.

The earlier female voice stepped into view. She was outfitted the same as the man, except a long tail of black hair escaped her cap.

"Now, Doctor," the man said. "A demonstration of what Nano

Keys has accomplished. Please remove your glove."

The doctor did as she was told, removing the plastic glove.

"The P9F file is familiar to you, yes?"

The doctor's eyebrow bowed in a frown. "Of course. Though, it rarely gives much."

The man adjusted his mask. "Ah, but you've never seen it where it was intended to go. Extend your hand please."

The doctor held out her hand.

In a matter of seconds, the man pulled a tiny blade from his coat pocket, and slashed the palm of the doctor's hand, and dropped the blade back into his pocket.

The doctor stifled a scream. A drop of blood trickled from the cut.

Nikki felt 88's hands go stiff.

"Now." The man leaned over Nikki. He removed his knife.

She grit edher teeth. Don't attack. Don't attack.

She felt the blade slice thorough her skin, on her upper shoulder. He then extracted a small towel, dabbed at her shoulder, and came away with it stained red.

The doctor scrunched her nose, holding her hand close to her. "What do you plan to do with that?"

"Heal you."

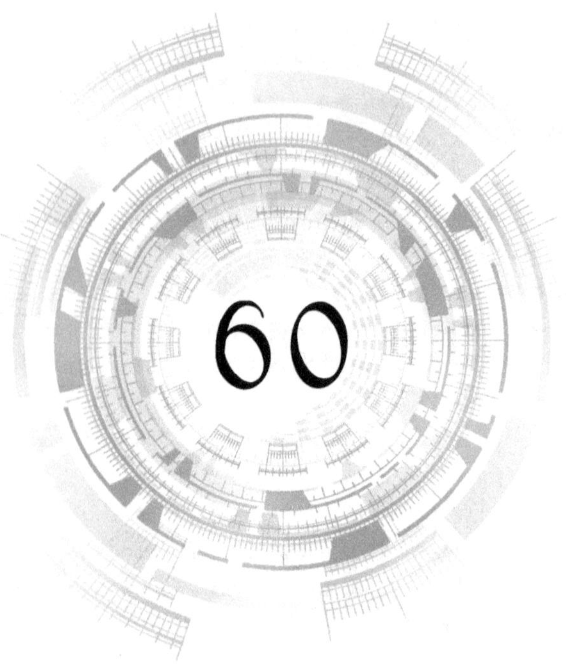

60

"He keeps coming in and out of consciousness. He only needed a bit of patching up for larger gashes. Luckily he's an Aviduous. Pretty strong one not to be crushed," a sergeant said, looking at Jack.

Jack couldn't meet his eyes. "Yes," he said to the floor.

"Sallow. We've done all we can. All there is left to do now is hope he can pull through." The sergeant smiled sadly and left the room.

Nikki paced nervously on the other side of the room, watching Jack. Miriam had fallen asleep on a bench in the room. Nikki felt obliged to thank her for everything she'd done for them. Miriam, Jack, and Taryn. Pain swelled in her throat thinking about them. What had become of Taryn?

"Nikki, you better go check on Taryn," Jack said quietly.

"She was being briefed on what happened to Kordin."

He was probably just trying to get rid of her, but she agreed anyway. She had cleaned herself up after the attack, though she couldn't seem to rid the awful dark lines from under her eyes. Felicity said they were a sign she was stressed and in need of sleep. She brushed it off.

It had been yesterday that she'd gotten Lincoln out of the rubble, and the world seemed to almost end. She'd heard, sitting quietly in on the endless conversations, that Orion was now being held in a cell in a high security prison, to be sent to the Capitol North. It didn't give her any sense of security. The Outown's had eventually managed to fight him off and Taryn had come back with help.

But that wasn't what concerned her the most. It was the flashback. The fact she willed a memory...without Avalon. That meant her memories were in her mind. But why couldn't she remember them?

She paused for a moment in the hall.

Did she want to? The younger version of herself she'd seen had so desperately wanted to get away, and now, five years later, she was. And somehow, she was sure of it, Avalon had to do with her escape from...wherever that place was.

Nikki continued down the echoing hallway, the only sound being the occasional footstep, soft voices, and the methodic beeping of machines. Taryn suddenly came from one of the rooms, a medic rushing to her. She shook her head, and they rushed into the room she'd just left. She was about to turn away when her gaze landed on Nikki.

Her eyes flashed to a lighter color, then shifted quickly back. Nikki wanted to ask, but she was sure she must have just been seeing things.

Taryn heaved a deep, tired sigh, rubbing her forehead. She

let her hands fall and sighed again. "It's fine," she said.

Nikki didn't believe the sergeant for even the slightest moment. The pain and hoarseness in her voice made it impossible for her to believe it was just 'fine.'

Taryn crossed her arms. "The Aviduous…Lincoln. He's still not awake?" she asked.

Nikki shook her head, her eyes shifting away from Taryn's gaze. "I-I came to check—"

"I'm fine," Taryn repeated, waving her hand. "Thank you for your concern."

Nikki nodded, beginning to turn away.

Taryn stopped her with a touch on her arm. "Walk with me," she said, gesturing for Nikki to follow her.

Nikki ran to catch up with Taryn, who already began to stride down the hall.

"How are you feeling, kid? About all this?" Taryn asked.

Nikki shrugged. "Hard to…understand."

"Confusing." Taryn nodded, laughing softly, through her eyes glinted with tears. "I feel the same."

Taryn looked to Nikki again, a line forming on her forehead as she examined her. "If you have any questions, feel free to…ask me."

Nikki's looked slowly up into Taryn's eyes. She flinched for a moment meeting her gaze, but relief swept over her when Taryn smiled.

Nikki nodded, itching to give her a smile in return, but not quite able to form one.

The hallway came to an end and Taryn began to turn. Nikki tried to call for her, but it fell short, caught in her throat.

Taryn stopped anyway. "Yes?"

Nikki reached into her pocket, holding the ring, delicately

wrapped in bandages. "The Key Ring."

Taryn's mouth gaped.

Nikki pressed it forward and Taryn snapped from her daze, taking it carefully from Nikki's hand. "You...succeeded. This is the reason the Oquelite didn't get out. You... retrieved it."

Nikki nodded. Thanks to Lincoln.

Taryn's eyes lingered on Nikki's, a small frown forming. Not one of anger, but of interest like she was trying to decipher her very DNA. Finally, Taryn relaxed. "Thank you," she said, with the tiniest fraction of a smile. She gave Nikki a slight salute.

Three fingers. The salute for a lesser, but still respect, nonetheless.

Nikki fumbled to give her one in return, but the two fingers turned into more of a frustrated fist. Taryn smiled and nodded, turning away down the hallway.

She uncurled her fist, her bandage coming loose. She needed to find a medic, but she desperately didn't want to ask one of the Defenders. She needed someone who could help Lincoln. She began to readjust the bandages around her raw fingers when an idea struck her. It was an awful idea. Life threatening, maybe.

She only knew one half trained, unofficial medic.

Yes, he might have tried to kill her friend, but he was also Lincoln's only chance. She looked down to her bandaged fingers.

Correction. *They* were his only chance.

61

RAY SCOURED THROUGH AN ABANDONED SHOP. HE HAD TO GET away. He had to *think*.

The whole place was in shreds, all the freezers shut off and fluorescent lights flickering. The open sign lay crushed on the floor.

He came in here mostly to calm himself down before he went crazy again. He couldn't hurt anyone else.

His stomach punched him again.

That's new essence running through you. New power. Zach's words rang through his head.

He yelled in frustration and kicked the stand closest to him. A flame formed in his hand, but he stopped himself. The essence of the killed Impure, those who probably hadn't even known what their blood contained, flowed through him now. No blowing stuff up. A bell like chime went off in the speakers of the shop. Ray glared at them and the speakers fell to the floor, melting into the ground.

"Ray?" Nikki said, stepping into the shop.

Ray jumped back, like a wild animal. "You shouldn't be here," he warned her.

Nikki shrugged. "Neither should you."

Ray growled. "Get out! Before I go crazy and kill you too!"

All the lights shut off at his command, the door flying shut behind her. Nikki stood still, her arms crossed. "Ray. I know you wouldn't hurt me."

"But I hurt Lincoln. Look. I'm different now. I'm crazy. Possessed. Crazy," Ray repeated, stepping forward.

Nikki stepped toward him as well, showing no fear. "Ray," she said. "Listen to me."

He stopped, meeting her eyes in the dark. "Just because you're an Oquelite, doesn't make you any more a monster than anyone else."

"I go insane at random moments."

"Then control it!"

"What if I can't?" he yelled, looking down at the blade in his hand. "I can't control *myself*. I can't even control the power in this stupid blade."

"Cole can."

Ray sighed. "Yeah, but Cole's different. He's older. Smarter."

"He's your brother."

Ray stopped talking. So, he hadn't been imagining it in his vague memories of Lincoln yelling at him. *Brother?* His head began to feel dizzy.

"I'm sorry. For killing Lincoln, for hurting…everyone,

and I…don't know how to say it. I can't fix it," Ray said, looking back up into Nikki's eyes.

"I do."

Ray frowned, putting his hands on his hips, laughing under his breath. "Alright how?"

"Healing him."

"He's not—"

"No. But he will be if we don't do anything about it."

"I can't do anything. I don't have any supplies."

"You said something about a super healing File. The plant."

Ray's eyes lit up. "Yeah, Phemonena Fleux—P9F File. You were listening? Nikki, the File is super hard to acquire. The plant hardly works. Can cure a scratch sometimes. It was a rare instance to make Tabitha breathe again. It's a super healing substance that my mother only got her hands on once—"

Without warning, she tore the bandage from her bloody hand, holding it out to him.

Ray frowned, moving his hand to hover over his. His mind burst with power, her essence tearing at him. He jumped back.

It was *in* her blood.

Ray gave a shaky laugh. "You're joking. That's not even remotely funny," he said. "You can't—"

He looked back to her hand. "How?!" he yelled. "They've tried inserting Files into humans for decades. That's an illegal practice. How?""

Nikki looked down at her bleeding hand.

"How?" Ray repeated. "I'll only do this if you can answer me."

Nikki whipped her head back up to him. "Only if you

agree to help. Come back and speak to the rest of them. Do you know how to use this?" She gestured to her hands.

Ray stared at his own hands. He could do unspeakable things, but this? "That's a big bargain."

"So is learning to control yourself. Being an Oquelite doesn't make you part of their army. Part of their war," Nikki said, turning to the door.

Ray thought for a moment, then groaned, running after her. "Okay, fine! I'll do it."

Ray immediately regretted his decision. His body was revolting, and the voice in his head that wasn't really his kept trying to kick him out. He stopped as they came into view of the Outown Manor. "No. Nope. I can't do this."

Nikki turned, giving him a frown. "Only way to make thing better." She turned and kept moving.

Ray hesitated for only a moment before letting out a groan of defeat. He was stubborn, but so was she. "Nikki, do you really think we can pull this off? I mean, what do they even think of me now?"

"The guy with the big camera said you were a criminal."

Of course, she was going to be straight forward. No sweet talk like 'Oh Ray! It's not your fault! I know you were just trying to do the right thing.' No. Of course not.

"Like a wanted criminal?" he asked.

"Like a criminal with a lifetime sentence criminal."

"Nikki! That means they'll put me in prison for the rest of my life," Ray yelled. "And the Defenders will probably...I don't know what. Betraying their base, defying the Council, and being an Oquelite—!" Ray broke off, quieting his voice as a guard on the street looked his way.

Nikki nodded. "You really have not been yourself."

Ray growled at her. "There isn't a point anymore!"

Nikki slapped him. "Where is Ray?" she demanded.

Ray blinked. "Sorry…" he muttered. "I told you I can't control it."

She rolled her eyes. "Your eyes grow to golden flames, your pupils nearly disappear, and your voice grows deeper," she whispered, looking off toward the Manor.

Ray opened his mouth to say something, but just looked away.

"We can't go through the front. You'll be spotted for sure," she muttered.

Ray's face lit up. "Where do you need to go, Princess?" he asked.

She raised her eyebrows at him, but he just smiled. "Parlor. Far east side of the manor," she said, pointing to the left side of the house.

Ray grabbed her arm awkwardly, and she moved a bit away from him. "You wanna get in, don't you?"

She nodded, but her arm tensed.

"Ready?" Ray looked at Nikki, who gave an unsure nod. He took that as enough agreement and leaped, sending them both into the black abyss.

Nikki fell to the ground, holding her head. Felicity, Tabitha, and Cole jumped up, the Illuminate in Cole's grip.

Nikki whipped her head up. "He's fine," she croaked. "I brought him here."

Ray gave her a smile and a nod of thanks.

"What did you do?" Felicity shouted.

"Teleported. Guess she's not used to it." Ray shrugged.

"Definitely not," Nikki gasped. She clasped her hand over her mouth.

Cole lowered his sword, glaring at Ray. "What got into you?" he shouted. "Why are you back?"

Ray took a step back, nervous now. "I can explain. I promise," he said.

Cole just shoved his sword back into the sheath. "You'd better get talking."

Ray explained everything at the best of his abilities. "I can't remember all too clearly, but I remember something calling me into the woods. Then someone telling me something, and it clicked, and I knew. That doesn't make any sense."

Felicity jumped from her seat. "Like when I left from Cole and Tabitha. I heard my name, and suddenly ... I couldn't think for myself."

"You're seriously trying to tell me we're now working with mind control?" Cole said. "You tried to *kill* someone."

Ray looked down. "Yeah, but please. Listen to me. I was trained to be a Medic. And Nikki has the P9F File in her blood."

"The what?" Felicity frowned.

"I mentioned it when Tabitha got attacked. A laboratory made healing File. It's in her blood. We can heal Lincoln. I can heal him. I can use my abilities and transfer it."

"How?" Cole raised a skeptical brow.

"I know how to transfer Files from my time with my mother, but I somehow integrate that knowledge with my essence, I can remove the tainted essence in her blood and transfer it to his own flow."

There was silence. Tabitha glanced to Nikki, who had her gaze closed on Ray.

He dug his heal into carpet. "Please. Let me prove myself. I can heal him. I promise. Believe me."

"We should trust him." Felicity stepped toward him.

"What?!" Tabitha's mouth gaped.

"Something is off here, Tabs. Something we can't fully explain. Something took control of my mind and led me away from you, and when you, Nikki, and I were in the room before our mission, we started hearing voices in our heads. Something about the … Lady of the Universe? Whatever it is, it's complicated. And we need to figure out. Together. We can keep a close eye on him, consult Taryn, but we need him. For Lincoln."

The awkward tension settled into silence.

"Fine," Cole finally said. "We'll trust him to heal Lincoln. And next we find the source of this … mind meddling."

Ray felt the non-Ray creep up on him again, the unnatural anger swelling inside him.

Nikki must have noticed his eyes shift because she was shaking her head at him.

Felicity turned to Nikki, her voice uneven and her hands shaking. "Nikki, are you sure you want to do this? You have a chemical in your blood that could—"

"Kill me, if it's activated for too long. But if it works, it could save a lot of people," Nikki said, glancing at Ray as if for back up.

Ray nodded.

"I'll stand guard," Cole said. "Tabs and Felicity, you will keep watch on entryways to the hallway. Warn me if you see Jack, Taryn, or anyone who could possibly be coming for Lincoln."

Ray breathed a tiny sigh of relief. His half-brother agreed with him, that was a good start.

They waited nervously for the coast to clear, then Nikki and Ray crept down the hallway, Cole close behind them.

As they cracked the door open, Ray held his breath. Nikki was flawlessly silent—it seemed to be a talent of hers. No one was in the room except for Lincoln, who lay silent on the bed. Guilt clenched in Ray's stomach. He had to fix this.

Nikki offered her hand to him.

He grabbed her hand, and she winced a bit. Nothing happened. "We need to expose the File—"

Nikki pulled away and clenched her fist. Even that small movement was enough to crack the scabs on her hand, and blood pooled to the surface.

Ray remembered his mother's words. As much as he's refused to accept her legends, now he had to trust in them. He found a small pair of scissors, carefully nicking his hand. Nikki's eyes widened.

He took another deep breath, clasping Nikki's hand. She stiffened.

Ray pressed his other hand against a wound on Lincoln's wrist.

His mind went blank. He could feel the File from Nikki's blood flowing through him.

The red on her hands began to shift to a dark violet, then Ray's vision went blank, gold flashing to silver, to amber, then red, then black. For a moment, he thought he couldn't breathe, then his mind whirled again, pixelating images he thought he should recognize.

The energy flowing through him grew into a pressure. Pain throbbed in his temples. A mash of voices flowed through his mind, but somehow the chaos was comforting.

62

THE WHOLE WORLD WEIGHED DOWN ON HIM, CRUSHING THE breath from him. Then slowly, the weight lifted, the world becoming light again. He thought he heard something crash, and he could feel his senses coming back gradually, like something was flooding through him, pricking all the nerves awake.

"Oh my gosh. It worked," a voice gasped somewhere above him.

He opened his eyes slowly and was grabbed in an unexpected embrace. Lincoln didn't even have time to ask what had happened. All he knew was that Nikki was hugging him. Memory filtered back in—Ray fighting him, the Tower falling—but the weirdest thing was still that Nikki was hugging him.

He hugged her back, trying to take it all in.

She finally let go, her face still pale and her breathing rushed and harsh.

Jack lingered by his side. *Jack.* Lincoln shot up, but his head suddenly grew lighting, and pain seared his chest. "You're alive?" he wheezed.

Jack just stared. "It worked. He repeated. You lunatics did it."

"I-I saw you—" Lincoln coughed. His mouth tasted gritty.

He looked first at Nikki and then to Jack, then to his hands. He moved his fingers, feeling the energy run through them.

"It worked," Jack repeated. "That insanely stupid idea worked."

Nikki shot him a look, though she didn't seem offended. Just quiet. There was blood on her hand.

Lincoln reached toward her hand. "Nik, w-what happen—"

"It's nothing."

Jack laughed. "Yeah. Nothing. Totally."

Lincoln sat up, and Jack jumped back in surprise.

"What?" Lincoln asked. What was wrong?

"Sorry, it's just that only twelve hours ago, you were beyond help, and then I walk into these two doing some...some...." Jack trailed off, scratching the back of his neck.

"I-I'm an Aviduous. Heal faster," Lincoln said, though he knew that couldn't have been the whole story. He looked over to Nikki. "I-I'm guessing that's not the o-only factor."

"I'll explain later," Nikki said, hiding her hand behind her back.

"And what is this about Ray? And how am I not a pancake?"

Nikki shrugged, her eyes sparkling with excitement. Lincoln smiled. He was alive. Yes, he had many questions, but he'd never seen her so…happy-like.

"You were crushed," Jack said. "Somehow your body remained intact, and the Ewyon spent hours looking for you and dragged your body out to safety."

Lincoln's eyes grew wide, turning to Nikki. She'd done that?

"You would have done the same," she said, shrugging.

"Then the Oquelite, Ray, was able to use the P9F File in her blood to heal you. And now…" Jack looked down at him, shaking his head. "Now you're healing…fast."

That was another surprise. "Ray?" Lincoln frowned.

"I'm guessing you don't want to see him," Jack muttered.

Lincoln shook his head, standing up, clearly shocking Jack even more than before. "Actually, the exact opposite."

He barely got a moment's peace after he stepped out the door. He collided with Felicity, and Tabitha gave him a strange pat on the head. Felicity's hug made him notice he wasn't fully healed. There were still some aches left.

"You're alright!" Felicity yelled, jumping back, then hugging him again.

"What can I say?"

"Maybe *sorry*? For freaking the flip out of us and nearly getting squished by a building?"

"Okay. I'm sorry for nearly dying." Lincoln laughed.

Felicity couldn't even pretend to be mad. She finally released him from her grasp, pouncing on her next victim, Nikki. Nikki flushed red, pulling away.

Felicity just laughed, her giddy excitement something Lincoln hadn't seen in her since before all this.

It seemed like every corner he turned he was surrounded by people he knew—which was a new concept to him. These people cared for him. Nikki had given her blood to save him, and Felicity proved it in her hugs, and Cole couldn't seem to shut his mouth—another pretty rare thing—trying to fill him in on everything.

Ray was all alone in the far parlor, which apparently, they had all stated in. Seeing Lincoln, he immediately looked away, rising. His eyes were normal again, and his hair wasn't fluttering in fiery wisps.

Nikki nudged Lincoln, like she was trying to remind him that Ray had saved his life.

Lincoln stepped right up to Ray, who looked up in surprise. Lincoln held his hand out. "It didn't happen."

Ray looked at him, his eyes wide and uncertain, but he slowly shook his hand. "I tried to kill you."

"Ray Mathews didn't try to kill me," Lincoln said. "He saved his life."

Ray broke out in a small smile, half amazed, half confused. He let out a shuddery sigh of relief. "You know, I am so glad I do *not* have your essence running in my blood!"

Laughter. Real laughter. Lincoln playfully elbowed him. "Doesn't mean we're totally friends though."

"Yeah, no way." Ray said, shaking his head, but unable to rid his grin. "I'm still taller."

Lincoln kicked him.

Ray shoved him back.

Lincoln's smile melted, his eyes slowly meeting Ray's, who's also had become solemn. "You have to tell Cole," Lincoln said.

"I know," Ray said. His eyes shimmered. "My memories might be foggy, but I remember...*that.*"

Lincoln nodded, pursing his lips.

"You really saw my mother?"

"She's an incredible woman."

Ray gave a small smile, looking off into the distance. "She is."

He turned his attention back to Lincoln. "Are—are you sure she said that? That would mean Cole knows my…"

Father. The word echoed in Lincoln's mind. The crazy eyed, killer boy with supernatural powers he'd seen days ago was nowhere to be seen. Now all he saw was an anxious boy, his eyes wide with anxiety, and shoulders hunched, at the subject of his unknown father.

"You can do it," Nikki said, her voice quiet, yet reassuring as he stepped closer to Ray.

Ray chuckled softly. "If he doesn't kill me first."

"That doesn't seem like Cole," Lincoln said, though he didn't fully believe his own words. He couldn't blame Cole if he held anger. Ray had attempted murder, even if it wasn't his own mind. He was still and Oquelite. A group who had done so much wrong to them in the recent past.

Ray's eyes fell. "I hope you're right."

"Your family," Nikki said, her eyes brightening, like that was the most fascinating thing in the world to her. Then she looked between them both. "I have to go...meet with Taryn."

"Good luck." Ray forced a smile.

Before Nikki could ask, he responded, "It's an expression."

"Well then, good of luck to you too."

Neither Ray nor Lincoln corrected her as she walked off.

Ray stood in front of the parlor doors, wanting to run. He'd promised he'd speak to Cole, but now that he saw the boy sitting, distracted by a tablet on the sofa, he couldn't breathe.

He could turn on his heel and run. Create a portal at his fingertips and go home.

But deep down he knew it wouldn't be the same.

It would never be the same.

Voices would still plague his thoughts. The anger and temptation would always plague him. He could still do terrible things at the will of his mind.

He couldn't run away.

He reached up, held his breath, and brushed his finger against the door. The sensor picked him up and swung the doors open.

Cole looked up.

Ray stood in the doorway. His heartbeat thundered in his ears. He opened his mouth, but the words caught in his throat.

"I know what you're going to say." Cole sat up.

"I don't think you do—"

Cole ran his fingers over his medallion. "He told me this morning."

"Who?"

"My—our father." Cole raised his eyes, clenching the medallion in his fist.

Ray's eyes heated. He looked away. "Oh."

Cole had *spoken* to his father.

Cole stood up and let out a heavy sigh. "So, this is awkward."

"Yeah."

Silence followed.

Ray dug the heel of his boot in the carpet. "We've been

lied too," he said, quietly.

"You can't lie about something you never mention."

"I was told my dad left us! But now, I'm told I have a half-brother, who's been living in the same region as me, and no one ever took the time to tell me about! A half-brother my father left to take care of!" A tear escaped, but he didn't care. "I feel lied too."

"I'm sorry," Cole said. His voice faltered, his arms falling to his sides, and away from the medallion.

"It's not your fault." Ray swallowed, tightening his fists. "It's mine. I screwed everything up. You're scared of me. I've nearly killed Lincoln. And what is my mom going to think? And Je—oh. I guess you have other siblings too."

Cole immediately perked up, his eyes sparking. "I do?"

Ray gave a small smile, his sight blurred by tears. "Yeah. Three, actually."

"There are four of you?"

Ray nodded, trying to casually brush away the tears.

"He said they kept us apart because of a threat an Oquelite gave a warning about a curse."

That was probably his fault. Had he been a nuisance since birth? Ray bit his lip.

Cole stepped closer. "But we're older now. We now have a fate that connects us. A curse and a council. And apparently...family?"

"I'm never going to get used to that," Ray said, quietly.

"Neither am I."

Cole's hand gently touched Ray's shoulder. "We're not going to let you lose control again. *I* won't."

Ray couldn't hold it in any further. He began to cry.

Arms wrapped around him and held him close.

Weight lifted from his shoulders, letting him breath for

the first time in what felt like ages. He was free.

Where to go? What to do?

There was no time for rest.

Taryn paced around the front of the window, watching the woods as they crawled farther, the trees and vines tangling and writhing like an ocean of green. This battle had ended, but the outcome was far from clear.

The defending officers were now in smoke. She knew the officials in the Capitol North were already beginning to reform.

They'd taken so much and left her with so little. But those thoughts no longer poisoned her mind.

Her uncle had been right about one thing. She had to move on eventually.

The words he muttered in his cot still lingered in her mind, whirling around meaninglessly.

Somehow it all led back to the new Council. She remembered the days when people had whispered about her team being the Council. The first five. She wondered where the other seven had been and if they had suffered as much pain as she had. Had there ever been a senior Council member alive to prepare the next Council?

In her memory, there hadn't been. Of course, it wasn't her responsibility, but she found the weight on her shoulders anyway. Some in the defending offices would gladly have the new members executed, just like her own, but Taryn wouldn't stand for that. She'd find a way.

This wasn't her fight anymore, but she could still fight for the others.

She had to let go of her impossible dreams and stresses. This was their fight to lead now. These kids were her only hope. The purest of the Impure.

She would train them, so at least she'd have some control.

The door burst open. Taryn gripped her pistol, pulling it from her belt, whirling around, and pointing it straight toward the new arrival.

Miriam and Jack stood in the doorway, their hands up in a salute.

She sighed, putting the pistol away. "Oh, it's just you two," she muttered. "Stop with the saluting."

Miriam scanned over the room, noticing the bags packed and stacked. "Leaving so soon, Sergeant?"

Taryn sighed. "There isn't much to do here now anyhow."

"Are you bringing your kids?" Jack added.

Taryn laughed, a cold, sharp laugh, that made both Miriam and Jack jump. "Of course, I'm bringing *my* kids, Sallow."

Jack gave a nervous grin and a nod. "I-I mean, w-we were thinking…well, thinking about—we're here to ask for dispatch—"

"To go search for other high-blooded Impure willing to join us," Miriam finished. "With an awakening…"

Taryn crossed her arms, raising her eyebrows. *More Impure.*

She scanned over Jack and Miriam with an intense stare, then released a long breath. She walked over to the bag on the windowsill, unzipping it and pulling out the two carefully leather-wrapped swords. Miriam and Jack's eyes grew wide in childlike excitement.

Taryn presented them each with one.

Jack hastily fastened the sheath to his belt, slowing down

a bit under Taryn's gaze. "Thank you, sergeant," he said, with a shaky salute, a wide grin spread across his face.

Miriam did the same.

"I usually do not allow Defenders to go out on such unusual, dangerous missions, especially this…young, but these are unusually dangerous causes," she said, placing a hand on each of their shoulders.

"Stay safe," she whispered.

Miriam's stern eyes, with the sincerity of her parents, reminded Taryn much of Aaron as the woman nodded firmly.

Taryn released them, giving them a salute.

Miriam and Jack went for the door, opening it, and another figure pushed through.

Nikki stood nervously in front of her.

Taryn nodded to Miriam and Jack, who left quickly, shutting the door behind them.

"Do you need something?" she asked.

Nikki began to shake her head but stopped herself and nodded. She clasped her hands behind her back and looked up to Taryn. "I-I have a question," she said.

Taryn smiled. So, she *had* been listening to her when she'd offered. "Ask away."

"Did any of…your friends…have family?" she asked.

Taryn frowned. "In what way?"

"Siblings? Living parents?" Nikki shifted her feet.

Taryn went through each of the old council members in her head. "There is Miriam. Her and Aaron's parents are still alive."

Nikki shook her head. "The others?"

"Zita Klirkpatrick…I'm not sure about her. She never knew herself," Taryn said. "Lyell had two sisters back in

Court Illegia. And Reyna…I think she has a sister. Caroline, if I remember correctly." A memory sprung to her. "I think she lives in North Cordell."

Nikki nodded. "Thank you."

"Why'd you ask?" Taryn said, her mind still whirling as she tried to remember the whereabouts of Caroline Wents.

Nikki shrugged. "Maybe you're not alone," she said, relaxing.

Taryn's lips parted, but no words came. She simply nodded. "No, maybe I'm not."

Nikki nodded again. "Thank you again," she said, rushing for the door and closing it carefully behind her.

Taryn scrambled for a screen, pulling up the file database for North Cordell. It lagged a bit, and Taryn chewed her lip impatiently, anxiety bubbling within her. The screen finally loaded, and she typed the name *"Caroline Wents"* into the database.

File does not exist currently.

Taryn scowled, tapping on the bar, entering Caroline Wents again, but into the Algery database. A small file popped onto the screen.

Caroline Wents Williams. No longer resident of Algery. Married. All available information.

Taryn clicked back to North Cordell entering 'Caroline Williams'.

She waited again, tapping her foot. Finally, a result came up.

Caroline Williams. Deceased.

63

She was winning, but no one expected any less from her.

Running was something Nikki took pride in, and relief. She was going back to North Cordell tomorrow morning.

With everyone else. Taryn. Her Council. Back to the place she belonged.

She looked over her shoulder and slowed down just a bit so the others wouldn't fall too far behind. The woods were crawling closer to the city, growing bigger every day. Amazing and horrifying at the same time.

They were heading for the woods that had grown overnight in the wasteland that stretched out behind the Outown manor. The voice had directed Felicity to the woods in the past, so at the first opportunity they got, they headed for the woods.

Ray suddenly appeared, running alongside her. "No one said using abilities was against the rules!" he called after her.

She rolled her eyes. "Who needs them?"

Ray jumped, disappearing again into thin air.

She felt that feeling again—the one she couldn't place. For a moment, fear wasn't pressing down on her, guilt wasn't eating away at her insides, and her mind seemed so light and free. She knew it would all come crashing back down on her, but for now she didn't think about it.

As they approached the woods, Nikki slowed down again. The others rushed to her side. The branches began to untangle themselves for the group to pass. The ancient woods held a reverent silence as they passed through. Ray reappeared; his amber eyes large in wonder.

"This is sick," Tabitha muttered under her breath.

Cole nudged her. "No one says 'sick,' Tabs."

Ray smiled. "I approve of 'sick.'"

Cole rolled his eyes, but a small smile breached his lips.

Light poured in through the gaps of the trees, and little eyes peered at them from the branches, but nothing attacked. The path grew a carpet of moss, leading them to an open clearing with a rushing river, vines, and overgrown branches hanging around the water. Colorful plants burst like paint splatters across the rocks.

Nikki was speechless.

"Now, this is sick," Tabitha muttered.

Cole groaned.

"It's beautiful," Lincoln corrected, his eyes wide open to soak in the view.

Beautiful. Nikki liked that word. It seemed fitting. This place was utterly *beautiful.*

They all moved closer to the river, though they couldn't seem to take it all in. Nikki placed her hand in the water. It was surprisingly cool. A refreshing type of cool though. Not cold, nor hot.

Another word joined her mind.

Safe and beautiful.

"Tomorrow. It's the day. We officially begin," Ray muttered in disbelief. "Can we even pull this off?"

Felicity laughed. "No. We're only half of the Council."

"Do you really think we can find six more?" Tabitha said. "I mean, we got lucky with just us six, but most of that was planned by Fate." She laughed at herself. "Never thought I'd say that."

"There was a lot of Fate," Ray said.

Nikki's chest swelled, but it was a good feeling. One she treasured. "Why did you have the Key Ring in the first place?" she asked, putting extra effort into making her voice clear and steady.

Ray's lips twisted. "They were looking for someone who could wield it. Orion could thousands of years ago, except his heart went…'cold' or something and he couldn't anymore. He used to be the Shadow Blade holder, but the Blade rejected him. They thought I would be able to."

"And were you?" Cole asked.

Ray shook his head. "I tried."

"So, the Key Ring *is* connected to the Council." Felicity eyes widened. "Perhaps you couldn't use it because we haven't united all the members."

"Six more," Ray sighed. "If they're out there…"

Everyone was quiet for a moment. Then Ray perked up again, and turned to Nikki, with a huge smirk on his lips. "Now don't you owe us an explanation?"

Nikki froze, putting her hands behind her back and looking down at the forest floor. She took a deep breath and lifted her head back up to the others. She could trust them. She knew them.

"I-I—" she stammered. How was she supposed to start this?

Lincoln looked around at the others, then stepped to her. "You okay?"

She felt herself loosen. Something about his nearness calmed her. "I don't know," she said, her voice cracking.

"You don't remember?" Lincoln said.

Nikki shook her head. "Bits and pieces. Blurry…I was injected. With a healing File. I was injected with Phenomena Fleux…the P9F File." The word was bitter on her lips, but it felt good to get it out.

"Isn't that illegal?" Felicity frowned, moving toward her as well.

Nikki shrugged. "I was taken."

Felicity frowned. "I can help you," she said. "And anyone else like you. If you remember anything, even just a little symbol, I could track these people down. My father could get them arrested easily."

Tabitha's eyes grew wide. "So that's how you saved my life?" she said, her hand going to her neck. "You enacted the Phenomena Fleux's healing capabilities."

"You're also not the only insane freak here," Ray added, sparks lining his fingers.

Felicity rolled her eyes at him.

"He is right," Tabitha said. "Since we're all being motivational and exposing ourselves and all, my favorite food is hot sauce."

"That is not a food," Cole groaned.

That lightened the mood. Nikki felt like she could breathe for a moment, like she could finally think clearly. The emotion bundled up inside her again.

"Come on, people," Tabitha said, rolling up the ends of her jeans and tossing aside her red converse. She stepped into the water. "Let's just relax! For one day, please?"

She cupped her hands full of water, splashing her nearest victim.

Cole flinched back as water sprayed over him but gave a playful frown. "I'll get you for that, Tabs." He shoved Tabitha backward into the water.

She came up soaking and laughing, as always. Nikki watched them curiously, finding her way up on a rock as they all soaked each other. What was it? That made them all like that?

Lincoln noticed her sitting alone. "Is that mind of yours giving you a break yet?"

Nikki frowned.

Then Lincoln did the unthinkable. He splashed her.

She startled; mouth open as water dripped down her face. She stood staring in disbelief, her arms frozen midair, and her shirt soaked.

Then she laughed.

They stared at her in disbelief. Never had they heard her laugh. Ever.

She jumped off the rock, throwing her boots aside, running into the water after Lincoln. She tackled him into the water, soaking him from head to foot.

That seemed to wash off the shock and he splashed her back again.

Nikki smiled, and it never felt so good.

*[Transmission from Year 2020 B.ES,
Citizen Lauren D. Fulter]*

ACKNOWLEDGEMENTS

This feels really weird. *laughs nervously*

Now you have learned the names of (most of) the people that occupy much more space in my mind than they should be allowed. I have to admit, I never thought this experience would be possible. I was 12 when the story first came to me, and I must say it was the Lord who pushed me to put it down on paper, and gave me the people to actually get it done by the age of sixteen (yes, I am sixteen). I've grown so much in my faith since starting this journey, and met some incredibly gifted, blessed people along the way.

First, I think it would be wrong not to mention my parents first, who dealt with this weird, anxious, hyper mess, and supported me, and disciplined my excessive screen time. Thank you to my father who first suggested the idea of publishing to me, and to my mother who wanted "fire" and "birds" on the cover. Next time, mom. Sorry it didn't work out.

Thank you to Ms. Tabor, who sat me down in eighth grade and told me to set a goal for the year. I chose "write a book" and here we are years later.

Thank you to Ellie, who read the book from the first drafts (when instead of the Inn there was a Dorm, and Felicity was an annoying little jerk … and Julianna existed). Thank you for always cheering me on, and making little comments on Google Docs.

EVERYONE, you have Ellie to thank for the reason Cole is still in the story!

Thank you to Anya. For always being the #1 TUQ fan, and giving me the much-needed confidence and friendship, I never knew I needed. So many weird inside jokes have probably made their way into this series....

To my fantastic betas: Allison, for being one of my first and only betas in the beginning to really pull through. Without you, this book would be like 700 pages long......

Emma, for "adopting" Silas, and making some fantastic "The Unanswered Questions" puns. They were cheesy, but very amusing. And turning in beta feedback even when a TORNADO went through your town. You are incredible.

Emerald, for being so. darn. supportive. How did I end up with a beta like you? Thank you for always rushing to my aide whenever I call for it, and giving me such fun and helpful feedback that's made the book so much better.

Molly and Shan, for being so eager to help out this struggling child who wrote a weird book, and being so entirely helpful, and getting me to where I am. Both of you deserve the world.

I want to also thank my street team, who made promoting TUQ way more successful than I could've ever imagined. Thank you, Hayley, Mary-Jacqueline, and Naomi, (and Naomi, thank you for the encouragement and constant support! And the beautiful bookmark! I will treasure it forever).

Thank you, Sofia, for being the reason I stayed sane during school, and thank you for stealing my notebook and reading my world building notes and pointing out the inconsistencies in the Lyntox society over lunch.

This book would've been published with an embarrassing

amount of errors without the watchful eye of Jane Maree, my fantastic editor. Sorry for all the emails with the repeated "thank you so much". I really meant it!

And to the amazing Beck Michaels and Klymenearts for making the cover as stunning and fantastic beyond my wildest dreams. My little self would be screaming over how amazing it turned out.

Thank you to every single human being who's followed me on social media, and hyped this book up more than I could've ever hoped for, and every single one of my friends and family that I don't have space to write the names of. You've all provided countless pieces of inspiration and teasing (Stella, I'm still scarred from that time you yelled "NIKKI!!!" in the church courtyard).

And to my brother, Dominic, who as of writing this, still hasn't read the book, but already has strong opinions on the characters. I hope Ray lives up to your expectations.

And to all of you, for picking up this book, and giving it a chance.

THE UNANSWERED QUESTIONS

BOOK TWO

COMING NEXT WINTER

[Message the Defending Department: You told me to let you know if there were any dangers to my mission. My only warning to you would be the source may not be reliable. Lauren D. Fulter, as she calls herself, might not be entirely truthful on her abilities and identity. The year of 2020 lies too far in the past for us to be sure. She is a good ally of transmission of stories to the past, but should not be trusted – N.B]

Lauren D. Fulter is an upcoming young American fiction author, publishing the first book of "The Unanswered Questions" series at age sixteen.

After learning the word 'author' at age five, she's been captivated by the art of storytelling, and the little people roaming her mind. Though she longs for the cold, she lives in the desert with her large family, spending her days drawing, dabbling in fictional dimensions, and attempting to make something edible.

www.ingramcontent.com/pod-product-compliance
Lightning Source LLC
Chambersburg PA
CBHW031043110726
47900CB00003B/794